"Peace," rumbled Kargrin. "Roban told me he thought you had the rage, and indeed I felt the presence of it when I tested your mark."

"A test?" mumbled Clariel. Her head ached, and she felt slightly nauseous. "You might have told me."

"It would not serve as a useful test if I told you," said Kargrin. "If I release you, will you keep that anger in check?"

"Yes," said Clariel. She slowly sat up and cradled her head in her hands. The ache intensified, a deep throbbing pain behind her eyes. "I've never . . . almost never let it get out of control like that . . ."

"You *are* a berserk," said Kargrin, in a very matter-of-fact tone. "It is not uncommon in the royal blood, and though rarer among Abhorsens, it does crop up from time to time. You have both blood-lines from your mother. It is curious that you have the rage, but not the usual affinity of your kin for the Charter. There is danger in this, for you, and for others."

"I've never . . . I've never let it get so far beyond . . ." faltered Clariel. "I've never hurt a . . . a person!"

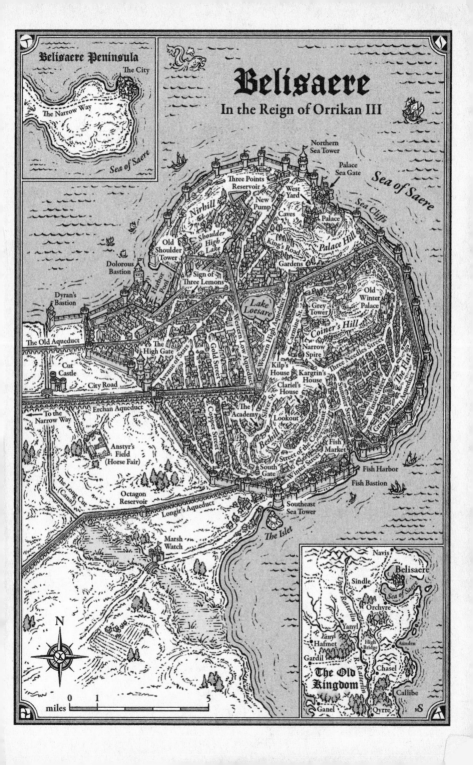

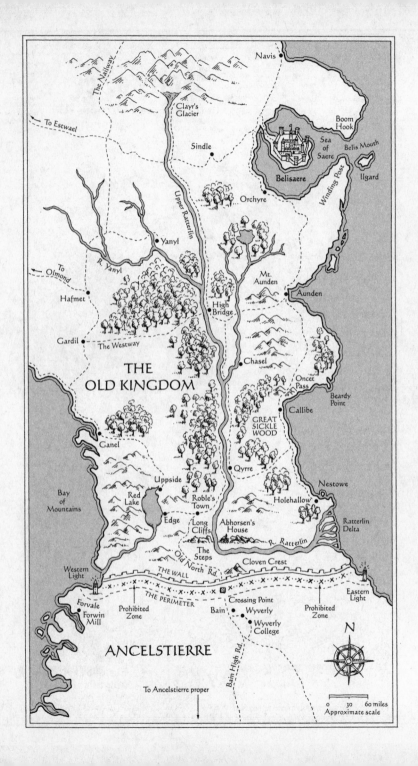

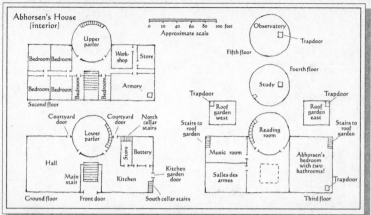

Abhorsen's House (interior)

Approximate scale: 0 10 40 60 80 100 feet

Fifth floor — Observatory, Trapdoor

Fourth floor — Study

Second floor — Bedroom, Bedroom, Bedroom, Bedroom, Bedroom, Bedroom, Workshop, Store, Armory

First floor — Upper parlor, Workshop, Store, Armory

Courtyard door, Courtyard door, North cellar stairs, Lower parlor, Store, Buttery, Kitchen garden door

Trapdoor, Roof garden west, Stairs to roof garden, Trapdoor, Roof garden east, Stairs to roof garden

Reading room, Music room, Abhorsen's bedroom with *two* bathrooms!, Salles des armes, Trapdoor

Ground floor — Hall, Main stair, Front door, Kitchen, South cellar stairs

Third floor

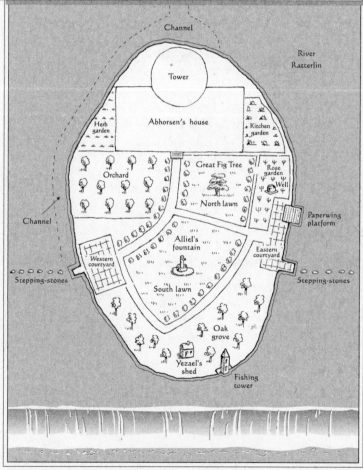

Channel

River Ratterlin

Tower

Abhorsen's house

Herb garden

Kitchen garden

Orchard

Great Fig Tree

Rose garden, Well

North lawn

Channel

Alliel's fountain

Paperwing platform

Western courtyard

Stepping-stones

South lawn

Eastern courtyard

Stepping-stones

Oak grove

Yezael's shed

Fishing tower

ALSO BY GARTH NIX

THE ABHORSEN SERIES
Sabriel
Lirael
Abhorsen
Goldenhand

The Creature in the Case: An Old Kingdom Novella

Newt's Emerald

To Hold the Bridge

*Across the Wall: A Tale of the Abhorsen
and Other Stories*

The Ragwitch

*One Beastly Beast: Two Aliens, Three Inventors,
Four Fantastic Tales*

Shade's Children

A Confusion of Princes

GARTH NIX

CLARIEL

THE LOST ABHORSEN

WITHDRAWN

HARPER

An Imprint of HarperCollinsPublishers

Library of Congress Cataloging-in-Publication Data

Nix, Garth.
  Clariel / Garth Nix. — First edition.
    pages cm
  Summary: "The story of how Clariel became a Free Magic Sorcerer, set 600 years
before the birth of Sabriel" — Provided by publisher.
  ISBN 978-0-06-156157-3
  [1. Magic—Fiction. 2. Fantasy.] I. Title.
PZ7.N647Cl 2014   2013047958
[Fic]—dc23   CIP
                                                                       AC

Typography by Henrietta Stern
Map of Belisaere by Mike Schley
16 17 18 19 20   PC/RRDH   10 9 8 7 6 5 4 3 2 1
❖
First paperback edition, 2016

To Anna, Thomas, and Edward, and all my family and friends

and

To the memory of poet, kind-hearted cynic, and good friend
Andrew Etheridge
1963–2012

THIS BOOK IS SET APPROXIMATELY SIX HUNDRED YEARS
BEFORE THE BIRTH OF SABRIEL.

Five Great Charters knit the land
Together linked, hand in hand
One in the people who wear the crown
Two in the folk who keep the Dead down
Three and Five became stone and mortar
Four sees all in frozen water

CONTENTS

Prologue

Old Marral the fisherman lived in one of the oddest parts of Belisaere, the ancient capital of the Old Kingdom. A proud city with high walls to defend against living foes, and rushing aqueducts to keep out the Dead, one tiny corner of the great metropolis lay outside the protection of both wall and water.

Known to all simply as the Islet, it was a rocky island just beyond the city's southeast sea tower. Joined to the mainland by a rough stone causeway save at the highest tides, the island was inhabited by the poorest of the poor, the fisher-folk who had lost their boats, or drank too much, or had suffered some calamity that kept them from the city's more prosperous fishing harbor farther to the north.

No one knew what had caused Old Marral to come to the Islet. He had been there as long as anyone could remember, living in a shack made of driftwood and torn sailcloth, distinguished from the dozen or so other hovels on the Islet only by its doorway, in which a heavy curtain made of hundreds of shark teeth knotted onto a discarded fishing net served as a door.

Old Marral made his living, such as it was, as a beachcomber. He walked around the Islet every morning, and if the tide was out, also went out along the rocks that faced the eastern seawall of the city proper. This could be very dangerous, for the tides in the Sea of Saere came in fast and high. In the old days, when the city walls were kept in constant repair, Marral would have drowned many times. Now, with much of the smooth outer face of the wall eroded, there were hand- and footholds enough to climb up out of the rushing waters, even carrying a small sack of whatever flotsam the sea had carried in on its blue-green back.

One particular morning, the sack held a real treasure.

Marral had thought it was a fisherman's glass float at first, lost from a net. The morning sun flashed off something bobbing in the water, sending back a greenish glint. But when a wave brought it close enough to snatch, he found it was a squarish bottle of thick green glass, not a float. It was empty, but neither the bottle nor the contents it once might have held were of interest to Marral. What caught his eye was the stopper. Though tarnished with age and immersion, he knew it for silver, and even better, the stopper was secured to the neck with bright wires still yellow and warm, gold resisting all tarnish.

Marral almost cackled as he saw it, but stopped himself. The cackling was an act for the city-folk, the few who thought he was some kind of small-time Free Magic sorcerer who could offer them an easier, and less equitable, path to whatever they wanted than the rigors of Charter Magic or non-magical hard work. The shark-tooth curtain was part of this act, but it was only an act, which delivered a few silver deniers every now and then, from those foolish enough to think a Free Magic sorcerer could set up so close to Belisaere, even if outside the city's walls and wards.

Hugging his find close, Marral retraced his steps along the wet rocks below the seawall, climbing up and around the deeper pools where the sea swirled dangerously, quick to whisk away and suck under anyone who fell in.

Back in his hut, he thought about what to do with his find, as he cleaned the silver with spirits of hartshorn and turpentine. There were a number of junk merchants on Winter Street who Marral dealt with regularly, but the silver stopper was too good for them, he thought. They'd never give him a fair price, not for something so finely worked. There was delicate engraving in the metal, tiny symbols like the ones he'd seen in a book once, the one from the dead sailor's pocket. Marral had gotten a good price for the book, despite it being so heavily water-stained and encrusted with salt.

After a few seconds peering at the symbols on the silver, Marral looked away. They unnerved him, somehow, almost like they were moving. Twitching about. It was the cleaning fluid, no doubt. Fumes.

Marral did not have a baptismal Charter mark, and thus had no connection to the Charter. He could not see the actual Charter marks twisting and moving around the engravings. He could not feel the binding spell that kept the bottle closed, and had done so for almost nine hundred years. Nor could he sense the entity trapped inside the bottle, though he did wonder a little why the glass continued to feel so cold, long after it had come out of the sea.

After he had been cleaning it for some time Marral thought perhaps it would be better to simply remove the stopper, and take it in to a goldsmith in the city. There was no need to take the whole bottle. After all, he'd seen dozens of solid square bottles like this one, and none had been worth more than a copper squid.

It felt like his own idea.

Very carefully, he prized off the first gold wire. His hands hurt as he unwound the gold, burning pains shooting through his fingers. It was the ague of age, he knew, though he'd rarely had it so bad. Marral thought of the goose grease which sometimes helped, but he had none of it, and anyway the pains lessened as the wire came off.

A stabbing pain struck his chest as he pulled the stopper out of the bottle. But he had had such pains before, and simply coughed, knowing it would pass in a moment. And it did, just as the stopper came out with a loud pop, as if the bottle was not empty at all, but contained the finest of the light sparkling wines from Orestery.

Marral held the heavy stopper in his hand, mentally calculating its worth as a lump of silver. It would pay for a new pot of goose grease, a keg of the dark ale he favored, and at least several chickens, a welcome change from a diet of fish and gathered crustaceans.

He was thinking of the chicken when he noticed there was someone else in the hut, though he hadn't heard the shark-tooth curtain
rattle, or even a single footstep on the rocky floor.

Marral's hand instinctively darted for the gutting knife at his
belt, but faltered even as his fingers gripped the worn bone hilt.

The stranger who had appeared so silently, and now sat opposite
him on a wooden crate, looked strangely familiar, but it was a familiarity only slowly remembered from long ago.

"Greten? But you . . . you drowned . . . nigh on thirty years
ago . . ."

The young woman smiled, a brilliant smile, her teeth white and
bright even in the shadowed interior of the hovel. Marral couldn't
help but smile back, and stretch out his arms to hug his long-lost
favorite sister, even as some part of his mind protested that even if she
had somehow escaped the sea, Greten couldn't possibly look exactly
the same as she had three decades gone.

Tears flowed down Marral's cheeks as they embraced, cutting
clear trails through the salt caked on his skin, trickling down to the
corners of his mouth. He laughed in delight, at all the goodness in
the world, which had brought him not only a valuable silver stopper
but also his little sister back from the sea.

The laughter ceased as Marral's heart skipped a beat and then
just . . . stopped.

But he had only a moment of fear and puzzlement, as Greten
somehow continued to move deeper into his embrace, disappearing
into his flesh.

The old man's eyes closed, and he slumped on his stool, and would
have fallen, save that something moved inside him and kept him
upright. Then his heart stuttered into action again, and began to beat
more strongly. Color flooded into Marral's skin, and his eyes cleared.
The white flecks in his hair and the stubble on his chin retreated, giving way to a deep brown not seen for many a year.

"I feel . . ." muttered Marral. He stopped, his voice sounding odd to his own ears. It was stronger, and he could hear more clearly.

"I feel young!"

"Somewhat," muttered a voice inside his head. Greten's voice. "I cannot do too much, for we must be careful. But I need you to be strong."

Marral laughed, a deep, bold laugh.

"Dear Greten!" he exclaimed. "I will be strong! Tell me what you need."

"First," whispered Greten, in a voice he alone could hear, "I need to know things. Who rules the Kingdom? How many years have passed since the second Dyran was on the throne? Do the Abhorsens still scour the land against the Dead and . . . others?"

The house was one of the best in Belisaere, high on the eastern slope of Beshill. It boasted five floors, each with a broad balcony facing east, and on top there was a pleasant roof garden which delivered a view over the lesser houses on the slope below, and past them across the red roofs of the buildings that clustered closely on the valley floor on either side of the Winter Road. Beyond the houses were the seven-tiered Great Eastern Aqueduct and its lesser companion, the city wall. The eastern wall had its feet almost in the water; beyond it lay the glittering expanse of the Sea of Saere, now dotted with those slower, straggling fishing boats that were coming late to Fish Harbor, hours after the rest of the fleet had returned to unload their catch with the dawn.

Clariel stood at the intricately carved marble railing on the edge of the roof garden, with the sun on her face and the cool sea breeze ruffling her shorn-at-the-neck jet-black hair, and wondered why she couldn't like the view, the house, or indeed, the whole city of Belisaere.

She was seventeen years old, two months shy of being eighteen, and up until their arrival in the city three days before had lived her entire life in the much smaller town of Estwael in the far northwest of the Old Kingdom, and more important to her in recent years, in and about the Great Forest that surrounded Estwael.

But Estwael and the Great Forest had been left behind, despite Clariel's entreaties to her parents. She'd asked to remain, to become a

Borderer, one of the wardens who patrolled the forests and woods of the kingdom. But her parents refused, and anyway the Borderers did not recruit youths, as Sergeant Penreth in Estwael had told Clariel numerous times, though always with a matter-of-fact kindness, for they were long acquaintances, if not friends. Nor would her parents accept any of her various other reasons for being allowed to stay behind.

Typically, Clariel's mother, Jaciel, had simply ignored her daughter's request, refusing to even discuss the matter. Jaciel's mind was rarely focused on her family. A goldsmith of rare talent, all her attention was typically on whatever beautiful gold or silver object she was currently making, or on the one that was taking shape in her head.

Harven, Clariel's father and manager of all practical matters in their family life, had patiently explained to his daughter that besides being too young to join the Borderers it was very likely that in a year she would not want to anyway. He had then added insult to injury by telling Clariel the move to Belisaere was as much for her benefit as it was for her mother, who had been accorded the honor of being invited to join the High Guild of Goldsmiths in the capital.

There would be many more opportunities for her in Belisaere, Clariel had been told repeatedly. She could be apprenticed herself, straight into a High Guild or one of the Great Companies. There might be a business the family could buy for her. Or she might make an advantageous marriage.

But none of these "opportunities" interested Clariel, and she knew they never would have left Estwael just for her benefit. Any advantage she might receive would be entirely incidental to her mother's desire for a much larger workshop, a greater variety of better metals, gems, and other materials to work with, and an increased labor force, doubtlessly including at least half a dozen more pimply apprentices who would try to look down the front of Clariel's dress at dinner.

A meaningful cough behind her made Clariel turn around. Her father smiled at her, the weak smile that she knew was a harbinger of bad news. It had made frequent appearances in the last few months, the smile. When people first met Harven they would think him strong, until his mouth turned up. He had a weak, giving-in smile. He was a goldsmith too, but was not particularly gifted in the actual craft. He was much better at managing the business of his wife's work.

"Have you come to tell me that by some stroke of good fortune I am to be allowed to go home?" asked Clariel.

"This is our home now," said Harven.

"It doesn't feel like it," said Clariel. She looked over the railing again, across all the white stone buildings with their red tiled roofs, and then back again at the ornamental shrubs in the terra-cotta boxes that made up their own roof garden, shrubs with pale bark and small, weak-looking yellow leaves. "There is nothing green here. I haven't seen a single proper tree. Everything is ordered, and tamed, and put between walls. And there are too many people."

"There are lots of big trees in the gardens on Palace Hill," said Harven. "We just can't see them from here."

Clariel nodded glumly. A few trees too distant to be seen, across miles and miles of houses and workshops and other buildings, and thousands and thousands of people, rather proved her point, she thought.

"Did you come to tell me something?" she asked, knowing that he had, and she wasn't going to like whatever it was. His smile gave that away.

"Ah, your mother had a meeting with Guildmaster Kilp yester-eve, and he made her aware of an opportunity for you that she . . . we desire you to take up."

"An opportunity?" asked Clariel, her heart sinking. "For me?"

"Yes, an opportunity," continued her father, raising his hands and lifting his shoulders to emphasize what a good opportunity he was about to reveal. "The Goldsmiths, the Merchant Venturers, the Spicers, the Northwestern Trading Company . . . all the High Guilds and most of the great companies, they send their children to the Belisaere Select Academy—"

"A school?" interrupted Clariel. "I've been to school! And I'm not a child!"

Clariel had indeed attended school in Estwael, from the age of eight to fourteen, and had been taught how to calculate using an abacus; keep accounts; write formal letters; supervise servants; ride in the great hunt with hounds and hawks; fight with dagger, sword, and bow; and play the psalter, zittern, and reed pipe.

She had also been been baptized with the forehead Charter mark shortly after her birth and taught the rudiments of Charter Magic, that highly organized and difficult sorcery that drew upon the endless array of symbols that collectively made up the magical Charter that described, contained, and connected all things upon, below, above, within, and beyond the world.

Indeed, it would have been very surprising if she had not been taught Charter Magic, given she was a granddaughter of the Abhorsen. The Abhorsen, chief of the family of the same name, both an office and a bloodline, descended from the remnants of the ancient powers who had made the Charter, codifying and ordering the Free Magic that had once been such a threat to all living things in its arbitrary and selfish nature.

The Abhorsens, like their cousins in the Royal Family and also the glacier-dwelling, future-gazing Clayr, were as deeply a part of the foundations and beginnings of the Charter as the more physical underpinnings: the Great Charter Stones beneath the royal palace in Belisaere; the Wall that defined the borders of the Old Kingdom to the south; and the Great Rift to the north.

In addition to the dame school in the town, Clariel had attended another, more informal, educational institution, largely without her parents' knowledge. Since she'd turned twelve Clariel visited her aunt Lemmin whenever she had a day free. Lemmin was an herbalist who lived on the fringe of the forest, in a comfortable house surrounded by her enormous, high-walled garden. Her parents assumed that Clariel stayed within those walls. But her visits to her relative rarely encompassed more than a hug and a greeting, for with her aunt's good-natured connivance, Clariel would go on out through the forest door, out to follow the Borderers into the deeper woods, or to join the hunters from the lodge. From them all she had learned the habits of animals, the nature of trees, and how to track, and hunt, and snare, to forage, to gut and skin, and make and mend, and live in the wild.

The wild . . . that was where she should be, Clariel thought. Not imprisoned here behind a great maze of walls, roped in by the vast net of streets, caught up in the thrashings of the multitudes of people likewise trapped—

"It's not like your old school," her father said, interrupting Clariel's thoughts. "It is a new thing, that they call a polishing . . . no, I mean finishing . . . a finishing school. And it's not for children as such . . . it's for the young men and women of the senior Guild members. You'll meet the best people in the city and learn how to mix with them."

"I don't want to meet the 'best people' in the city!" protested Clariel. "I don't particularly want to meet anyone. I'm quite happy by myself. Or at least, I was, back home. Besides, who is going to help you?"

Clariel had assisted her father for several days each week for a long time, working on all the aspects of being a goldsmith that Jaciel ignored, which included money-changing, some minor loans and financial dealings, and the administration of the workshop, particularly the detailed accounts of the raw materials bought, how they were used, what they were made into, and how much profit they returned when sold. She had liked doing this, mostly because she was left alone, and it had been quiet and peaceful in Harven's old study, a high tower room with tall windows that gave a wonderful view of the forested hills that surrounded Estwael. It also only took her a dozen hours a week, leaving her plenty of time to wander in the green world beyond the town.

"The Guild is sending me a senior apprentice," said Harven. "One who is suited for the . . . less . . . ah . . . someone with the . . ."

"With an eye for numbers and good penmanship?" suggested Clariel. She knew that her father felt diminished by his lack of talent in the actual craft of goldsmithing, though he tried to hide it. He had not made anything himself for years, probably because he could not come even close to his wife's genius, though he always lamented how the business took up all of his time, leaving nothing for the craft.

"Yes," said Harven. "Though I expect I will still need your help, Clarrie, only not as much."

"Or at all, from the sound of it," said Clariel. "How much time do I have to spend at this school?"

"Three days a week, until the Autumn Festival," said Harven. "And it's only mornings, from the ninth hour until noon."

"I suppose I can survive that," said Clariel. It was already several weeks past midsummer, though the days were still long and the nights warm. "But what happens after the Autumn Festival? Can I go home then?"

Harven looked down at the sharp-pointed, gilded toes of his red leather shoes, fine footwear for the consort of the city's newest and probably most talented High Goldsmith. Along with the smile, looking at his shoes was a well-known telltale. He had a habit of shoe-gazing when he was about to lie to his daughter, or wanted to avoid directly answering a question.

"Let us see what paths appear," he mumbled.

Clariel looked away from him, up at a lone silver gull flying toward Fish Harbor, going to join the flocks that endlessly circled and bickered there, mirroring the people below.

She knew what her father wasn't saying. Her parents were hoping she would find someone who wanted to marry her, or more likely, wanted to marry into the family of Jaciel High Goldsmith. An apprentice from a Guild family, or one of these "best people" from the school. This would solve the problem of a daughter who didn't want to be a goldsmith herself, or take up any of the other crafts or businesses deemed suitable.

But Clariel didn't want to marry anyone. She had once or twice—no more—wondered if she was naturally a singleton, like the russet martens who only came together for the briefest mating season and then went their own way. Or her own aunt Lemmin, for that matter, who chose to live entirely alone, though happily for Clariel could stand visitors provided they amused themselves.

They had talked about solitude and self-sufficiency once, Lemmin and her niece, soon after Clariel had first chosen to lie with a young man and had found herself quite separate from the experience, and not caring one way or another about repeating the act itself or the emotional dance that went with it.

"Perhaps I don't like men," Clariel had said to her aunt, who was pulling garlic bulbs and delighting in her crop. "Though I can't say I have those feelings for women, either."

"You're young," Lemmin had replied, sniffing a particularly grand clump of garlic. "It's probably too early to tell, one way or another. The most important thing is to be true to yourself, however you feel, and not try to feel or behave differently because you think you should, or someone has told you how you must feel. But do think about it. Unexamined feelings lead to all kinds of trouble."

Clariel examined her feelings once again, and found them unchanged. What she desperately wanted to do was get out of the city and, since the Borderers wouldn't let her join them, purchase a hunting lodge or forester's hut outside Estwael, to go hunting and fishing and just *live* in the quiet, cool, shaded world of the forest valleys and the heather-clad hills that she loved. But that would require her parents' permission, and money, and she had neither of these things.

At least not until she worked out how to get them . . .

"There is one other matter," said Harven cautiously. He was gazing over the railing now himself, which was a slight improvement from staring at his shoes, though he still wouldn't look her in the eye. "Well, a few other matters."

Clariel lost sight of the seagull, who had joined the flock and been absorbed by it, all individuality gone in an instant.

"Yes?"

"This school . . . uh, the Academy . . . it doesn't teach Charter Magic."

"And this means?" asked Clariel, encouraging the bad news out. Her father's smile was spreading across his face again, so obviously there was more unpleasantness to come.

"Apparently it's not the fashion these days, or something," muttered Harven. "The best people don't practice Charter Magic, they hire people to do it for them, if absolutely necessary."

"These 'best people' sound rather lazy and stupid," observed Clariel. "Do they get awfully fat from not doing *anything* for themselves?"

She herself was slim, and up until relatively recently, could easily pass for a boy. She still could, with a bit of preparation and the right clothes. It was quite useful, and had made it easier to follow the truffle-hunting pigs, tickle trout in the Wael River, hunt the small puzzle deer, or do any of the things that she liked but weren't proper for a well-brought-up child of the merchant elite. She thought this potential for deception might come in handy in Belisaere as well. Particularly for leaving the city.

"No, don't be silly," said Harven. "In any case, your mother wants you to further your Charter Magic studies—"

"Why?" asked Clariel. "She never wanted me to before. Is it something to do with Grandfather?"

Her mother was a Charter Mage, and certainly used her magic in her goldsmithing, but she made no display of it outside her workshop. This was presumably because she was estranged from her family, the Abhorsens, and the Abhorsens were very much a living embodiment of some aspects of the Charter and tended to be powerful Charter Mages. In fact, Jaciel's father was the current Abhorsen, but Clariel had never met him, because of a never-spoken-about rift that had occurred when Jaciel was young.

"Possibly, possibly," muttered Harven, which suggested to his knowing daughter that it probably *didn't* have anything to do with the Abhorsens. But he seized upon it as a possible explanation to her, adding, "The Abhorsen or the Abhorsen-in-Waiting do come to Belisaere upon occasion, there are ceremonies and so on, so we might well have to meet either your grandfather or your aunt—"

"My aunt is the Abhorsen-in-Waiting?" asked Clariel. "I didn't even know Mother *had* a sister!"

Her parents never talked about Jaciel's family, so this was all interesting information. She hardly knew anything about the Abhorsens really, apart from the childhood rhyme everyone learned about the Charter:

Five Great Charters knit the land
Together linked, hand in hand
One in the people who wear the crown
Two in the folk who keep the Dead down
Three and Five became stone and mortar
Four sees all in frozen water

The Abhorsens were the "folk who keep the Dead down," which as far as Clariel knew meant they hunted down necromancers, and banished Dead spirits that had somehow returned from Death to Life.

Abhorsens could walk in Death themselves and like necromancers used Free Magic bells to command and compel the Dead,
though the Abhorsens' bells were somehow not Free Magic as such
but bound to the Charter.

Not that the Abhorsens did much keeping the Dead down in
the present era, as far as Clariel knew. She'd never heard of the Dead
causing any trouble in her lifetime. Nor for that matter did the Clayr,
the fourth of the Great Charter bloodlines, seem to see very much
into the future. If they did, they kept it to themselves, just as they
kept themselves remote in their glacier-sheltered fortress far to the
north. Even the King, head of those "who wear the crown" didn't
do much ruling anymore, though Clariel had never really been interested in who ultimately was in charge of the various institutions that
effectively managed the kingdom.

Abhorsens, Clayr, the King: they all seemed to be relics of a
bygone past, just as the "stone and mortar" of the rhyme meant very
little in the present day. This referred to the Wall to the south, to
Clariel merely a curious landmark she'd heard about but never seen;
and to the Great Charter stones she knew only as they were depicted
in a mummer's play: big grey man-size puppets painted with gold
representations of Charter marks. In Estwael they had become part
of a comic turn in the Midsummer Festival, tall rocks that crashed
into each other, fell over, got up again, and then repeated the whole
process numerous times to gales of laughter.

"Of course you knew about your mother's sister," said Harven,
as if they talked about Jaciel's family all the time, instead of never.
"Anyway, we may be seeing her or your grandfather, and then there's
the King, who is your mother's second cousin after all, and they all
are . . . well . . . you know, very big on Charter Magic."

"I thought you said the 'best people' don't do Charter Magic anymore because it's too much like hard work or they'll get their fingers

scorched black or something. Are the King and the Abhorsens not the best people?"

"Don't be silly," said Harven. "They're more . . . more kind of separate, particularly these days. Out of the way. Modern times, you know, and different ways and means, things change . . ."

"What *are* you talking about, Father?" asked Clariel.

"You are to have lessons in Charter Magic," rallied Harven, getting back to the subject at hand. "We have arranged for you to take afternoon lessons with a Magister Kargrin, whose house is on the hill below us, possibly you can see it from here, I believe it is quite distinctive—"

Clariel looked over the railing. There were hundreds of houses on the western slope of Beshill, and many more beyond, all crowded together.

"Where?" she asked.

"Somewhere downhill," replied Harven, waving vaguely. "The house with the sign of the hedgepig on the street of the Cormorant . . . anyway, your guard will lead you there—"

"My guard?"

"I thought I told you about the guards already?"

"No you did not," replied Clariel sternly. "What guards?"

"The Guild has sent us some guards, for the house and the workshop, and also to . . . look after us. The family."

"Why do we need guards?"

"I don't think we need them particularly," said Harven, but he was looking at his shoes again. "It's just something they do here. In any case, one will be guarding you. To and from the Academy, and so forth. His name is . . . um . . . well, it's slipped my mind for a moment. He's waiting to meet you downstairs. Also your mother wants Valannie to help you with your clothes."

"What's wrong with my clothes?" asked Clariel. She was wearing what she wore most ordinary days in Estwael, basically her own version of a Borderer's uniform: a short-sleeved doeskin jerkin over a knee-length woolen robe with long sleeves dyed a pale green with an inch of linen trim at the wrists and neck; woolen stockings and knee-high boots of pig leather, made from the first boar Clariel had hunted and killed herself, when she was fourteen.

Admittedly, leather and wool was a little too heavy to be comfortable in Belisaere. The sun was hotter and the winds warmer here by the sea, compared to Estwael, which was situated in a high valley and surrounded by the wooded hills of the Great Forest. There was a term used disparagingly in other parts of the kingdom—when it was unseasonably cold, they called such days an "Estwael Summer."

"Women wear different things here," said Harven. "Valannie will help you buy whatever you need."

Valannie was Clariel's new maid. She had been waiting for them at the new house, and like it, had been provided by the Guild rather than being hired by the family. Jaciel didn't care about choosing her own servants, particularly since Valannie was immediately competent and useful. But Clariel had refused her help as much as possible so far. She was determined to do without a maid, since she could not have the help of her old nurse, Kraille, who had chosen to retire to her son's farm outside Estwael, rather than brave the horrors of the city.

"So you need to come down," said Harven.

Clariel nodded, without speaking.

"I'm sorry, Clarrie," said her father. "But it will all be for the best. You'll see."

"I hope so," said Clariel bleakly. "You go, Father. I'll be down in a minute."

Clariel's new guard was standing in the courtyard, near the front gate, watching two of Jaciel's workmen stacking sacks of charcoal. She was rather surprised to see he was both shorter and even thinner than she was, and much older, probably at least thirty, if not more. His eyes were hooded, and he did not look at all agreeable. As Clariel left the stairs and walked closer, she saw he had a Charter mark on his forehead, the baptismal symbol that was the visible sign of a connection to the Charter. So he was at least capable of wielding Charter Magic, though the forehead mark itself meant little without a lifetime devoted to learning and practice.

But the guard's forehead mark was mostly concealed by the red bandanna he wore, and would be totally hidden when he put on the open-faced helmet he held at his side. His surcoat showed the golden cup of the Guild, but it was done in a dyed yellow thread, not even a part-gold alloy. The hauberk of gethre plates he wore under it was short, reaching only to mid-thigh, and did not meet his knee-high leather boots. A sword hung in its drab scabbard on the left side of his broad belt, and thrust through the belt on the right side was a narrow club of some dark, heavy wood.

He turned as Clariel approached, bowed his head and snapped to attention.

"Good morning, milady," he said, without a flicker of emotion in his eyes or face. "My name is Roban. I have been assigned by the Guild to guard you when you go about the city."

"Thank you," said Clariel. "Um, why do I need to be guarded? We got here without any guards."

"Actually, we were with you from several leagues outside the High Gate, milady," replied Roban. "Incognito, being as the Lady Jaciel wasn't yet admitted to the guild."

He didn't look at Clariel, but at a point somewhere above her right shoulder. It almost felt like he wasn't talking to her, but reporting to some invisible officer who was hovering above her head.

"Did you really follow us in?" asked Clariel. "Why?"

"Orders, milady," replied Roban, not actually answering the question.

Before Clariel could continue, she was interrupted by the

bustling arrival of Valannie, who was always bustling, constantly on the move, busy doing something or organizing other people to do things. She was probably only ten years older than Clariel, and certainly did not *look* prematurely aged, but there was something about her which made her seem much older than anyone else around. She reminded Clariel of her grandmother, her father's mother, who had been just such a managing person.

"Lady Clariel, I am so sorry to keep you waiting," she declared, pausing only to insert her arm through the crook of Clariel's elbow. "Everything is arranged. We will go to Parillin's first, for cloth, then to Mistress Emenor, she has by far the best dress-cutters. Then Master Blydnen for shoes, or perhaps Kailin's, and I think Ilvercote for some scarves and suchlike. Oh, that reminds me. Take this for the time being. Don't worry, you'll soon have something more fetching."

She held out a blue shawl of some shimmering cloth. Clariel looked at it, but didn't take it.

"What's this?"

"A silk scarf, milady!" exclaimed Valannie. "To cover your head."

"I have hair for that," replied Clariel. "And a perfectly good hat inside I can get if you think it's going to rain. It doesn't look like it to me."

"No, no, no! Hats are for ordinary folk! You must wear a scarf, Lady Clariel!"

Clariel opened her mouth to say something about no one wearing scarfs on their heads in Estwael, but stopped as she saw her mother come out of the workshop door, trailed as always by apprentices and forge hands. She was not wearing her simple linen working clothes and leather apron, with its pockets full of files, hammers, pincers, rules and the like, but a kind of layered robe of blue and pale gold silks. She also wore a blue headscarf, though Jaciel's was embroidered with small golden coins that caught the sunshine and flashed it back, proof of real gold.

The lack of an apron was a bad sign, thought Clariel, because if Jaciel was not working, then she might take an interest in her daughter.

This proved to be the case. Jaciel stopped in mid-progress toward the men who were unloading the charcoal and changed direction, coming straight at Clariel. As she approached, Roban stood even more stiffly at attention, and Valannie quickly put the scarf over Clariel's hair, pulled it down to cover the Charter mark on her forehead, and knotted the ends under her chin.

"Clariel. You have come down."

"Yes, Mother."

"No more tantrums then?"

"I wasn't having—" Clariel started hotly, before biting her lip. She never could seem to have a normal conversation with her mother. "That is, I am quite reconciled to my fate, thank you."

"Your fate?" asked Jaciel. "Rather portentous, don't you think? In any case, I am pleased. I see you are about to go and purchase your new clothes. Make sure you pay attention to Valannie."

She turned her imperious gaze to the maid and continued. "Please see that Clariel has everything appropriate that she will need for the Academy and the house, Valannie. Do not let her pursue any . . . sartorial whimsy."

"Yes, milady," said Valannie, with a curtsy.

"And you are Roban?" Jaciel asked the guard. "The senior of the detail assigned by the Guild?"

"Yes, milady!" snapped Roban.

"Formerly of the Royal Guard, I see," said Jaciel. How she knew that, Clariel couldn't tell.

"Yes, milady."

"Then I must presume you to be adequately trained," continued Jaciel. She turned back to Clariel.

"In addition to your clothes, Clariel, you will need to purchase a small gift for the King. We have an audience in three days."

For the first time, Clariel saw emotion on Roban's face, a flicker of surprise at this announcement. Valannie actually looked stunned, her eyes widening for a moment before she managed to school her face into its normal, attentive guise.

"We do?" asked Clariel. She didn't know much about King Orrikan, save that he was very old, and the gossips in Estwael said he had become a recluse since the death of his wife and the disappearance of his granddaughter and heir, Princess Tathiel. According to common wisdom, he saw no one and now played almost no part in the governance of the kingdom. Which, Clariel had heard said, was an improvement from when he had taken an occasional interest. "Why do I have to buy him something?"

"Because you are his youngest kinswoman," said Jaciel. "The kin-gift is a tradition, when you first call upon him."

"But what can I get for the King?" asked Clariel. "I mean he can have whatever he wants, can't he?"

"Something small and personal, as is befitting for a gift from a young lady," replied Jaciel. "I'm sure Valannie will advise you."

Valannie looked surprised. Clearly some things were outside her otherwise vast sphere of competence.

"Uh, milady, I am well versed in the fashions of the Governor's court, but the King, I really don't, I mean he's hardly even been seen these last five years—"

"I'm sure you will find something," pronounced Jaciel. "Now, where is that Allin?"

"Here, milady!" called one of the senior apprentices, quickly moving to the front of the small crowd that had been waiting a few paces behind Jaciel.

"I am going to look at your design for a long-handled spoon now, Allin," said Jaciel. "Come to my study. Rowain, Errilee, you will come too. Bring your workbooks and drawings. The rest of you, be about your duties."

There was a sudden whirl of activity, with apprentices and work-ers moving quickly back to the huge, arched door of the workshop on the other side of the courtyard, and Jaciel and her chosen appren-tices going to the smaller of the two doors on the house side, that led directly to the chambers that Jaciel and Harven had taken for their private offices. Jaciel's, of course, was by far the larger room.

"Well, I suppose I had better go and find a gift for the King," said Clariel. "Where do you suggest we start, Valannie?"

Valannie frowned.

"I really don't know, milady," she said. "As I said to your mother, if it was a gift for the Governor, or one of the councilors, that would be a different matter. Who knows what small thing the King would like?"

"He likes fish," said Roban. "Or he used to like fish."

"To eat?" asked Clariel. She liked fish too, particularly trout she had tickled herself from one of the creeks that ran into the Estwael. Bled immediately, filleted, and pan-fried with wild garlic and shal-lots on a campfire, fresh-caught trout was one of her favorite meals. Yet another thing she would miss now they lived in Belisaere.

"No, bright fish from far away," said Roban. "Alive. He has them swim inside huge glass orbs. He likes . . . or he liked . . . to watch them."

"And you saw this when you were a Royal Guard?" asked Clariel.

"Yes, milady."

"Why did you leave?" asked Clariel, before immediately regret-ting the question, as Roban's neck tilted back and he once again looked up and past her shoulder at his invisible officer. Perhaps he was dismissed, she thought, for drunkenness or some dereliction of duty. "Oh, I'm sorry, that is a . . . a silly question."

"I didn't leave as such, milady," said Roban slowly. "When the guilds took over our duties in the city and beyond, most of the Guard was disbanded, there only being a few score needed for the palace alone. Quite a few of us joined up with one or other of the guild companies."

"I didn't know about that," said Clariel. "I suppose I don't know much about the city and . . . everything. Uh, why did the guilds take over from the Guard?"

Neither Roban or Valannie answered, but Clariel detected a kind of tension within them, as if both would like to speak. But Roban continued to stare at the sky, and Valannie reached up to make a quick and barely noticeable adjustment to Clariel's scarf.

"Well, it's useful to know about the fish, thank you," said Clariel, into the silence. "Do you know where I could buy one . . . or some . . . of these bright fish?"

"The fish market does sell live fish and unusual catches," said Valannie, wrinkling her nose. She looked at Roban. "Is it safe today?"

Roban nodded.

"Safe today?" asked Clariel. "What do you mean? And no one has told me why I need a guard in the first place."

"There is some unrest in the city, milady," said Roban. "Disaffected workers and the like. There have been some . . . minor disturbances . . . and the fish market is close to the Flat, where the day workers live."

"Day workers?" asked Clariel.

"Those who do not belong to guilds and are hired—or not—by the day," explained Roban patiently.

"Nothing to do with *us* and nothing to worry about," added Valannie brightly. "The guilds look after their own. Oh dear, that scarf still isn't quite right. Please, allow me, milady."

Clariel reluctantly lowered her head and let Valannie retie the scarf. It was clear to her there was a lot going on in the city that she didn't know about, and probably needed to know, but neither Valannie nor Roban were going to tell her about it.

Not that she intended on staying in Belisaere for a moment longer than was necessary. Not once she had worked out how to get back to Estwael, and how she might be able to live with only limited support from her parents. Or perhaps no support at all, for she was reluctantly coming to the conclusion that they would never countenance her ambitions. She would have to devise her own plans for the future.

"Very good," proclaimed Valannie, interrupting Clariel's thoughts of independence with a last, tiny tug on the corner of her scarf. "By tomorrow, milady, with the right clothes, I believe you will be a credit to your family and the High Guild of Goldsmiths."

"Good," mumbled Clariel, just for something to say, since she didn't care about clothes or being a credit to anyone. "I suppose we had better go and buy these clothes, then. But first, a bright fish for the King."

Chapter Two

COLORFUL FISH AND COLORFUL CLOTHES

The fish-buying mission was not a success. Clariel almost couldn't bear the crush of people in the fish market, the noise, the swift traffic of carts laden with fresh-caught fish, and the overpowering smell. Even with Roban leading the way, his presence somehow making people move aside despite his small stature, it was hard to proceed along the narrow alleyways that were lined with booths selling all manner of fish, crustaceans, seaweed, and who knew what else. Everywhere there was constant shouting from the sellers, and shouting back from the buyers, and yelling from the cart-pushers, a cacophony of sound such that Clariel had never experienced before.

To cap it all off, there were no bright fish. Such things were sold from time to time by the fish merchants at the northern end of the market who specialized in live eels, fish, and exotic fare like rays. But none of them currently had the bright yellow or orange fish that Roban said were the ones the King favored. Indeed, it was unclear where such fish came from, save that every now and then a sailor or a fisherman would come in with one or two, and more often dead than alive.

"You could try over at the Islet," said one of the sellers, who wore a bronze badge above his ringmail apron that identified him as an Undermaster of the Guild of Fishmongers. "They pick up oddities from time to time. In any case, I'll spread the word."

"I need one soon," said Clariel. "It's to be a gift for the—"

"Oh, look at that eel!" screeched Valannie, pointing at a huge, toothy eel that was flicking and coiling itself out of a nearby barrel. At the same time, Roban said, "We'd best be getting on, milady. It's almost noon."

"Uh, yes," said Clariel. "Thank you. I will try the . . . uh . . ."

"The Islet," said the fishmonger. "It's a little rocky island, not far past the South Tower. Outside the walls. Bit rough and ready, but safe enough in daylight."

"Thank you," Clariel repeated. "If a fish does turn up here, please let me know."

The fishmonger inclined his head. Before Clariel had even turned around he was shouting at one of his workers, "Get those eels sorted, you lazy gudgeon!"

It was a little quieter outside the fish market, but still much noisier than Estwael ever was, even on its biggest market day, during the harvest festival. And the people walked fast, as if whatever they had to do could not wait a moment. Clariel felt that if it were not for Roban, she would be swept up by the tide of hustling, shoving, catcalling people and carried away into some crammed alley, to be trapped there for all time.

"Shall we go to the Islet now?" asked Clariel. She was very tempted, because it was outside the walls, and anywhere outside the walls had to feel better than being within them.

"Oh, no time for that now," said Valannie. "We simply must get you some proper clothes!"

Clariel sighed and nodded, and held to the thought that this was all only temporary. Soon enough she would be free of all the people, the noise, the smells, and be back in the cool green world of the forest. She just had to figure out how she could earn her own living. She was honest enough about her skills as a hunter, and the difficulties of that life, to know she might survive a summer well enough, but winter would be another matter. Besides, bare survival had little charm.

She would need at least a moderate sum of coin to get herself set up, with title to a lodge or a cottage on the forest edge. Her parents could well afford to purchase this for her, of course—

Roban interrupted her daydreaming with a hand on her elbow, as she almost put a foot through an iron grille covering the access way to a sewer below. Despite being well-flushed with water from the aqueduct that bordered the fish market, the tunnel below carried with it a noisome mass of fish guts, offcuts, and scales, and she could easily have broken her ankle in the broad mesh of the grille.

"This way, milady."

Roban led them up the broad avenue of Summer Street, which Clariel was slightly heartened to see was lined with trees, though they were thin, bare, and grey compared to those in the forests she knew. The trees were some kind of ash, she thought, but neither Roban nor Valannie could identify them to Clariel.

They left Summer Street before it began to climb through the somewhat elevated valley between Beshill and Coiner's Hill, turning east instead into a narrower way. A hanging sign at the intersection there showed a faded picture of something unidentifiable, which Valannie assured Clariel had once depicted three needles and some thread.

"Three Needles Street," she explained. "Merchant Tailors Guild territory. We'll go down to where it crosses Shearer's Lane, which is Clothworker's, that's where Parillin's shop is. The best shops for cloth and the best tailors are all around the cross."

The street was busy, though not nearly so busy as the fish market. Most of the traffic was on foot, for horses were forbidden in the city for all but a few special purposes. But there were palanquins being carried by sweating porters, and many of the ubiquitous handcarts, though here they were loaded with bundles of clothes, rolls of uncut cloth, barrels of buttons, and giant spools of thread, and did not reek of fish and the sea.

The street broadened again as it continued west, and the houses grew larger, and began to have signs indicating the businesses within, most of them tailors. Unlike at the fish market, Clariel also started to see other people accompanied by guards, wearing the livery of various guilds.

"Am I supposed to say hello?" Clariel asked Valannie doubtfully, as she caught the eye of one imposing-looking woman coming down the street toward them, who was wearing the only other blue headscarf Clariel had seen, though many women wore scarves of other colors. This woman was also preceded by a bodyguard, resplendent in a sur-coat bearing the mortar and pestle sign of the Apothecary's Guild.

"No, no, you're not dressed yet!" replied Valannie quickly. "Look the other way! Don't give her a reason to notice you."

"But I am dressed," protested Clariel.

"Not properly!" hissed Valannie. She moved to interpose herself between Clariel and the apothecary. "Just keep walking!"

Clariel kept walking, but peered at the apothecary as she passed, just to see what on earth Valannie was talking about when she said she was not properly dressed. She'd seen women wearing all sorts of clothes, some like her own. But the apothecary was wearing what looked like several tunics of differing length. The main outer one was a dark yellow silk, but with at least three others of different colors beneath, the layers showing at the knee and wrist.

Belatedly, Clariel realized that this was pretty much what her own mother had been wearing that morning, but in different colors again.

"Do the colors mean something?" she asked. "And the blue scarf?"

"Of course," replied Valannie. "Guild colors for the two outer and two inner dresses, in the right order, and the blue scarf without embroidery means a close relative of the guild, a spouse, son, or daughter, not a Guild member yourself."

"Different colors for every guild?" asked Clariel. "How many are there?"

"Seventy-four guilds," replied Valannie. "And the five Great Companies. Don't worry, milady, you'll learn to recognize all the combinations at the Academy."

Clariel was about to say she probably wasn't going to be in Belisaere long enough to bother, when she was suddenly grabbed by Roban and thrown violently to one side. An instant later, she saw the bright blur of a blade swish through the air near where she'd been, wielded by a man whose face was hidden by his shabby hooded robe.

Before he could strike again, Roban was on him, grabbing the man's knife-hand at the wrist with his left hand as he punched him in the stomach very quickly twice, accompanied by a gasping wheeze from the young man as he arched back, avoiding the main strength of the blows.

Then Roban twisted and threw the attacker across his hip, sending him sliding across the road, between several astonished bystanders. The knife went clattering, more people started shouting and screaming, and Clariel added to the tumult with a scream of rage as she leaped after her attacker, the slim knife from her boot in her hand, though she had no recollection of drawing it.

The man was still on the ground as she stabbed at his thigh, her knife deflected at the last moment by the surprising intervention of Roban's sword, blades screeching as he forced her strike aside.

"No, milady!" he said urgently, distracting her just long enough for the attacker to roll away under a handcart, his hood falling away from his face. Clariel saw him clear for a moment, a handsome young man with fair hair. Their eyes met, hers so brown they were almost black, his as blue as a painted sky. He winked at her, crawled under the cart, sprang up, and fled down a side alley.

Roban kept Clariel's knife engaged with his sword and his hand gripped her elbow. She twisted against his hold, and tried to disengage her knife, a red rage filling her with a violent strength, so strong Roban had to fully exert himself to hold her back.

"Milady!" he shouted. "No!"

Clariel heard his shout as if from far away. She ignored it, and turned into him, her knife slipping under his blade, coming up again to gut him, fast enough he had to release her and step back, ready to parry or even riposte, and then her blow faltered as the viciousness suddenly left her.

She slowly lowered her knife, but Roban did not step closer.

"I had him!" she protested. "Why did you stop me!"

"Everything isn't always what it seems," said Roban quietly, watching her with wary eyes. "I didn't know you had a knife. Or that you could use it."

"I'm a hunter!" spat Clariel, too loudly, the force of her words helping rekindle the anger she had tamped back down. She took a breath, slowly releasing it, expelling the rage as her lungs emptied. This anger came upon her rarely, but she knew she had to be careful of its consequences. She had kept it suppressed since she was old enough to realize what it could lead her to. In the rage, Clariel was not herself.

"I see," muttered Roban. "Are you all right?"

Clariel knew what he really meant was "Have you got yourself under control?"

"Yes," she said, sheathing her knife back in its special place inside her boot. Her hand was trembling, and she felt strangely weak, as if her knees might fold and she would tumble to the ground. She took a deep breath and managed to stand fully upright, but she was very wobbly on her feet.

Only then did Roban come closer. He put his hand under her elbow to steady her and leaned close to whisper.

"Just go along with this for the moment. All right?"

"Only if you explain why you stopped me."

"Later," he said hurriedly. "Not safe here."

"Oh, milady," cried Valannie, hurrying over. She was the only one heading toward Clariel. The previously crowded street was emptying fast. People were disappearing into shops and houses, or retreating back up the street, a tide of humanity most definitely on the ebb.

Valannie looked at Roban, who gave a slight nod, filled his lungs, and shouted.

"Goldsmiths! Goldsmiths! To me! A Guard! A Guard!"

His cry was answered swiftly. Far more swiftly than would usually be the case, suspected Clariel. Shouts came from several directions, repeating his words, and within a few minutes the heavy tramp of many boots upon the paved street could be heard, accompanied by the clatter and jangle of arms and armor.

"What is going on?" asked Clariel. She could feel her strength returning, and stepped away from Roban's supporting hand.

"A vicious attack upon a goldsmith's daughter," said Valannie. "Terrible it is. You were lucky not to be killed."

"No I wasn't," protested Clariel. "It was a—"

"Shock," interrupted Roban urgently. His right eye half closed in a desperate, slow wink. "You've had a nasty shock. But you're safe now. Look, here come the Guard."

"Faked," whispered Clariel, low and to herself. The cut had missed her by a body's width at least. If the young man had really wanted to hit her, he would have stabbed her in the back. And if Roban had really thought he was an assassin, he would have had his sword drawn and through the man in an instant, instead of punching and throwing him, and he certainly wouldn't have blocked Clariel's own attack.

She was wondering what this was all about as two score or more of armed soldiery came around the corner, marching in step. Though all wore hauberks of mail or gethre plates, their surcoats varied, showing different guild insignia. There were gold coins for the goldsmiths, stylized ships for the merchant adventurers, bright blue drops for the dyers, upright swords for the weaponsmiths, and other blazons Clariel did not immediately recognize.

They were led by a tall and imposing man of middle age, who wore a long, very white surcoat over a hauberk of gilded mail, not gethre plates. The surcoat was embroidered with the tower and aqueduct symbol of the city of Belisaere, with a smaller badge above his heart, the coins of the goldsmiths again. It was cinched tightly at the waist by a very shiny belt of gold, supporting a gold scabbard that held a rather impractical-looking but very decorative sword with swan wing quillons and a jewel in the pommel. He looked to be forty or thereabouts, and no doubt had been very handsome when younger, as much of it still remained in his even features and thick, dark hair. But as he drew closer, Clariel noted his eyes were narrow, sharp, and distrustful, the eyes not of a hunter, but of a vicious predator. He reminded her somewhat of a stoat. A sleek and powerful stoat.

"Guildmaster Kilp," whispered Valannie in Clariel's ear. "A middle bow to him usually, guild relative to guildmaster, but as he's governor of the city as well, a full bow please, milady."

Clariel bowed low as the Governor approached. She kept her face impassive, but inside she was trying to figure all this out. The attack on her had been staged, but for what purpose? Clearly something organized by Kilp, because why would he be so close by otherwise?

"Ah, the young lady Clariel, daughter of my most gifted colleague Jaciel," said Kilp, returning her bow with a slight inclination of his head. As he straightened up, she saw he had no baptismal Charter mark on his forehead, or if he did, it had been very cleverly hidden with powder and paint. He smiled as he spoke, but though his lips curled, she felt no warmth or kindness in his smile. "I trust you have taken no harm?"

"No, sir," said Clariel shortly. She almost said something else, but Roban had edged into her vision and his eyes, at least, were alive with an emotion, one she recognized as apprehension, perhaps even fear. She shut her mouth, and saw Roban's throat move slightly, a barely noticeable gulp of relief.

"I am pleased to hear it," said Kilp. He lifted his head and raised his voice, speaking not to Clariel, but to the few people still around, and no doubt to the others listening behind shutters and doors in the shops and houses nearby. "If you had been injured, or Charter forbid, killed, then we would not rest to bring the assassin to justice. Indeed, should any of *my* guildmembers suffer such an attack again, we would be forced to close off the location, forbid all business, search all within, and take any further action that might be warranted."

He looked at Clariel and smiled again. She smiled back, the smile she used for customers who were trying to sneak bad coins in payment, pass an alloy as pure gold, or otherwise cheat her parents' business.

"Perhaps I can escort you home, Lady Clariel?" he asked. "To be certain of your safety."

Clariel shook her head. She didn't know what was going on, but she was certain she didn't want to spend any more time in Kilp's company than was absolutely necessary.

"No thank you, Guildmaster. We have not yet completed our purchases. Valannie, please, let us continue."

Valannie looked frightened now, more fearful than Roban had done a few moments before, as if declining Kilp's invitation was akin to Clariel putting her head on the block. Or maybe Valannie's head, since Clariel doubted the maid was at heart concerned with anyone other than herself.

"Oh, milady! After such a terrible ordeal, surely you should accept the Governor's kind offer and go straight home? I can buy everything you need, I have your sizes and—"

"I prefer to do it myself," said Clariel. "By your leave, sir?"

She bowed to Kilp again, and took a step backward.

"You are brave," said the Guildmaster. "If perhaps a little head-strong. We must take care nothing happens to you. Roban, take two of my guards. Whomsoever you please. Lady Clariel, till we meet again . . ."

He inclined his head, and strode past, a couple of his men running ahead, while most of them fell in behind. As they passed, Roban gestured to a tall man with a scarlet-dyed beard, who stepped out and waited, and then again to a woman with a scar across her chin that drew the corner of her mouth down, who also left the marchers.

"Heyren and Linel," Roban said shortly. "Used to be Royal Guards, like me."

"Milady," said Heyren, the red-bearded guard. Scar-faced Linel simply bobbed her head.

"What was that all—" Clariel started to ask, but Roban shook his head again, and looked meaningfully at Valannie, who was staring after the departing Governor. Perhaps sensing Clariel's attention, she turned, and cocked her head in the attitude of a faithful servant agog to hear the next command.

"Such a wonderful man," she said, following it up with an annoying laugh. "He's quite revitalized the city government, the Guild . . . everything! Now, where shall we . . . yes, Parillin's first. There is much to do!"

She bustled away. Clariel, flanked by her three guards, followed thoughtfully. Only a few houses along, Valannie turned into an open doorway hung with curtains of a rich velvet, tied back with broad bands of a saffron-colored cloth. Evidently this was the house and shop of Parillin the cloth merchant.

As Valannie entered, Clariel pretended to slip on the paved street. Catching Roban's arm for support, she whispered close to his ear.

"I want to know what is going on."

"Soon as I can, milady," replied Roban, out of the corner of his mouth. "Can't talk just anywhere."

When Clariel joined her father at the head table for dinner, above the mass of apprentices and servants on the longer table below, he didn't mention the attack on her. She chose not to bring it up for the time being, because she didn't know what was behind it, or the complications it might lead to, when she wanted to keep everything as simple as possible before she could escape the city. Jaciel, as was not unusual, was absent from dinner, no doubt working on something she did not want to leave.

In any case, there wasn't much opportunity to talk, with the apprentices becoming rowdy and needing quelling, and Harven's very vocal dissatisfaction with some of the courses, most notably the grilled eels that were served poking out of a giant pastry shaped as sea coral. Everyone else ate them with relish, while Harven summoned the cook to complain about the spices used, or not used. Clariel didn't bother to listen, and ate steadily, her thoughts far away as usual, imagining a life in the forest.

After dinner, Clariel went to the roof garden, to watch the sun set and get away from the organization of her new wardrobe, which Valannie had entered into with considerable fervor. It had taken all afternoon to buy a vast array of cloth, get tediously measured numerous times, and order what seemed like dozens of items of clothing, in addition to picking up ready-made clothes that Valannie thought would just serve until the new clothes could be made. It all cost a huge amount, more than forty gold bezants, a sum Clariel thought she could have lived on for a year or more in the forest and so in her opinion was a ghastly waste of money.

"Milady."

The whisper came from the top of the stairs. Clariel turned quickly, ready to draw her knife. But it was Roban. He was obviously ill at ease and would not climb the last few steps to the roof garden. He remained in shadow, only his face illuminated by the light from the ancient Charter-spelled lantern of filigreed silver that hung on a tall pole at the stairhead.

"Only got a minute," he said. "Watch change in a moment, I'll be off home. And I can't tell you much, milady. It's all politics and plots, beyond my ken. All I know is I was ordered to take part in the mummery with Aronzo—"

"Aronzo? Is that the name of the young man who attacked me?"

"Yes, and on no account to hurt him, not that I needed to be told twice, him being Guildmaster Kilp's son—"

"His son!"

"The older one. The younger brother's an ox, good-natured and not like his father, whereas Aronzo is too much like—fair-looking he is, but as cold and vicious as an eel, and as quick to strike."

"I don't understand this at all," protested Clariel. She frowned. As far as she could tell, Roban was speaking truthfully. There was a Charter spell to compel plain-speaking, but she didn't know it. In fact, she knew very few Charter Magic spells and hadn't cast even the ones she did know for months. Besides, Roban doubtless would be offended to have his veracity questioned.

"Kilp has staged similar 'attacks' before, making excuses to intervene in the business and territories of other guilds. I think that's what it was about . . . but there might be more . . ."

He hesitated, and shifted on the step, clearing his throat as if it had suddenly gone dry.

"What?"

"I'm only guessing," muttered Roban, "and smarter folk than I might guess otherwise. But Kilp is Governor because he is Guildmaster of the goldsmiths, and it is the middle of the goldsmiths' turn, with three years to go. But the goldsmiths have an election coming up *this* year, and Kilp could be unseated, say by the most famous goldsmith in the Kingdom. No longer Guildmaster, no longer Governor."

"You mean Mother?" asked Clariel. "But she doesn't give a . . . a grain of copper . . . for politics!"

"Your mother is also the King's cousin," said Roban. "In a Kingdom where the King does not care to rule, and none know where his heir has got to, maybe not even the King himself—"

"Princess Tathiel? I thought she was dead. Years ago."

"She may be. Who knows? The King cannot or will not say."

"You think Mother wants to be Guildmaster, and Governor, and . . . and Queen?"

"I don't know, milady. But perhaps Kilp thinks she does, and that attack on you was a warning—unless she limits her ambitions, harm will come to those she holds dear."

"Holds dear? Me?" asked Clariel. "Mother wouldn't even notice!"

"I think you'll find she would," said Roban. "Any mother would."

Not my mother, thought Clariel. She has been lost in her craft my entire life.

"There is one . . . other matter . . . milady," said Roban hesitantly. He was watching her carefully now, no longer looking down.

"Yes?"

"Begging your pardon, but I've seen berserks before, and . . ."

"What?"

"I think you might have the fury, milady. It is oft found in the royal blood, and you're a cousin . . ."

"The fury? Me, a berserk? I'm not old enough to be anything!"

"Age is of no import," said Roban carefully. "May I suggest you talk to Gullaine, the Captain of the Guard. The rage can be shepherded, kept in check, and she knows about such things."

Clariel wrinkled her forehead. "I do get angry sometimes, but I've never . . . almost never . . . completely lost my temper. I'm sure I'm not a berserk."

"As you say, milady," said Roban. "By your leave, I'll be away to my bed."

Roban quietly slipped away down the stairs, leaving Clariel to think about many things. She wanted to dismiss the suggestion she was a berserk. They were rare fighters, almost monstrous in their rage, which fueled them to great feats of arms, shrugging off blows and wounds, exhibiting the strength of several men and the like. And they were always men, as far as she could remember, from the tales she'd heard or read. Clariel had never seen an actual berserk.

But she had experienced a similar feeling of uncontrollable anger years before, when she had been surprised and attacked by a wild sow. It had slashed her leg through her leathers and got her on the ground, which was the worst place to be. Clariel remembered the sudden onset of the fury, starting from a moment of intolerable exasperation at letting herself get in such a predicament. Then the anger blew up like a forest fire. The sow had swung around to come back and attack again, and the next thing Clariel knew she was standing over its dead body, gripping a trotter in each hand, having literally torn it apart. And she'd still been so angry she'd thrown the pieces down, ripped up a sapling, and whipped the remains until suddenly coming to her rather appalled senses, followed soon after by a great weakness, not to mention a feeling of revulsion.

So she couldn't dismiss the notion she was a berserk as easily as she wanted to . . .

Roban's other suggestion, that Kilp was sending a warning to thwart her mother's ambition, was easier to disregard. Clariel very much doubted her mother could have changed so drastically without her noticing. Surely if Jaciel *was* plotting to become Guildmaster of the goldsmiths, and Governor, and then Queen, she would have stopped making things, or at least would be less fanatical about her art?

"I suppose I had better *try* to talk to Father," Clariel whispered to the sky. Unlike in the Great Forest, it was a vast and bare expanse of stars, lacking the comforting shadows cast by the mighty trees. It made her shudder to look upon the cold emptiness above, and shudder again as she dropped her gaze and looked out upon its opposite, the crowded, fettered houses jammed together, mimicking the night sky and its stars with lanterns and Charter lights in a thousand, five thousand, ten thousand windows . . .

Clariel went down the stairs. Even the cool, dead wood of the stair rail gave some comfort under her hand. It was not a living branch, but it still had some connection with her true home, and it had been cut and shaped by a master. One day, Clariel told herself, she too would fell trees for a house, and take axe, adze, plane, and saw to timber, and fashion a dwelling in the greenwood that would enrich her spirit, not leech the life from it, like all the cold, dead stone around her now.

Harven was in his study, his elbows planted amid a pile of papers, his hands close to his face, turning something in his fingers so it caught the light from another ancient Charter light on his desk, this one a cube of translucent stone with the marks set within a central hole inside it, so it gave a softer illumination.

He turned as Clariel entered, smiled, and then looked back to the tiny golden object he was studying. His daughter came close, and gazed over his shoulder at the teardrop of gold he held. It was no longer than the nail on his little finger, though a third its width.

"It is a perfect tear," said Harven reverentially. "Burnished so cunningly it reflects light from all angles, and appears liquid, for all that it is solid metal. Even as I hold it, I fear it will run between my fingers, and splash away into nothing. And yet your mother made it quickly, and will make dozens more this night, and yet I . . . some other master goldsmith could never make such a thing, no matter how long they labored. She has the skill of the ancients in her hands and eyes, rival even to Dropstone or Kagello the Old—"

"She is truly gifted," interrupted Clariel. "Now, Father, I need to talk to you about something important."

"Perfect," sighed Harven. "As the others will be, and all together in a necklace. It will be a wonder of the age."

"Father!" snapped Clariel. "I said I need to talk to you about something important! Very important!"

Harven reluctantly put the teardrop down. But even as he half turned in his chair to face his daughter, his eyes were dragged back to the golden object.

"Father, I was attacked today. In the street."

"Attacked?" asked Harven. "I heard there was some kind of horse-play, a . . . a jape or jest, on the part of Aronzo, the Governor's boy."

"It wasn't a jest," protested Clariel. "There was a point to it. Tell me, is Mother planning to wrest the Goldsmith's Guild from Kilp? To become Guildmaster, and thus Governor of the City?"

She had all Harven's attention now. He sat back and blinked, then gave a brief chuckle.

"What?" asked Clariel. "What's so funny?"

"I was imagining your mother dealing with all the dull business that comes before Kilp every day, as Guildmaster and Governor!"

He laughed again, and wiped his right eye with the back of his hand.

"Jaciel has barely looked beyond her workbench since we arrived! She cares naught for politics, or business, or any of these things, only her work . . ."

He stopped laughing as he said this, perhaps realizing its powerful truth, that it applied not just to politics and business, but also to Clariel and to some degree, himself.

"She wanted me to get clothes, and buy a present for the King," said Clariel. "Why? I can't believe she really cares whether I visit him or not, or about some old tradition about cousins handing over gifts."

Harven's smile came creeping across his face, till Clariel stamped her foot suddenly and shouted.

"Don't lie, Father! Tell me the truth!"

The smile vanished in an instant. Harven looked at the golden teardrop, and bit his lip fussily.

"The truth, Father," said Clariel, more calmly.

Harven still couldn't look her in the eye, but his smile did not come back.

"There is a salt cellar in the Palace, in the shape of a great shell, made from gold, silver, and electrum, set with emeralds and malachite. Each fluted rib is a container for more than a stone weight of salt, pepper, saffron, ginger, and more, sufficient for the grandest table that could ever be set! It was made many centuries ago by one of the greatest goldsmiths who ever lived, though we do not know his . . . or her . . . name, only the spell they signed their work with, which when the visible mark is touched shows a stone dropping in a pool, and the ripples coming from it. We call the few things that survive Dropstone-work. Jaciel saw the salt cellar as a young girl, and wishes to see it again. She believes she is ready to re-create such an object, to equal or surpass the work of the ancients, of Dropstone. I believe so, too, and she will prove herself not merely the greatest goldsmith of the Kingdom, but of all time!"

"What's that got to do with me giving the King a present?"

"It is not easy to enter the Palace now, even for a cousin, with the King holding himself aloof from the city and the people. Yet he does still observe some of the most important of the age-old customs, and Jaciel thought that the kin-gift would gain us admittance and so it has proved—"

"So I am nothing but a ticket of entry," interrupted Clariel bitterly. "Another useful tool for Mother."

"No!" blustered Harven. He seemed at a loss for a moment, once again glancing toward his feet. "It is simply combining two things. It will give you . . . um . . . honor and prestige to have been presented to the King, which will be helpful to you, in any . . . any—"

"Marriage?" asked Clariel quietly. "Do you and Mother have someone in mind? Have you had someone in mind all along?"

"Well, it is only natural we should think on it," continued Harven. "We want you to be well-established, Clarrie. If you chose to be a goldsmith, then of course you would be apprenticed, or any of the other high crafts, but if you aren't interested . . . and failing a craft of your own, a marriage seems the best course."

"I don't want to be married. I'm like Aunt Lemmin. I am happiest by myself. I would like to live by myself."

"Lemmin is a very good woman, and has been a good sister to me, but she is not a *usual* person, Clariel. Even when we were children she was not at all—"

"Father, I am not a usual person either! Can't you see that?"

"You are just young," said Harven. His smile flickered across his face for a moment. "I daresay you haven't met the right young man. There are far more eligible young men here—"

"I don't want a young man, eligible or otherwise!"

"You don't know what you want!" snapped Harven.

"I *want* to be a Borderer," said Clariel forcefully. "I *want* to live in the Great Forest. The best course for me would be if you supported this ambition!"

"Clarrie, don't be silly. You are our daughter, a familial member of the High Guild of Goldsmiths in Belisaere! You cannot just go and live in the woods!"

"It is what I want," said Clariel. She could feel anger rising inside her, a heat kindling that she knew she must not feed. She took a deep breath, held it for a second, then calmly said, "It is all I ever wanted."

"You are too young to know what you want," repeated Harven, as if repetition might make it true. "In any case, you owe us, you owe your family, to do the right thing and forget about this child's dream! You would not last more than three days in the Great Forest, and you know it!"

"How little *you* know me, Father," said Clariel. The anger was not rising, but rather ebbing, being replaced by a deep sadness. "I have spent many days and nights in the greenwood, since before I was even thirteen. All those times you thought me at Aunt Lemmin's house, I was where I wanted to be. In the forest."

"What?" asked Harven. "Don't be ridiculous and don't try to present your aunt as some ally of your fancies, just because you slipped away from her for an afternoon or two. This is an ill-considered dream, too long prolonged. And we have spoken enough of it. You go to bed. Tomorrow you begin your lessons at the Academy, and I trust that you will soon learn to become a proper young lady who respects her parents as she should!"

"As I should?" asked Clariel. "Perhaps I have respected you too highly!"

This was too much, even for Harven, who usually shied away from any confrontation. Pushing his chair back violently, he stood up and raised his hand.

"To bed!" he shouted.

Clariel gave no ground, and met his gaze, discovering for the first time with some shock that she was now slightly taller than her father, and that neither shout nor raised hand made her quail and want to flee to her room.

"I will go, Father," she said quietly. "But I tell you now, that one day I will go to the Great Forest, and make my home there, and then . . ."

Only at this last did her nerve fail her, the sadness welling up so high that tears filled her eyes, and one, never so perfect as the golden teardrop on the desk, splashed upon the floor. She ran out the door, crying out words she hadn't used for many years, because they never came true.

"And then you and Mother will be sorry!"

Chapter Four

GETTING READY FOR SCHOOL

The next morning dawned bright and clear, and even more detestable to Clariel than ever. The sunlight seemed to penetrate everywhere, accompanied by the dull, ever-present noise of the city, and there was no quiet, cool place to hide, no forest glade to shelter in. After a simple breakfast, taken alone in her room, Valannie appeared, chivvying her to the bath chamber in the lower part of the house, where other servants had labored in the dark to light the fire that heated the hot water reservoir, and work the pump to fill the cold pool. Clariel offered no resistance to the routine of steam and oiling, and plunged into the cool pool as instructed, and stood to be toweled dry without complaint. But inside she was once again wondering how she might escape the city, and get back to Estwael . . . or not Estwael exactly, but some part of the Great Forest near it where she would not be so easily found. But finding a practical means of carrying out what was essentially a daydream was no easy task.

"You seem tired, milady," said Valannie, as she helped Clariel dress in linen underwear and the multiple layers dictated by her guild status and affiliation, alternating tunics of silk, white and gold. "Are you well? You were not too alarmed by yesterday's—"

"No," said Clariel. "I am just thinking about . . . things."

"May I suggest, milady, that at the Academy, it would be well to smile, and to talk with the other young folk," said Valannie.

"Why?" asked Clariel. "I have no interest in them. I consider this

Academy a mere duty, and a dull one."

Valannie tied a blue scarf over Clariel's head.

"It will be easier for you, milady, to . . . um . . . make a pretense of interest. A smile, a simple question, these ease the way with people."

"To what end?" asked Clariel.

"To make friends," said Valannie, with a smile that Clariel found very condescending. "Surely, you wish to find some new friends here, milady?"

"I have friends in the forest, and in Estwael," said Clariel. "I will rejoin them soon enough."

But as she said this, she thought that in fact she had very few friends, and the ones she had were unusual for a woman of her age and station. Her aunt Lemmin was the closest. But she was almost more like an older sister, an ally against her parents. Lemmin provided a useful alibi for her forest adventures, and was also an uncritical listener to retellings of her exploits, rarely offering a comment, let alone an opinion. She supported Clariel, and loved her, and that love was returned, but they didn't really talk . . .

Then there was Sergeant Penreth of the Borderers, a tough and silent woman who had let her trail along and learn by observation since she was thirteen . . . but again, she didn't talk much, and Clariel had never felt the need to smile at her, or make conversation.

There were childhood friends as well, of course, people she had played with when small, or had shared the experiences of the dame school. But she hadn't really kept in touch with them, save to say hello, or perhaps share a glass of wine if they happened to run across each other in the town.

Clariel had never felt much need for friends, but then she had also never felt alone, even when she was at her most solitary. The forest filled her up, she needed no more. Here, things were different. Perhaps she *should* seek to make some friends . . . at the least, they might be able to help her work out how to escape the city . . .

"So I should talk to the others," she said abruptly. "What about?"

"Oh, that is easy!" exclaimed Valannie. "About clothes, of course, and at the moment, comical songs are very fashionable, the minstrels who excel at this are in great demand, as is Yarlow the balladeer, who writes such sly verses. Oh, and always, betrothals and weddings, and the alliances of the guilds, and in some quarters, among the more sober, the course of business, the price of grain and suchlike, though I expect that this is more for the *older* students—"

"I cannot talk about clothes and comical songs," said Clariel. "I suppose I could support a conversation about business, at least as it is done in Estwael."

"Oh, best not talk about Estwael!" cried Valannie, throwing up her hands in horror.

"Why not?"

"It is in the country," whispered Valannie, bringing her painted face close to Clariel's, so that for the first time she noticed her maid had no eyebrows of her own, just cleverly painted streaks of black. "No one speaks of the country in Belisaere!"

"I will," said Clariel. "Estwael is a fine town, and the Great Forest beyond an even finer place. Better than any part of this noisome city!"

"Oh, milady, I beg you not to speak such! Not at the Academy! Not anywhere! It will serve you ill."

Clariel sniffed. Valannie's pleading seemed very sincere, and though she burned to hear criticism of Estwael, perhaps it would be sensible to follow the maid's advice. She had learned long ago not to rush ahead into who knew what, but to go silently and hidden, to spy out the lay of the land.

"I will try not to speak of . . . of the country," she said.

"Good, good, milady!" said Valannie, with a heartfelt sigh. She bent down to do up Clariel's sandals, ignoring Clariel's own motion to bend and do them up herself. "No, no, milady. I will fix these on properly. You will see, it is not too difficult to make conversation. The young gentlemen and ladies will be keen to meet you, being the daughter of so famous a goldsmith."

"Will they?" asked Clariel. It was interesting that Valannie did not say that her connection to the King, or the Abhorsens, would make her popular. Her father had been strange about this as well, with his talk of the "best people."

"Tell me, Valannie, should I mention that my grandfather is the Abhorsen? Or the King my mother's cousin?"

Valannie stopped doing up the left sandal for a second. Clariel looked down at the top of her maid's head. The foremost part of hair, that part not covered by her scarf, was so shiny and stiff that she realized it must be coated with lacquer, or a varnish.

"Perhaps not unless it is brought up first, milady," Valannie said cautiously. "There, the buckle should rest just above the ankle, no higher, and turned out so."

"Why?" asked Clariel.

"The buckle is very fine work, and gold, so should be shown. If it were pinchbeck or mere gilt, then you would hide it—"

"No. Why should I not mention my connection with the King or the Abhorsen?"

Valannie looked up and gave the tinkling laugh that had already annoyed Clariel on several occasions.

"Oh, politics, milady! That is for your elders, I think—"

"I wish to know," said Clariel sternly. "If you will not tell me, I shall ask at the Academy. I shall ask everyone I meet."

Valannie snapped back like a bowstring freed of its arrow, and took Clariel's hands anxiously in her own.

"No, no, my dear. You mustn't do that!"

"Then explain to me. What are the politics? What is going on in the city?"

Valannie scowled and dropped Clariel's hands.

"Oh, milady, you are a hard mistress. I will tell you, but you must not let on that it was I. Your parents do not want you worried, and there are . . . well it is not right for a young girl to be drawn into troubles that are of no concern—"

"They are of concern!" snapped Clariel. "I wish to know."

Valannie pursed her lips, and looked to the door, before lowering her voice.

"Some years ago, the King went mad, or so they say. He is very old . . ."

"And?" asked Clariel, as Valannie faltered.

"He stopped . . . he stopped ruling, I suppose. He lets no one enter the Palace for any serious matter, only if it be for one of the old rituals, and then only upon rare occasions. He will not hear his officers, he will not read letters or petitions, he will not sit in the Petty or the Greater Court, or sign or seal any document of state. He dismissed most of the Guard, keeping only two score, so that the city was left bereft of soldiery and order, till the Governor and the guilds stepped in. There was trouble with lawless folk, and the common- ers who have ever caused trouble against the guilds, and the King to blame for it all! Now no one knows what is to come, for he does not abdicate, and Princess Tathiel is who knows where, and all must fall upon the shoulders of Governor Kilp and the High Guilds!"

"I see," said Clariel. "I suppose this is also why Charter Magic is frowned upon now? Because the King is part of the Charter itself?"

"Oh no, magic has been ever so unfashionable for years!" exclaimed Valannie. "It is so tedious to learn, all that time memoriz- ing marks to make spells, and then if you get one wrong, your eyes might bulge out of your head or your hair catch on fire, or some- thing even worse. Best left to those who have the time to waste on learning it all, I say!"

Clariel nodded. Valannie did not have the baptismal Charter mark, so she had no real idea of what she was talking about it, though it was true that Charter Magic could twist against the wielder. But it fitted with what she had seen so far of the city, that if some difficult service could be bought instead of learned, that would be preferred.

"And the Abhorsens?" she asked. "They are seen as allies of the King who has caused such trouble to the city-folk?"

Valannie looked up and shook her head.

"No . . . the Abhorsens rarely come here. I doubt anyone thinks much of their connection with the King. I don't want to speak ill of your relations, milady, though how your mother, the artist that she is, came to be born from . . . from . . ."

"From what?" asked Clariel curiously. Back in Estwael, though they did not often come up in conversation, the Abhorsens were held in high regard, as past defenders of the Kingdom against the Dead, Free Magic entities, necromancers, and all manner of evils. Not that any of these things were considered current problems, nor likely to be in the future.

Valannie pursed her lips and tucked her chin in, before reluctantly speaking, almost out of the side of her mouth.

"Well, just as Yarlow said in that ballad, they get rid of unwanted things, so they're really rather like rat-catchers, or even night-rakers—"

"Enough!" snapped Clariel. "That is even more stupid than being too lazy to learn Charter Magic."

Valannie shrugged angrily. "It is what everyone says, milady."

"You'd better make sure my mother doesn't hear it," said Clariel forcefully. Though even as she said that, she wondered if that was true. Jaciel was estranged from her father, the Abhorsen Tyriel, and the whole clan who lived somewhere to the south in a sprawling house or series of houses collectively called Hillfair. The reason or reasons for that estrangement had never been explained to Clariel. She'd never asked about them, either, and in fact hadn't ever really thought about it.

Maybe Jaciel felt so badly toward the rest of the Abhorsen family that she wouldn't mind them being called rat-catchers or night-rakers, the folk who back in Estwael emptied cesspits, but here apparently worked in the great sewers far beneath the city, keeping them working to carry away the vast ordure of so many people in one place . . . Clariel's nose wrinkled at the very thought of it.

Valannie was saying something about never speaking so in front of Jaciel, but Clariel ignored her, as she was suddenly struck by the question: What had made Jaciel separate herself from her parents? Quite possibly it was exactly the same problem Clariel faced now, that her mother had wanted to be a goldsmith, and her parents hadn't wanted to let her follow that ambition.

I need to find out, thought Clariel. If I can just get her to understand . . .

Far off in the distance, carried by the sea breeze, the bells on the tower of the Southeast Gate began to sound, ringing out the hour. A few seconds later, like a distant echo, Clariel heard other bells farther into the city follow. She did not know them all at present, but would soon learn their distinctive tones: Grey Tower, Old Shoulder, the Narrow Spire, and the clear chime of Palace Hill.

"Eighth hour already!" exclaimed Valannie. "We must bustle!"

"Where is the Academy?" asked Clariel. "More than an hour's walk away?"

"Oh no, it is not far, just over the top of Beshill, a little way down the western side, on Silver Street, that was once called Janoll's Way, and to tell the truth still is by the uneducated folk who can't read the new signs the Governor has put up. It is a very good address, and no more than an easy walk at a comfortable pace."

"Why the hurry then?" asked Clariel. "We have plenty of time."

"No, no, no," cooed Valannie. "We haven't painted your *face*. Come over to the window, here is a little stool, and turn toward the light. Please, milady!"

"No one paints their faces back—" Clariel started to say, but she bit back the words, and sat down as instructed, tilting her head so that the over-bright sun could fall full upon her. She shut her eyes and thought of home, of the Great Forest. There had to be a way she could bring her parents around, or failing that, escape from them . . .

Almost forty minutes later, her eyes wider than they had been, her lips much more red, and her forehead Charter mark almost invisible under something skin-colored that Valannie had painted on very thick so it felt unpleasantly like a scab, Clariel was walking up the broad steps that led to what she was told was a "viewing garden" atop Beshill. From there they would go down the other side via another series of steps to Silver Street, where the Academy occupied a very large house that had once belonged to a past Guildmaster of the Dyers, who had fallen on hard times.

The viewing garden had no living plants, Clariel saw with distaste as they reached it. There were marble sculptures of trees instead, arranged in a ring, with wooden benches between them, and in the middle there was a Charter Stone, a monolith of dark basalt, its surface only somewhat relieved by the slight luminosity of the Charter marks that swarmed and swum all over it, their light faint in the morning sunshine.

Clariel noted the stone, but not with any particular interest. She'd seen other Charter Stones dotted here and there about the city, but just as in Estwael, where there were three within the town, they were such a common sight that they seemed a natural background. She could feel the power within this stone, but was not particularly drawn to it. Despite her birth as an Abhorsen, her baptismal Charter mark, and early education, Clariel had no real interest in the Charter, or Charter Magic. Whenever she had a few hours to spare she had always taken to the forest, rather than spending time in the laborious process of learning marks and then practicing recognizing and drawing them out of the constant flow of the Charter, and its seemingly endless variety of marks.

"In the evening, young couples come here to watch the sun set," said Valannie archly, almost winking at Clariel, who looked away in distaste. It was true the top of Beshill did have a tremendous view to the west, and only a slightly lesser prospect to the east. To the north, the higher Coiner's Hill blocked the sightline, so that only the western edge of Palace Hill beyond it was visible.

There were trees below the Palace, Clariel noted with something very like hunger. A band of green between the great swathe of white stone, red-tile-roofed buildings that seemingly filled up everything for miles, and the high, bright walls of the Palace on the hilltop.

"Come, milady," said Valannie. "We must hurry, while not, of course, being seen to hurry. Roban!"

Clariel ignored her, and looked at those distant trees for another full minute, as Valannie made a noise rather like a squirrel being kept away from a toothsome nut by a dog.

"Milady, we should move on," said Roban apologetically. He was still accompanied by the two extra guards, Heyren and Linel, or as Clariel mentally referred to them, Redbeard and Scarface. Roban had not been able to tell her whether they were permanently assigned or not, or whether they were there primarily to protect her, or report on her to Guildmaster Kilp. Or something of both, most likely.

Clariel nodded, and turned to follow Valannie, who was talking as usual, gossip about the dyer and his house, and how he had been lucky that the Governor had allowed him to hand over his house in lieu of his truly enormous debts, and then in his generosity Kilp had given it to the city, for use as an Academy, one being sorely needed . . .

Clariel stopped listening. As they descended she looked out to the southwest, out beyond the walls of the city, to freedom. There was the great field of the horse fair, mostly empty at the moment, for it was only Dyrmday, and the horse-trading ran from Belday to Astarday.

If she could buy a horse there, Clariel thought, then she could be quickly away, following the road that ran straight as a sword-blade alongside Erchan's great aqueduct, till it met that even greater road, the Narrow Way, which was broad enough for six carts to pass abreast and had got its name from the peninsula it traversed, not from being a meager track.

Here the daydream hit a familiar obstacle. She had no money to buy a horse. There was one simple solution to this, which she had been considering for some time: to steal some from her parents. This wouldn't be difficult. She could help her father in the counting house, take the money she needed and make the necessary adjustments, a few silver deniers subtracted in one column, a few from another. Her father probably wouldn't even notice a dozen gold bezants disappearing if the bookwork looked right.

But it would be *stealing* . . . and she wasn't quite ready to take that step. Not yet.

"Watch these steps, milady," said Roban, interrupting her thoughts. "Some of 'em are cracked at the foot."

Clariel stopped thinking about embezzling money and looked to her feet, just in time to avoid slipping on a crescent-shaped gap in the next step, that wasn't so much a crack as a great bite out of the edge of the worked stone.

"I cannot believe these steps haven't been repaired!" exclaimed Valannie, again with her annoying laugh as special punctuation. "I'm sure when the Governor hears that *you* will be coming this way so often then he will speak to whoever is meant to keep this quarter in full repair!"

Clariel didn't respond. She was still thinking through the events of the day before, and the things she had been told by Roban, Valannie, and her father. She needed to know more, particularly if one of the likely possibilities she'd thought about needed to be averted.

If her parents got her married off, then she would *never* escape from Belisaere.

"Almost there!" said Valannie, as they reached a road cut into the side of the hill to make a long terrace. There were houses built all along its outer edge and down the slope, presenting one story at the road level, but three or perhaps four going down the hill, where there was another, lower road along another broad terrace. "Look, the house of blue gables there, that is the Academy."

The house was impressive, the white stone façade newly cleaned, with thin blue lines painted to delineate each course of blockwork. The crow-stepped gables of the central roof and its two lesser companions were indeed edged with a stone that had a faint bluish sheen, of a kind Clariel had not seen before. The entire building was larger even than Jaciel's new house, the front spreading at least eighty paces along the road, with a great arched gate and two lesser doors, and it ranged three stories up and at least another four below to the next terrace, the whole of it occupying as much space as Clariel's old home in Estwael *and* all six of its neighbors, and those houses had been the best and largest in the town.

There were a dozen guardsmen standing outside the open gate, three wearing the familiar blazon of the Goldsmith's coins, the others different badges: a black anvil for the Ironmongers; a slender purple bottle for the Vintners; three stacked square stones of white for the Masons; a gold-hooped barrel of red for the Brewers; a blue lozenge with silver roundels for a guild Clariel didn't know but guessed to be the Upholders who made cushions and stuffed chairs; and a silver pepper-pod for the Spicers. The guards bore man-high oaken staves in addition to the swords at their sides, and looked ready to use them.

Clariel noted that three men who were approaching veered to the other side of the street and increased their pace. Judging by their worn leather aprons they were probably journeymen or simple workers. The guards watched them go by with an attention that was almost menacing, before switching their collective gaze to another group of men who were pushing a handcart laden with small kegs that were marked with distinctive pokerwork: the triple interlinked "O" that signified they held the fiery spirit the Borderers called "Triplex" and highly valued, though more for cleaning wounds than actual drinking.

"A Goldsmith!" called Roban, as they approached the gate, but it was not a shout for aid, just the raised voice of routine ceremony.

"We see you!" called one of the Goldsmith guards. "Advance and be recognized."

This too was clearly routine, as even as he spoke, the six of them shuffled into two lines of three, and saluted with their staves, raising them up and then grounding them with a sharp synchronized crack on the paved road.

"Straight through, milady," said Valannie breezily. "Roban and the others will await our return here."

The guards had come with other students, Clariel realized. Students she would soon be meeting. New people. She had no desire to meet new people, but like everything else in Belisaere, it had to be endured until she could leave. She set her face in an expressionless mask, and walked through the gateway, with Valannie close at her heels.

Chapter Five

MISTRESS ADER AND THE ACADEMY

The gateway led into a large hall that had a musician's gallery or internal balcony under a very high, vaulted ceiling, and stone staircases in each corner, spiraling up and down. The hall itself was newly whitewashed, and was very clean and empty, save for a writing desk right in the very center, with a slender curved-back chair of mahogany that had a black cushion on the seat. Standing very straight and still next to the chair was a short and rather bony woman wearing the fashionable multiple layers of tunics, but hers were cream and white, and she had a black scarf on her head. Clariel did not know what guild or organization these colors signified.

"Mistress Ader," whispered Valannie, very softly.

"What did you say? Adder?" Clariel whispered back. "Like a snake?"

"No, no, 'ay-der,'" whispered Valannie. "Now we must be quiet, and give her a low bow."

The name still sounded like "adder" to Clariel. Mistress Ader didn't look much like an adder, she thought. Clariel quite liked adders. They left you alone if you left them alone. In fact, she quite liked snakes in general. They had their place in the woods and among the rocky hills. Also you could eat them; they were quite tasty cooked on hot stones in the corner of a campfire.

Up closer, Mistress Ader was a lot older than Clariel had thought she was. Her face was so heavily caked with the white, claylike stuff

Valannie called "astur" and in Estwael was called "esture" that from a distance she looked about thirty-five. Up close, the wrinkles under the white were visible, so Clariel upped her age estimate by at least thirty years. If she had a Charter mark, it was invisible under the clay.

"Lady Clariel," said Ader, making a low bow herself. "Welcome to the Belisaere Select Academy."

"Thank you, Mistress . . . uh . . . Ader," said Clariel, hoping that she'd said it right.

"We are delighted you could attend," said Ader. "Valannie, you have done well, Lady Clariel is presented adequately. You may join the other maids in the Paneled Chamber, until you are summoned."

Valannie, for once, didn't say anything, but simply bowed and retreated.

"Now, stand straight, Lady Clariel, and we shall talk," said Ader.

Clariel thought she was standing up straight, but she pushed her shoulder blades back a little and moved her feet apart a few inches. Ader sat down in her chair, though her back remained completely straight and she did not relax at all.

"This Academy prepares the young of the notable families of the Kingdom to move in polite society," she said. "Before a student takes their place in it, Lady Clariel, I like to discuss with them the path they intend to take, for this may shape some elements of our teaching."

"The path?" asked Clariel.

"Your plans for the future," said Ader. "Do you wish to be married soon? No? Many of the young ladies here do, and if that is so, then they have more lessons concerned with the supervision of a household, selection of a doctor, on childbirth, on setting up a nursery, and so forth."

"I have no desire to be married," said Clariel firmly. "Or to have children."

"You do not?" asked Mistress Ader. "You prefer some more

unconventional arrangements?"

"No," said Clariel. Her forehead wrinkled as she tried to think of the best way to explain. "I . . . I like to go my own way, without needing anyone else."

"Very few people need no one else," said Ader.

"I mean I don't need to be *with* someone, married, or tied down," said Clariel.

"Marriage need not be a shackling together of the unwilling," said Mistress Ader. "But it is not impossible that you are a natural singleton. You are not apprenticed, I believe? You do not wish to follow in your parents' footsteps? Or is it that you have no ability?"

There appeared to be no insult in Ader's voice. Just calm curiosity. Clariel felt as if she was an object, being weighed up and examined, and, once identified, to be put in the appropriate place, just as she herself had often sorted coins by type and weight and mint, and placed them in the correct niche within the great chest in her father's office.

"I have done some work with my mother, but not to her satisfaction, so it seems that I lack the native talent to be a goldsmith," said Clariel, not bothering to mention that she had deliberately sabotaged her own work, because she did not want to be like her mother, did not want to be trapped inside by forge and workbench. "Though I do assist my father in the exchange of monies, lending, the keeping of accounts, and so forth."

"That is good," said Ader. "If you did not already know how to read a book of accounts, we would have to teach you. But tell me, is there no other craft you wish to follow? Your parents could surely have you indentured wherever you would choose."

"No trade," muttered Clariel.

"Please, you must open your mouth and speak clearly," said Ader. "At all times. This is a rule of the Academy, but also a good guide in life. Speak clearly and you will never be misunderstood."

"I do not wish to be apprenticed to any trade," said Clariel, quite loudly. "I do not want to belong to any guild."

"You are fortunate to be of the Goldsmith's Guild, by blood," said Ader. "Much more fortunate than you seem to be aware. I shall ensure that you are taken on a tour of the Flat, where the day laborers live. But the question remains, if we are to teach you most effectively, we need to know your intentions for the future. Do you, for example, wish to become a guard?"

"No," said Clariel. "I can fight, if need be, with sword and dagger, and I am considered an able archer. But I have no desire to march about, and bellow orders, or take them for that matter. Or live among many, in barracks."

"You would, of course, be an officer, and not live in barracks," said Ader. "The Goldsmiths maintain a large company, and there would be a place for you. But if that was your intention, then I would send you there at once, for soldiering is a trade best learned young. So tell me, is there some path that you *do* wish to follow?"

"Yes," said Clariel reluctantly. She hesitated, sure that she was about to invite the scorn of this elegant, poised woman, then said, "I want to join the Borderers, and live in the Great Forest."

One painted eyebrow rose a fraction of an inch, but there was no other obvious reaction and no immediate outpouring of derision.

"Curious," said Ader, at last. "Perhaps I begin to understand more of your desire to be solitary."

"In the right place," said Clariel. "The forest."

"Your parents, I presume, do not support you in this ambition?"

"No."

"I am not overly familiar with the organization of the Borderers," said Ader. "Their chief house is near Hafmet, is it not?"

"Yes," said Clariel, surprised that Ader knew even that. The Forest fort called Greenstilts was only a few leagues from the town of Hafmet, and it was there that the Borderers' senior officers dwelled, the stores and records were kept, a hospital maintained, and most important as far as Clariel was concerned, recruits were trained.

"But they do not take in anyone who has not already been a forester, wood-warden, or suchlike for some years," said Ader. "Five years, if I remember aright."

"You do, Mistress," said Clariel eagerly. "But I have worked as such, off and on, since I was thirteen. If I can only plead my case at Greenstilts, and show my skills, I think there might be a chance they will take me."

Ader looked at her for a moment, then slowly shook her head.

"No. This is not achievable. Not now."

"Why not?" asked Clariel. "I am as good . . . almost as good a hunter and tracker as Sergeant Penreth, I have learned a great deal of herblore from my aunt Lemmin, I—"

"Stop," said Ader, without raising her voice or changing her tone. "It is not simply a matter of your skills. While it is very unlikely the Borderers would enlist someone so young in normal times, they simply could not enlist you now, no matter if you were half-beast yourself and the finest hunter ever seen."

Clariel opened her mouth to ask why not, but Ader held up one forceful finger and continued to speak.

"They could not, because like all the royal institutions, they have no money, and their future is in doubt. In fact, if the King does not reassume his authority, or if the Guilds do not take over the Borderers as they have done the Royal Guard and the Wall Garrison, then the Borderers must eventually be disbanded, when they run out of whatever funds they still possess."

"But that would be madness!" said Clariel. "The Great Forest alone needs constant attention, lest it run totally wild, and there is the West Wood, Great Sickle Wood . . ."

"Madness is unfortunately not incompatible with government," said Ader. "So. You cannot join the Borderers, not now, perhaps not ever. What else might you do?"

Clariel was unable to answer. She stood there, cold inside, part of her grappling with the idea that the Borderers might not be there to join, that her dream was even more foolish than she'd thought, while another part of her wanted to erupt in fury, to show this over-calm old woman that she *would* be a Borderer, that she *would* make the King pay them again, though she didn't know how she would do that . . .

"What else might you do?" repeated Ader.

"I can still be a hunter," said Clariel. "Live in, and off the Forest. Make what coin I need on top of that by guiding those from the town or the city who wish to hunt, but do not know the woods."

"You will need capital to establish such a business," said Ader. "It would be slow to start, particularly at your age, but it is not an impossible notion. If you can talk your parents into supplying say . . . at least fifty bezants a year, for your first five years, I would adjudge it an achievable ambition."

"Really?" asked Clariel. "I thought you would . . ."

Her voice trailed off. She did not want to say that she thought that the Academy was the kind of place that would make its pupils only want one kind of life.

"You thought that we limit the choices of our students?" asked Ader. "We do not, but it is a sad fact that the great majority limit themselves. You might find it best to keep your ambition secret, Lady Clariel. Many here would consider it too small, a thing to be made fun of. However, all I am concerned with is that we equip you both for the possibility of other futures, and for the one you yourself envisage."

She lifted the lid of her writing desk and removed a piece of thick paper, which had a list of twelve things printed in a large legible type in bright blue ink down the middle, leaving a very generous margin to the top, bottom, and either side. Closing the desk again, she put the paper down, carefully inked a quill, and drew two nearly perfect lines through two of the items on the list. Then she renumbered the list from one to ten with large numerals in the margin, not in the order they were originally written.

"This is our standard curriculum for those young people who will be venturing into their own business or enterprise," said Ader. "I think two subjects would be superfluous in your case. You will attend the other ten lessons, starting with number eight, as that is about to begin, and work your way through each day. Each room in the Academy has a name, you will find the location of each lesson in this list, and the name of each instructor. Your immediate class is in the Three Window Room—take the southwest stair there down two floors, walk twenty paces along the hallway, and the door will be on your left, with a nameplate. After your lesson today, I suggest you to walk around and learn the names and locations of all the rooms; there are only nineteen."

Clariel took the paper, running her eyes quickly down the list of lessons. The two that had been crossed out were "Keeping a Count of Monies, the Twice-Written Method" and "The Calculation of Cost of Making Stuff and the Setting of Prices Thereof," both familiar to her from her work with her father. The remaining ten were:

> On the Writing of Letters, Reports, Epistles, Writs, Bills, and
>   Such
> The Proper Obtainment, Direction, and Discontinuance
>   or Severance of Servants, Apprentices, and Partners-in-
>   Business
> Music and Dancing, Courtly and Otherwise
> The Role of Each Person in Households, Great to Small
> The High, Middle, and Low Guilds and Great Companies of
>   Belisaere

The Direction of Feasts, Celebrations, Festivals, and Fairs
Geographical Understanding and the Flow of Trade
The Serving of Tea
Matters of Law, Royal, City, and Guild
The Exercise of the Body, Martial and Merely Aesthetic

"The Serving of Tea?" asked Clariel. She knew what tea was, a new herbal drink that had been introduced to the Kingdom from somewhere far off five or six years before, though she had never drunk it herself. There was even a teahouse in Estwael that had been open a year with little sign of it becoming a permanent fixture. "How can that be helpful to anyone?"

"Go and find out," said Mistress Ader. "I shall see you again in due course, to discuss your progress. You may go."

Clariel hesitated, then bowed and turned around, heading for the southwest staircase. She had just taken her first step down when Ader called after her.

"Lady Clariel. One more thing."

Clariel looked back from the top of the stairs.

"I understand you are to study Charter Magic. It is a good thing for one of your heritage to study Charter Magic, as ignorance of it may prove fatal. Please pass on a message from me to Magister Kargrin when you see him this afternoon. Tell him I said, 'None have yet passed through, but I shall keep watch.'"

"None have yet passed through, but I shall keep watch," repeated Clariel. "What does that mean?"

"It is a private message," said Ader. This time, perhaps because of the angle, even at the greater distance, Clariel saw that there was a Charter mark on Ader's forehead, showing through the whiteness. Or was there? When she blinked and looked again, she couldn't see it.

As she stood there, staring, Mistress Ader raised one eyebrow, and this was enough to send Clariel quickly down the stairs. It was odd, she thought, that she should feel more nervous about going against that raised eyebrow than she had when facing down a boar armed with nothing but a boar-spear, trusting to its cross-guard to stop the boar running up the shaft and slicing her to death with its tusks, teeth, and sharp trotters.

She didn't feel particularly nervous about the class she was going to, because she didn't care about the people, or about the subject. "The Serving of Tea" sounded like an awful waste of time, but Clariel supposed she could endure it.

Particularly as she now had a plan with a definite object. Fifty bezants a year. It wasn't a great sum compared to the amounts her parents earned in the business. And there might be a simple way to get it. Clariel had always presumed that her *mother* was the stumbling block for her desire to become a Borderer, but perhaps it was really her father. Now she thought she had been wasting her time trying to get Harven to agree to her going to live in the Great Forest, when she should have been talking to Jaciel. Not that she ever really did talk to Jaciel, Clariel had to confess to herself. But surely this same question had arisen for her, and led to the falling-out with her father the Abhorsen. So she should be sympathetic.

The big question was when to talk to Jaciel, or more important, how to get her to pay attention. Timing was everything, and it would depend upon what she was working on at the moment. If the necklace of golden tears was close to being finished, then there would be an opportunity soon, as Jaciel typically did not start a new major work for a few days after finishing the previous one. Not that she stopped work, she just didn't pursue it with the same level of intensity.

Clariel was thinking about this, and going through various lines in her head, wondering which would work best to broach the subject, when she reached the door that had a bronze plaque set squarely in the middle with the words engraved upon it in an ornate script

"Three Windows Room." The door was ajar, and she could hear the murmur of conversation on the other side. Clariel pushed it open and walked in.

Five heads turned toward her, and the conversation stopped. Four of the heads belonged to people roughly her own age, somewhere in the vicinity of sixteen to twenty years old. There were two young men and two young women. The women wore the layered tunics of differing length in their Guild colors, and had their scarves tied around their necks rather than on their heads. The men had sleeves cut to show the inner lining of different colors and were bareheaded. None of them wore swords or daggers, or carried any obvious weapons at all.

The fifth person was much older, perhaps fifty, and reminded Clariel of a crane, for he was very tall and thin, his nose was long, and he had tufts of grey hair that departed his head at angles that made them reminiscent of wind-ruffled feathers. Wearing a long coat of banded white and cream, clearly the colors of the Academy, he immediately stepped forward and gave a middle bow to Clariel and said, "Welcome. You are the last to join us. I am Master Dyrell, and this class is The Serving of Tea. Before we begin, we shall practice polite introductions. You have entered the room, therefore it is to you that we look to begin."

"My name is Clariel," replied Clariel, speaking to the room at large, without really looking at anyone other than Dyrell. "Daughter of Jaciel High Goldsmith and her consort Harven."

"No, no, Lady Clariel," said Dyrell. "One at a time, one a time, beginning with the person of the highest order in the room."

"Who would that be, then?" asked Clariel. "And how am I supposed to know?"

"It will be a trifle difficult before you have met many people," admitted Dyrell. "But you can begin by looking at the indication of guild, which will narrow the possibilities. Here, you see, there is but one High Goldsmith other than yourself, so naturally that person will be of the highest—"

Clariel interrupted him with a kind of snort that would not have been out of place coming from a disturbed boar, as she properly looked at the person in the white and yellow of the Goldsmiths. A young, handsome man with fair hair and strikingly blue eyes. Familiar eyes, that had winked at her the day before, just before the young man had made his escape after the mummery of his supposed attack upon her.

"You!" she said, following the snort.

"I don't believe we've met," said the man, with a smile that was nearly a smirk, and very annoyingly, the shadow of a wink. "I am Aronzo, son of Kilp, Guildmaster of the High Goldsmiths and Governor of Belisaere, and his consort Marget."

"You see, that is how it is done," said Dyrell, with a curious glance at Clariel and then back at Aronzo. "Then we have . . ."

"Actually I believe I should have precedence, even over High Goldsmiths," said a slighter, shorter young man with badly cut dark hair that made his fringe slant from left to right, above regular but not particularly handsome features, and skin rather too white to look healthy. He wore simpler clothes than Aronzo, dark blue on top with dull silver stripes showing through the cuts in his sleeves, with no other indicator, save a small silver badge of a single key high on his left arm, so unobtrusive Clariel almost missed it. "Being the Abhorsen's great-nephew—"

"Rat-catcher!" said Aronzo, making it sound enough like a sneeze for Dyrell to be able to ignore him, though like everyone else present he must have heard it.

"—and a cousin of the King," continued the pale young man, ignoring the interruption.

"Yes, yes, we have been over this," said Dyrell testily. "This is not the old times, and in the modern age, certainly for the last very many years, it has been the custom in the *city* for guild rank to take precedence, save in some of the old ceremonies—"

"It's all right, Dyrell," said the black-haired man. "I'm just showing my cousin how things are."

He made a bow to Clariel and she saw a glint of mischief in his eye. Aronzo pointedly yawned and made a faint show of covering it up by turning his head a fraction, as the pale young man continued.

"Greetings, milady. I am Belatiel, and as we are kinfolk, please call me Bel," he said. "Unfortunately, since I cannot claim a guild-member for a parent, I am something of a nuisance here. They never quite know what to do with me. I welcome a relative and—"

"Now, Lord Belatiel, please, there are introductions remaining to be done, and there is a correct order to matters, tea to be poured, and so forth, before we can make conversation. Lady Clariel, the ladies present are of the Spicers Guild, red and yellow alternated in double bands; and the Vintners, purple, green, and silver. In the order of precedence as I have given them. Please introduce yourself."

"But they've already heard who I am," said Clariel.

"Please, Lady Clariel," said Dyrell. "Once learned correctly here, you will never be embarrassed anywhere in the city."

"I don't get embarrassed," said Clariel frankly. "I think it's because I don't really care—"

"Please!" beseeched Dyrell, with a flutter of his hand. "I do not wish to send you back to Mistress Ader."

"Oh," said Clariel. She didn't want to be sent back to that formidable woman either, though the whole thing seemed ridiculous. She turned to face the young woman from the Spicers, who was tall, blond, and even featured but not particularly attractive. Her nose was out of proportion to her face, and she made herself more unattractive as far as Clariel was concerned by looking down that long nose in a supercilious fashion.

"Greetings. I am Clariel," said Clariel quickly. "Daughter of

Jaciel High Goldsmith and her consort, Harven."

"Well met, Lady Clariel," said the Spicer, though her face gave no indication that it was indeed a happy meeting. "I am Yaneem, daughter of Guildmaster Querem of the High Guild of Spicers and her consort, Wihem, also a Spicer."

Clariel immediately turned to the next young woman and rattled off the same greeting again, ignoring Dyrell's wince as she sped through it. The Vintner looked a bit friendlier, Clariel thought. She was also tall and dark-haired, and perhaps could even be described as beautiful, or would be in a few years, as she had not yet grown into herself. She actually looked at Clariel as she replied, and there was warmth in her eyes, which were somewhere between blue and green.

"Well met, Lady Clariel. I am Denima, daughter of Haralf of the High Guild of Vintners and his consort Jonal, Undermistress of the Guild of Upholders."

"Now, please my lords and ladies, be seated around the tea table," intoned Dyrell, indicating a fairly low, hexagonal table of pale timber with a tiled top, set with an unlit spirit burner, a small tin of friction lights, a highly polished metal kettle, an enameled box that was open revealing tea leaves, a white ceramic teapot, and six very pale yellow ceramic cups on even paler saucers. The table had six curiously foreshortened chairs around it, as if like the table, it was made for people a foot smaller than usual. "Highest precedence to the north chair, there, then clockwise around."

Aronzo immediately sat in the north chair, and patted the seat next to him.

"Here, Lady Clariel, before Bel tries to sit down."

Clariel didn't move. She didn't like the way Aronzo was patting the seat, like he was calling a dog to come and sit by him.

"I will sit last, as Dyrell insists is the current mode," said Bel. "Yaneem and Denima, I am sure you will be happy to sit before I do."

"Conversation after the tea service," pleaded Dyrell. "You know that! Silence and decorum, please. A slight nod, a gesture, no more!"

Yaneem and Denima sat in the approved fashion, without speaking, leaving Clariel and Bel standing. Aronzo patted the adjacent chair to his left again, and smiled at Clariel in what he obviously intended to be a winning fashion. He was very handsome, she noted without favor. Combined with being Kilp's son, that probably meant he was used to getting his own way with women as much as in anything else.

"I am also close kin to the Abhorsen," said Clariel. "Perhaps I should sit in the least chair."

"No, no," beseeched Dyrell. "You are a *Goldsmith*. It really isn't difficult, Lady Clariel. You sit *here*, to the left of Lord Aronzo."

He went and stood behind the chair, pulling it out a little. Aronzo slowly removed his hand. Clariel hesitated, then walked over and sat down, pulling the chair in herself before Dyrell could push it in from the back. Bel went to the sixth chair, leaving a gap after Denima, so he was next to Aronzo but on the right side, in the position of lowest precedence.

"Please," sighed Dyrell, raising his eyebrows. Bel laughed and moved across one seat so there was no gap.

"Now that everyone is *correctly* seated," said Dyrell, "we may begin the service of tea. Lord Belatiel, you will light the burner; Lady Denima lift the kettle; Lady Yaneem pass around the cups; Lady Clariel, you will measure the tea in the pot, three spoons; and then when the kettle boils, Lord Aronzo, you will fill the pot."

"What is the point of all this?" asked Clariel.

"The point? It is a ceremony, to quiet the mind, before conversation; and like all such ceremonies, is best done properly or not at all," replied Dyrell, his voice unable to hide his agitation.

"Best go along," whispered Bel to Clariel, across Aronzo. "It's quicker that way."

As he spoke, he reached and began to sketch a Charter mark at the top of the wick of the spirit burner, only to be interrupted by a screech from Dyrell.

"No, no, Lord Belatiel! The friction lights! Only a servant uses magic!"

Chapter Six

TEA AND ARGUMENTS

R eally?" asked Clariel. "I thought that couldn't possibly be true."

"Magic is tiresome and menial. It is work that only befits a servant," said Aronzo, pushing the metal box of friction lights to Belatiel. "Or a rat-catcher."

"Please do be explicit, Aronzo," said Belatiel sweetly. "Are you saying that the Abhorsens are rat-catchers?"

"Would I insult such an . . . ancient and illustrious . . . family?" asked Aronzo. "I was merely thinking of an old rat-catcher who used magic to herd rats to their . . . death."

"My lords!" exclaimed Dyrell. "Please! Be civil, let us get on with the tea service, there is not much time remaining in this lesson."

Bel shrugged, took out a bright yellow-headed friction light, and struck it on the table. It lit instantly, spewing white smoke that smelled strongly of phosphorus and sulfur. Bel applied it to the wick of the spirit burner, then opened the other side of the box and dowsed the friction light in the black sand that filled it, before laying the burned-out stick on the table next to the burner.

Denima immediately put the kettle on the trivet above the burner, and adjusted the wick so that it would heat the water more swiftly. Before she had finished Yaneem was passing around the cups and saucers, very deftly balancing two at a time.

Clariel shrugged and transferred three spoons of tea from the tin to the pot, noticing that Dyrell winced at her inelegant motions and not very well-regulated measures, the first spoon heaped and the other two not even full.

Everyone then sat in silence, waiting for the kettle to boil. Clariel stared straight ahead, not wanting to look at any of the others, or at the nervously hovering Dyrell. She couldn't believe that she was stuck here in an absolutely ridiculous class, with people she had no interest in whatsoever. It made escaping to the Forest even more imperative, and then and there she determined that she would talk to her mother that night, even going into the workshop if that proved necessary, though this would be akin to entering the lair of a monster.

As soon as the kettle began to whistle, Aronzo took it off and poured the water into the pot, put the kettle back, turned the wick of the burner down till it went out, and put the lid on the teapot.

"Now what?" whispered Clariel. "Who pours the tea?"

"We pour for each other, for whoever we choose to show favor today," said Aronzo. "Isn't that right, Master Dyrell?"

"Yes, milord," said Dyrell, more respectfully than he had spoken to anyone else. "Whenever you wish to proceed."

"I thought the form was to let it steep for a measured five minutes," said Belatiel, ostentatiously consulting a blue crystal timepiece that glowed with Charter marks. "And I can tell you, it has only been three since the water was poured."

Aronzo ignored him. Taking a gold-cased and jewel-encrusted clockwork watch of the newer egg type out of a pocket in his sleeve, he flipped it open and watched it with an air of civilized boredom till the appointed five minutes had passed. Snapping the watch shut, he replaced it in his pocket, picked up the teapot, and leaned past Clariel to pour Yaneem a cup. She simpered, and when the pot was set before her, poured Aronzo's cup in return, before passing it to Clariel.

"I don't even drink tea," said Clariel.

"You don't have to drink it, milady," said Dyrell. "Simply pour for someone who has not yet received a cup and when you are poured for, do not drink."

Clariel looked at Denima and then at Belatiel.

"I suppose since you're some sort of cousin I should pour for you," said Clariel. "Since I cannot choose from any other knowledge who is most deserving of the honor, such as it is."

"How very sensible of you, cousin," said Bel, as Clariel poured his cup and passed the pot to him, whereupon he poured for Denima, who smiled as she poured Clariel's cup in turn, finishing the process. Clariel noticed that the smile was particularly for Bel, whose eyes sparkled in return.

Bel and Denima certainly seemed friendly, but Clariel couldn't tell whether they were amused at her or at the stupidity of this tea business. She similarly couldn't tell whether the hostility between Bel and Aronzo was real or some kind of playfulness between old friends, or at least old acquaintances. All in all it made her feel tired.

Clariel did not like trying to make friends, or the business of keeping up with them. As far as she was concerned, people might hunt with her, for example, or otherwise work cooperatively. She had no time for simply talking or the lounging about doing nothing together that had seemed to her one of the prerequisites of the groups of friends back in Estwael to which she had never really belonged. Here seemed no different, save that she could not escape these enforced sessions of conversation or whatever was supposed to happen.

"Now, as you sip your tea, considered conversation," said Dyrell. "A suitable topic might be the weather, or any striking matters of business observed in the market or suchlike."

"I observed something in the clothier's quarter yesterday," said Clariel, turning to look at Aronzo, who once again annoyed her with the faintest wink. "A strange attack upon a Goldsmith's daughter. A piece of mummery and—"

"No, no, Lady Clariel," interrupted Dyrell. "That is not an appropriate topic. Lady Yaneem, perhaps you might start?"

"I thought today less hot than yesterday," said Yaneem, slowly and without emotion. "And the day before that was hotter."

"Odd that it should be growing cooler so soon," added Denima, also speaking slowly, again without energy or feeling. But Clariel noticed the corner of her mouth quirked up, showing some effort at not laughing at herself.

"We must hope that it doesn't rain too much," continued Aronzo, his deadpan delivery slightly spoiled by a sideways glance at Clariel, who looked away.

"Excellent, that is the way it is done in the best houses," said Dyrell. "Please continue, till the Academy bell tolls the eleventh hour. I have something . . . some work I must attend. Lord Aronzo, I deputize my authority to you."

Dyrell was hardly out of the door before Aronzo spoke.

"Fussy old fool. And tea is a disgusting drink. Whoever thought up all this rigmarole should have been thrown off the seawall at the Shark Pool."

"But you go along with the rigmarole . . . when anyone's watching," said Belatiel.

"I don't lack for sense, unlike some people," said Aronzo. "There are advantages to having our elders think well of me."

"Why did you attack me yesterday?" blurted out Clariel. "What was the point of that?"

Aronzo yawned.

"Must you keep harping on about that?"

"What attack?" asked Belatiel and Denima at almost the same time.

"A faked one," said Clariel. "Aronzo, under a hood, pretended to take a dagger-swipe at me, then ran off while his father came up with a whole troop of men and made a speech about not attacking

Goldsmiths, which seemed to be the whole aim of the stupidity."

"We shouldn't be talking about this sort of thing," said Yaneem stuffily. "Dyrell could come back, or Mistress Ader might come in."

Everyone else ignored her. Aronzo shrugged at Clariel.

"That *was* the point of it. Father wanted an excuse to warn some of the weavers and tailors who've been talking trouble. I merely volunteered to help out, and you happened to be a convenient target. Besides, I wanted to take a look at you."

"Why?" asked Yaneem, with a sniff that suggested no one would want to look at Clariel at any time. Particularly not if they had her to look at instead.

"Sometimes one wants to . . . see something new," said Aronzo, with a sigh. Yaneem colored and pursed her lips while Denima and Belatiel exchanged a swift glance. Clariel noted all this and inwardly sighed, though she was careful to show no outward emotion. Back home in Estwael she had avoided becoming involved or even necessarily knowing about all the complicated romantic entanglements of her former school-fellows, simply by not being around.

Clariel's own sexual experimentation with a twenty-two-year-old Borderer the previous year had happened out of curiosity, not love, or even very much desire. She had liked Ramis well enough and he had certainly desired *her*, but though she had slept with him three times to be sure of what she was feeling—or not—she had not particularly cared when he was posted away, and neither had she sought out a new lover. Though her aunt Lemmin had suggested her feelings might change as she grew older, Clariel wasn't so sure. She simply felt she had better things to do. Or she did have, when the Forest lay close by.

But though Clariel was not a captive to such feelings, it seemed to her that Yaneem was in the grip of just such emotion. Clearly Aronzo and Yaneem had some history as bedfellows, and Yaneem considered the relationship to be more important than Aronzo did.

"I trust your curiosity has been entirely satisfied," said Clariel coldly. "You were lucky I didn't kill you."

"Oh, I don't think you could have done that," drawled Aronzo, displaying massive—and to Clariel, deluded—self-confidence. "I was a little surprised to find you so suddenly beclawed."

"I would have liked to have seen this combat," said Belatiel. "My money would be on my cousin if it happens again."

"Oh, I'm sure we could find better things to do together than fight," said Aronzo, looking at Clariel and smiling. He was very handsome, and his teeth were very white, so white that Clariel found herself wanting to smack him in the mouth with her teacup, for his assumption that she would swoon and lie back when he paid attention to her.

"I doubt it," she replied, through gritted teeth. "I doubt I shall see you at all outside of this ridiculous Academy."

"Of course you will," soothed Aronzo. "We are both Goldsmiths, and your mother and my father are working so closely together, we're practically family already."

"What do you mean 'practically family already'?" asked Clariel. Her fingers were tightening on the teacup, knuckles almost white. She could feel the anger growing as she thought about what he was implying. Her mother and his father . . . it was an insult that could not be borne. She half rose out of her chair, the teacup shattering in her hand. She held a jagged segment of china, and then Denima was calling out—

"Clariel! Don't react! Aronzo likes to tease and cause trouble, he likes people . . . women in particular . . . to get upset."

Aronzo chuckled and deliberately leaned past to say something to Yaneem, who laughed in turn. Clariel, standing above, for a brief, white-hot moment of anger considered punching down with the sharp ceramic shard, straight into his neck, but the moment passed as quickly as it came. Frightened by the intensity of that sudden emotion, Clariel slowly subsided into her chair and let the fragment drop onto the table.

"It's true, Aronzo is like a troublesome thorn in the foot," said Belatiel. "A little prick—"

"Shut up, rat-catcher," said Aronzo. He leaned back in his chair and smiled again at Clariel, this time more easily, showing less of his ever-so-white teeth. "I apologize, Lady Clariel. It is true that I like a jest or jape, sometimes too much. I most humbly beg your pardon."

"I accept your apology," said Clariel shortly. Inwardly she decided to keep away from Aronzo. She just didn't understand this stop-start behavior, or what his true intentions were.

"Where is it you have come from?" asked Yaneem, apparently politely returning to the proscribed small-talk for a tea party.

"Estwael," said Clariel, with a pang. What she would give to be there now, and be able to walk out through the town gate, and leave the high road a hundred yards south and take the track that wound up into the hills, into the Great Forest—

"I'm not even sure where that is," tittered Yaneem. "Do you know, Aronzo?"

"Of course I do," said Aronzo. "Haven't you ever looked at a map?"

Yaneem flushed again, and was silent.

"Another delightful lesson," murmured Belatiel.

"Don't *you* be mean, Bel," said Denima. "We might as well try to be nice to each other, since we'll be doing this till the Autumn Fair."

"What!" exclaimed Clariel. "This same tea business every week?"

"Or more," said Denima. "If Mistress Ader thinks we need it."

"So we will be seeing each other," said Aronzo. "Won't that be amusing?"

Clariel didn't answer him.

"In fact, why don't you come and take supper with me this

evening?" continued Aronzo. Yaneem turned her face away as he spoke, and Clariel heard her bite down on a sob. "So I can make amends for my bad behavior?"

"No thank you," replied Clariel. "I'm afraid I will be busy."

"Tomorrow then."

"I shall be busy tomorrow evening as well."

"Come to luncheon. Starday tomorrow, no Academy."

"I will be busy," reiterated Clariel.

"Doing what?" asked Aronzo.

"Being busy," said Clariel. "As I shall be busy on any other day you might ask me to luncheon or supper or any such thing."

"I'll just have Father ask your parents to have you visit," said Aronzo. "They're very keen we should . . . acquaint ourselves."

"Does your father do everything for you?" asked Clariel. "I trust you can at least wipe your—"

Her words were lost in the sudden tolling of a bell, ringing in the corner tower far above, its echoes reverberating through the floor. But Aronzo caught the gist of what she was saying, and his handsome face flushed red with anger, and he spat some insult back that Clariel did not hear, and could not guess from watching his mouth. He made to lunge at her, but suddenly stopped as she drew her smallest dagger, a leaf-shaped blade the length of her little finger, from its sheath inside her left sleeve.

Clariel smiled, stood up, and pushed her chair with the back of her knees, to give herself space. She backed away another two paces as the bell continued to toll through its eleven strikes, marking the hour. The others also stood, but none drew weapons or reached for hidden arms, though Clariel noted that Belatiel's right hand was clawed back in a gesture typical for preparatory spellcasting, though whether any spell would be directed against her or Aronzo she couldn't tell. Perhaps it would be purely defensive.

As the last note of the bell faded away, Denima clapped her hands suddenly and called out, "Dyrell will be back in a moment. Please sheathe your blade, Lady Clariel, and sit. You too, Aronzo. None of us want to be dragged up before Mistress Ader."

"I do not take orders from cushion-sewers," said Aronzo. "But to show I bear no grudge, Lady Clariel, I will sit down."

He sat down and turned away from Clariel, pointedly looking at the empty chair next to Belatiel.

Clariel slid her small dagger home into the sheath along her left wrist, under her sleeve, and also sat. Yaneem, Denima, and Belatiel sat down as well. There was complete silence for a moment, then Denima suddenly laughed.

"That was more interesting than most tea service lessons!"

"It's not supposed to be like this," muttered Yaneem. Whether she was talking about the lesson or her relationship with Aronzo was unclear, thought Clariel, though the spiteful glance she then received suggested it was the latter. An enemy found without wanting one, with little chance of repairing the situation. Yet another reason to be away from the city as soon as possible.

They sat in silence for a minute, until Dyrell came in, holding a great sheaf of papers and appearing quite flustered. He looked at the table, saw the broken cup in front of Clariel, dropped the papers, and flapped his hands around in what in other circumstances might have been the beginning of some kind of dance but here was an expression of great upset.

"You broke a cup!"

"It was an accident," said Denima as Clariel said, "I didn't mean to break it!"

"It's only a cup," said Aronzo. He carelessly reached into the purse at his belt and withdrew two gold bezants, throwing them on the table. They rang true as they hit and one rolled on its edge over to Belatiel's saucer, clanging again as it struck.

"It is not the cost of the cup, Lord Aronzo," said Dyrell. He took a deep breath and bent down to pick up his papers, continuing to speak as he crouched on the floor. "It is the principle. The opportunity for such a breakage should not have occurred. You must aim for greater delicacy when handling a teacup, Lady Clariel, really you must try harder."

Clariel bit back an extremely rude response as she saw Denima smile and shake her head, just a little bit. It was a warning and a friendly gesture and as soon as she saw it Clariel realized that entering into any kind of discussion with Dyrell would only prolong the awfulness of this tea service lesson.

"I will try my best," she said primly.

"Thank you," said Dyrell. He put half his papers on the table and bent down to pick up more, but continued to speak, so that his voice appeared to be emanating from the floor. "Now, you may go to your next lesson. Please do not dawdle or delay."

Everyone pushed back their chairs. Clariel waited a moment, letting Aronzo stalk out first as he clearly expected to do. Yaneem was close in his wake, trying to catch up with him, one hand almost plucking at his elbow, but not quite landing there, as if she didn't dare to make that touch. Both Belatiel and Denima stayed back, and followed Clariel close as she went out into the corridor.

"What is your next—" began Belatiel, as Denima said, "What have you got next—"

They stopped talking at the same time and both gestured to the other to continue.

"Please, go on," said Belatiel, but Denima was saying, "After you, sir."

Clariel took out her paper, consulted it, and said, "I have Matters of Law, Royal, City, and Guild in the Crooked Room. But I don't know where it is."

"That's my next lesson too," said Denima. "I'll show you the way. Come on, we don't want to be late."

She started off, with Clariel and Belatiel following, the latter talking as he walked.

"I've got Money Counting," said Belatiel, making a face. "Tower Room, with Master Fincher. But I really do want to talk to you, cousin, about . . . about a very important matter concerning our family, the Abhorsens, that is. I hesitate to ask, after Aronzo, but my motives really are straightforward and honest, so I wonder if we could meet after the lessons today . . ."

"I really am busy," said Clariel, giving him the benefit of the doubt. "I have Charter Magic lessons this afternoon, and tomorrow I have to go to the Islet to try and find a colorful fish."

"So you don't hold with only servants doing Charter Magic," said Belatiel, with a pleased look. As before, Denima spoke at almost the same time, so their words overlapped: "A colorful fish? Who for?"

"The King," said Clariel. "I'm not much of a Charter Mage and I don't particularly want to be one, but I don't think it should be left to servants . . . what?"

Denima had stopped in mid-stride and swung around to face Clariel so they nearly ran into each other, and Belatiel had also crowded close, and they were both staring at her.

"The King?"

"You're seeing the King?"

"The day after tomorrow," said Clariel. "The fish is for a kin-gift. It's traditional, apparently."

"But no one sees the King," said Belatiel. "Not for years."

"No one," repeated Denima.

"I was told he keeps up some of the old traditions," said Clariel, uncomfortably. "Like the kin-gift, and I'm his cousin so I have to see him to give him the present—"

"I'm a cousin too, and I've never been able to get an audience," interrupted Belatiel. "I was supposed to present the kin-gift when I first got here last year, but the King refused to see me. Or someone refused on his behalf."

"Mother seems to think we'll get in," said Clariel. "I wish I understood what is going on here. There's clearly all kinds of machinations afoot and I really don't want to get caught up in them before I can . . ."

Her voice trailed off and she looked down at her shoes, before realizing she was doing exactly what her father did when he wanted to avoid talking about something difficult, so she jerked her head back up to see Belatiel and Denima looking at her, not unkindly. For the first time she realized that they both had forehead Charter marks, albeit disguised under the same sort of thick paint as her own. But Aronzo and Yaneem didn't have marks, or at least she didn't think they had.

"Before you can do what?" asked Denima.

"Make my own plans," said Clariel.

"You're right about the machinations," said Belatiel, lowering his voice. "There are things you should know, that's why I want to see you after the lesson. Be very careful of Aronzo, for one. His father effectively rules the city now, and that pretty much means the Kingdom as well—"

"Does it really matter who rules the city, or the Kingdom for that matter?" interrupted Clariel.

"Perhaps it doesn't matter so much who actually rules," replied Belatiel. "But the Royal Family don't just govern the Kingdom. They also embody part of the Charter, and are charged with its preservation, in all its manifestations. Which begs the question, who . . . or what . . . also gains if the King is overthrown?"

Chapter Seven

THE EDUCATION OF A CHARTER MAGE

I f the King is *overthrown*?" asked Clariel. "What do you mean?"

"We can't talk about it here," said Belatiel. "I'll meet you straight after class, and we can go—"

"You shouldn't be talking about it at all," interrupted Denima. "Best you leave it alone. Come on, Clariel. Law is taught by Mistress Gurlen and she's a very different proposition from old Dyrell."

"Wait for me after class!" called out Bel, as Denima took Clariel's hand and dragged her away. "It is important! Very important!"

"They always say that," said Denima. She darted a look at Bel that Clariel couldn't interpret: part angry and part wistful. "Men!"

Clariel wondered if it was as simple as that. Bel wasn't obviously trying to set up a flirtation, he appeared sincere about having something important to tell her. And she felt she should know more about the situation in the city and what was going on with the King, and the Guilds and all that, despite another part of her wanting to keep separate from it all. If she could convince her mother, she might be away within days, off to the Great Forest, and then everyone could fight over who ruled to their hearts' content.

As for the Charter, Clariel thought it ought to be fine without assistance from the likes of Belatiel or herself. She didn't really know what the Royal Family had to do for or with the Charter, the childhood rhyme about the Great Charters not being very informative on a detailed level. Apart from the Royal Family, the Clayr, and the Abhorsens having some role, she did know Charter Stones were important for keeping the whole thing together. There were several Charter Stones in Estwael, and every village had one, and she had seen a number in the city, often at crossroads or other such places as well as the one in the hilltop garden near her house. All of them looked extremely old, and from her limited perception of the marks that shone and crawled upon the stone, the magic within them was ancient too, so it didn't seem that the current King or any of his immediate predecessors had very much to do with them.

"Come on, we'll be late!" urged Denima. She started to run, and Clariel ran with her, up one of the corner stairs, along another bare, whitewashed corridor, and then into what was clearly a later addition to the house, the stonework changing to brick, the ceiling lower, and the angle where the walls met something less than true.

"Crooked Room," said Denima, slowing to a walk. "Better lesson, better teacher. You might even like this one. Sit by me . . . if you like."

It was a better lesson, and Clariel did sit by Denima. The group was larger, but there was no nonsense with introductions, apart from Clariel meeting Mistress Gurlen, a surprisingly young woman with a commanding presence, bright eyes, and a penetrating voice. She lectured from a podium and drew with chalk on a huge slate board, and the students sat in rows behind small desks. Every desk had two key reference books chained to it, books that Gurlen expected everyone to be able to hunt through and find any indicated text at a moment's notice.

Clariel almost enjoyed it, for it suited her idea of how things should be. There was a clear aim, potentially useful knowledge, a confident leader, and no time to waste. If only the class had taken place beyond the walls, in some sun-dappled glade, she would have enjoyed it completely. But even grappling intently with questions of law and the differing interpretations of the texts and a third opinion from Mistress Gurlen, she could never entirely forget the brick walls that hemmed her in, and the oppressive weight of the city beyond that.

It was a relief when the class was finally over, and they were dismissed. Though many of the students were slow to leave, chatting to one another, Clariel went straight for the door. Denima half raised her hand as if to call her back, but Clariel didn't even notice. She needed to get out under the sun again, away from the weight of stone and the smothering attention of other people.

In her urge to escape the confines of the house, she also forgot that Belatiel had asked for her to wait.

Roban, Heyren, and Linel were standing around outside the front door. There were even more guards there now, two score at least, showing many different Guild badges. Though they straggled along the wall of the house, most leaning against the stonework or sitting on some upturned barrels, Clariel noted that even in this apparently relaxed attitude they still watched the street, and all passersby. At the moment this included workmen pushing barrows of sand to a building site; women returning from a market with their large baskets full of foodstuffs, mostly a kind of purple root vegetable Clariel didn't recognize; and a peddler and his family engaged in propelling a handcart laden with small puppets, traditional figures from the various festivals, like the Midsummer Bird of Dawning and the Fall Fair's Moon-Moth.

"Let's go," said Clariel to Roban. "Magister Kargrin's house. I want to get the next lesson over and done with as well."

"Ah, milady, your maid . . . Valannie," said Roban. "She probably wasn't expecting you to come out so quickly, she's not—"

"Here I am!" pronounced the penetrating voice of Valannie, almost as if she had been summoned by Roban speaking her name. She followed this with her annoying laugh, and added, "You sped past so quickly, Lady Clariel! I had thought you might lunch with some of the other pupils . . ."

"I would like to go to my Charter Magic class," said Clariel.

Valannie visibly blenched as Clariel said the words "Charter Magic" and made a frantic shushing gesture, waving two fingers across her mouth as if fanning something too hot to eat.

"Lady Clariel, please, let us speak quietly of this," she whispered. "As I have told you, it is not the done thing to be, to do, to study magic!"

"Well, whether it is or not, can we get going to my next lesson?" asked Clariel. "Street of the Cormorant, house with the sign of the hedgepig, I think."

"I know the house, milady," said Roban. He turned to Heyren and Linel and indicated for them to fall in behind Clariel. "Follow me, please."

"But luncheon, the other pupils, I'm sure we should—" protested Valannie.

"I'll have a late lunch," said Clariel firmly. "Lead on, Roban."

The Street of the Cormorant was not far below Clariel's parents' house on Beshill and the houses that lined it were almost but not quite as large as her parents', each being three or four stories high, with the familiar red-tiled roofs. They also had balconies, but these were on the far side of the street, looking east to the sea.

The house with the sign of the hedgepig was completely different to all the other houses in the street. Clariel saw it before she knew it was her destination, poking up above the red roofs like a tall daisy among a crop of beetroot. It was really a tower, not a house at all, and looked much older than the other buildings around it. It was at least six stories high, and was built of a dark yellow stone, not faced in white ashlar like almost every other building in Belisaere. The tower was crowned with a crenellated wall surmounted by a cupola room, its roof clad in copper green with verdigris.

"It's a guard tower, part of the old wall," said Roban, correctly interpreting Clariel's cricked neck and long stare. "From a long time ago, when the city was smaller. There used to be more towers, and a few stretches of the old wall, but most of it has long since been pulled down."

"Very sensibly," said Valannie. "That tower really does not fit in at all with the other houses."

"And on that account I am disposed to like it," said Clariel. Valannie darted a glance at her that perhaps, if she had not been a servant, might have become a scowl of distaste, but vanished so quickly into her usual, bland, pressed-flat expression that Clariel wasn't even sure she'd seen it. Perhaps it was just how she imagined Valannie was feeling inside. Seething at having to put up with a yokel mistress who would do nothing to her maid's credit, not even in taking a conformist line on the city architecture.

There was an iron hedgepig sign, a flat, rusty thing cut from a plate, dangling aslant from two equally rusty chains of unequal length from an iron rod that was set into the keystone of the arch above the house's front door. Or gate, rather, since in keeping with its origins as a tower, there was a massive, bolt-studded gate of two leaves, together at least twelve feet wide and eighteen high. But there was also a lesser door set within the gate, a sally port perhaps, which was of significantly smaller size, not even high enough to admit someone of average height without stooping. Roban went to this door, and thumped his fist upon it three times, rattling the bolts on the inside.

A moment later, the bolts were withdrawn with a screech, indicating the ironwork of the gate was as rusty as the hedgepig sign. The door opened slowly, but Clariel could not see who had opened it. Roban stepped inside, bending low. Clariel followed, then Valannie, but Heyren and Linel remained outside.

The sally port opened onto an enclosed bridge over what appeared to be a very deep pit or even crevasse, with an arched ceiling overhead whose most prominent feature was a series of holes the size of oranges, clearly for the application of heated oil or pitch onto unwelcome visitors.

"Murder holes," said Roban, again noting Clariel's stare. "Stopped up now. I had to check once. Long ago, when the . . . well, I had to be sure it was safe."

Clariel blinked, accustoming her eyes to the relative darkness. There were some dim Charter marks for light set into the ceiling, but they did not illuminate very much. The bridge crossed some fifteen paces over the pit and led to another great gate, with another smaller sally port set into it. This door was half open, though she didn't think there had been time enough for a doorkeeper to run back from the outer door.

"I don't like this place at all," pronounced Valannie as they crossed the bridge. "It's no wonder that the Governor wants it knocked down."

"Does he?" asked Clariel. "Why?"

Valannie immediately reverted to the smiling ignorance she displayed so well to any of Clariel's significant questions, and shrugged her shoulders.

"Who opened the door?" asked Clariel.

"You'll see, milady," said Roban, as he hunched down to go through the inner door.

Clariel followed him into a small hall that took up most of the tower's lower floors, the vaulted ceiling and the beams studded with many bright Charter marks for light some thirty feet above her. Unlike the dilapidated exterior, this large room was clean, tidy, and in good repair, though furnished in an eccentric fashion. There was a very long table of some dark, dense timber, bearing many scars and scratches. It could easily seat twenty people or more, though there were now only two old benches drawn up to it, and a single high-backed chair at the very end. A chair that had once been very grand, for it still showed patches of gilt here and there, the rest having been long worn away.

There were no windows as such, but there were arrow slits every four or five paces around all four walls, about twelve feet up, with a few broken beam ends protruding from the stonework to indicate where a wooden walkway had once given archers somewhere to stand.

There was a stairwell in the northeast corner, but it was filled with rubble, great stone blocks that had tumbled down and blocked it completely, so that only three or four steps poked out, leading nowhere. If the upper floors of the tower were still standing, they could not be reached by that stair, and Clariel could see no other entrances or exits. One corner of the room was out of sight, partitioned off by a folding screen of six hinged panels, each section painted with a scene that all together told a story, though it was so faded and damaged that it was unclear whether the narrative was of a great hunt, a parade or festival, or perhaps a battle.

The opposite corner had a workbench and a very tall glass-fronted bookcase of four doors with a hooked ladder to reach the higher books. There was a man standing at the bench, so intent on whatever he was doing that he did not look around or greet the visitors. He was tall and very broad-shouldered, bald on top but with hair braided down his back. His arms were also extremely muscular, well displayed by the sleeveless leather jerkin he wore atop leather riding breeches that were not paired with the usual boots, but slippers of a bright blue cloth, which were turned up at the toes and ended in sharp gilded points.

"Don't interrupt!" he called out, still without turning around, his voice loud and commanding. "Stay over there."

Clariel and her entourage stopped near the end of the long table as instructed, an instinctive response to the authority in the man's voice. For a moment Clariel wondered what he was doing, then she saw Charter marks begin to glow and appear around his hands, a great stream of them that moved and roiled over the bench, and wrapped themselves up his arms to his elbows. They were directed at something on the bench, but Clariel couldn't see what it might be, as it was blocked by the man's body. By Magister Kargrin's body, since he could be no one else. Clariel hadn't expected a magister who looked like a tavern brawler, but then she had never met a fully fledged magister before. The Charter Mages who had taught her the fundamentals of magic back in Estwael were healers, with the additional lessons on defensive and offensive marks from the town's sergeant, who had served with the Wall Garrison.

They stood in silence for a few minutes, Valannie shifting nervously by Clariel's side, clearly discomfited by seeing the evidence of magic at work. Eventually the Charter marks subsided down Kargrin's arms, fading as they retreated into his hands, until they disappeared completely. The magister turned around, and Valannie shrieked as she saw he was cradling a large brown rat in his hands, its pink tail dangling down over his wrist.

"Well met, Roban. And Jaciel's daughter, whose name I have forgotten," said Kargrin. "And Valannie, isn't it? You'd best begone, lest you see something truly disturbing."

"I will stay with my lady—" Valannie started to say, ending in a shriek as a hand touched her elbow, a hand made not of flesh, but of thousands of Charter marks, close together, giving the illusion of skin. The hand belonged to a robed and cowled figure. Its face, if it had one, was hidden deep in the shadow of its hood. It gestured at the door.

Clariel had never seen one before, but she knew what it was, from many stories and legends. The robed figure was a Charter sending, a magical creature created for a specific purpose, usually a servant of some kind, a guard, or a messenger.

"Amda will show you out," said Kargrin.

Valannie's mouth moved, but only a kind of strangled clucking sound came out. Avoiding the Charter sending's helping hand, she dashed for the door.

"Remind me of your name, Jaciel's daughter."

"Clariel."

"You will address me as Magister," replied Kargrin, in a conversational tone that nevertheless brooked no opposition. "So you wish to learn Charter Magic?"

"No, Magister," replied Clariel. She met Kargrin's enquiring gaze, his eyes dark beneath large and very bushy eyebrows, above a face that once again did not match her expectations. It was a forceful, almost ugly face, and his nose had been broken and set somewhat awry. "My parents wish me to learn."

Kargrin nodded thoughtfully, lifted the rat near to his mouth and whispered something to it. Clariel saw small Charter marks like sparks come out with his words, to be answered by glittering reflections across the rat's skin, and realized the rat too, was a sending. The magister gently set it down on the floor, and it ran to the wall and slipped through a triangular crack between two stones.

"So your parents wish you to learn," he said, rumbling over to her, his slippered feet making the floorboards groan. He was even taller and bigger than Clariel had thought, up close, perhaps six and a half feet tall and proportioned more like a bear than a man, with a long waist and short, tree-trunk legs. "I will test your mark, if I may."

He raised one massive finger and reached toward Clariel's forehead, where the brand of her baptismal Charter mark suddenly flared into life. She remained still as she felt the slightest touch of Kargrin's fingertip, and without really thinking about it, did as she had been taught long ago, reaching up to touch the Charter mark on Kargrin's forehead in turn.

It was like falling into deep water. All of a sudden the world ceased to exist. She was surrounded entirely by Charter marks, brilliant, shining, blinding marks that swirled and swam all around her, through her and inside her, marks that she did not know and felt she could never know, thousands, tens of thousands, millions of Charter marks—

Clariel gasped and stepped back, breaking the connection. Kargrin lowered his hand and looked at her thoughtfully.

"It has been a long time since you joined with the Charter," he said, his voice a deep rumble from the cave of his chest. Clearly he had seen a great deal into Clariel's connection with the Charter in the moment of their exchange. "And you do not practice the little magic you have been taught."

"No, I don't," admitted Clariel.

"Hmm," said Kargrin. "Roban?"

He raised his hand again, and he and Roban reached out at the same time, almost like a salute, reassuring each other that their forehead Charter marks were true, and not some disguise of Free Magic. At one time all those who bore the Charter mark would have greeted each other this way, but no longer. Clariel belatedly realized that she had not seen anyone perform this traditional greeting since she had come to Belisaere.

"Do you have any news, Roban?" asked Kargrin.

"Nothing beyond my earlier communication, Magister," replied Roban, with a sideways glance at Clariel, so slight she almost didn't notice it. "If I do, I will send word at once, or come myself."

"Speaking of messages," said Clariel. "Mistress Ader at the Academy asked me to tell you, 'None have yet passed by, but I will keep watch.'"

"Thank you," said Kargrin. He nodded at Roban and made a slight gesture with his hand. The guard stood at attention, inclined his head, whipped around in a parade-ground-perfect about-face, and marched out. The magister turned his gaze back to Clariel, who suddenly felt shorter, younger, and more vulnerable.

"Conjure me a Charter light," said Kargrin. "A small one, on your fingertip."

Clariel nodded, took a breath, and reached out for the Charter once more. It was a little easier this time, because she could kind of sidle into it, rather than being inundated via Kargrin's own immersion. But even so, she found it difficult. Starting with a few very familiar marks, she thought of more, visualizing them as a chain reaching back into the full flow, but all too quickly there were more marks than she could cope with. So many marks they threatened to swamp her, and it took all her concentration to just select the one she needed, a minor mark for light, pull it out of the swim, and coax it to her fingertip.

Light flared there, but only for a few seconds, as Clariel broke away from the Charter too soon for the light mark to be established on its own. She took another breath, and wiped away the sweat that had suddenly broken out on her forehead.

"Curious," said Kargrin. "I wonder what you would do if—"

His fingers arched and suddenly shards of sharp metal spat straight at her, shards made not of true metal but of Charter marks, conjured so swiftly that he must have already had most of the spell put together and hidden on his person, awaiting only a single mark to activate it.

Clariel reacted instantly, ducking under the shards, but even so she felt the heat of their passage above her head.

"What are you doing?" squeaked Clariel. Raising her voice, she shouted, "Roban! Help!"

"Use the Charter," bellowed Kargrin, his eyes intent on her own. "Defend yourself!"

His fingers arched again, and more red-hot shards spat forth, missing Clariel's shoulder by a hairsbreadth as she twisted violently aside and collided with the edge of the table.

"Use the Charter!" Kargrin shouted again, stamping his foot.

Charter marks blew up under his heel, forming a swirling cloud that rolled over Clariel, enveloping her in a choking mist. She dived onto the table, slid across it on her stomach, and went over the other side, ending up on all fours on the floor, her knees and hands smarting in pain, but with the cloud behind her.

Kargrin came around the end of the table, advancing upon her, his hands out in a spellcasting gesture. Clariel retreated, stood upright, and backed away. Anger was building inside her, anger fueled by pain and humiliation. Her knife was in her hand now, though she did not remember drawing it.

How dare he suddenly attack her, she thought, and why should she use Charter Magic anyway? She wanted to charge straight at the great bull of a man, and twist this way and strike, the knife parting his throat on the diagonal. Even before she knew it she was sliding forward, her arm going up, moving as swiftly as she ever had, fast as a kite dropping on a vole in the grass, but somehow when she twisted and her arm came across, Kargrin's throat was not there.

Clariel whirled around but she could not see him anywhere in the hall.

Suddenly a plate dropped on her head, a china plate that shattered into pieces, though its surprise impact hadn't really hurt. Clariel screeched a war cry, her head going back, and saw Kargrin standing tiptoe like a dancer on one of the broken beam ends way above her head.

"Use the Charter," cried Kargrin. "Defend yourself!"

Rage filled Clariel. Her nostrils flared open as she exhaled and almost closed shut as she breathed in. She picked up one of the massive benches and threw it up at Kargrin, but he jumped away, across twelve feet or more to the next beam end, an impossible jump were he not aided by some magic. Clariel dropped her knife and ran toward him, raging. She swarmed up the wall, her fingers thrust into the tiniest cracks between stones, dislodging ancient mortar, but even so she could not find enough hand- and footholds. She fell back, immediately circling to find a weapon, something to throw at the enemy above her. But even as her hand closed upon a fallen piece of stone the size of an apple, a glowing net of Charter marks fell on her from above, wrapped itself around her three times, and bound her as securely as a spider ever tied a fly.

Clariel thrashed in her binding, enough to bruise herself more, and perhaps would even have dashed her own brains out on the floor if Kargrin had not dropped lightly by her side and laid a spell for sleep upon her brow, quickly followed by another, stronger spell when the first one was shrugged off by the anger that shone from her like the heat from one of her mother's forges, busy smelting gold.

Chapter Eight

COMPLICATIONS AND OPPORTUNITIES

C lariel came to her senses to find herself lying on the table in Kargrin's hall, with a cushion under her head. For a moment she was disoriented, then she remembered what had happened. Her hand went into her sleeve for her dagger again, only to find nothing there, and her wrist gently but firmly clasped by the magister.

"Peace," rumbled Kargrin. "Roban told me he thought you had the rage, and indeed I felt the presence of it when I tested your mark. But my attacks, save for the plate I dropped on your head, were illusory. Part-formed sendings that I would have expected even a half-trained Charter Mage to see through, particularly one of your heritage."

"A test?" mumbled Clariel. Her head ached, and she felt slightly nauseous. "You might have told me."

"It would not serve as a useful test if I told you," said Kargrin. "If I release you, will you keep that anger in check?"

"Yes," said Clariel. She slowly sat up and cradled her head in her hands. The ache intensified, a deep throbbing pain behind her eyes. "I've never . . . almost never let it get out of control like that . . ."

"You *are* a berserk," said Kargrin, in a very matter-of-fact tone. "It is not uncommon in the royal blood, and though rarer among Abhorsens, it does crop up from time to time. You have both blood-lines from your mother. It is curious that you have the rage, but not the usual affinity of your kin for the Charter. There is danger in this, for you, and for others."

"I've never . . . I've never let it get so far beyond . . ." faltered Clariel. "I've never hurt a . . . a person!"

"It is not simply the rage itself, and the violence that may come with it," said Kargrin. "It is also an indicator of an affinity with Free Magic, which is governed by emotion and raw will. All those who have the blood of the Five have some natural ability with Free Magic, but it is usually counterbalanced by an innate connection and under-standing of the Charter, a desire to be part of its all-encompassing nature. Tell me, do you like to be alone?"

"Yes."

"You would prefer to be alone, than to be in company?"

"Yes . . ." said Clariel slowly. "But I do not feel alone, not in the Forest. I feel part of it, though I may have no company save the beasts and the birds. But in this city . . . I feel surrounded, and seek solitude. Or I would, if anyone would let me!"

Kargrin's brow furrowed slightly as he took Clariel's hand and helped her stand. She felt weak and a little dizzy, and had to sit on the bench. It was the one she had a dim memory of throwing, now back in its place. But how could she have thrown such a heavy piece of furniture, that must weigh three times what she did?

"Free Magic often appeals to the solitary, those who wish to order their lives without the constraint of others. The rage is similar, in that it throws off the constraints of your normal self, your normal physicality, rationality, and emotion. In fact, it is possible that the berserk state is itself a form of Free Magic, or is derived from some ancient effect of that magic."

"I never really understood what Free Magic actually is," said Clariel. "Our teacher just said it was evil, something to fear, and warned us to seek help should we ever encounter any. Not that she told us how we would know."

"You would know," said Kargrin. His teaching voice was coming on again, and he gestured with his huge hands. "Free Magic is not necessarily *evil* as such, it is merely unconstrained, though this difference may be hard to understand. It is a raw power. It resists consistent ordering and may be shaped and directed by will alone. Most so-called Free Magic constructs or entities are relics or leftovers of an ancient age, things that for various reasons were not subsumed in the making of the Charter. They tend to see anything of the Charter as their enemy, which is to effectively say all life. To make it worse, over time many such entities have become impressed with a limited range of human feelings, usually the baser ones, without any counterbalancing better nature. But it is their desire for total freedom, regardless of others—including other Free Magic creatures—that leads them to kill and wreak havoc."

"I don't want to kill or wreak havoc," mumbled Clariel. "I just want to live in the Forest, and be left alone."

"Yes," said Kargrin. "But how far would you go in order to live as you want to, alone in the Forest?"

"Not very far, obviously. I wouldn't even be here if I wasn't so obedient!" snapped Clariel. "I'd be in the Forest already."

"Yes . . ." mused Kargrin. "That does indicate you have some measure of control over your anger, and your desires. Perhaps, with some training, it will be enough."

"Enough for what?" asked Clariel.

Kargrin's nose twitched, and he rubbed it thoughtfully, but did not immediately answer. Clariel repeated her question.

"Enough for what?"

"I suppose you need not remember this, if necessary," said Kargrin. He spoke quietly, almost to himself, but Clariel caught the implication very clearly. For a brief moment she felt a shock of sudden fear, that he would kill her if he thought it was required. Then she realized that as an accomplished Charter Mage he was talking about erasing part of her memory. This did not greatly lessen her fear.

Memories were part of what defined a person, and who knew what might be taken away with a memory?

"I am in the habit of keeping secrets," she said quickly. "We do not talk much in the Forest."

"Very well," said Kargrin. "There is a possibility that you might be able to assist us . . . to assist me . . . with a particular problem that has arisen in the city."

"What kind of problem could I help with?"

"There is a Free Magic creature in Belisaere," said Kargrin flatly. "And we need your help to find it."

"What! But . . . how? I thought that the aqueducts kept out the Dead, running water . . ."

"Running water does protect against the Dead, and some lesser Free Magic beings," said Kargrin. "But there are things that can pass under the aqueducts, or even cross a great river like the Ratterlin. Creatures with power to remain unseen, save by careful scrutiny of Charter Magic. We suspect one such entity is here, within our walls and aqueducts."

"But how can I help?" asked Clariel.

"Like many of the Abhorsen line, you have a strong affinity for Free Magic, and great potential to wield it," said Kargrin. "The rage is one indicator of that, and there are other signs within you. Like seeks like, and once it becomes aware of you this creature will seek you out in order to augment its power. It is the nature of such things that they must test each other, and the lesser fall under the will of the greater."

"Like seeks like . . ." said Clariel. Her thoughts immediately went to her experience of the hunt. "You mean to use me as bait? Tethered like a goat for a wolf-hunt?"

"Not tethered," said Kargrin. "But that is the general idea. You are also well suited for another reason."

"Which is?"

"We . . . I suspect a connection between the creature and Governor Kilp," said Kargrin. "But until we find the creature, we cannot prove it, and as Kilp has grown very powerful these last few years, we cannot move openly against him. But you will be able to look where we cannot, since Kilp has chosen you to marry his son—"

"What!" exploded Clariel, standing up so quickly that she almost fainted and had to quickly sit back down again. "Me? Marry Aronzo?"

"Ah," said Kargrin. "I thought you were cognizant of that plan. It is part of some overall scheme of Kilp's to seize power and replace the King . . ."

He paused as Clariel stared at him, her jaw partly open and a look of total disbelief upon her face.

"You don't know any of this?" asked Kargrin. "Didn't Belatiel tell you?"

"Oh," said Clariel. "He wanted me to meet him after the last class. I forgot."

Kargrin shook his head.

"Bel was not born to be a conspirator. He talks too much when he's not supposed to, and clearly not enough when he is."

"What *was* he supposed to tell me?" asked Clariel. "Because I need to know and I'm *really* tired of being a . . . a game piece moved about by my parents, or Kilp, or you and your . . . conspirators!"

"We're not absolutely sure," said Kargrin, suddenly defensive. "But from what my rats have been able to gather, and other sources, we think Kilp intends for you to become the Queen—"

"What!" shrieked Clariel, leaping to her feet again, swaying and having to sit down yet again.

"If you keep interrupting I'll never be able to explain," said Kargrin. "And you'll pass out. The rage is always followed by weakness, you should know that. Now, Kilp can't put just anyone on the throne, it has to be someone of the royal blood, who can assume the wardenship of the Great Charter Stones . . . though the bigger question is why would a Free Magic creature want to help Kilp set a puppet Queen upon the throne. What would it gain from that . . . what?"

Clariel had raised her finger questioningly, not wanting to stand again.

"What are the Great Charter Stones?"

"Didn't your mother teach you anything?" said Kargrin testily. "You know the rhyme, don't you? You must have learned it as a child!"

"Oh, you mean the one about the five Great Charters?" asked Clariel. "I guess I never thought it meant anything."

"Never thought it meant anything!" exploded Kargrin. "What is the world coming to? The Great Charter Stones in the reservoir beneath the Palace are part of the physical embodiment of the Charter, created by the Wallmakers and infused with their power. They are a foundation for the Charter, along with the Wall and the bloodlines of Clayr, Abhorsen, and the Royal Family; surely you must know this?"

"I suppose I must have been taught something about it all sometime or other," said Clariel doubtfully.

"Bah!" exclaimed Kargrin. He threw up his hands and continued, "Where was I?"

"Kilp making me Queen," muttered Clariel.

"Yes. We think that Kilp plans to put you on the throne, with Aronzo as your consort, but Kilp will rule."

"So I would be trapped in Belisaere for good," whispered Clariel. Her face twisted in distaste. "And married to the slimy Aronzo . . ."

"It's an educated guess," continued Kargrin. He scratched one of his massive eyebrows as he returned to his ruminations about the nature of the connection between Kilp and the suspected Free Magic creature. "I just cannot think what the motive is . . . I mean for the creature; it is not so unusual for such as Kilp to seek greater power. But Free Magic entities usually flee concentrations of Charter Magic, and there are none greater than here. Kilp is not himself a sorceror, nor can we identify one in his service. So the creature is not bound, and I cannot think why it would want to just *help* Kilp make himself the effective ruler of the Kingdom. Other than hatred of the royal line, I suppose . . ."

"I don't care why they're doing anything," protested Clariel. "As long as I can avoid it. I particularly don't want to marry Aronzo, or be Queen!"

"There is some doubt whether you would in fact be recognized as Queen by the Charter," mused Kargrin. His manner was very much a teacher's, considering some long-ago historical matter, not something of supreme importance right now to Clariel. "Even if King Orrikan is dead and Kilp installs you in the palace, the Great Charter Stones might reject you, because Princess Tathiel is presumably still alive somewhere. Also, your mother does have a higher claim, and there are the cousins on the other side who might have a better right . . ."

Clariel groaned and rested her head in her hands.

"I don't care about the Charter! I just want to live in the Great Forest, be a Borderer, and be left alone!"

"And you may be able to, one day," said Kargrin. "We might also be wrong. Up until yesterday I was sure it was your mother that Kilp wanted to put on the throne as his puppet, and her invitation to the High Guild of Goldsmiths was simply a pretext to get her to the city. But on investigation she is highly esteemed in the guild, and her . . . ah . . . lack of interest in politics and so forth is well attested. Then we learned of your intended marriage to Aronzo and all became clear."

"Not that clear. Roban told me he suspected Kilp was afraid my mother would displace him as Guildmaster, and she would become

Queen of her own doing," said Clariel. "So maybe you're wrong as well."

"Roban, like all of us, is trying to make sense of what is happening, and what might happen," said Kargrin. "But he did not then know what we know now."

"Who is 'we'?" asked Clariel.

"An informal society," said Kargrin. "Intent on the preservation of the Kingdom. We were all formerly employed by the King, either in the Guard or some other capacity. I myself was once Castellan of the Palace."

"Why aren't you still?" asked Clariel. "I just don't understand why the King got rid of everybody."

"The King is . . . ill," said Kargrin. "A darkness is on his mind, and he sees no joy in anything, and no relief. It is a consequence of a long life bearing the great burden of kingship, until the weight of it grew too heavy. He wished to pass that burden on, but his daughters were dead, and his grandchild lost to him, so he simply set it aside, refusing to make decisions. Part of that was a belief that if he did so, Tathiel would return and take the throne. But that has not happened yet. For want of any other authority, the guilds—under Kilp's leadership—have usurped much of what was the royal prerogative and power."

"Why does he think Tathiel will return?" asked Clariel. She had always been interested in the story of the missing princess, though there was no definitive version of the tale. Some said she had deliberately run away, others that she had died in an accident, or even that she was imprisoned beneath the Palace. The only thing the various stories agreed on was that Tathiel had not been seen for almost a decade.

"The Clayr have seen her, back in Belisaere, upon the Palace walls, in enough visions to make it very likely it will happen," said Kargrin. "She is clad as if for war. But as is common, they do not know when, save that she looks to be of an age somewhere between twenty and thirty-five. That is to say, anytime from now up to the next ten or fifteen years. Or more probably twenty, given the difficulty of determining any woman's age, let alone one wearing a helmet. They could also have mistaken someone who merely looks like Tathiel."

"I'm supposed to be seeing the King the day after tomorrow," said Clariel. "To give him a kin-gift. If I can find a bright fish on the Islet, that is."

"Yes . . . Roban mentioned you would be going to the Islet. This is also of interest to us."

"What? Why?"

"There is a man called Marral in Kilp's service, who has come to our attention these past few months. Indeed, it is he who first led us to suspect that there is a Free Magic creature within the city."

"How?"

"We have numerous friends in Kilp's service. One noticed that this man Marral had become a new favorite, often closeted with the Governor on secret business. So we had him followed, and quickly learned that he goes to and from the Islet, but much more significantly, goes a very particular way that avoids all Charter Stones. Once we heard that, I cast various spells on his footprints, places he had passed and so forth, and by this means discovered he is tainted with Free Magic. As is Kilp's house, at least those parts I can easily investigate. I suspect that the creature either inhabits Marral, as some such things can wriggle within a mortal body, or he is transporting it in some container that keeps its true nature and force hidden, so leaving few signs. A casket of lead or gold, perhaps a bottle of green glass . . . in any case, Marral went to the Islet yesterday and has not yet returned. It seems likely that he has taken the creature to its lair or holt upon the Islet. If you go there, it will be unable to resist the temptation to reveal itself to you—"

"Like a dog taking the scent of a fox," said Clariel. "Perhaps with similar results for the quarry. I have no desire to confront any Free Magic creature. Nor do I want to be involved in any politicking or anything that might stop me getting out of the city and back where I belong!"

Kargrin's eyes narrowed.

"It is your duty," he said. "You are of both the Abhorsen and the royal blood."

"My blood is of no consequence," said Clariel. "I simply want to be a hunter, a Borderer in time."

"Your heritage is of great consequence, whether you wish it to be or not," said Kargrin. "And we do need your help. The creature hides most cunningly and we have not been able to draw it out. Who knows what its plans are, underlying Kilp's own treason?"

"It is not my affair!" protested Clariel. "As soon as I can, I am going back to Estwael and the Great Forest!"

"Hmmm," said Kargrin, fixing her with his piercing gaze. "You say you came to the city in obedience to your parents. Yet now you say you will leave. If this is so, why did you come and what holds you back?"

"I suppose I have the habit of doing what they ask and . . . I didn't realize how much I would hate . . ."

Clariel threw her hands up as she tried to find the right words, as if she might somehow pick meaning from the air. "Hate it here. The city oppresses me, the noise, the closeness of everything, the . . . the torrents of people in the streets. I have no money of my own . . ."

She stood up, ignoring the wave of dizziness, bunched her fists together, and brought them down on the table.

"But I am going to get out of Belisaere, no matter what I have to do to escape!"

Clariel had finally decided. She would steal from her parents after all, take a few bags of coin from the strongbox, a gold bar from

the stock waiting to be worked, some of the lesser jewels that were
waiting to be set . . .

"You need money," agreed Kargrin. "But you will also need help
to leave the city, to evade Kilp's people here and on the roads."

"Kilp's people?" Clariel asked. She'd thought of her parents sending someone after her, but hadn't considered anybody else would. If
Governor Kilp ordered her arrest, then there would be all manner of
guards and agents and guild people after her, in every town on the
way, and the major roads. "I didn't think anyone would bother . . ."

"Perhaps we can help each other," said Kargrin. "We can provide
you with money and a Charter spell to change your countenance.
Clothes and weapons, a horse . . . in return you will help us lure the
Free Magic creature into revealing itself."

"I need two hundred and fifty gold bezants," said Clariel, mind-
ful of the amount Mistress Ader had said would be required for
her first five years. It seemed an enormous sum. Considering Ader
was calculating on Belisaere rates, she'd probably need a lot less in
Estwael. But as in all bargaining Clariel thought she might as well
start high, and be prepared to settle for whatever she could get.

As she said the amount, Clariel felt like she had finally stepped
over a threshold where she had been dallying for weeks, neither
turning back nor going ahead. Whatever sum of money they arrived
at, or even if she had to steal from her parents, the decision was made.
She would leave Belisaere. Leave her family. Start the new life she
had always wanted.

The only thing was, now that it seemed likely to be possible, she
was not as sure she wanted it.

"Done!" boomed Kargrin.

"What?" asked Clariel.

"You are a brave and sensible young woman!" declared Kargrin.
"Now, we must focus your mind on Charter Magic, for there is no
small danger in the task ahead, and you are currently ill-prepared. I

believe we have another two hours of your time today, do we not?"

"We do," sighed Clariel. "But . . ."

"No buts!" cried Kargrin. "Do not fret. It is simple stuff we will do, the very foundation work you have neglected!"

The prospect of studying Charter Magic for two hours was not something Clariel relished. But despite that she felt a fizzing excitement, for at last she had a plan of escape that was more than just a daydream. She could see a path forward now, out from behind the walls that loomed so high above her, back to the quiet, green world of the Great Forest.

All she had to do first was be the bait in a trap for a Free Magic creature . . .

Chapter Nine

OLD SECRETS, NEW PLANS

That night, Jaciel came to dinner, surprising not only Clariel but also her father. They had already sat down, and the score or so younger apprentices and forgehands at the lower table were drawing in their benches when Jaciel appeared with two of the senior apprentices following subserviently, as if they were holding an invisible train on her dress. This appearance required everyone to stand up again, and the apprentice who had been just about to place the gravy boat in front of Harven spilled it, sending a flood of thick, spiced sauce across the high table.

"Be seated," said Jaciel. She had been working when Clariel had returned from her magic lesson, smoke billowing from the workshop, but had washed and changed since then. Now she was wearing another multilayered dress of gold and white, this one trimmed with tiny, paper-thin gold coins at sleeve and neck. "Sillen, don't stand there gaping, scrape the gravy back in the boat and return it to the kitchen. Cook will give you a fresh service. You—Kellil—come up here and help her."

"Hello, Mother," said Clariel. Before she had agreed to help Magister Kargrin she had thought to ask her mother about why she had left her family, in the hope of finding some common ground. But now she had a definite way out on her own, she considered it best to stay quiet. Similarly, she had also decided not to talk about any plan for her to marry Aronzo, mostly out of fear that there really was a plan, and that by bringing it up she would make it more real, make it more than Kargrin's suspicion. A polite exchange of greet-ings, followed by silence, seemed the best policy, as it had been so often in the past.

"Clariel," replied Jaciel, taking the high seat, which here in their new house was almost a throne, a great thing of gilded wood, set with semiprecious stones: garnets and amethysts and chrysolite. Back in Estwael, she had been content with a high-backed chair. "Harven."

"Hello, my dear," said Harven. "I trust your work goes well?"

"Well enough," said Jaciel, leaning back so yet another appren-tice on table duty could fasten a napkin around her neck, the snowy linen suspended from a cord of twisted gold. "I will speak to you later about the latest delivery of the blue natron, which is not of the first quality. Clariel, you went today to the Academy, and then to Magister Kargrin, did you not?"

"Yes, Mother," said Clariel.

Jaciel stabbed a long spear of poached asparagus with her silver fork, one she had made herself, as she had made all the cutlery on the high table.

"And?" she asked, turning to look at her daughter as she bit off the top of the asparagus and flicked the woody stem back on her plate.

"I . . . attended, as I have been asked to do," said Clariel.

"You met other young people," said Jaciel. "Including Aronzo, our Guildmaster's son?"

"Yes," said Clariel, her mouth tightening. It was typical that hav-ing decided not to bring up the subject herself, her mother unerringly did so for her, as if she could sense her daughter's caution.

"Good," said Jaciel. "I wished you to meet him. You and he are of a similar age. I believe he is a useful journeyman in his father's workshop and will soon be admitted as a goldsmith in his own right."

"Will he?" snorted Clariel. "I doubt he works very hard at it."

"Do not judge others by your lack of application," said Jaciel.

"Have you found a present for the King?"

"Not yet," said Clariel. She could feel herself growing angry again. It was somehow closer to her now, after her berserk fury earlier that day, and she had to try harder to keep it in check. "I hope I will have something tomorrow. Even though I know it's just an excuse to get you in the Palace to look at that Dripstone work or whatever it is."

"Dropstone work," said Jaciel coldly. "It is very important that I see it, and given the King's attitude, your presentation for the kin-gift was the only way to do so. You should be pleased to be able to help me toward what I intend will be a truly great creation of my art."

"That's all you care about it, isn't it?" snapped Clariel, rising to her feet and throwing down her knife and fork, so they clashed on her plate, a meeting of arms like a harbinger of battle. "Your art! You can't even see that other people have things they care about just as much, but *you* won't help them!"

"Clarrie . . ." warned her father, raising one ineffectual hand.

"I suggest you retire," said Jaciel, apparently unperturbed by her daughter's outburst. "I am making allowances for you, Clariel. I know that our removal here has disturbed you, but please do understand that I . . . that we . . . simply know far better how to arrange your future. You will be grateful, in time."

"How can you say that?" asked Clariel, her cheeks white with suppressed anger. "You ran away from your home to do what you needed to do! How can you not understand that I want something different from you too!"

Jaciel's eyes had half closed as Clariel spoke, hooded as if she was momentarily lost in thought. She opened them wide and stared at her daughter, a powerful, disturbing stare.

"I did not run away from my home to become a goldsmith," she said very quietly, so that despite craned necks and obvious attention the lower table could not hear. "I was already apprenticed, and would have stayed at Hillfair. Many Abhorsens have been metalworkers, particularly bell-founders, of course. I left because . . . because . . ."

"You do not need to speak of it," said Harven, covering her hand with his own. For once, he was not looking at his shoes. "It is enough to say that things happened there that were misunderstood . . ."

"No," said Jaciel softly. "You should know, for it may help you understand that your own problems are petty ones. And you may meet your grandfather and aunt soon. They may wish it so, even though we do not, and will not ever, speak."

She paused and looked down at the lower table, where everyone suddenly turned away and started eating again with faked enthusiasm.

"Go," said Jaciel, only a little louder than she had been speaking before, but her words carried through the hall like a trumpet. "Take your plates to the courtyard. All of you. Go!"

There was a moment when no one moved, followed by a sudden clatter and bustle as everyone moved at once, eager not to be the last one to leave the room. Several apprentices crashed together in the door and fought to get out, doubtless inflicting minor injuries with the deliberately blunted knives and three-tined forks that were all they were allowed, given their propensity for using them on one another.

When they were gone, the hall strangely quiet, Jaciel continued as if there had been no interruption.

"I will tell you this once, and once only. I left Hillfair because my father believed that I had killed my brother."

Clariel heard the words, but it was as if she couldn't understand them, they were some strange language that might as well be grunts and coughs. Surely she had misheard? She opened her mouth to say so, say that she didn't understand, but her mother was talking again, not looking at her, but staring into the air as if it were a window to a time long past and, as much as possible, forgotten.

"Teriel was the youngest of the three of us. I am eldest, then

Yannael, who is Abhorsen-in-Waiting now, then Teriel. Back then it was Teriel who was the greater Charter Mage, the only one of us who wished to become the Abhorsen, the one who delved in those arts . . ."

She paused for a moment, her eyes unfocused, seeing who knew what.

"Teriel alone sought to learn the use of the bells, to venture into Death and back again, to command and banish the Dead. But he sought too deeply, for one day he came to my forge. His eyes were strange, reflecting no light . . . I saw that he was no longer my brother, but instead something that wore his flesh like a coat."

Jaciel fell silent for a moment, the silence like a sudden chill.

"He . . . it saw that I knew, and attacked me. It would have slain me, for my dagger turned against its flesh, but at the last I managed to fling a crucible of molten gold against it, gold I had prepared with magic. But in its dying, the thing that had inhabited Teriel was released and fled, leaving the body behind."

Jaciel paused again, her brow wrinkled, her eyes still distant.

"My father could not or would not believe me that the body was not really Teriel's, that his favorite son could have succumbed to some fell creature. Father thought I had killed Teriel in a rage, for we argued often, about many things and . . . I did not hold my temper well in those days. So I was banished. Gladly banished, for I had no desire to stay among my close-minded and foolish relatives."

"In a rage . . ." whispered Clariel. "Mother, I . . ."

"I do not wish to speak further on this matter," said Jaciel stiffly, as controlled as ever, her eyes suddenly hard and sharp again. Her mother's constant control, Clariel suddenly realized, must have much to do with a lifetime of suppressing the same berserk fury that lived within herself. "I have told you what you need to know and you may count yourself fortunate that you have not grown up with parents who can know you so little as to think you a kinslayer and murderer!"

Jaciel stood up, tore the napkin from her neck, gold button flying off to dance across the table, and stalked out. Harven stood more fussily and rushed after her, his napkin still fast around his neck.

Clariel picked up an asparagus spear with her fingers and dipped it in the spilled gravy, since no one could see. Chewing it, she tried to sort through what she had just heard, adding it to the other revelations of the day. Coming to Belisaere had opened up not opportunities, but certainly secrets. Secrets and plots that she wanted no part of, that threatened to complicate her life far beyond anything she had ever dreamed might be possible.

Her mother had killed her own brother . . . or was thought by the rest of her family to have done so, even if she believed she had only killed something in the shape of her brother, himself already dead and gone.

Then there were Governor Kilp and Aronzo and the Free Magic creature. Whatever their plans were, she didn't want to be any part of them, particularly if it involved marrying Aronzo.

Even the visit to the King was a bit of a mystery. Why had the King agreed to see her, when he wouldn't see anyone else? Bel had not been allowed to present his kin-gift.

"The sooner I get out of here the better," she whispered to herself, thinking of the gold Kargrin had promised, and the disguising spell that would help her away.

But first she had to help find the Free Magic creature on the Islet. That task was to be done next morning. Which meant that there was a chance Clariel could be away tomorrow afternoon. The next time she sat down for her evening meal, it might be under a tree by the roadside, out in the open air. Leaving all these problems, these mysteries and plots, behind her.

Clariel smiled, took another asparagus spear, and bit into it with a great deal of satisfaction.

With the need to rise well before the dawn and sneak out before Valannie awoke, Clariel had a very restless night, waking every hour or so to take a panicked look at the Charter-magicked crystal by her bedside that marked the hour. Finally, at the fourth hour past midnight she got up, dressed in her familiar hunting clothes, and buckled on a falchion, a heavy broad-bladed sword she had used in the past to good effect to finish boars or to fight off wolves. With her smallest knife in her sleeve and the medium one in her boot, she felt well armed to face a mortal enemy. She was less confident about confronting a Free Magic creature, but then Magister Kargrin and his companions would be there for that.

Roban was waiting for her in the courtyard, near the front gate, a dim shadow she recognized by his size more than anything else. He spoke to the other gate guard, who Clariel couldn't identify in the dark, and the woman strode over to the workshop doors and rather ostentatiously rattled the great chain and padlock. The workshop was locked until the dawn, when whichever senior apprentice was keybearer this week would come yawning to open up, kicking the junior apprentices ahead to fire up the forges. Jaciel herself would not come down until the ninth or tenth hour.

"Heyren is outside," whispered Roban. "He'll look the other way. Follow me."

Like the magister's house, there was a small sally port set into the greater gate. It was already unbolted and the hinges had been newly greased, so that it opened without a sound. Roban looked out and made a clicking noise with his tongue, which was returned in kind by someone a few paces away. Reassured, he stepped through, Clariel following close behind.

It was strange to be out on the street in the relative darkness of the night. There were lights in and outside some of the houses along the street, Charter lights for the most part, though here and there a few duller, more yellow spots of illumination were the result of oil lanterns hung over front gates or doors.

It was quiet too, but again it was only a relative quiet. Though it was an hour yet till dawn, Clariel could hear carts farther down the hill, and voices raised in complaint or irritation carrying in from somewhere lower down and to the northeast.

"Let's go," said Roban. He set off, walking a little more slowly than he would during the day, his head carefully turning from side to side as he watched the doors and openings ahead. Clariel noted that he held his sword drawn at his side, the blade darkened with soot so that it did not catch the light. She wished she'd thought to do the same with her falchion, but settled with loosening it in its sheath, and kept her hand upon the hilt.

Magister Kargrin was waiting outside his house under the sign of the hedgepig, accompanied by a woman who wore a knee-length hauberk of gethre plates and a surcoat dappled with the golden castles on scarlet indicating the Royal Guard. The sign above their heads was swaying slightly, as the dawn breeze had just begun its whispering journey into the city from the east, and there was already the faint glow of the rising sun on the horizon, and the sky was noticeably lighter. But apart from their own small group, the street was empty and still.

"Clariel, this is Captain Gullaine, who commands the Royal Guard."

"What's left of it," said Gullaine, her mouth quirking up in something that was not quite a smile. She wore a mail coif close around her face, as well as a helmet, so it was difficult for Clariel to guess her age, but she thought she must be forty, perhaps older. The captain took off one glove, parked it under her elbow, tilted her helmet back, and pushed the coif up, to show her forehead Charter mark. "Lady Clariel, if I may test your mark, and you do likewise?"

Clariel moved closer and briefly touched Gullaine's mark, as the guardswoman returned the gesture. After her lesson yesterday, mostly just refamiliarizing herself with simply connecting to the Charter, it was easier, but still the vast flow of marks threatened to overwhelm her, so she was glad that the contact only lasted a second or two.

"Best to be careful," said Gullaine. She stepped back and looked over Clariel's outfit, her expression indicating some unhappiness.

"I wish we had a coat of gethre plates for you," she said. "If it comes to fighting, they resist the stuff of Free Magic better than leather or iron."

"I trust Clariel will not be getting so close," said Kargrin. "If we are wishing, I would wish for the particular robes the Abhorsens wear when handling such creatures. But we have neither the robes nor an Abhorsen."

"I believe we will have the next best thing," said Gullaine, with a smile. "Once or twice removed, perhaps."

As she spoke, Roban was already turning toward the sound of running booted footsteps, his sword raised. Clariel followed suit. But Roban lowered the weapon as he recognized who it was, and a moment later Clariel did so as well. It was Belatiel, who slowed down and walked the last few paces to join them under the sign, puffing out something that was obviously meant to be an apology for being late but was basically incomprehensible due to him being so out of breath.

"Ran all the way from the Palace," he managed to get out eventually. "Hello, Clariel."

Bel was also wearing a hauberk of gethre plates, though it was somewhat too big, as was the surcoat of faded blue with silver keys that went over it. He had a sword at his side, but in his right hand he held something Clariel didn't recognize at first, till he turned his hand and she saw it was a musical instrument: a set of reed pipes, seven tubes of different lengths joined together. Except these pipes were not reeds, but silver, or silver-plated bronze. Clariel had seen foresters play reed pipes, often bringing them out at the campfire after a day's work.

"Why the pipes?"

"I don't have a set of bells," said Belatiel, as if that explained everything. After a second or two, Clariel realized that it did. The Abhorsens used seven named bells to command and control the Dead, as did Free Magic necromancers, though the Abhorsen's ones were different, imbued with the Charter. She peered closer at the pipes in Belatiel's hand and saw the faint sheen of Charter marks moving in the silver. So this seven-voiced instrument must be a similar magical tool to the bells.

Something about Clariel's expression made him go on to answer the question she hadn't actually voiced.

"This is Abhorsen business, you know. Dealing with Free Magic creatures. There might be Dead things too. And I *am* in training to be a proper Abhorsen, even if I do only have the pipes."

"Training? Attempting to learn by yourself is not training," said Kargrin, but his words had no sting in them. "I would have preferred your great-uncle or cousin, but it seems the Abhorsen and the Abhorsen-in-Waiting are too busy, or at least too busy to answer my entreaties. I suppose in the circumstances we should be glad to have any assistance. Even that of a self-taught, self-proclaimed Abhorsen-in-Waiting-Waiting, if I may call you that. Gather close now. I wish to set a spell of unseeing upon us all."

They huddled together, shoulders touching. Kargrin looked along the street to make sure no one was about, then took a small tin box out of a pocket on the inside of his dark red cloak. Opening it, he reached in with two fingers and spoke three words, words that were imbued with a complex chain of Charter marks, some of them visible in his breath as he exhaled, others running down his arm and fingers, joining with many more marks that began to froth out of the box. Kargrin pinched them together and slowly drew out a faint, shimmering net of lights that was composed of thousands of marks.

"Closer!" he commanded, and they all leaned in, helmets and heads touching. Clariel felt the cold steel of Gullaine's helm against her forehead as Kargrin's hands flew up, casting the net of thousands of faintly glittering marks into the air. The shining tracery spread out above the group like the branches of a sheltering tree, then faded into nothing. Kargrin grunted. He waited a moment, stepped back, and indicated for the others to do likewise.

"What was that meant to do?" asked Clariel, for she could see no change in anyone. They were all perfectly visible. Surely a spell of unseeing would cloak them in darkness or something, at the very least?

"It was *meant* to divert attention from us," said Kargrin. "As it will. Onlookers will see us but make no note of it, nor remember our passage, unless we actually bump into them, or make physical contact. So be sure you don't. It should be easy enough until after first light, when the streets get busy."

"But I can see everyone clearly," protested Clariel.

"You are inside the spell," said Kargrin. "Trust me. It worked. The marks are still around us, if you look carefully. Squint, and stare upward, that may help."

Clariel narrowed her eyes and bent her neck back. At first she couldn't see anything, but as her eyelashes brushed together, lids almost closed, she saw the marks, suspended in the air above her like falling leaves caught in an instant, never to descend.

"If you're satisfied, perhaps we can be on our way?" asked Kargrin. "Roban, take the front."

Roban nodded, and stepped outside, sword still held ready. His wariness made Clariel think of other hunts, and the seriousness of the hunters, and she remembered something Sergeant Penreth of the Borderers had told her long ago.

"Never underestimate your quarry, be it boar, sow, deer, or even fox. I have seen hunters slain by all of them, fast or slow. A fox bite gone bad in the deep forest can be as much a death blow as having your guts torn out by a boar's tusk, or your head broken by a stag."

I'm not any kind of Abhorsen-in-Waiting really," Bel confided in Clariel as they walked next to each other along the Street of the Cormorant and turned left to take the sloping alley known as the Little Steps down to the next street below. "I expect you know that they don't take the family business very seriously back home. Great-uncle Tyriel thinks it's just a title, and I doubt Cousin Yannael has even read *The Book of the Dead*. They're all mad for hunting—"

"Hunting?" interrupted Clariel, her interest sparked, even though she thought it would be better to stay silent.

"The Grand Hunt," said Bel, rolling his eyes. "Hundreds of people on horseback, with hounds and beaters and tremendous rigmarole, whole days wasted charging backward and forward and stupid ceremonies and lots of drinking afterward. Instead of our proper business as Abhorsens. But I intend to make sure at least one of the family is properly prepared to deal with the Dead, or Free Magic or whatever comes up, or out, as the case may be. It is very unusual for the Kingdom to have had no trouble for so long. Do you read history?"

"No," said Clariel.

"There's a lot to be learned from history," said Bel. "I read other things too. Have you read *The Binding of the Free*?"

"No," said Clariel shortly. She wished he would stop talking. Nobody else was, and she had been enjoying the relative quiet of the city so early in the morning. Though now as the day edged closer, and they descended toward Winter Street, there were more people about, working people going to jobs or beginning to carry out early morning tasks like sweeping in front of houses that were probably merchant's shopfronts, or would be in a few hours when they opened the shutters.

"I haven't either," continued Bel. "I have seen a copy, at the Abhorsen's House—the old place, you know. But there isn't one at Hillfair or in the apartments here. Pity. Still I guess the magister knows how to bind this thing, if we do find it."

"Yes," replied Clariel, not turning her head to look at Bel as she spoke. Hopefully he would get the idea and shut up.

"I'm annoying you, aren't I?" he said ruefully. "Sorry about that. I suppose I tend to talk too much when I'm enthusiastic about what we're doing. I mean, a Free Magic creature hasn't been seen for decades, maybe longer!"

Clariel nodded absently, hoping this would be taken as an understanding gesture that would also end any further conversation.

It worked. Bel stayed silent at her side as they continued toward the southeast, not taking Winter Street itself, but a series of smaller back streets, where they would be less conspicuous, just in case the spell of unseeing failed. Clariel wondered what people would think if they did notice the strange quintet: Gullaine, Captain of the Royal Guard; Bel in his faded Abhorsen's coat; the huge Magister Kargrin striding ahead with a great staff of yew in his massive hand, which was topped with what looked like a thistle, presumably an arcane weapon of some sort and not an eccentric piece of costumery; the slight but deadly Roban, a Goldsmith's guard; and herself.

In such company, if the spell should fail, Clariel was fairly certain she herself would not be memorable, and that was how she liked it to be. A hunter should stay unseen as much as possible, but if not unseen, at least unremarked.

They came to the South Gate with the sun still not high enough to reach past the city wall, though it was now light enough to see well. The breeze had dropped again, as it so often did, and it was already warm. Clariel was glad she was not wearing an armored coat, though the thought did cross her mind that she might think otherwise later, if the Free Magic creature was found. Not that she intended to fight it, nor did she plan to be as constricted as an actual tethered goat.

Walking a little faster, she left Belatiel and moved next to Kargrin. Gullaine was a little farther ahead, using a key as large as her hand to open a small sally port set into the wall about thirty yards west of the South Gate proper, which would be shut until full dawn. There were two guards nearby, but they stayed facing the other way, talking quietly to each other. Clariel guessed this was not because of the spell of unseeing, given the noise the door made when it squeaked open, but because both guards, despite the surcoats showing the golden bee and bowl of silver of the Confectioners, were ex–Royal Guards and part of Kargrin's association.

Clariel caught up with Kargrin inside the narrow zigzag tunnel through the wall, just before a rusty portcullis that looked like it hadn't been fully lowered in years.

"What will this Free Magic creature look like?" asked Clariel quietly. "Will it use weapons? What else should I know about it?"

"It may look like any number of things," said Kargrin. "If it fully reveals itself, its very presence will sicken you, and the air around it will smell like hot metal. But I do not expect that to happen. It has hidden itself well, leaving few signs and traces. But your presence should make it rise more to the surface of whatever . . . or who-ever . . . it hides within; it will not be able to resist the temptation."

"So how do I bait the trap?" asked Clariel.

"I will tell you in a moment, and Belatiel, for you will both be part of it."

He slowed as they reached a small guard chamber beside the outer door, where Gullaine was waiting, another key in the massive, bronze-bound lock, but not yet turned, and the two bars above and below still in place. "We will pause here a moment. Gather round.

"When we go out, the Islet lies to our left, some three hundred and fifty paces away, the last hundred across a causeway that will be a little awash, the tide being on the ebb but not yet low. The path is marked by large stones; stay within them. Now, I am going to draw the spell of unseeing off Clariel and Belatiel, for it is you two who will go to Marral's hut, looking for bright fish—"

"Bel is to accompany me?" asked Clariel. "But Roban is my guard."

"We will need Roban to help if the creature does come forth in its full strength," said Kargrin. "If it does, you and Bel should withdraw and observe. If we are overcome, you must retreat, back to the main South Gate, not this postern. The guards there are with us, and will protect you. Get under the aqueduct, for this will also lessen the creature's power."

"You mean we just back off and leave you, Roban, and Gullaine to fight it?" asked Bel. "I didn't come along to flee at the first—"

"Belatiel, you promised to follow orders," said Gullaine, in a voice that brooked no opposition.

Bel opened his mouth, and raised one hand falteringly, then lowered that hand and shut his mouth.

"Good," said Kargrin. "Now. As I have said, Clariel and Bel will go first, and will be seen. There will be people about on the Islet. Ask them where Marral's hut is, though so you know, it is the farthest hovel on the northern side, set somewhat apart. It has a kind of curtain made of shark teeth in its doorway. We will follow, unseen. When you get to Marral's hut, do not go in. Ask him to come out. If, as I suspect, the creature is within Marral, it will reveal something of itself to Clariel."

He paused and bent his head to look directly at Clariel, speaking with measured force.

"You may feel it in your mind, Clariel, or see something that wasn't there beforehand. As soon as you do, call out and back away. We will either bind it quickly, or if not, you will soon see the way matters go. If they go ill, as I have said, run for the South Gate. Run as fast as you can, and do not look back. Do you understand?"

"Yes," said Clariel and Bel together.

"Gullaine, Roban, you know the spells we discussed?" asked Kargrin. Both nodded. "All of us should also ready arrow wards and spells to deal with mortal enemies. Such a creature as we seek can easily dominate folk who do not have the Charter mark. Also, given Kilp's possible involvement, there is much that can simply be bought with gold from the inhabitants of the Islet. There are known murderers and others of such ilk there."

"I can't remember the marks for an arrow ward," said Clariel. "But I can duck."

"I can cover us both," said Bel. "I've been practicing."

"I trust it won't be necessary," said Kargrin. "Stand together, you two."

Clariel and Bel stood close. Kargrin reached across, above their heads, and with the same two fingers he'd used before, began to draw in the almost invisible threads of the concealment spell. Watching him, Clariel saw the lines of tiny marks being drawn in as a fisherman might haul on his ropes. The threads of the net broke into many scattered marks as they left Clariel and Bel, only to re-form as they joined the other marks that still hung suspended over the other three.

When the last of the marks left, Clariel felt a sudden dizziness. She blinked, and her hand went to the falchion at her side, for she saw three strangers suddenly appear, strangers that she found it hard to look at, her eyes sliding off them . . .

"You'll find it easier to look away," said Kargrin's familiar voice, though Clariel couldn't tell where it came from. "Go out the door. We will be close behind. Don't stop suddenly!"

"Yes," said Clariel. She looked directly at the door, and found it was easier. "You ready, Bel?"

"Yes," said Bel, for once not embellishing his answer.

Clariel lifted the bars, first the bottom and then the top, and turned the key in the lock, the mechanism clicking three times, the sound to her unpleasantly like some portent of doom.

It's only a hunt, Clariel thought. I've hunted dangerous animals scores of times. It's only a hunt . . .

But then she had never before been called upon to be the bait.

The postern gate opened out into a ditch that had once been much deeper and clean-cut, but lacking repair had fallen in on itself to a great degree. Clariel clambered over some fallen stones and found a broken series of steps on the opposite side. Climbing up into the open air, she felt her moment of doubt fade. The sky above was much brighter, and just being able to see its great expanse, unhampered by walls and buildings, lifted her heart.

They had come out near the corner of the wall, and the sea was close, the crash of the waves loud in Clariel's ears and the scent of salt and weed strong on the breeze. She glanced eastward to the bridge over the ditch that led into the South Gate, but there was no one watching, and no one was on the road. It was probably still an hour until the gate opened.

Climbing over the lip of the ditch, she saw the sea and the cause-way to the Islet. The rocky island was smaller than she had expected. It looked to be not much more than three hundred paces across, in all directions, and though it rose out of the water to twice her height, it was much lower than she'd imagined it to be. In a storm, surely the dozen or so shanties and huts that clustered on it would be swept away?

"Keep going," whispered Bel. "They're right behind me."

Clariel started forward, not realizing that she had completely stopped. The ground fell away quite rapidly toward the narrow beach that led to the causeway, and up ahead there was a well-trodden path that joined up with the road behind them. She strode over to it, and started down.

Despite the hour, there were already a few beachcombers following the tideline, looking for flotsam. The closest was a woman, bent and old, clad in a raw woolen dress hitched up very high on her bare thighs and tied around her waist with a fraying rope. She had a sack in her hand and was wriggling her feet in the sand. A moment later she lifted one foot with a long worm caught in the grip of her toes, expertly transferring it to her sack without needing to use her hands.

As Clariel and Bel trod closer across the sand, the old woman turned toward them, and bowed her head.

"We're looking for Old Marral," said Clariel. "Can you direct us to his . . . his hut?"

"Take you there for two squid," said the old woman. "What do you want with Marral?"

"Business," said Clariel. She reached into the small change pocket inside her tunic and drew out one of the large copper coins that in Estwael were called simply "rounds," and in Belisaere were called "squids," apparently because some long ago issue had featured something supposed to represent magic streamers and had been misinterpreted as a squid's tentacles. "One squid."

The old woman's mouth quirked, but she shrugged and took the offered money.

"Follow me," she said, swinging the sack to her back. "Stay inside the rock markers, or the sea'll take you."

They followed the old woman along the beach to a point where a broad black rock emerged from the sand, the visible part of some greater mass below. It was like a great stone doormat marking the entrance to the causeway. The old woman stepped onto its worn surface and went straight out into the wash of the sea. Clariel and

Bel followed, both letting out a slight gasp as the cool water splashed around their legs, the wavelets coming around the Islet sometimes washing up as high as their thighs.

Looking down through the swirling water Clariel saw that they were standing on a kind of bridge of stone that was at least a foot higher than the surrounding sand. At the lowest tide, it would be completely dry, but judging from the tidemarks on the beach and the green stain on the city wall some hundred paces away, at the flood the Islet would be cut off by deep water. It would certainly be well over Clariel's head, and the tidewash would be powerful.

As both Kargrin and the old woman had said, there were stones marking the sides of the causeway, which was about twenty paces wide. Roughly pyramidal, the markers were obviously man-made, but had been worn long in the sea. They were covered in green weed and the purple-grey shells of lippets, shellfish that could be eaten or used as bait for fish, though neither humans nor fish were particularly fond of the strong-tasting bivalve.

"Good defense against the Dead," said Bel quietly to Clariel when they were about halfway across. A bigger wavelet had just swept past them, drenching them up to their waists. "Sea currents and waves are as effective as a strong river flow."

"But the sea doesn't stop whatever this Free Magic thing is," said Clariel, keeping her voice low, so the old woman ahead couldn't hear them.

Bel shrugged. "Maybe it crosses when the causeway is dry."

"The aqueducts don't dry up," said Clariel. "And apparently it passes under them as well."

"Yes, there is that," replied Bel. "Look, I'm not going to run if we do find this creature. No matter what."

"Then you're an idiot," said Clariel.

"You don't understand," said Bel. "I'm an Abhorsen, this is what we do—"

Clariel stopped, and turned to face the young man, both of them briefly rising up on tiptoe as another wavelet washed past them.

"I don't care if you get yourself killed. But don't mess things up. My parents keep going on about opportunities for me in Belisaere. This represents an opportunity for me to get *out* of Belisaere and it might be my only one, so don't spoil it!"

Bel looked surprised. Before he could answer, Clariel waded ahead, catching up to the old woman, who had kept plodding on. She was so bent the water was almost up to her chest, but she paid it no attention, just cricking her head back whenever a wave threatened to reach her mouth.

Clariel glanced back to make sure Bel was following. Behind him, about a dozen paces farther back, she saw three typical inhabitants of the Islet. But her eyes skittered away from them, and she felt dizzy again as her thinking mind knew they must be Kargrin and the two guardsmen, but some subconscious part insisted they were just beachcombers and not worth looking at.

Two-thirds of the way across, the causeway started to slope upward, and soon the sea was merely knee-deep and then just a foamy wash around their ankles. The Islet seemed taller than it had from the beach. There were steps cut into the rock face immediately in front of them. The old woman began to climb these, pausing halfway up to beckon to Clariel and Bel.

"This way, this way," she said. "Another squid when we get there, I think you said?"

"No, I didn't," said Clariel.

"I might have forgotten which is Marral's house," said the woman.

"Then I'll ask at every one," said Clariel. "Maybe I should do that anyway."

"Can't blame a body for trying," grumbled their guide. "It's easy enough to spot, anyway. Got a door made of shark teeth. Over there, take the second left."

"Second left what?" asked Clariel, as she climbed to the top step, and then added, "Ah."

The Islet had appeared to be one big rock from a distance, but now she saw that it was made up of about twenty stone hillocks thrusting up like pimples out of the huge plate of black stone below. There were channels between the hillocks, most of them high enough to be dry, but some cut deeper and so open to the sea. A broad channel lay straight ahead, almost cutting the island in two, with many lesser branches running off to either side.

All of the hovels and shelters were built upon the hillocks, some joined by bridges of driftwood across the channels. Others had steps cut into the stone to reach them, or ladders lashed together from whatever the sea had brought the builders.

"Follow the second channel on the left, go as far as you can, there are steps up," said the woman. "I'm going back to the worms."

Clariel nodded, and started down the steps on the other side, into the main channel. Bel followed her warily, looking around as he did so.

"Easy place to be ambushed," he said.

"Yes," agreed Clariel. She was also thinking that it would be a difficult place to leave quickly, if they had to get away.

There were no people moving around. A few of the huts had smoke coming out of them, usually through a hole in the roof rather than a proper chimney, but it was otherwise impossible to tell if they were inhabited. It was very quiet, save for the regular crash of the waves against the island, and the sound of their own footsteps on the rock.

The second left channel was narrow, not even wide enough to stretch out both arms, and the rock above rose higher, easily twice Clariel's height. She kept glancing up as they moved cautiously along, thinking about some attack from above. But there were no sounds of movement, and they passed two hillocks without event, before reaching the end of the channel and a series of steps cut into the mount ahead.

Clariel loosened the falchion at her side again. Bel did the same with his sword, and took out his pipes.

"Do you feel anything?" asked Clariel. "Smell anything?"

Bel shook his head. "I can smell only the salt from the sea, and the deaths are old and long-ago. Drowning, and murder from behind, but I can sense no Dead here. Too much swift water."

Clariel started up the steps, comforted by the knowledge that Kargrin and the guards must be close behind. For the first time in any hunt, she felt less than confident. She didn't like not knowing what to do, or what might happen.

On top of the rocky mount, there was a hut made of driftwood, canvas, and odds and ends, a fish-drying rack with no fish hanging from it, and a firepit built into a natural depression that had been smoothed into a bowl shape. Wood was laid there, ready for a fire. The doorway of the hut was closed by a curtain made of hundreds and hundreds of shark teeth tied to a heavy, close-meshed fishing net, so it was impossible to see inside.

Out of the shadowed channel, the sun was now fully visible just above the horizon, and its warmth was welcome, particularly since they were both sodden from the waist down. Clariel thought of sitting down to empty her boots of seawater, but decided it would be too risky, and there was no point. They would be crossing back soon enough, or so she hoped.

"I suppose we should call out to Marral," she whispered to Bel. But he was looking around them anxiously and didn't immediately answer.

"I can't see the others," he whispered back after a long pause.

"You're not supposed to be able to see—" Clariel started to say, then stopped. Of course, they should be able to see *something*, even if their minds wanted to accept it as part of the background. Kargrin and the others should look like beachcombers or fishermen or something . . .

"Even if they are there, how can they surround the hut? There's not enough space up here and there's no point being down in the channels."

Clariel drew her falchion. Bel drew his sword, and they instinctively stood back to back.

"They were behind us on the causeway," said Bel.

"Well they're not anymore," answered Clariel.

Chapter Eleven

OUT OF THE BOTTLE

Maybe we should shout out," said Bel nervously. "Call them."

"I can't see anyone at all," said Clariel. She was slowly looking from left to right, watching for any movement outside the huts on their higher outcrops of stone, or perhaps the glimpse of a head in one of the channels. "Nothing, no . . . there!"

She pointed at a sudden movement as someone leaned around the corner of a hut some fifty paces away, there was a flash of sunlight on metal—

"Down!" shouted Clariel.

She grabbed Bel as she threw herself down. But she was a moment too slow, and with a hideous thumping sound a quarrel suddenly flowered in Bel's shoulder and he screamed in shock and surprise and then both of them were in the firepit, the prepared wood scattered everywhere.

"Spelled quarrel," gasped Bel, as he rolled onto his back and gripped the shaft, which was wreathed in acrid white smoke. Aided by Free Magic, the quarrel had gone straight through his armored coat, breaking the protective spells and boring a neat hole through one of the gethre plates. Clariel measured the distance from his shoulder with her fingers together.

"Three fingers under your shoulder bone," she said. "Not fatal, unless the magic is . . . is like poison."

"N . . . no," said Bel, getting the word out through a grimace of pain. "I don't think so, just some sort of power to cut through Charter-spelled armor . . . can you break off the shaft, close as you can?"

"Yes," said Clariel. She knew not to pull it out, because that would make the bleeding worse, but breaking off the shaft would make it easier for Bel to move around. If he could. Shock would be setting in soon. "I'll do it in a minute."

She said that, but broke it off immediately, holding it as tightly as she could against his chest so not to move the embedded point around. Bel screamed again, and fainted.

"Roban! Kargrin!" shouted Clariel. "Gullaine!"

She heard several shouts in reply, but couldn't tell where they came from, or what they were saying. They sounded distant, as if the others were right over the far side of the Islet. Maybe down in one of the channels and not on a hillock. The sound was strangely faint, and difficult to locate.

Clariel risked propping up on her elbows to have a look, but there was still no sign of life around the other huts, and she couldn't see anything where the sun had reflected off the quarrel before. It had been a murderer's shot, a sudden attack from hiding. She'd been lucky to see the slight movement before the assassin fired.

"See anything?" croaked Bel muzzily. "Kargrin?"

"No," said Clariel.

"I can't . . . concentrate," whispered Bel. "Can you cast . . . healing marks . . . on my wound?"

"I can't remember the spell," said Clariel. She was desperately trying to work out what they should do. Where could Kargrin and the others have gone? What could have happened to them? She didn't have time to try and cast a Charter spell that she only dimly remembered learning. "I've forgotten the marks, I'm sorry, I was taught them a long time ago."

"I'll try in a minute," said Bel. He was even paler than he

normally was, even a little blue around the lips, Clariel thought. He needed help quickly.

"Kargrin! Roban! Captain Gullaine!"

She heard no shouts in answer, but a moment later a great column of fire erupted on the far side of the Islet, appearing so suddenly that Clariel didn't know whether it had come down like lightning or had erupted upward, exploding one of the huts into thousands of burning pieces, some of which started falling around them, though none were big enough to be dangerous.

There was no sound from the fire, though from her experience of forest fires Clariel knew something burning like that would be roaring, popping and crackling loud enough to be heard from a half a league away.

"Kargrin," whispered Bel. "Casting a fire spell. Why can't we hear them?"

"Because I don't choose to let you," said a soft voice behind them. A woman's voice, but something about it did not sound entirely human. With the sound, so sudden, came a choking stench of hot metal that was both like and unlike the smell of Jaciel's forges.

Clariel moved even as she heard the voice, springing up regardless of any chance of being shot by a crossbow, the falchion in her hand. But there was still no one visible. The shark-tooth curtain had not moved. As far as she could tell, there was just her and Bel on that particular hillock of stone.

"Where are you?" she said. "Face us!"

Bel tried to get up too, but he only managed to raise his head slightly before his eyes rolled back and he slid down. He was either unconscious again or close to it, and the dark, black stain of blood around his shoulder was spreading.

"I am here," said the voice again, seemingly behind Clariel. She spun around, swinging her falchion, but it cleaved empty air. The smell grew stronger, more acrid, biting into Clariel's mouth. She coughed and spat as if she could somehow rid herself of the taint that was slowly rolling down her throat.

"Interesting," said the voice. "So you are . . . *Clariel.*"

Clariel spun around again, so fast she was dizzy. The voice was nowhere, everywhere . . . it was inside her head . . .

The Charter. Kargrin had told her to reach for the Charter, that simply by joining with it she would gain some protection, even if she couldn't remember the marks for a particular spell. *Just reach for it, fall into it, let it wash over you,* Kargrin had said.

With her free hand, Clariel traced a Charter mark in the air. One of the first marks she'd learned, nothing by itself, but a mark that could be used to find a way into the flow. She tried to visualize it deep inside her mind as she drew it, thought of where it could go, the marks that it traveled with, and there they were, glowing inside her mind. She called them to her, and more, and found herself drawing them in the air with her left hand, and the point of her falchion. They weren't marks that she knew how to join up to make a spell, but they surrounded her and caught her up in the eternal current of the Charter, blocking out that insidious voice, the woman she instinctively did not want to hear—

"The Charter is a prison," said the voice, suddenly breaking through the golden glow and single-mindedness of the marks. "A maze to pen you in, to make you go certain ways. You do not need marks and spells, Clariel. There is a power within you. Direct it, by your will alone. I will show you, guide you, be your friend—"

"No!" screamed Clariel. "Kargrin! Roban!"

She staggered to the edge of the rock, swinging wildly with her falchion, but cut only air. Charter marks hovered around her like bees bewildered by smoke, without direction, and she did not have the skill or knowledge to make the marks into anything, to cast a spell that might reveal her enemy.

"Lady Clariel!"

A human shout, followed by the rush of footsteps on stone. Roban came charging up the steps, sword in hand, silver fire leaping along the blade. At the same time something else rose up out of the very rock, almost under Clariel's feet. At night, from a distance, it might be confused for a woman, for it was vaguely feminine in shape. But this close, it could be seen that the slender legs ended not in feet, but narrowed to become sharp, bony blades the color of yellowed teeth; its arms had two elbows a handsbreadth apart; and its spadelike hands had three fingers each ending in a curved-back claw. Its hair was not hair, but a mass of brilliant tendrils of white light that flowed around its head and cascaded down its shoulders and back, and its face, if it had one, was an absence of light in the middle, a dark, oval void without features of any kind.

Below its shining head, its skin was entirely the color of old, dried blood.

Claws raked at Roban. He parried, Charter marks blazing on his sword, sparks flying. But the creature was far stronger. Roban was forced back and then flung down the steps. Swatted like a fly, he disappeared into the shadow as if he had never been.

As Roban fell, Clariel swung her falchion two-handed at the creature's back. But the steel did not even break that strange, blood-red skin. It melted as it hit, the metal roiling away in molten drops, as if Clariel had cast a cup of quicksilver against the creature rather than struck it with a finely tempered blade.

The creature turned, and tilted its head quizzically.

"Not even an ensorcelled sword? But true, *you* do not need such things. Let me show you how to find the power within yourself. I will guide you, but first let me dispose of this small Abhorsen . . ."

It strode over to where Bel lay half in the firepit, its blade-feet striking sparks from the stone as it trod. It raised one of those feet above Bel's head, and was about to bring it down when Clariel screamed and dived forward, grabbing that unearthly, spiked foot with both hands to hold back the killing blow.

The moment she touched it, she felt a shock through her whole body. Her heart raced in panic as some unseen force flowed from the creature into her. It entered her mind, exerting a sudden mental pressure that made her want to let go, to open her hands and let the spike drive down, to *help* it strike—

"No!" shrieked Clariel. "No! I won't let you!"

It took all her willpower to keep her hands closed, and all her strength to stop the spiked foot. Yet despite everything she could do, it kept pressing down, coming closer and closer to Bel's forehead and the Charter mark there, as if that was the spot where the young man's skull was thinnest.

"You are strong," said the voice inside Clariel's head. "But not strong enough."

The thing leaned into its stomp, yet still Clariel managed to keep the spike a bare fingerbreadth above Bel's forehead. Every muscle in her body was quivering, her head was burning with the effort of resisting the creature's will. Blood began to trickle from her nose, and she knew the creature was too strong, the spike would smash into Bel's head and kill him and then it would kill her, she just *wasn't* strong enough . . .

Not by herself.

She needed the fury. Yet all her life Clariel had kept the anger in check, rather than trying to call it up. Now she was far more full of fear than anger and the berserk rage felt impossibly far away.

"Not strong enough," mocked the voice in her head. "But good enough to keep as a slave."

Clariel gripped even tighter, working her hands against the sharp edges of unnatural bone. The spike slipped down, so close that its very tip broke the skin on Bel's forehead and brought a bead of blood to the surface. Just one drop, like some hideous sweat. But Clariel stopped the spike from spearing through more skin and the bone beneath, even though her palms were sliced open and pain was shooting through her, and a terrible pressure in her head plucked at nerves, muscles all over her body twitching and rippling as the creature slowly gained control over her arms and hands.

The pain helped combat that invader in her mind. Clariel welcomed the hurt, and bit her lip as well, hard as she could, so that the blood filled her mouth. With the salt tang of blood fresh on her, she finally felt the fury. She could sense its source deep inside her, a banked fire that just needed fuel and air to rise up. Clariel welcomed it, summoned it, fed it with pain and fear and the necessity of action. It rose like a tide on the flood in answer.

She screamed again, but this time the scream was not one of fear, but of incandescent rage.

In that moment, she felt the power that had invaded her from the creature suddenly ebb back, and then a moment later, *she* was inside the creature's strange mind, and it was trying to resist *her*, as she gripped it with her will and demanded that it do her bidding. They were locked together, two intelligences in fierce, internal combat, the rest of the world forgotten, all thought and senses concentrated on the battle of wills between them. One must surrender soon—

A thistle-head suddenly appeared, sticking out of the creature's chest, the other end of the spear-shaft in Kargrin's powerful hands. Deep inside the creature's mind Clariel felt as if her own chest had been pierced, but it was a distant, walled-off agony. She held on tighter with both mind and body, now intent not just on stopping the thing from killing Bel, but on making it bow down to her, to obey her in all things, to become her slave . . . it was slowly giving in to the pressure of her will, she could feel it weakening . . . and then it spoke to her, mind to mind, no longer dominant and jeering but pleading with her, begging her for mercy.

"Help me! They will imprison me, trap me in a bottle, bind me again! You know what it is to be bound, contained against your will! Help me, sister!"

Dimly, Clariel was aware that Kargrin was weaving some sort of mighty Charter Magic spell. She could sense the Charter very close, like a great reservoir of power dammed high above, with Kargrin about to open the floodgates to let that power rush through him and his thistle-head spear, enveloping the creature in bonds it could not escape.

And once bound, Kargrin would force her—for Clariel found herself thinking of the creature not as it but she—into some less solid shape, and then contain her in a glass bottle or some vessel of pure metal, reinforced with spell after spell, all the weight of the Charter to hold the creature inside for forever and a day.

"Help me, Clariel," whispered the creature, the two of them still wrapped together deep in the thing's mind. "My name is Aziminil."

Clariel let go. Let everything go, her mental stranglehold, her grip on the sharp, stabbing feet, her rage, just released everything, even as Kargrin came to the final marks of his spell, an instant before he spoke the master mark. The mark that would bring everything together, combining all the thousands and thousands of marks that shone like a great galaxy of stars in the air above his head and swam the length of the thistle-head spear, striking great gouts of silver sparks wherever they touched the creature's blood-red flesh.

But Kargrin was just a second too late. As Clariel let go, Aziminil jumped high, wrenching the spear from Kargrin's hands. The creature stumbled against the wall of the hut but then leaped again, a great leap that took her to the next rocky hillock some thirty paces away. There she tore the spear from her body, threw it toward the sea, and vanished into the stone like water soaking into sun-parched soil.

"Blast it!" roared Kargrin. "Gully! Gully! I got it with the spear but I was too slow with the binding! It's gone into the stone."

"I know!" came an answering shout from Gullaine. "I'm following!"

Clariel looked at her bloodied hands, staring at her slashed palms.

She was on her knees, but even that felt too hard to maintain, so she let herself slump sideways, landing heavily next to Bel. Her eyes felt weighted with iron, so weary that she could barely keep them open. She looked out at the sun-drenched world sideways, and saw Kargrin's boots approach and then his face as he crouched by her side.

"No," she muttered. "See to Bel. Badly wounded. I'm all right . . . just my hands . . ."

But Clariel knew it wasn't just her hands and she wasn't all right. Something had changed inside her, during the struggle with Aziminil and in the moment she had let the creature go free. She had let a monster escape, and not only because she could not bear to think of anything sentient imprisoned in such a way.

Kargrin ignored her, quickly rolling her wrists to look at her wounded hands. Seeing the cuts were deep, but not immediately life-threatening, he did turn to Bel.

Clariel watched dully through half-closed eyes, still lying on her side, as bright Charter marks swirled around Kargrin's fingers. He called them into the air, where they hung like tiny stars. He arranged the suspended marks into a pattern and sent this shining constellation into Bel's wounded flesh, the marks sinking through the gethre plates of his hauberk, leaving a golden afterglow behind. Nothing happened for a minute, then the broken quarrel started to move, the barbs of the head becoming visible before the point popped out with a quickly stifled gush of bright red blood.

"Where . . . where were you," croaked Clariel, as Kargrin turned back to her and carefully lifted her hands.

"We were caught in a spell ourselves," Kargrin said, as he began to cast a healing spell upon Clariel. "The hunters trapped. It took me a few minutes to even realize we had been diverted to the other side of the Islet, and then longer to break free of the illusion. We are not dealing with any lesser creature, not a Margrue or Hish. This is one of the more powerful entities, though I do not yet know which one. And there was someone helping it, a mortal, probably under its dominion."

Clariel cried out as pain shot through her hands, a bitter ache that ran through the bones of her wrist and up her arms and ended explosively in the middle of her forehead with a sharp agony right under the Charter mark.

"Embrace the Charter," said Kargrin. "It will make it easier. You touched the creature, and some of its taint is on you, resisting the healing marks."

Clariel gave the slightest nod, because it hurt to move her head too much. She tried to visualize one of the common marks, to use it to find the Charter, but she just couldn't make it appear in her mind. She needed to sketch the mnemonic used to remember the mark, but Kargrin held her hands, and it was . . . all . . . too . . . difficult . . .

"Is she badly wounded?" asked Roban, who was himself holding his broken right arm, his face pale from hurt.

"Not physically," said Kargrin. There was sweat on his brow as he forced the final mark of the healing spell into the unconscious Clariel's left hand. It had taken all his skill and power to set the spell in both hands, and neither had worked as completely as they usually did. She still had partly healed cuts across her palms and the lower joints of her fingers, which would need to be bandaged to complete their healing at a natural rate. "But she held the creature for some minutes, protected by her blood and her berserk fury. I suspect in anyone else their flesh would have boiled away."

"She's a brave lass," said Roban. "I hope Kilp and that viper son of his don't get their hands on her."

"Indeed," said Kargrin. "Her great desire is to leave the city and go back to the Great Forest and I am thinking that is a very good idea, and soon. We need to keep her away from the creature, in any case."

"Will it return here?" asked Roban, looking over the Islet, his good left hand on the hilt of his sword.

Kargrin shook his head.

"I don't think so. It has been greatly weakened by the spear, and the spells it laid on the people and place here are broken now. I think it will go into the city . . . or try to . . . which means there is still a chance that we'll get it today . . . I was so close to the binding! Another few seconds . . . we have to hope that—"

"No point moaning over might have beens," interrupted Gullaine, leaping nimbly up the step. She had a crossbow over her shoulder, a very sandy crossbow that she had just picked out of one of the channels. "I lost the creature near the causeway, deep in stone."

"But you got the assassin?" asked Kargrin. "Who was it?"

"No. Only the crossbow," said Gullaine, placing it down on the stone. "It may tell us something. The shooter swam ashore, made a diagonal to the wall, and then was away along the rocks under the wall. An excellent swimmer, and I would say a young man, but I couldn't see who it was. How are our younglings?"

"Bel took a spelled quarrel under the collarbone," said Kargrin. "A few weeks' rest, he'll be fine. Clariel has some deep cuts to the hands, where she held the creature's bladed feet."

"Really?" asked Gullaine. She walked carefully to the hut as she spoke, and parted the shark-tooth curtain with her sword. "She *held* the creature?"

"She stopped it from killing Belatiel," confirmed Kargrin. "Aided by the fury, which shielded her from the thing's corrosive essence. She is a true berserk, Gully, she'll need help with that. And quickly, for I want to get her away from the city before a week is out."

"Why so fast?" asked Gullaine, who was now inside the hut, poking about with sword and boot, not touching anything even with her armored, gloved hands. "We might need to hold on to her; as a potential heir she could be useful—"

"She *held* the creature," said Kargrin. "That is something beyond the physical strength of any mortal. It was her will that held it, and that is how Free Magic sorcerers are made. If she should meet the creature again, and dominate it, find how . . . simple it would be to wield the powers the creature would give her . . . it is a great risk as long as that creature is free."

"She *is* the Abhorsen's granddaughter," said Roban doubtfully.

"The Abhorsens bind Free Magic creatures," said Kargrin. "They do not dominate them and take them into service."

"True," came Gullaine's voice from inside the hut. "But she strove against it to save another, not herself. Surely that is not the way of a sorcerer?"

"Few begin truly selfish," said Kargrin. "But all Free Magic sorcerers end up that way, suffering no check upon their actions. None, of any kind."

"Ah," said Gullaine, but it did not seem to be in response to Kargrin's words. She came out of the hut, carrying a brass-bound wooden bucket in her hand, and set it down by Roban's feet, some water slopping over the side. The guard and the huge Charter Mage looked down curiously.

"What in the Charter's name?" asked Kargrin. "Why bring that out?"

"Bright fish," said Gullaine, tapping the bucket with her sword, making the two brightly striped orange and red fish inside circle nervously. "For Clariel to give to the King. So at least we achieved *something*."

Chapter Twelve

THE EDUCATION OF A BERSERK

Clariel awoke in her own bed, her hands bandaged in clean white linen. The room was filled with soft, reddish light, and she had a moment of disorientation because the last thing she remembered was the Islet and the bright sunshine of the early morning. Now it was near dusk, the sun was low, and would soon be out of sight behind the expanse of the city to the west.

She looked at her hands. They hurt, in the way of minor wounds that are partially healed. Not a sharp pain, but an ever-present and unwelcome ache. Her lower lip hurt too, and was swollen and had bumpy lines where she'd bitten it. At least with her mouth closed, the scab wouldn't show, she thought.

Her hurts cataloged, Clariel sat up.

Pain stabbed her in the forehead, and then spread into her eyes. But it faded after a moment, so she swung her legs over the side, put her feet into the slippers there, and thought about getting out of bed.

But the thought did not translate into the deed. Clariel continued to sit, staring at something that did not belong in her bedroom and hadn't been there before. A knee-high glass bowl with a beaten gold rim next to the door, two-thirds full of water, with two very brightly colored fish swimming around in it.

"Bright fish," said Clariel wonderingly. "Where did *you* come from?"

Her rhetorical question was answered by a knock on the door, and her father's voice.

"Clarrie? Can I come in?"

"Yes," said Clariel. She sat up straighter and tried to remember exactly what had happened and what might be the best thing to tell her father had happened, which were not at all the same thing. "Do."

Harven edged around the door as if his very presence might cause Clariel to fall back on her sickbed, and only came in a few paces before stopping, but at least he did look at his daughter rather than his own shoes.

"I wanted to see that you are all right," he said. "I was assured you are, but to see you lying unconscious was a terrible shock! I never thought that you would actually be attacked, or that we really need the guards—"

Clariel held up her hand to stop him.

"What . . . ah . . . actually did happen?" she asked, hoping that he had been told something less upsetting than the truth. "I can't quite remember all of it. Roban was hurt . . ."

"Roban is fortunate to only have broken his wrist," said Harven. "And you . . . we . . . are fortunate that he could fight equally well with his left hand. I still find it unbelievable that a gang of unemployed laborers would attack a Goldsmith, and in daylight too! It is quite shocking. Nothing like this ever happened back in Estwael!"

"No," agreed Clariel. So that was the story. It was certainly better than telling him she'd been used to try and trap a Free Magic creature who was working with the Governor in a plot to overthrow the King. But it was also interesting that this tale of laborers attacking her was perfectly credible to Harven, despite his words. She knew that there was unrest among the day workers, who were not guild members, but like so many other things about Belisaere she had not yet found out what that was all about.

"Well, that's by the by," said Harven quickly. "In future you will have three guards at all times. Roban will be off for a few weeks of course, but his compatriots, ah . . . the woman with the . . . and the fellow with the red hair . . ."

"Heyren and Linel," supplied Clariel. Seeing her father unable to remember the names of people who might have to give up their lives for the family, she was ashamed that she had been thinking of the two guards as Scarface and Redbeard.

"Yes, well, Governor Kilp is sending over someone else to join them, and increasing the house guard as well. So you make sure you don't leave the house without them, young lady!"

"I doubt I could, even if I wanted to," said Clariel. She was thinking that she *would* want to leave without them in the near future and this could be a problem. She would need to evade them to get out of the house, and then out of the city. Presuming Kargrin paid up, despite not capturing the creature . . . or perhaps he had captured it, she thought. She couldn't remember anything after collapsing . . .

"How is Belatiel?" she asked.

"Who?" asked her father.

"Uh, no one," stammered Clariel. "I'm a bit confused. I don't even remember getting the fish for the King. Um, that is . . . I presume I did get them?"

"They were brought back with you," said Harven. "That's another thing we can count as fortunate, it would have been so easy for those . . . those scum . . . to spill them from the bucket, and our visit has been confirmed for tomorrow. I meant to tell you, we will leave for the Palace an hour after you return from the Academy. Valannie will dress you properly. I mean, presuming you are feeling well enough for the Academy and a visit to the Palace . . ."

"I am, Father," said Clariel quietly. Harven was smiling again, that pathetic smile. Even if she wasn't well enough, Clariel thought her father would prop her up in a palanquin, do anything to make the visit happen. His daughter's health was of so much lesser importance than getting Jaciel into the Palace to have a look at the Dropstone treasure.

"In fact, you have a visitor in that respect," continued Harven. "A Captain Gullwing or somesuch, of the Royal Guard. Apparently she has to talk to you before you can see the King tomorrow. I trust you are up to receiving her?"

"Yes," said Clariel eagerly. "And . . . I think her name is Gullaine."

"Yes, that's right, Gullaine," said Harven. "Strange-looking woman. Now you're sure you are feeling well enough . . . I mean now, and for tomorrow."

"Yes," said Clariel.

Harven fidgeted with his belt, gazed down at his shoes, looked up, edged two steps closer, and then finally looked at Clariel.

"I know you feel that this visit is just for your mother," he said. "But I really do think it will help you, Clarrie. I do . . . I do want you to be happy, you know."

"I know," said Clariel. He did want her to be happy. Provided her happiness didn't conflict with Jaciel's work, or wasn't too difficult to achieve.

"Also," continued Harven. "Your mother, last night . . . telling you about Teriel . . . I'm sure it was a shock. She still feels very strongly about the injustice done to her by her father and the family. Anyway, best not to bring it up with her. Or with anyone. Private family business, you know."

"*I* won't talk about it," said Clariel. She was still coming to terms with the whole idea of her mother killing anyone, let alone her own brother or—if she was to be believed—some creature that had assumed her brother's shape. And "in a rage" was another eye-opener. Her mother the berserk. An inheritance which she had passed on to her daughter without explanation or help.

"Good, good," said Harven.

"How is Mother?" asked Clariel. "Did she already come to see me while I was unconscious?"

"She is very busy," said Harven quickly. "She would come up, but there is a process, a type of annealing, very delicate work she began this morning, that cannot be interrupted . . ."

He stopped talking, perhaps aware that he was trying to excuse the inexcusable, before bending down to kiss Clariel on the top of her head, something he hadn't done for quite a few years. Her eyes glistened as he straightened up and retreated, pausing to offer a tentative wave at the door. She remembered when her father's kisses on her head had been unalloyed with her resentment of his weakness, the weakness that always put his daughter last. But that was many years gone, when she was just a little girl and her father was a big, strong refuge from the world at large. She had known for years he was a flimsy shelter at best, that she could not rely on him for anything important.

It still hurt, when she remembered what he had once been to her, however false that was.

Captain Gullaine came in a few minutes later, armed and armored as she had been that morning, except she carried her helmet, revealing a completely hairless head. Gullaine had gleaming, dark brown skin, no hair or eyebrows at all, and her sharp blue eyes were a starker blue than Clariel had remembered, seen now out of the shadow of the woman's helm.

"Lady Clariel," said Gullaine formally, with an inclination of her head. "I hope you are recovering."

"I am, thank you, Captain Gullaine," said Clariel. "Only . . . what happened? I mean after I passed out?"

"I think you can call me Gully now," said the guardswoman. She came over and sat down on the end of Clariel's bed, with a stretch and a sigh. "Ah, I've been running backward and forward all day. Do you want the long or the short version?"

"Um, I'm not sure," said Clariel. "Perhaps the short to begin with."

"The creature got away from me," said Gully. She stretched again and looked away as she spoke. "It can move through stone, albeit not that quickly, but I couldn't track it once it went deep. Kargrin says the thistle spear weakened it, which was less than he hoped. Evidently the thing is of the second or third order of such entities at least, not something weaker."

"Do . . . does Kargrin know what it is?"

"Not yet. He's scouring bestiaries, but that could take a long time. We've sent to Hillfair for the Abhorsen's advice. He should know more, but Charter knows he doesn't easily stir himself, even for this sort of thing."

"That's what Bel said. But isn't that what the Abhorsens are for?"

"Yes," agreed Gully. "But old Tyriel lives for his horses and the Grand Hunt, and cares little for anything else. His daughter and the rest of them take their lead from Tyriel. Except for Bel, of course. He's a throwback to the old days, or would like to be."

"Is Bel going to . . . going to be all right?" asked Clariel.

"He'll live," said Gully. "Bed for a few days, a sore shoulder for a few weeks. He was lucky. A handsbreadth closer to the throat or chest and he'd have been killed instantly. Not to mention Magister Kargrin getting to him quickly. He is one of the most expert healers in the city. Among other things."

"Who shot Bel? It can't have been the creature, could it?"

Gully shook her head.

"A mortal follower, likely someone mazed into obeying the creature. It had laid numerous spells on both the Islet and the people there, spells of command and beguilement, reinforcing them over time. I think it's been here longer than we thought. A year, at least. We should have looked over the Islet long before now."

"And is it connected with Governor Kilp?" asked Clariel.

"Kargrin still thinks so," said Gullaine. "But I have yet to see solid evidence that this is so. There are traces of a Free Magic presence by his house, but many people come and go there. Certainly Kilp has enough ordinary reasons to plot, without Free Magic being involved. The King withdraws his authority, Kilp moves in, as far as he is able. That is the nature of power."

"The King," said Clariel. "Who I am to visit tomorrow."

"Yes," replied Gullaine. "The ostensible reason for my visit. We will discuss that a little later, if you will, it is simple enough, in terms of ceremony. The King, though old and sometimes crotchety, is not a difficult man. But more important right now, I wanted to talk to you about being a berserk."

"I'm not a . . ." Clariel started to say, then stopped. There was no point trying to deny it, particularly to herself. Gullaine waited patiently for her to continue. Clariel took a deep breath and said, "Yes. Yes. I *am* a berserk."

"I, too, am a berserk," said Gullaine. She smiled, a faint smile that was not one of happiness, but of troubled memory. "My mother was a Clayr, and my father a third cousin of the King. So we are distant relatives, Clariel. Both the Charter and the rage are strong in my bloodline, but I had the Sight very weakly and was never called to the Nine-Day Watch. So I joined the Rangers who patrol the glacier and the lands about it. The rage rose in me the first time I fought bandits, and then again against norn-bears, and it grew inside me like a fire spreads in dry straw until I would snap at the mildest provocation. But I was lucky. There were books about berserks in the Great Library of the Clayr, and sisters and cousins to quite literally restrain me and make me read those books. So I learned early how I might govern myself. To keep the fury in check, but also how to call it up when necessary."

"I called the fury today," said Clariel quietly. "I didn't know what else to do. I couldn't stop the creature killing Bel . . ."

"You did what had to be done," said Gullaine. "But having roused your berserk nature, you *must* learn how to master it. I have brought you the book that helped me most. Read it, and return it to me when you can. One day it must go back to the Great Library of the Clayr, under the glacier."

She took a small, leather-bound book from the pouch at her belt and handed it to Clariel, who glanced at the title, the gilt type deeply embossed on the front cover: *The Fury Within: A Study of the Berserk Rage and Related Matters.*

"It is an old book, but then berserks have been around a long time," said Gullaine. "It contains directions for various exercises of the mind, which can be tedious, but work well. There are also some Charter spells that help contain the fury, though you will need help learning those, I think. Read the book soon."

"I will," promised Clariel. She meant it too, having been alarmed by her recent experiences. She had experienced the rage twice in three days . . . it felt as if it were closer now, easier to call upon. Or worse, likely to rise up and boil over at any time, like a stew that had now been moved to a hotter part of the kitchen fire.

But it wasn't only the berserk fury that troubled Clariel. It was her experience with the Free Magic creature Aziminil, the sense of triumph she had felt when she had entered the creature's mind, when it had begun to bend to her will. She'd never felt anything like it before, nothing so ecstatic, not even after a day stalking a deer and then the perfect true flight of her arrow, striking exactly the right spot . . .

Clariel shivered.

"Are you feverish?" asked Gullaine, with concern.

"No," said Clariel. "No. Just . . . thinking about what happened today."

"Few people have encountered such a creature and survived to speak of it," said Gullaine. "You did well."

"Well enough for Kargrin to keep our bargain?" asked Clariel. "To help me leave Belisaere?"

She had another reason to be gone from the city now. Clariel did not want to meet the Free Magic creature again. Not because of what the creature might do to her, but because of what she might do to it.

"Yes," said Gullaine. She hesitated then added, "You will be paid, and you will be helped on your way. Kargrin thinks it would be best that you leave. After you have seen the King."

"I suppose," said Clariel. "The creature . . . do you think you will find it, and bind it?"

"I am sure of it," said Gullaine, who was indeed very sure, for reasons not yet to be shared. She watched Clariel carefully as she spoke, but the younger woman didn't notice. She was looking at her bandaged hands.

"It won't . . . it won't come looking for me?"

"It is extremely unlikely," said Gullaine. "If it does, five of the dozen guards in your house tonight used to be in the King's service, all bear the Charter mark, two are quite accomplished Charter Mages. There is also no easy path to get to this house without passing one or more Charter Stones, and the creature cannot or will not do that."

"I wonder . . ." Clariel said slowly. "I wonder if I should stay to help you find it."

"That won't be necessary," said Gullaine. "Don't you yearn to be free of the city? Magister Kargrin certainly thought you did."

"I do, I do," confirmed Clariel, but there was the slightest tinge of doubt in her voice.

"Presuming you still wish to leave, we will help you," said Gullaine. "After you have seen the King. Speaking of that, let me tell you of the manner of your presentation tomorrow. It is quite straightforward . . ."

The Captain spoke on, and Clariel listened, taking in what she needed. But part of her mind was thinking back to Aziminil, remembering the moment when she felt the raw power within the creature.

Power waiting to be called upon, waiting to be directed, waiting to be used.

Power waiting for her . . .

The Academy was not so daunting the second time, now Clariel knew she would be free of it within days. In fact the most difficult part of the morning had been the walk over, with Valannie going on and on about the perfidious day laborers and their attack upon her, and her poor wounded hands—despite the fact they had already scabbed over and the unsightly scars were hidden under the thinnest doeskin gloves, bleached whiter than Belisaere stone.

Clariel had even enjoyed the first lesson, The Exercise of the Body, Martial and Merely Aesthetic, which on this occasion had been mostly aesthetic, practicing some of the dances the students would perform as their part of the Autumn Festival. Denima was in that lesson. She came over to Clariel at once to ask her what had happened to her the day before, since rumors were flying all over the city. Clariel stuck with the official story of being attacked by a gang of disaffected workers, which Denima also appeared to accept without demur, indicating that such attacks were a lot more common than anyone had wanted to tell Clariel, and the guards a necessity.

The second lesson, On the Writing of Letters, Reports, Epistles, Writs, Bills, and Such, was considerably less enjoyable, mainly because Aronzo was in it. As soon as Clariel came into the Second Hall, where the lesson was held, he approached her with a smirk on his face.

"Lady Clariel," he said, with an exaggerated bow. "I trust you are well?"

"Well enough," replied Clariel, moving to step past him and go to the closest empty desk. Aronzo blocked her path, so she stopped and looked at him with a withering gaze.

"You hurt your hands I believe," said Aronzo. "Those annoying rebels from the Flat are becoming too troublesome."

Clariel nodded and stepped sideways. Aronzo stepped sideways too, the smirk changing to a full-blown smile, showing off all his white teeth.

"And poor little Belatiel," continued Aronzo. "Got stuck in the shoulder. More than a little prick, I hear."

Clariel's eyes narrowed and she felt the anger rising. Her right hand was halfway to her sleeve before she even knew it, fingers reaching for the hilt of her knife. She stopped the movement and breathed in very slowly through her nose, counting silently to three, and out her mouth, counting again. As Gully's book had told her, she imagined the anger blowing out with the air.

"I suppose you could say he was very lucky," said Aronzo, still smiling.

"I suppose you could," replied Clariel coldly. Inside, her mind was putting pieces together and not liking what she made from them. Denima had not asked about Belatiel, and Clariel was sure she would have done so if she'd known he was injured. Clearly Belatiel's presence at the supposed attack was not part of the general rumor, though it would be now, since everyone else in the room was watching and listening intently.

So how did Aronzo know Belatiel was wounded, and that it was in the shoulder?

"Please allow me to take my seat. I believe we are about to begin our lesson."

Aronzo arched his eyebrows in mock surprise.

"So keen to learn, Lady Clariel? I had not thought you so intent on your *lessons*. It gives me hope."

"Hope for what?" spat Clariel, the anger rising again, till she clamped down on it and resumed the steady breathing, slowly in and slowly out, slowly in and slowly out.

"Hope is a wonderful thing," said Aronzo. He turned and walked away, only a few steps, before looking back over his shoulder. "We can discuss it at dinner tonight."

"I'll be otherwise occupied!" said Clariel, louder than she had intended, causing some gasps and titters among the rest of the class. Clariel ignored them, sat down at the nearest desk, and selected a quill from the three or four that had been cut and put there by the Academy servants earlier, trying to stay calm as she inked it and tested it on a piece of scrap paper.

My temper is my own and answers to me, she wrote. *My temper is my own and answers to me.*

She was writing the phrase for the third time when the teacher came in, a middle-aged man who had inkstains on the sleeves of his shirt, and a pleasant but slightly absent face. Clariel noted he had a Charter mark on his forehead not very well concealed by the same sort of paste Valannie applied expertly to Clariel's skin. He stopped to introduce himself to Clariel as he went past. She flipped over the piece of paper as he bowed, so he couldn't read it.

"Master Kaernon," he said. "Scribe by profession, teacher upon occasion. Welcome to the Academy, Lady Clariel."

It was a fairly perfunctory greeting and he did not wait for an answer, proceeding straight to the lectern at the front of the hall, where he opened a book and called out, "Pages fifty-two to fifty-five, *Heribert's Misleading Letters*, read the piece on appearing to agree while not agreeing at all, and then we shall discuss."

Clariel found the book under the lid of her desk, one of the three books there, opened it, and began to read. But while her eyes took in the words, she did not retain them, nor think about the content. She was wondering what Aronzo meant by "we can discuss it at dinner tonight," whether he was a good shot with a crossbow, and how well he could swim. She was also thinking about collecting her money from Kargrin and getting out of Belisaere, what she would say to the King in just a few hours, the possibility of meeting Aziminil the Free Magic creature again and what she might do if that happened . . . there were so many things that were more important than writing misleading letters.

But she had to listen to the discussion about such letters, and then write one, all of which seemed to take far longer than two hours. In part to avoid Aronzo and in part because she simply couldn't bear being cooped up again, Clariel raced away as soon as Kaernon dismissed the class.

Denima hurried after her, and caught her by the front gate.

"Clariel! Aronzo said that Bel was hurt? Is he all right?"

"Yes," said Clariel hurriedly. After a moment's reflection she added, "At least as far as I know. I've been told he is . . . injured . . . but recovering."

"But what happened? Was he attacked too?"

"I can't talk now," said Clariel. "I have to go. Sorry!"

She rushed out through the gate. Valannie was already waiting, and rather than trying to encourage Clariel to stay and lunch with her fellow students, this time she was anxious to get her back home as quickly as possible.

"We must hurry, Lady Clariel," she said. "You need to dress and I will have to repaint your face as best as I can, indeed I don't know how I can make it last to this evening! If only I'd been told earlier!"

"Told what?" asked Clariel crossly, as she led the way into the street, with Heyren, Linel, and the new guard—an older, very tough-looking woman called Reyvin—rushing to keep up.

"That you would be dining at the Governor's house tonight," said Valannie. "And going straight from the Palace instead of coming home first!"

"I see," said Clariel grimly. "Am I to go alone, or with my parents?"

"Oh, with Lady Jaciel and your father, of course," prattled Valannie. "It is a signal honor, you know, to be invited to dine with just the Governor's family. But no surprise. Of course, it would have been easier tomorrow night, what with you going to . . ."

Her voice dropped and she looked around nervously before adding in a much quieter tone, "Going to see the King. I do hope he doesn't keep you long, but with him as mad as he is, who can say?"

"That's enough!" snapped Clariel.

Valannie gave her a mulish look, but didn't speak for the rest of the hasty walk home, via the stone garden on the ridge. Clariel noticed that the steps had indeed been freshly repaired, a wooden framework still around the broken piece of stone to keep the new work in place.

There was a great bustle back at the house, with many extra guards in the livery of the Goldsmiths formed up loosely outside the gate, and several palanquins and bearers inside the courtyard. Apparently Clariel and her parents could not risk getting dusty and hot by walking to the Palace. Or perhaps couldn't get dusty and hot for the visit after their royal audience. The Governor's dinner continued to occupy Valannie's thoughts and speech as she rushed Clariel upstairs to dress in the new, made-to-measure clothes that had been delivered just in time from Mistress Emenor. She also repainted Clariel's face, once again burying her Charter mark under the thickest paste, smoothed with a brush and a curious light stone. Clariel had to admit Valannie was an extremely skillful lady's maid. Even if she was also a spy for Governor Kilp and couldn't be trusted at all.

When Clariel came back downstairs an hour later, she felt more like a painting of herself than herself, a thought that caused her to begin to smile until she remembered that this would crack the plasterwork on her face or some such thing. She had on no less than five

silken tunics, but they were so light she hardly noticed any weight
or constriction and had to admit that in the warm and humid air of
Belisaere they made much more sense than her normal clothes. She
still had her small dagger in her sleeve.

"There you are," said Jaciel as Clariel entered the courtyard. Her
mother was attired similarly to herself, but was also wearing the new
golden necklace of teardrops that she had made, and her gold-dotted
scarf was fastened with a large golden brooch set with sapphires and
diamonds in the shape of a swooping hawk, also her own work. "You
will go in the first palanquin with Valannie."

"Yes, Mother," replied Clariel. Jaciel did look very regal, she
thought. She *was* proud of her mother, as a truly great goldsmith
and artist. But she had often wished that she could swap this grand
personage for someone easier to get on with. Her aunt Lemmin,
for example. Jaciel would actually be a better aunt than mother, she
thought. Good for gifts and visits and influence, without needing to
offer much actual love or time . . .

"Milady?"

Clariel blinked. Valannie was holding back the red and gold curtains of the nearer palanquin, and a block had been placed to make it
easier to climb inside. Clariel had never ridden in a palanquin before,
it seemed stupid to her to be carried by people when you could walk
yourself. But as Captain Gullaine had explained to her the night
before, it was the usual protocol to arrive at the Palace by palanquin,
or on horseback if given leave to ride within the city, but this was
usually reserved for royal couriers or other special messengers.

The interior of the palanquin was padded with cushioned velvet
on all surfaces, so much so Clariel wasn't sure exactly where she was
supposed to sit. She climbed in and positioned herself at one end, discovering that there was a depression amid all the cushioning, though
it made her not so much sit as recline. Valannie climbed in the other
end, carrying her cedarwood case of cosmetics, and twitched the
curtains closed. There were small holes to see out, disguised on the

outside as gold coins against the red, but they didn't offer much of a view. Or let in much air, so it was quite stifling inside.

"Please remember to keep as still as possible, milady," said Valannie anxiously. "I will retouch your face of course, but please *do* try to keep it undisturbed."

"I'll do my best," muttered Clariel. She settled back and slowly turned her head so she could see out through one of the small holes. One saving grace about being trapped in a palanquin with Valannie was that the maid probably wouldn't talk too much, not wanting to crack her own face paint, or encourage Clariel to answer and destroy the last hour of her work.

There were eight bearers carrying the palanquin. Clariel could hear them whispering a kind of marching song to one another to help them keep in step and make sure the ride stayed level. She smiled as she recognized the chant; it was a song the Borderers sang, though with ruder words.

I once loved a lover but I left . . . right . . . left
Never find another as right . . . left . . . right
Should I have left . . . right . . . left . . . right . . .
I once loved another but I left . . . right . . .
Should've listened to Mother right . . . left . . . right
But I'd still have left . . . right . . . left . . . right . . .

Even with the steadiness of the bearers' steps, there was a small amount of swaying and tilting, rather like being on a barge. Clariel had been on a barge once, when she traveled with her father along the Metal Canal that took silver ore from the mine at Mount Shulle to Ponstayn, where it was smelted and refined. She had not particularly enjoyed the experience, disliking the mine and the metalworking town. They were far to the west of her beloved Estwael and surrounded by clear-felled dales, the nearer woods gone for lumber long ago. Her father had liked it though, perhaps because he was seen as a significant figure there, being an important buyer of silver and not just Jaciel's husband.

There wasn't much to see out the closest coin-size hole in the palanquin's curtains apart from even more houses of white stone. There weren't even many people, probably because they were being herded out of the way by the guards that accompanied the palanquins on every side. Despite the presence of the guards, Clariel regretted that she had only her smallest dagger, and nowhere to hide a larger weapon, since she'd been forced to wear slippers of a soft silver mesh fabric rather than boots.

With nothing to see, Clariel turned away from the peephole, remembering to do it slowly so as not to invite criticism from Valannie for cracking her face paint. She hoped this would be her first and last ride in a palanquin, because it was getting even more airless, and the slight swaying motion was making her feel sleepy, but not in a good or comfortable way.

It should be one of the last, at least, she told herself. She would go to Magister Kargrin tomorrow, get her money and a disguise, and leave. It would probably be best if she were disguised as a man, which she had done before herself, without the aid of Charter Magic. She smiled as she suddenly thought of what a magic disguise might do. If she was bespelled to look like a man, would that go so far as to give her the parts of a man, to look at, at least? That would dissuade even the most suspicious, if it came to that kind of inspection . . .

The sudden, sharp sound of metal on metal brought her out of this amusing daydream and she shot upright with her hand on her knife, legs swinging toward the curtain, before Valannie managed to raise her hands in alarm and cry out.

"Milady! It's only the metal stars in the road, under the guard's hobnails!"

Clariel's hand slowly came out of her sleeve, but she did not lie back.

"What stars?"

"We are on the Avenue of Stars," said Valannie. "There are many tiny stars set in the flagstones. It is a wonder of the city."

"I see," said Clariel. She leaned forward and gently pulled the bottom of the curtain up and leaned over to look out. The palanquin rocked more than usual, and there were a few grunts as the bearers adjusted to the shift of weight. Clariel peered down at the road, and indeed saw many tiny stars in the stone, reflecting the afternoon sun like bright sparks fallen from a fire, though these would never fade to cinders.

The metal clicks continued for quite a long time. Clariel looked out, but again couldn't see much, apart from the fact that the Avenue of Stars was at least twice as wide as most of the regular city streets, and that the guards were still keeping people well back, forcing them to stand aside. Most of them looked at the passing palanquin with unhappy or angry faces, making Clariel think again about the "minor trouble" with "unsettled workers." She'd not really noticed before, the mass of people in the city being simply too large for her to focus on as anything other than "huge and frightening crowd," but seeing individuals from within the palanquin, it became clear to her a great many people were not happy to see rich Goldsmiths and their guards arrogantly force their way past.

There were some shouts ahead, but not in alarm or trouble, just the same sort of ceremonial call as Roban had given when they'd arrived at the Academy, calling out "Goldsmiths!"

"Are we there already?" asked Clariel, puzzled. "I thought there was some sort of park, a band of trees below the Palace . . ."

"Not yet, milady," answered Valannie, who was trying to speak without opening her mouth too wide. "We're turning onto the King's Road. There are guards, to keep the commoners out of the gardens."

Clariel frowned at this, and wondered why the commoners were being kept from the gardens. In Estwael, there was a town park much frequented by the more timid folk who didn't like the forest beyond the walls. She'd loved it as a small child, before transferring that love to the wilder woods.

Through the spyhole, she saw a large crowd gathered as close as they could get to the great iron gates that had been opened to allow the palanquin's passage, gates in a high fence of iron topped by spikes that had once been gilded, remnants of gold still showing here and there.

As Clariel looked out, she saw one of the people, obviously poor from her sackcloth dress, lift her arm back to throw something. As she did so half a dozen others followed suit.

"They're throwing things!" cried Clariel, instinctively crouching and once again reaching for her dagger.

But the thrown objects had no weight, bouncing off the roof and sides of the palanquin, and neither the guards nor the bearers paid any attention to the missiles or the throwers. Whatever they were hurling, it was soft and harmless. Clariel saw one missile bounce onto the road near her and partially unfurl.

"They're throwing crunched-up paper?"

"Petitions," said Valannie, with a sneer. "They hope to get their petty grievances to the King. Don't worry, the guards at the gate will pick the papers up and record the names on them for later attention."

"To address their wrongs?" asked Clariel, but even as she asked the question she knew that would not be the case.

"No! To make further enquiries, to see if they are troublemakers," said Valannie. "It is a small set of rabble-rousers causing all the problems. Most folk are loyal to the Governor."

"You mean loyal to the *King*," said Clariel, but Valannie didn't answer, nor would she meet Clariel's gaze.

It wasn't her problem, thought Clariel. Let others politick and plot and counterplot. She would be away from the city soon enough, and in the Great Forest within a week. If the Borderers continued to exist, then she would join them in a year or two, when she had proved herself as a hunter and guide. If by some stroke of governmental foolishness the Borderers were disbanded or discontinued through lack of funds, then so be it. She would remain a hunter and try to carry out some of the good work the Borderers did on her own account, tending to the woods, its animal inhabitants, and the men and women who lived or traveled there. "Tending" being a word that covered all manner of activity, from clearing overgrown paths, protecting young deer from poachers and travelers from wolves and bears, culling populations of animals that threatened the balance of the Forest . . .

A shadow fell across the palanquin. Clariel reacted to it instantly, her head going up, her nose sniffing the air. She knew the shape and feel of that shade, she could smell the great tree that cast it. Ignoring Valannie's decorous and ineffectual attempt to stop her, she leaned forward and pulled the curtain open.

They were in the Palace gardens, being carried along a gently rising road that ran straight as a blade between great oaks, whose branches intermingled above them to form a canopy of green, the occasional crunching sound underfoot from the treading of fallen acorns.

There were lawns behind the oaks, and stands of other trees, silver birch and rowan, ash and beech, interspersed with beds of white flowers, bordered in red brick, a warm and welcome sight compared to all the cold stone of the city.

Off in the distance, for the gardens stretched around the Palace Hill and continued out of sight, a stag raised his antlered head to watch the procession. The rest of his herd, a half-dozen hinds and half-grown fawns, followed his motion a moment later. They were cautious, but not overly so, and Clariel knew they were not hunted, but mere ornaments of the royal garden, or perhaps an aid to keep the grass down.

"Do close the curtain, milady!" protested Valannie again. "It is not seemly."

"I don't care," said Clariel, breathing in the clean, soft air with its scent of earth and wood and natural decay, the work of wind and rain, not of mortal action.

Valannie muttered something else, but Clariel paid her no attention. She was drinking in the vista, the air, the whole park, reinforcing her spirit for whatever lay ahead.

One of the guards, a man Clariel hadn't seen before who was walking close by, looked over at her curiously. She knew she must seem an odd sight with her head thrust out of the curtains, staring into the distance. But he said nothing, falling back a step or two, so as not to intrude upon her view.

The road they were on—the King's Road, Valannie had said— took a sharp turn to the right and began to climb up Palace Hill, which Clariel saw had been terraced into six levels, the road switch-backing up, first right then left and back again. The gardens continued on each terrace, the closest one with wildflowers growing in the retaining wall, a profusion of starflowers, a mixture of the white and yellow varieties. Starflowers did not grow in Estwael, the climate did not suit them. They were late even here, Clariel considered, so close to autumn.

The bearers swapped positions seamlessly as they climbed up the road, a pair from the front moving to the back, to help hold the palanquin level despite the inclination of the road. It wasn't that steep, but enough to cause problems for palanquin bearers. For a moment Clariel thought about hopping out and walking once again, but she gave up that idea after considering the likely lecture from Valannie and possibly from her mother, who never seemed to care about etiquette and the like except when it concerned her own inter- est. If they weren't allowed in the Palace because Clariel had walked up, and Jaciel thus didn't get to examine the Dropstone gold work, then there would be a storm indeed. It wasn't worth the risk.

At the top of the final terrace, the King's Road ended in front of a massive gatehouse that projected out from the high, white walls of the Palace. Clariel didn't wait to be invited, climbing out of the palanquin even before one of the bearers could put down a step.

The Goldsmith guards marched around and drew themselves up in formation, four ranks deep. There were forty of them all together, Clariel noted, which seemed like a lot of guards for only three people. There was a certain tension among them too, she saw, as if something more than ceremonial escorting might be required.

There were half a dozen Royal Guards present too, on the bridge that ran over the narrow, but very deep moat before the gatehouse. In fact it looked like not so much a simple moat but a dark crevasse that might go all the way down through the hill to sea level. The guards wore the same long hauberks of gethre plates as Captain Gullaine, with red-and-gold surcoats and blackened steel helmets. They held poleaxes and had swords at their belts. Clariel noticed another ten or so above on the walls, looking down. These had short bows like the Borderers used, holding them strung and ready, but without arrows nocked. There were more still behind the portcullis at the end of the bridge, in the arched entryway to the gatehouse. Clariel also noted the portcullis was halfway down, sitting just above the level of the guards' heads, so it could be quickly dropped.

All of which added up to a high level of suspicion on the part of . . . well, it had to be Captain Gullaine since the King was supposed not to take an interest in anything . . . Clariel wondered again about the number of Goldsmith guards they'd brought.

"You go ahead, Clariel," said Jaciel, as she alighted from the palanquin with imperious ease. "Your father and I will follow. Where is your gift?"

Clariel looked around for the bearers who were supposed to be carrying the gold-rimmed bowl with its bright fish. After all the effort to get the fish, she'd forgotten to check that they had joined the procession and had a moment's panic, assuaged when she saw the two men behind the palanquin with the bowl—wrapped in cloth-of-gold to hide its contents—suspended under two stretcher poles, as if it were a palanquin itself.

"Bring the bowl over, please," Clariel called out, waving to the bearers. "Take it to the guards . . . oh, here they come."

Gullaine—or Gully, as Clariel now tried to think of her, at the Captain's request—had told her that no one would be allowed to enter the Palace proper, save for herself and her parents. Royal Guards would take the gift and convey it inside for the presentation. Everyone else would have to wait by the gatehouse until they came back out.

Of all the guild guards and servants, only Valannie made an attempt to stay with Clariel. She fell in behind her mistress as they crossed the bridge, but they'd only gone a few paces when Captain Gullaine stepped out of the shadow under the gateway and took Valannie by the elbow as if leading her in a country dance, swinging her around to send her back again. It happened so quickly she barely had time to squawk in indignation.

"King's guests, only, madam," said Gullaine. "Lady Clariel, Lady Jaciel, Master Harven, I welcome you on behalf of His Highness."

"Oh, I never meant—" bleated Valannie.

"Best wait with the others," said Gullaine. "Refreshments will be sent out."

Clariel noted a general stir among the guards and bearers, a movement of positive approval. Evidently the Palace did not stint on refreshments to visitors' entourages, even if they were not trusted and required to wait outside.

Gullaine led Clariel and her parents through the gatehouse, under a broad pattern of murder holes that looked as if they might have been tested recently, judging by the fresh scorch marks around each opening, and the evidence of scrubbing on the pavestones beneath. After they passed the portcullis, it slowly groaned down behind them.

"Expecting trouble, Captain?" asked Harven. He sounded nervous, Clariel thought. Jaciel paid neither the closing of the portcullis nor her husband any attention, striding on ahead to a metal-studded gate that glowed with many slowly crawling Charter marks.

"We always expect trouble," said Gullaine, with a smile and a wave of her hand. "This tends to work out better than never expecting any."

At the inner gate, Gullaine drew a Charter mark in the air—yet another one Clariel didn't recognize—and spoke something very quietly under her breath. The marks on the gate glowed more brightly in response, and one leaf slowly opened, just enough to admit the four of them, in single file. As soon as they passed through, it shut behind them, leaving them in an octagonal guardroom that had gates on all but one side. Each of the seven oaken gates was decorated in cut bronze and silver, showing various scenes from the kingdom. Clariel recognized the Wall, the Clayr's glacier, a house on an island in a river, Belisaere itself, two rural scenes that could be almost anywhere, and a forest setting that was most likely in the Great Forest but could be in one of the lesser woods.

A guard stood in front of the gate decorated with the walls, aqueducts, and houses of Belisaere. He bowed as they entered.

"Ah, Kariam," said Gullaine. "Lady Jaciel, Master Harven, you will be escorted to the Upper Hall, while I take Lady Clariel to the King."

"What?" asked Jaciel, suddenly sharp. "We are not to see the King?"

"I fear not, Lady Jaciel," said Gullaine. "The King is old and tired, and visitors tax his strength. He has agreed to see Lady Clariel for the kin-gift, as ancient tradition demands, but that is all."

"I demand to see him," said Jaciel. "We are second cousins, after all."

"His Highness has given strict orders that allow no variation," said Gullaine. "However, perhaps I should also tell you that a number of items I believe you wish to see have been placed in the Upper Hall, to . . . ameliorate your disappointment at not seeing His Highness."

"What items?" asked Jaciel.

"Items I believe are of particular interest to one of your craft, Lady Jaciel. The Dropstone-work salt cellar and the swan dish," replied Gullaine.

"Ah," sighed Jaciel, the sound of a starving person finally being offered food.

"Also a water ewer that is believed to be Dropstone work," continued Gullaine. "Though it is unfinished and does not bear the mark."

"Unfinished?" asked Jaciel. Now her whole body stiffened to attention like a dog catching that first scent of a fox. "I did not know . . . I must . . . I *must* see it!"

"Kariam will take you there now," said Gullaine. "Lady Clariel, please, this way."

Though she didn't appear to do anything, the gate marked for the Clayr's glacier swung open, again only just enough to admit Clariel and Gullaine in single file. There was a narrow winding stair on the other side, and here they could walk side by side, though Clariel's shoulder brushed the wall. It should have been dark, enclosed by stone with no windows, but there were bright Charter marks in the walls. Marks that grew brighter as Clariel drew nearer and faded as she passed.

"Are we going to some sort of throne room or something?" asked Clariel. "Or a great hall?"

"No," said Gullaine. "We go to the battlements of the North Wall, facing the sea. The King likes to look out from there in the afternoon, if the day is warm. In a moment we will have to pause a little. Do not be alarmed."

She said this as they reached a landing, a small room that had two doors leading to left and right, while the stairs continued up. The room was empty, save for a bare wooden chair in one corner. The walls, unlike in the lower stair, were plastered rather than bare stone, and painted a pale yellow.

"Sit on the chair, please," said Gullaine. "This will only take a few minutes."

Clariel sat on the chair, and looked at Gullaine.

"Why do I need to sit here?"

"One of the King's Guardians must look you over," said Gullaine. "They are Charter sendings, of a kind. It won't take long. Here comes one now."

Clariel looked up and down the stairs but couldn't see anything. Then she noticed a faint ripple in the faded plaster of the wall opposite, a ripple that spread up from the floor. As she watched, tiny Charter marks blossomed and began to outline . . . something . . . that was about eight feet long and four feet high and took up most of the wall. Slowly the outline began to become more distinct, until Clariel saw it was some sort of catlike beast, but far larger, longer, and thinner, and it sported a feathery tail.

The outline flashed bright as sunshine on a mirror and an actual beast, albeit one made of Charter marks, stepped slinkily out of the wall. It shook itself as if to become fully awake and opened its impressively betoothed jaw, hopefully in a yawn and not in anticipation of a meal. It stood taller than Clariel sitting, and as the beast shook itself it became more and more solid-looking, its color darkening to something like a sweet white wine, and faint shadows grew thick upon its back and flanks like spots.

Clariel sat extremely still and resisted the twitch of her right hand toward the knife in her sleeve. She doubted any normal blade would be much use against a sending like this one anyway.

The Guardian finished its yawn and extended its flat, rather triangular head toward Clariel, sniffing up her left leg, across her body, and then down her left arm. When it reached the sleeve it stopped and a great paw came up, claws extended, and it delicately pulled back the material to reveal the small, sheathed knife.

"I said no weapons," chided Gullaine, but she sounded calm enough. Clariel tried not to breathe as the sending opened its mouth to show those great teeth again, and bent forward to bite—the hilt of her knife, pulling it out of the scabbard. Clariel expected it to drop the weapon on the floor for Gullaine to pick it up, but instead the cat-beast tipped its head back and swallowed the knife whole, apparently with great satisfaction and no ill-effect.

"What . . . will I get that back?" whispered Clariel. It was a very fine knife, and it was hard to get one of such quality so small.

"I doubt it," said Gullaine. "I'm not actually sure where things go when they eat them. I trust you have no more hidden weapons?"

Clariel shook her head, very slowly, so as not to antagonize the Guardian. But it kept sniffing up and down her body, and along her arms, paying particular attention to her hands, nudging Clariel to open them when she unconsciously balled them into fists. Once they were open and flat on her knees, palms uppermost, the sending sniffed for a long time at the still-healing cuts and then surprised Clariel with two sudden licks, which sent a jab of pain right through her arms to her forehead. She jumped, but the sending wasn't finished. It rose up on its haunches and its paws came down on her shoulders, fortunately with claws retracted, and gave Clariel one more lick, right across the Charter mark on her forehead.

Not that it felt like a lick. It was a sudden immersion into the Charter, her head submerged in a vast sea of marks for a second and then just as rapidly they were gone again and the cat-beast sat back down and let out a purring noise similar to a house cat satisfied with its current lot, only much louder. As it purred, small, almost transparent Charter marks fell from its mouth and nose.

"Never seen one lick anyone before," said Gullaine, with interest. "I suppose it's because you're a relative. But it's passed you, so we can go on. Up three more flights."

Clariel stood up and followed Gullaine. She had only taken three or four steps up when she noticed the Guardian was following her, though its large paws were completely silent on the stone.

"Does it . . . normally come along?" she asked.

"They're all different," said Gullaine, who was taking the steps three at a time, making Clariel rush to keep up. "Some wander about, some keep to particular rooms or places. They are all very old. Magister Kargrin says they are of a higher art, now lost to us."

"But he has sendings," remarked Clariel. "A doorkeeper, and rats."

"Oh, yes, there are mages who can make sendings, but not ones so strong, or that will last as long. These are *hundreds* of years old, and still very powerful. Here we are."

The Captain opened a regular wooden door with a key, the sea breeze blowing in and sunshine streaming past as the door opened. A guard on the other side stepped away, pulling his poleax back to parade rest by his side.

"All well, Ochren?" asked Gullaine.

"All well," confirmed the guard. "His Highness is drinking his tea."

"Oh please, *not* a tea ceremony," muttered Clariel. Gullaine smiled and indicated for Clariel to go ahead of her, out into the sunshine. Clariel went, blinking at the brighter light, and found herself on the wide battlements of a very high wall. It was built directly above the sea cliffs, and the waves rolling in below delivered a regular, dull thud like a muffled drum. There was another tower some forty paces ahead but she paid it little notice, for King Orrikan III was close by, sitting on a well-cushioned chair pulled right up next to an embrasure.

He was smaller than she'd expected, and looked older, if that were possible. He had a red-and-gold skullcap on his head, tilted back to show his Charter mark, with wisps of pure white hair escaping out from under the cap, his long beard flying over his shoulder, caught by the sea wind. His skin was red and quite shiny, particularly his nose, which was long and rather pointed. His eyes, when he looked over at Clariel, were dark brown and very weary.

"Come, child," he said, passing his teacup to a servant in red-and-gold livery who stood behind his chair. A faint smile crossed his mouth as the cat-beast loped past Clariel and sat on his feet. The sending had gotten smaller, Clariel noticed, which was just as well. It wouldn't have been able to fit between battlements and chair otherwise.

"They know the family," said King Orrikan. "But you have more of the look of the Abhorsens, I think. Not much of my side from your grandmother, my cousin Leomeh."

"I never knew her, Your Highness," said Clariel, coming close and bowing low.

"Yes, she died quite young," said the King. "Many of the best do. It is only old relics like myself who hang on too long. Now, where is that drawing?"

"Um, what drawing . . ." Clariel started to say, when the servant who'd taken the teacup silently proffered a scroll to the King, evidently the drawing in question. He took it and unrolled it slowly, his bent, arthritic hands barely able to hold the paper.

"Ah," said the King, as he finally got it unfurled. The finely detailed drawing showed a woman in armor on a wall, standing with one foot up in an embrasure, looking out. "Go and stand just so, girl, over there."

"Yes, Your Highness," replied Clariel, stepping up into the embrasure. She turned about and gave Gullaine a puzzled look, but the older woman didn't say anything.

"Give her your helmet, Gully," called out the King. "Can't tell otherwise."

Gullaine unbuckled her helmet and held it out to Clariel.

"It's to see if you look like someone," the Captain said. "In the drawing."

"No, it isn't," said the King, who despite his great age obviously wasn't deaf, for Gullaine had spoken quietly. "It's to see if you *are* the woman in the drawing."

"Oh," said Clariel, finally understanding, or at least thinking she understood. She took the helmet and put it on. Despite her lack of hair, Gully clearly had a bigger head, for the helm was a little loose.

"Turn a bit, that way!"

Clariel copied the pose in the drawing, and looked out across the sea. There was a large trading ship some distance off. It was much fatter and higher and carried far more sail than the fishing boats she usually saw to the east, from her roof garden.

A loud wheezing noise made her glance back again. The King, supported by his servant, had risen from his chair to look at her more closely. Now he was holding the drawing out to Gullaine.

"Doesn't look like her to me," he said. "But my eyes are old, and perhaps I wish not to see. You look, Gully."

Gullaine held the drawing up with both hands, so it couldn't flap around in the breeze, and looked over it at Clariel for some time. Then she rolled it up and handed it to the servant.

"No, sire. She is not the same. Clariel could not be mistaken for Princess Tathiel."

"Good, good, there is hope left then," said the King. "Though your family do see things wrong from time to time, don't they, Gully?"

"Not wrong exactly," said Gullaine. "The Clayr See many possible futures. Some are clearer than others, and more likely to come to pass. Others depend upon long chains of chance . . . or mischance."

"Can I get down now, Highness?" asked Clariel. She had already taken off the helmet and now passed it to Gullaine.

"You may, girl, you may," said the King, settling back in his chair. "I mean you no ill when I say I am relieved that you do not look much like my granddaughter."

"Did the Clayr do a drawing of their vision for you?" asked

Clariel. Like most people in the kingdom she was interested in the ice-dwelling farseers, but had no experience of them and did not really know what they could do. "Of Princess Tathiel standing on this wall?"

"They did," said the King. "As they Saw her in the ice. One day she will stand where you stood. One day she will be Queen, and the sooner she realizes it and comes home the better!"

"Where is she now?" asked Clariel.

"Who knows," said the King grumpily. "Bah! I am tired of it all. Where is my tea?"

"A fresh cup is coming, sire," said the servant soothingly. He looked back to the West Tower. The door there sprang open and a servant came out quickly, carrying a tray with a teapot and, Clariel was glad to note, a single cup.

"You've seen me now, and I've seen you," said the King. "I hear you've given me some fish for a kin-gift, so I suppose I should give you something too. What do you want? That ghastly salt cellar those goldsmiths are always so eager to look at, Charter knows why?"

Clariel shook her head, thinking furiously. She hadn't realized that the kin-gift worked both ways. She was surprised her mother *hadn't* told her to ask for the salt cellar, but perhaps Jaciel had not expected the King to offer a gift.

"I . . . I would like you to . . . give the Borderers the money they need to continue their work," she said. "To keep on looking after the Great Forest, and all the woods—"

"No, no," said the King, shaking his head so much his beard whipped around to his other shoulder and his lower lip stuck out. "I don't want to be bothered with anything like that. Fifty years I've had of it, and that's enough! Tathiel should be taking care of all that stuff. She's a good girl, as soon as she hears of my troubles, she'll come back. I'm sure of it. Another week, perhaps, and then she'll be here . . ."

"There, there, Your Highness," soothed the servant, with a poisonous glance at Clariel. "Drink up your tea, you'll feel better in a moment."

"No I won't," cried the King. "I'm all upset. Ask for something sensible, girl."

"I did ask for something sensible," replied Clariel.

"Don't argue with me!" snapped the King. "Do you want to upset me?"

"Maybe you need some upsetting," said Clariel, feeling her anger mount. "Are you just going to let Kilp and people like him do whatever they want?"

"It's Tathiel's problem, not mine," muttered the King. His head had sunk into his chest and he looked more and more like a sulky child. "She should have come for the crown long ago. Let Tathiel tussle with Kilp and the Guilds and all the petitioners and difficulties. I want some peace! I've earned some peace!"

"Do you know what's happening to Belisaere and the Kingdom while you stare out at the sea up here and drink *tea*?" asked Clariel.

"I don't care!" shouted the King. He was almost sobbing. "I've had to care for too long and I'm past caring! Why does everything depend on me? Gully, give her that salt cellar. Anything! Just get her out of my sight!"

"I'm ashamed to be your cousin!" said Clariel, her voice growing louder with each word till she was nearly shouting too. "If you won't act like a King you shouldn't be one!"

"Come away, Lady Clariel," said Gullaine very softly, near her ear, with her hand firmly on Clariel's elbow. "He is very old, remember. Come away."

I didn't mean to get cross with him," said Clariel to Gullaine as they made their way back down the stair, this time without the cat-beast following along. The Charter sending had remained behind, curled up on the King's feet.

"You are a royal cousin," said Gullaine. "So I suppose I can consider it in the light of a minor family dispute, rather than treason."

"Treason?" asked Clariel, suddenly worried that she'd done something that would get her stuck in the city. This time in a prison cell.

"No, not really," sighed Gullaine. "I understand your frustration, and I know that you do not plot against the King, nor wish to become the tool of those who do."

"Like Governor Kilp."

"Yes. I even understand Kilp, to some degree. We are in an odd situation, the King withdrawing from power but not actually abdicating."

"He should abdicate," said Clariel. She had firm ideas about people not doing their jobs, learned at the shoulder of Sergeant Penreth in the Great Forest.

"No," said Gullaine. "It's both too late and too soon for that."

"What do you mean?"

"He should have abdicated ten years ago, when Tathiel was sixteen, and still here," said Gullaine. "But he didn't want to then. Now, he's let the royal power ebb away, and there is no clear line of succession. Very few people believe Tathiel is still alive. We just have to hope that the King can hang on until she does come back, and try not to let matters get any worse."

"Things seem pretty bad already," said Clariel. "If the day laborers are attacking guildmembers, and Kilp really is planning to make me or my mother Queen when the King dies . . ."

"It won't be up to Kilp," said Gullaine, her face set. "Nor will it be soon. The King may be old, and his mind in a dark place, but he is surprisingly strong in body. And he is well protected here."

"Good," said Clariel. "The sooner I'm out of all this, the better."

Gullaine stopped on the step below and looked back up at Clariel.

"Are you sure about that?"

"Why?" asked Clariel.

Gullaine hesitated, and looked up and down the stairs.

"It is true that you are one of the closest potential heirs to the throne," she said carefully. "One way out of our current problem might be if we could convince the King to appoint a regent . . ."

"A regent?" asked Clariel. "Like a caretaker?"

"Yes. A member of the family to hold the throne, until Princess Tathiel returns. Or if not, assume the crown themselves. Someone young and promising to give the people hope."

She looked meaningfully at Clariel.

"Me?" asked Clariel.

"You would be supported by a regency council . . . that would be myself, and Magister Kargrin, and some other folk who think as we do," said Gullaine hastily. "You won't have to marry Aronzo, or anyone for that matter. You could take on Kilp with the power of the throne behind you, set matters to rights—"

"How do I know what's right?" asked Clariel. "Is this some sort of test? I already told Kargrin I just want to get out of here and go back to the Great Forest!"

"It is not a test," said Gullaine. "I think you would be a worthy

Regent. You took on that Free Magic creature, you have courage, and we would be behind you!"

"I have no desire to be your puppet any more than Kilp's," said Clariel. "I want to make my own life, not be stuck on a throne inside a great stone building, trapped behind walls forever."

"You would not be a puppet," said Gullaine. "Nor would we be puppeteers! That is something that Kilp could never promise you, even if that Free Magic creature isn't involved, with some darker purpose."

"No," said Clariel firmly, shaking her head.

"Think on it," said Gullaine. "You may be glad of the choice, in time to come."

"In a very short time I will be in Estwael, and the Great Forest," said Clariel. "My answer is final. No."

"I hope matters work out as you wish," said Gullaine lightly, but for the first time Clariel caught an air of menace in her words. "As we all wish. Perhaps Princess Tathiel will turn up tomorrow, as the King so fervently dreams. Come, I will take you to your parents."

"Mother's not going to be happy," said Clariel, as they began to descend again. "I'm sure she thought she'd have hours looking at the Dropstone gold, while I chatted away to the King."

"On the contrary, I imagine she will be very happy, provided you let her look after his gift," said Gullaine. "Unless you intend to keep the King's present to yourself, or even sell it?"

"What? The salt cellar . . . but he just said that when he was angry and wanted me gone!"

"He said it, and the King's word must be obeyed."

"But it must be worth a fortune!"

"A small fortune," agreed Gullaine. "I would not recommend traveling with it. Too much temptation for thieves."

Clariel blinked, but did not answer. This was yet another complication, though possibly one she could use to her advantage. She

could offer Jaciel the salt cellar in return for being left alone . . . or
perhaps she could threaten to take the salt cellar away if her parents
didn't let her go . . .

"Through here," said Gullaine, opening a door that led to a long,
narrow corridor of bare stone. The corridor had no windows and was
dark, save for a few scant pools of light from Charter marks set in the
walls. There was another door at the far end, some fifty paces away.

Clariel had only just started along the dark corridor when she
realized Gullaine had fallen in behind her, when before she had
led the way. She felt a stab of fear, suddenly wondering if Gullaine
thought she was lying about wanting to be Queen. Maybe the Captain
thought Clariel had thrown in her lot with Kilp and Aronzo, that she
was going to try and claim the throne, and was going to get rid of her
once and for all. She started to walk faster, her shoulder blades itch-
ing, as if any moment a dagger would fall. Perhaps she should turn,
and . . . and what? She was unarmed—

"This is a shortcut, we're inside the Western Wall," said Gullaine
from close behind, making Clariel jump. "I haven't used it for a long
time, I'm sorry it's so dark. There's always somewhere in the Palace
that needs the light spells cast anew, and we no longer have enough
Charter Mages to keep up. If you just turn that knob, Lady Clariel,
a door will open."

Clariel's hand shook slightly as she turned the bronze knob. A
wooden panel slid aside revealing a large, bright room where large
windows let in the afternoon sun for full effect. The walls were paneled in a light and lustrous timber, there was a thick carpet of red and
gold on the floor, and a divan or daybed sat in the middle of that carpet. A young man with badly cut black hair was lying on the divan,
dressed in a robe of blue and silver that was too large for him, reading
a book that was also too large to be easily held so he had propped it
up on his stomach. A young woman in the purple and green of the
Vintners was sitting next to his feet on the far end of the divan, also

reading. A bowl of grapes lay on the floor between them, with more empty stems than ones with fruit.

"Bel! Denima!" exclaimed Clariel. "What are you doing here?"

"I live here," said Bel. "In the Palace. Didn't you know?"

"I'm visiting Bel," said Denima, with a blush. "I wanted to see he wasn't . . . I wanted to make sure he was not too badly hurt."

"But Bel . . . you said you couldn't see the King!" protested Clariel, stepping down into the room. The hidden door to the passage was at least two feet higher than the floor here, indicating the confluence of two different epochs of palace construction.

"I can't see him," said Bel. "I live here, the Abhorsen's apartments, in the west wing. The old chap never visits and I'm not allowed in the rest of the Palace. Gully said she'd bring you over to say hello."

"She didn't tell me," said Clariel, with a glance at Gullaine, who gave her an enigmatic half smile. Out here in the sunshine, she felt a bit ashamed of her sudden flash of fear in the darkened corridor. Gullaine would protect the King's interests, or perhaps the Kingdom's, but surely she wouldn't do anything like just kill a potential traitor . . .

I'm just jumpy, Clariel told herself. Understandably nervous, given all the things that are going on . . . I need to stay calm.

"Bel said he wanted to talk to you," said Gullaine.

"I see," said Clariel. She still felt tense, and supposed that she would continue that way until she managed to get away. It was like being caught in the rapids, with currents tugging every which way, and a great waterfall ahead. But which way to swim to get clear, and avoid being dashed on the rocks?

"Yes, uh, I do . . ." said Bel. He glanced at Denima, and added, "It's family business, Denima. Abhorsen stuff . . . I don't mean to be—"

"I understand," said Denima flatly. She got up and bowed to Clariel, then to Bel.

"I'll escort you to the Abhorsen's Gate," said Gullaine. "Your guards await you there, I believe?"

Denima nodded. Gullaine turned to Clariel and said, "I will return to take you to your parents in a short time, Lady Clariel."

"Thanks for the grapes, Denima," said Bel, lifting himself up on one elbow with a wince. "Uh, this really is an Abhorsen matter, it's not . . . not personal."

"Absolutely not personal," added Clariel, with a meaningful glance at Denima. She liked the other young woman, and wanted to make it clear she had no designs upon Belatiel, since she didn't and it was clear he and Denima had some understanding. Or Denima hoped they were going to have an understanding.

"Oh," said Denima. She lost some of the frozen look in her face. "I'm so used to those bitches like Yaneem at the Academy. I know you're not like that, Clariel."

"Definitely not," said Clariel, with some feeling.

"Hey, neither am I," said Bel, with rather less authenticity.

"I know," said Denima. She hesitated, then bent down quickly and kissed Bel on the cheek, before rushing from the room.

"We're . . . um . . . good friends," said Bel. He tried to sit up even more but grimaced, pain evident on his face, and settled back. "What I really wanted to talk about was simply to say thank you. For saving my life. Twice. If you hadn't dragged me down, the quarrel would have got me in the head, and Kargrin told me . . . he told me that you *held* the Free Magic creature and stopped it from finishing me off."

"I should have been quicker to spot the crossbow," said Clariel. She hesitated for a second, then added, "I think it was Aronzo."

Bel was silent for a moment, a frown passing across his face.

"That makes sense. Unfortunately. I know Gullaine doesn't believe it, but Kargrin is certain the creature was working with Kilp, even if for its own ends, whatever they may be. Aronzo hates me and . . . he kills for fun."

"Kills for fun?" asked Clariel. "What, animals?"

"People," said Bel. "I know he's killed several day laborers, supposedly in self-defense. But the way he talked about it . . . it was clear he enjoyed the killing."

"Great," muttered Clariel. She remembered Sergeant Penreth of the Borderers, telling her about tracking a wolf that had started to kill for pleasure, a rogue that had been banished from its own pack. Penreth had said such rogues were among the greatest dangers in the forest, for their unpredictability and bloodlust. "We're having dinner with them tonight, and I'm fairly certain my parents really do want me to marry Aronzo."

"But you won't!" exclaimed Bel. "Will you?"

"No," said Clariel. "I'm getting out of here. Soon. Going back to Estwael and the Great Forest."

"What? Why would you want to do that?"

"Because that's where I'm supposed to be!" said Clariel. "That's where my proper *life* is!"

"Oh," said Bel. "Sorry."

"Don't worry," said Clariel. She sat down on the end of his divan with a long sigh. "Nobody else understands it either."

"No, I think I do understand," said Bel. "I'm just a bit slow . . . it's like me wanting to be an Abhorsen, a *real* Abhorsen. Everyone at home thinks it's a bit of a joke. That's why I got sent here."

"Why?"

"My great-uncle . . . your grandfather . . . the Abhorsen, he got tired of me asking about things he couldn't or didn't want to answer, and then when I started asking Cousin Yannael, the Abhorsen-in-Waiting, she got really cross. All that lot care about is Grand Hunts, you know, the full thing with horses and dogs and a hundred beaters that go on for days on end . . . so Great-uncle Tyriel got rid of me."

"What about your parents? Surely they—"

"They're dead," said Bel. "An accident, when I was very little. Drowned."

"I'm sorry," said Clariel. "My parents annoy me, but it would be terrible . . ."

"I never knew them," said Bel, with a shrug. "I doubt things would be any different if they were still alive. Whatever Great-uncle says goes for everybody, so when he wanted me out that was it. I'm supposed to be an ambassador from the Abhorsen to the city, a presence here when such is needed. Only ceremonially, of course, not for anything important. There's not even much ceremony now the King is . . . avoiding everyone."

"But you do things with Magister Kargrin," said Clariel.

"I'm a student of Magister Kargrin's," said Bel, his pale face lighting up. "He's about the only person who's ever taught me anything useful. I mean, I've had to learn everything else by myself, from books, and from asking Mog . . . from asking someone, but that's never straightforward. Kargrin shows me the marks, and how to put them together, and to swim in the flow of the Charter. I've learned more Charter Magic from him in the last six months than from all my relatives in ten years!"

"My best teachers are far away," said Clariel. "Sergeant Penreth and the Oddsby Beacon Hunters and Aunt Lemmin and her herbs. But I'll see them soon."

She stood up and went over to the window, looking out. They were still high up, some fifty feet or more, and the view was into an interior courtyard and across to a wall on the other side, rather than the gardens she had hoped to see.

"I hope you can get away," said Bel. "From Kilp and Aronzo, I mean. It's a pity you aren't going to stay though, since I'm sure there will be more trouble and we need everyone. But at least we got that Free Magic creature."

"What?" asked Clariel, spinning around in surprise. "But we didn't!"

Bel laughed, then grimaced as he reached for a grape, the movement pulling his wounded shoulder.

"Well, when I say we, I mean Kargrin's people in general."

"What happened?" asked Clariel. "No one told . . . Gullaine didn't tell me."

"Kargrin's a sly one," said Bel, tossing a grape up to catch in his mouth, and missing so that it rolled down his chest. "Oops. He had Mistress Ader and that snaggletoothed servant of hers hidden on the beach—"

"Mistress Ader! From the Academy?"

"Yes," said Bel. He paused in the act of popping the recalcitrant grape in his mouth. "She's a mighty Charter Mage. Didn't you know?"

"No," said Clariel. "I don't even know who her snaggletoothed servant is. I guess I don't know very much."

"You've only been here a little while," said Bel, reaching for another grape and wincing again. "City's complicated. Very complicated."

"Yes," said Clariel grimly. "Too complicated for me. So Mistress Ader ambushed Az . . . the creature."

"Caught it in a storm of Charter marks, forced it into a bottle," said Bel. "Least, that's what Kargrin told me this morning. Very difficult, those binding spells. I'll learn them one day. I know some of the master marks, but you have to build up to them. They'll kill you otherwise, burn your throat or blast your fingers off."

Clariel turned back to the window, and looked out at the blue sky and the sun. So Aziminil was back in a bottle, trapped by magic in a tiny prison, never to emerge. She shivered, thinking of such confinement herself. But at the same time she told herself Aziminil *was* a Free Magic creature, something inimical to mortal life. She had to be captured and imprisoned.

Didn't she?

"When are you going?" asked Bel.

"As soon as I can," said Clariel. "I have to see Kargrin first, to get my money and some help out of the city. Maybe tomorrow."

"Tomorrow!" Bel nearly choked on his grape. "When you said soon, I thought you meant a few weeks, or months. Tomorrow . . ."

"If I can," said Clariel. She looked back at Bel, who was staring at her. "What?"

"Oh, I just thought," muttered Bel. "I . . . ah . . . thought perhaps we could get to know each other better . . ."

Clariel frowned. She knew this kind of talk from young men, and that it had to be nipped in the bud.

"I'm not interested in romance," she said. "Love, marriage . . . none of that. Besides, what about you and Denima?"

"We're friends," protested Bel. "And I just, you know, I like you, I thought we have things in common, being Abhorsens—"

"I don't think the rest of your family would consider me an Abhorsen," said Clariel. "Do you know why my mother never speaks to them?"

"Not really," said Bel. "Only I thought it was they don't speak to her. It's pretty easy to cross Great-uncle Tyriel, he's a mean-spirited old curmudgeon. What did she do? Steal his favorite horse when she ran away from Hillfair?"

Clariel shook her head.

"No. It's not for me to speak of it. Enough to say that there is a great divide, one that I'm sure extends to me as well."

"*This* Abhorsen sees no divide and is very grateful to you," said Bel. "I hope we can stay friends, Clariel. I'm not the bothersome kind, it was just a momentary rush of blood to the head, you understand."

Clariel laughed. A short, almost sardonic laugh.

"You don't look like you've got much blood anywhere. You're paler than ever."

"I am a bit tired," said Bel. He hesitated, then added, "But you know I'm pale because I've walked in Death, right?"

"No . . ." said Clariel, looking at him again. "I have heard people speak of it a few times. That the Abhorsens can enter Death, and return."

"Yes, we can," said Bel simply. "You probably could too. It is also your heritage. With proper training, of course. It is very dangerous."

"The living world is enough for me," said Clariel. "That is, a world really alive. Not surrounded by all this stone, hemmed in and confined. Ah, I wish I was back in the Forest!"

The creak of the door announced Gullaine's return.

"Thank you once more, for my life," said Bel. "Travel safely. Perhaps we'll meet again one day. As friends."

"Yes," said Clariel. "As friends. Take care of your wound."

"Your parents await you," said Gullaine to Clariel. "I believe your mother is most anxious to talk to you about the King's gift."

"That's no surprise," said Clariel. She left the room thinking about Bel being an orphan, and what it would mean to her parents when they found her gone. Perhaps it would be a blow to them, even to her mother, though she suspected her absence would soon be forgotten amid Jaciel's work. Besides, she told herself, she had little choice. The city was drawing her in like a whirlpool, a devourer of ships, with so many different tangles and plots and dangers.

If she stayed in Belisaere, she was sure it would kill her. One way or another.

Chapter Sixteen

THE GOVERNOR'S DINNER

It was growing dark by the time they tore Jaciel away from the Dropstone gold and returned to the palanquins. A light rain had begun to fall by then. It was not much more than a mist, but it made the evening unpleasantly clammy. Yet even this did not weigh on Jaciel's mood. She was happy, possibly as happy as Clariel had ever seen her, and certainly the most visibly happy she had been with her daughter for a very long time. This was entirely due to the rosewood box she had just shut back in the Palace, which contained the Dropstone salt cellar in the shape of a ship, to be transported to her workshop the next day. There Jaciel's apprentices would draw it from every angle, and she would study it till she discovered all the secrets of its making.

"You will ride with me," Jaciel told Clariel as Gullaine bowed farewell at the end of the bridge. "Harven, you take the other palanquin. Valannie, you may walk with the guards."

"Yes, dear," said Harven.

"But I need to repaint Lady Clariel's face, milady!" protested Valannie. Probably because she didn't want to walk or get damp, Clariel thought.

Jaciel looked at her daughter, and Clariel felt as if her mother was actually seeing her for the first time in years. There were faint beads of mist on Clariel's scarf and a lock of hair had escaped it on the front. Jaciel carefully tucked the errant hair back under the scarf, a maternal gesture Clariel had not experienced since she was a little girl. It made her feel quite odd now, because she knew it stemmed from her mother's love of her art, her excitement for the work that lay ahead, and not from a pure love of Clariel herself.

"I think Clariel looks fine as she is, thank you, Valannie. You did a very good job earlier."

"Yes, milady," said Valannie mulishly. Jaciel ignored her, climbing into the palanquin and settling in among the cushions. Clariel followed more slowly. She wasn't keen on the dinner ahead, and she was particularly not keen on sharing the enclosed space of the palanquin with her mother.

"You did very well today," said Jaciel as the palanquin was lifted and the bearers began their whispered chant. "I had not thought there was any possibility that the King would let the salt cellar leave the Palace, even temporarily. He must have liked you."

"I don't think so," said Clariel honestly. "We kind of . . . had an argument."

"He must have liked you despite that," said Jaciel. "Captain Gullaine tells me that he may be open to a regency. That *you* might be Regent, Clariel. Guided and aided by the appropriate people of course, a Regency Council. Your father would be good on that."

"And Governor Kilp, I suppose," said Clariel bitterly, seeing a new web being woven around her. She'd thought Gullaine at least something of a friend before this visit.

"No . . . we won't need Kilp now," mused Jaciel. "I thought I might need his assistance to even get a look at the Dropstone salt cellar . . . but if you are Regent, then there will be no problem with getting at the other works. I know there are more in the Palace, unattributed, of course. A full inventory will be required."

"I don't want to be Regent, Mother!" protested Clariel.

"Don't be silly!" snorted Jaciel. "It is a wonderful opportunity, far better than anything else we could arrange."

"Really?" asked Clariel. "If I took it, I'd probably be dead in a week, and you and Father too. Do you think Kilp is going to stand by and let someone else take the power he's been aiming for?"

"Bah, Kilp! He's simply the governor of the city, and I'm sure he's happy with that," said Jaciel. She wasn't looking at her daughter now. Her eyes were out of focus, dreaming of some unseen, distant object, almost certainly the Dropstone salt cellar or the imagining of a work of her own that would surpass the ancient master. "You make too much of this, as always, Clariel."

"No, I don't," said Clariel calmly. "You are immersed in your work, Mother. You have no idea what is going on in the city. I admit that I don't know enough either, but I do know that I don't want to be part of the politics and the plotting. I'm going to go back to Estwael. I'm going to live in the Great Forest as a hunter."

"Don't be ridiculous!" snapped Jaciel. "We've been over this before. No! Not another word on the subject. I am grateful to you for procuring the salt cellar, but do not imagine this gives you license to behave like a spoiled five-year-old!"

Clariel opened her mouth, her lips almost curving into a snarl, but she managed to shut it again. Anger boiled up inside her, the rage threatening to take hold. Clariel forced it back by will alone, starting the breathing exercises she'd learned from *The Fury Within*. There was no point in continuing to talk, Clariel thought. She would simply go to Magister Kargrin's tomorrow, take the money, allow him to disguise her with Charter Magic, and flee.

The whispered chant of the bearers provided a backing rhythm to her breathing exercises. Her breath came slowly in and went slowly out, as she imagined the calm place the book told her was of central importance in restraining the fury. She pictured her favorite glade in the forest, where two clear, cold creeks met, and two ancient willows curved overhead to make an arch. She had often lain there on her belly, tickling the trout under the red stone ledge . . . there she was, the dappled sunshine on her back, her arm in the water up to her elbow, still as a stone herself, the fish brushing her fingers . . .

It only occurred to her much later that Jaciel was probably doing the same thing, and her mother's calm place lay in her work. There they were, two people who were so much the same, retreating into their inner worlds, one of the forest, one of gold. Both steadying their breathing, slowing mind and body as they restrained the fury that was their birthright.

Kilp lived in the Governor's House, a vast mansion of six levels that with its broad outer courtyard took up all the space between the Western High Aqueduct and Carmine Street. It was built typically of white stone and red tiles, but unlike other houses in Belisaere it boasted a fifteen-foot-high curtain wall around its grounds, and the house itself had a tower on each corner, topped with cupolas of greenish bronze.

The courtyard was full of a great number of guards, from many different guilds. There were scores of them, sitting, standing, wandering around, eating, drinking, talking . . . all clearly waiting for something, their halberds, spears, bows, helmets, and other weapons and paraphernalia of war stacked in neat piles around the courtyard, under guild flags that had been thrust into barrels of sand.

"Why are all these guards here?" Clariel asked one of their own, as she was handed down out of the palanquin.

"There's rioters gathering in the Flat, milady," said the guard. "Troublemakers going to march on the Governor, so they say. Don't expect they'll hang about when they see us waiting for 'em."

"Why are they rioting?" asked Clariel.

"Couldn't say, milady," replied the guard, his face wooden. Before she could ask more, he'd stepped back and joined a file waiting to escort them to the house proper.

"Come along," said Jaciel. "Harven!"

Harven ran up to Jaciel's side and took her arm, and they swept on up to the broad front steps of the house, Clariel following along behind. The flickering light of oil lanterns lit their way, with no Charter Magic illumination to be seen, not even the soft sheen of the old marks that must have been in the stone of the steps and the railings, and so must have been chipped away or painted over.

The rain began to fall more heavily as they reached the front door, which stood open, Goldsmith guards standing on either side. A servant, dressed entirely in cloth of gold, bowed low as they stepped through to the entrance hall. This again was lit only by lanterns, and crowded with yet more guards, mostly officers of the various Guild Companies, in fancier clothes and armor, many sporting expensive decorations on the hilts and scabbards of their swords.

The cloth-of-gold-clad servant, some kind of majordomo, coughed gently to get their attention and said, "Welcome, Lady Jaciel, Master Harven, Lady Clariel. The Governor wishes to apologize for the unusual circumstances in the house. Please follow me to the Governor's study."

The majordomo led them through the crowd of officers, some pausing their conversations to bow or salute, though many of them hardly noticed the new arrivals. There was an air of excitement among them all, the kind of energy Clariel had often seen before a hunt, the expectation of adventures to come. Here she found it distasteful, the powerful and rich about to descend upon the weak and defenseless, as if a full array of Borderers were about to attack a rabbit hutch. All these sleek soldiers, and the massed ranks outside, up against the kind of folk who'd thrown the scrunched-up papers at the Palace gates . . . it had all the trappings of a nightmare, a nightmare bounded by the city walls.

"This way," said the majordomo, opening a small door in the corner, revealing a narrow, winding stair. He took a lantern from its hook above the door and started to climb, his shadow flickering behind him across the steps. "This is the Governor's private stair."

The door at the top of the steps was open, a bright rectangle lit by many candles within. Kilp himself stood there. He was wearing armor, a coat of gilded mail with no surcoat over it, and his sword with the swan-wings hilt was at his side.

"Well met, well met! Come on up! I'm sorry we shall not have too much time to dine, as no doubt you saw there is serious business afoot tonight. But the Governor's office is ever busy."

He stood aside as they entered a surprisingly large room, the narrow stair being truly a private entrance, as there were large double doors at the other end. The place was lit by candlelight rather than Charter Magic, two huge chandeliers of golden filigree hanging from the timbers of the vaulted ceiling, each carrying a hundred candles. Beneath them was a table of deeply polished walnut, set for six, with a great array of gold and silver cutlery, gold goblets, and silver-rimmed glasses, and a massive salt cellar fashioned in the shape of Belisaere itself, or an abstraction of it, a thing of aqueducts and walls with a few key landmarks like the Palace, all of it shining gold and silver and massive gemstones. It was quite remarkably ugly and the weight of metal alone would make it worth a fortune.

Aronzo came in through the main doors as Clariel stepped in from the small, private way. He also was armored, in blackened mail, and he wore a dark gold surcoat over it, a sword and long dagger on his belt. He smiled, his blue eyes bright in the candlelight.

"Lady Jaciel and family. Good evening."

Clariel returned his bow, a second slower than her parents. She was thinking about Kilp and Aronzo armed and armored, and her empty sleeve and generally weaponless state. But surely there could be no real danger . . . not when they had arrived so openly, and Jaciel an important figure in the Guild . . . if there was danger, it would not be a danger that could be met by a dagger from her sleeve or boot.

But still she felt wary, more on edge than ever, and the edginess would not leave her, no matter that she told herself she was jumping at shadows. She just had to get through the dinner, and the night beyond. In the new day she would see Kargrin and get out.

"Please, be seated," said Kilp. He clapped his hands. Four servants entered in answer, each carrying a tall silver ewer of wine. They did not ask what the guests would prefer, but simply filled the four goblets in front of each of them. A waste, Clariel thought, but typical of the showing off that Aronzo seemed to like. He'd obviously inherited the trait from his father.

"I wanted us to have a small, private dinner," said Kilp as they sat. Aronzo was next to Clariel, but she edged her chair away and angled her legs, so that Aronzo's questing foot could not touch her own. "The two leading families of the city."

"Will your lady wife be joining us?" asked Jaciel, indicating the empty chair. "I have not seen her for some time."

"I fear Marget is ill," said Kilp, with a sigh that did not alter the coldness of his predatory eyes. "As you know, the poor dear suffers from many ailments."

"You are equipped for battle," said Harven. "And the Trained Bands have been called out. Should we postpone this dinner? I . . . we would not wish to get in the way of whatever . . . whatever is occurring."

Kilp waved one hand in a relaxed dismissal.

"It is nothing of any great consequence. A rabble of rioters has proclaimed they will march upon this house and present their 'demands' to me. Malcontents from the Flat, who have no stomach for honest work. But they could be annoying, damage property of guildmembers and so forth, so we will essay forth and . . . contain their protest . . . before they get anywhere important. Let them stone their own windows and burn their own hovels, I say. We will keep them penned in, have no fear of that!"

"What are their demands?" asked Clariel.

"Who knows," said Kilp. "They want this and that, changing by the day or even hour. They complain of too much work, or not enough . . . the truth is they need firm handling. But enough of this, these troublemakers will occupy too much of my night as it stands. Let us talk of other things, and begin to eat."

He clapped his hands again. Four more waiters entered, bearing trays of oysters, mussels, and eels, which they set upon the table. Again, there was far more food than the five of them could possibly eat, and Clariel knew it would only be the first of many courses. She had no appetite, aware that Aronzo was watching her all the time, and Kilp too, that she was of no account to them save as a playing piece in their game of power, and they were preparing to make a move.

"You come from the Palace," said Kilp, opening an oyster with gusto, using the short, blunt knife provided among the array of cutlery in front of him. "How was the King?"

"We did not see him," said Jaciel. She speared a mussel from its shell with a needlelike implement of finely chased silver. "He met with Clariel, to receive the kin-gift."

"And gave one in return," said Harven quickly, clearly wanting to be in on the conversation. "A most notable gift."

"He did?" asked Kilp, with a darting glance at Clariel.

"The Dropstone salt cellar," announced Harven cheerfully. "We will have it in the workshop tomorrow."

"Really?" drawled Aronzo. "I would like to see that. I have heard of it, of course, but to look at it closely . . ."

"You must," said Jaciel eagerly. "It is a remarkable work. Kilp, you too. There is so much that we can learn from it."

"I fear I am overburdened with matters of state, rather than matters of craft," said Kilp. "It is too often the way, but then I was never as skilled as you, Jaciel. Aronzo will undoubtedly benefit from a study of the work, though I must say I am greatly pleased with his journeyman piece. It will go before the Guild assayers next week."

"Next week?" asked Jaciel. "Congratulations, Aronzo. You will be one of the youngest masters ever."

"Should the work be accepted," said Aronzo with, Clariel was sure, entirely false modesty.

"It will be. You will be a Goldsmith of the High Guild," said Kilp. He gave Clariel a slight bow. "And a guildmember should be married. When Aronzo sets up his own house and workshop, I would be delighted to see his wife by his side."

"So should I," said Clariel sweetly. "Who are you marrying, Aronzo?"

Kilp laughed. Aronzo transformed the beginnings of an angry scowl into laughter as well, a second too late.

"You are playful, Lady Clariel," said Kilp. "It would be good to plan for the wedding soon, as I fear we will all be busy with the current difficulties, which can only be exacerbated by the King's ill health—"

"The King is perfectly well," interrupted Clariel. "And plans for *my* wedding are much ahead of any likelihood of there being one."

Kilp raised his eyebrows and opened another oyster, tipping the shell back to let the meat inside slip down his throat. He tossed the oyster shell back on his plate and looked at Jaciel.

"Lady Jaciel? I thought this matter was agreed?"

"Not quite," replied Jaciel smoothly. She looked at her daughter, but Clariel couldn't tell what she was thinking. "Clariel and I have many matters we must talk about. Let us discuss other things. Your son Aronzo's work, perhaps. I would like to see his masterwork, if I may."

"It is not quite ready, I regret," said Aronzo. "A matter of some minor polishing remains, and there is the question of etiquette, that only the assayers should . . ."

"That doesn't matter," said Kilp. He turned to the servant behind him and snapped, "Fetch Lord Aronzo's goblet from the workshop."

"Father, it's *really* not . . ." Aronzo started to protest, but Kilp merely looked at him. The young man stopped, picked up one of his goblets instead, and took a hefty swallow.

"The King is well, you say," said Kilp, after a minute of awkward silence, though at least Jaciel and Harven had started eating.

"He seemed well enough, though very old," said Clariel. "He was very kind to give me . . . us . . . the salt cellar."

Kilp grunted, but did not add anything else. He continued to look at Clariel as he ate, until she became uncomfortable and resorted to helping herself to a portion of eel. She pushed this around on her plate, cutting it into smaller and smaller sections with a knife that was considerably blunter than she thought it should be. She also couldn't hold it tight enough, because the wound on her palm still hurt.

"You do not intend to be a goldsmith yourself, do you, Lady Clariel?" asked Aronzo blandly, as if they had just met. "What are your plans for your future?"

"I have not been in Belisaere very long, Lord Aronzo," said Clariel. "I am still assaying the true value of many things here. Sometimes there is only the thinnest layer of gold upon the lead."

"That's true," said Harven. "Remember those counterfeit bezants from that gang in Navis, they skimped on the leaf so much the coins could hardly pass between two hands before it came off."

"True coin is an ornament of the state," said Kilp pontifically. "And yet another responsibility of we Goldsmiths. Ah, here we are!"

His exclamation was for the arrival of Aronzo's masterwork, which, if passed by the guild examiners, would allow him to become a full member of the guild. It was a goblet, carried in the white-gloved hands of the cloth-of-gold-clad majordomo, self-evidently a much more senior servant than the man sent to fetch it, who could not be trusted with an item of such value.

It was a very beautiful piece, Clariel noted with reluctance. A slim goblet of beaten gold raised upon a long stem set with small rubies, arranged so that a red glow wrapped the cup above and the circular foot below, which was also rimmed with rubies or tiny chips of ruby.

Jaciel's eyebrows rose as she saw it.

"Show me!" she demanded, rising from her seat. Aronzo stood too, and both moved around opposite sides of the table toward the majordomo.

"It *really* isn't ready, Lady Jaciel!" he said, in his most charming manner. "Please don't touch—"

Even as he spoke, Jaciel put out one finger and touched the foot of the goblet. It was the slightest touch, a mere graze of her fingernail, but as it passed, tiny white sparks flew from her hand.

"You didn't make this alone," said Jaciel, her voice harsh. "This was made by a Dwerllin or Hish, it was forced by Free Magic from the raw gold!"

"True," sighed Aronzo, and drew his sword in one swift motion. A moment after he did so, Kilp thrust his chair back and drew also. The servants, all save the majordomo, drew daggers. Clariel pushed her chair back, but before she could rise there was a dagger at her throat held by the servant who been standing behind her, and another servant had her weapon at Harven's neck. Bewildered, he looked from side to side as two more servants moved in front of Jaciel, their daggers ready, though they did not lift them.

Jaciel stood very still, clearly unarmed in her white and gold silks.

"I'm sure we can forget this," said Kilp. He darted a sharp glance at his son, who looked down and bit his lip. "So my son had some help. It is of no great importance. Let's sit down and talk, there are many arrangements we need to make—"

"I beg to differ," interrupted Jaciel. She stood tall and imperious, speaking as she might to a forgehand who had spoiled the work of days. "You have knives at the throats of my husband and daughter. You deal with Free Magic. No."

She spoke a word then that could not be properly heard or understood, a word that Clariel saw emerge from her mouth in a flash of golden brilliance. A Master Charter mark that was linked to hundreds of other marks, that came out of her mouth all together like a sudden storm of rain, but here the drops were molten gold, spraying out at neck height, passing over Clariel's head so close she felt the burn of their passage. If it were not for her scarf, her hair would have caught on fire.

The servants in front of Jaciel and the ones behind Harven and Clariel screamed and fell as one, their faces dappled with burning holes. Jaciel stooped and picked up two daggers, wielding one in each hand. She lunged at Aronzo who frantically backed away and parried, and Kilp ran back to the doors and shouted, "To me!"

"Flee!" screamed Jaciel, parrying a riposte from Aronzo with one dagger as she drew Charter marks in the air with the other. The marks were bright as the sun, shining in the air with such brilliance they left afterimages in Clariel's eyes. She pushed her chair back but the legs stuck against the fallen servant, so she had to writhe under the table to get out, and then drag at her father's hand. Harven was still sitting there, his mouth open and face aghast.

"Father! Come on!"

She pulled his hand hard. He rose from his chair and they stumbled away. Clariel still had the small, blunt knife that she'd been using to cut the eel. She let go of her father's hand and charged toward Aronzo's back, aiming for his neck above his armored coat, but he saw her coming from the corner of his eye and stepped away, and she was only saved from his counterattack by Jaciel parrying with a dagger.

"Go!" screamed Jaciel. She was still tracing Charter marks with her left hand, even as she parried with her right. Clariel had rarely seen her mother practice her swordcraft, but somewhere along the line Jaciel had been taught very well indeed. "Take the small stair!"

"Don't kill them, especially the girl! Shoot to wound!" shouted
Kilp as he opened the doors, a dozen or more of his guardsmen pour-
ing in around him.

But even as he spoke three eager arbalesters fired their crossbows.
Quarrels shot through the air, all three aimed at Jaciel. Yet they did
not strike true, instead colliding with some invisible, or near invisible
barrier, for Clariel saw Charter marks flash as they struck.

Though the quarrels did not strike home, they did distract Jaciel
for the barest instant. In that moment, Aronzo landed a cut across her
arm. Blood flowed through the silk, spreading quickly.

"You cut as easy as any, for all your magic," taunted Aronzo,
stepping back so he could watch Jaciel and Clariel together, his blue
eyes flickering. Harven was still gaping, his hands raised imploringly
as if someone might step in to save them.

"Do I?" asked Jaciel. She leaned over and licked the blood from
her shoulder, the smear of it frightful around her mouth. She laughed,
a laugh Clariel had never heard before. A laugh that made her shiver
from crown to toe, the laugh of something being released after a
long, long captivity.

Another crossbow twanged, this time the arbalester aiming low
at Jaciel's legs. The quarrel struck the back of a chair, deflected off
it at an odd angle, and struck Harven in the middle of his chest. His
hands fell, the imploring gesture broken. He fell to the floor, blood
pumping from the wound like a flooded gutter overflowing at the
eaves.

Clariel felt him die. It was a sensation she knew well from hunting, though she had never realized it was the death sense of the
Abhorsens, because she had never been so close to a person in the
moment of their death. With animals it was like a fleeting, frozen
touch in her mind. Here it was an icy gale that blew through a door
that slammed shut again, all in one terrible instant.

A moment later Jaciel's left-hand dagger flew through the air and
the crossbowman who'd fired choked and gargled and plucked at the

steel in his throat. Clariel felt his death too, another brief, icy waft deep inside her head.

"Clariel! Go!"

Jaciel's command was laced with Charter Magic. Before Clariel could even think to fight against it, she found herself at the small door, wrenching it open, the narrow stair below her dark. She turned sideways as she stepped through, fighting the spell, and saw Jaciel throw her second dagger at Aronzo. He parried it too slowly and too close, so the blade spun across his handsome face, opening his cheek from chin to ear. Aronzo screamed and dropped his sword, his hands clutching his face, the blood running out between his fingers.

Clariel had one last glimpse of Jaciel preparing to launch herself at Kilp and his guards. Her mother was casting a spell, a forge spell drawn with a single Master Charter mark, sketched in the air. Flames grew from her fingers as she traced it, long white-hot flames like curving swords.

Jaciel's daughter saw no more. The spell forced her away, turned her head and sent her stumbling down the stair.

Clariel did not see her mother charge her enemies.

Kilp fled before her, his guards closing ranks behind him. Jaciel killed one, cutting him almost in two. But she was struck herself twice, a terrible wound in her side, and another above her knee. She merely laughed again. Bloody foam dribbled from her mouth as she spun and hacked and drove steadily deeper into the panicked guards, her fiery blades hissing as they cut through armor, flesh, and bone.

The guards fought back, chopping and stabbing in blind desperation at this terrible enemy who wielded fire and would *not* die.

Jaciel was almost through to Kilp when a blow from a halberd took her and the head of the greatest goldsmith and finest artist in the Kingdom flew from her shoulders, to roll bloodily across the floor.

Chapter Seventeen

SEEKING REFUGE

Clariel ran. She stumbled down the stairs, compelled by the spell. All she could think of was flight. She had to get out of the dark, enclosed stair, get out of the Governor's House, get out of Belisaere!

Get out! Get out!

She collided with the door at the bottom, and frantically felt for the lever, handle, or bar. But there was nothing, just smooth wood. She hammered on it with the eel knife, screaming, "Open! Open!" until finally someone did open it and she fell out into lantern light, her clothes splattered with blood and the top of her head singed. Hands clutched at her, but she fought them off and ran, ran as fast as she could for the front door through people shouting questions, and then all-too-slowly beginning to run after her.

Then she was outside, the door behind her. Out in the courtyard, crowded with soldiers, and there was an instant, just an instant when no one noticed because it was noisy and everyone was excited with the coming battle or riot or whatever they wanted to call it.

That moment passed as Kilp shouted behind her.

"Stop her! Catch her! Do not use steel!"

Clariel didn't slow down. Even as everyone began to react, she was running, this time for the gate in the curtain wall. She was half-way there when she heard Kilp again, closer.

"Stop her! Catch her!"

A grinning guardsman stepped into her path, the grin gone

instantly as she kicked him in the groin and ducked past, cursing the flimsy shoes she wore instead of her proper boots.

She was almost at the gate when one of her own guards, the grim-faced Reyvin, stepped out from the shadows and thrust her spear-shaft at exactly the right point between the young woman's knees.

Clariel came crashing down on the flagstones and lost her eel knife. She rolled quickly and got onto her knees, just as the spear shaft came down again, this time to tap her quickly on the back of the head.

It was meant to knock her out, but it didn't. Clariel rode the blow down, flipped over on her side and kicked up at her attacker, getting Reyvin just under the knee. The guard cursed and went down herself, sprawling on the pavement. Clariel dove onto her, whipped a dagger from her belt, and was up and away again, still compelled by her mother's spell, Jaciel's shouted *Go!* echoing in her ears.

She was through the gate before any other guard came close, and then sprinting down the road faster than she had ever run, faster than on any hunt, this time the quarry rather than the hunter. She ran without conscious thought for any ultimate destination, seeking only darkness to shield her, turning off the well-lit roads that were illuminated by Charter-Magic lanterns suspended on iron poles, choosing always the darkest street at every intersection.

Halfway along a dim lane, her mother's spell began to fade a little. This allowed Clariel to think for moment instead of simply running. She paused to look up at the stars to get her bearings. But there were no stars. The clouds hung dark and low, and a light rain was falling, less wet than the tears already on her face.

There was a great hue and cry behind her, so she went the opposite way from the noise, running not quite so fast, saving her strength. There were people on the streets, as there always were, but few now, for it was full night. They parted before her, as soon as she was close enough to be seen in whatever light fell from house windows or street lanterns. No one wanted to get in the way of a bloodied, crazed-looking woman cradling an unsheathed dagger to herself as if it were a precious jewel.

Eventually, the compulsion faded completely. Clariel came to her senses, or what passed for senses, given the hammerblow of her parents' murder. She was shivering with shock, her hands ached, her feet were cut and bruised, her soft shoes in ribbons. She looked around wildly, seeing only the dark outlines of tall houses, relieved here and there by the glow of lamps and Charter lights. She was in a residential street, a good one, judging from the size of the houses near her, but she had no idea which one.

Or where she should go. At least it was quiet. Wherever her pursuers were, they were not close. Perhaps she was no longer even pursued . . .

Clariel looked around again, studying the skyline, the patterns of lights. Then she saw it, sticking up above the other houses, the darker, taller shadow of a tower. One of the towers of the old wall.

Perhaps even Magister Kargrin's tower. This could be . . . it looked like it was . . . the Street of the Cormorant . . . somewhere she had run to unwittingly, her deeper self knowing where some hope of safety lay.

The gold and a disguise, thought Clariel dully. Now I have to go, for there is nothing . . . no one left to me here.

Nothing but death and trouble.

Limping, she walked up the street, keeping to the shadows, crossing the road when a particularly well-lit house cast too bright a light out its many windows.

Near Kargrin's tower, she slowed, pushing the shock and grief away, forcing it deeper, till some other time. Kilp might well have Kargrin watched, she thought, as a known opponent. She might have to fight her way to the gate, and if it were at all possible, it would be

CLARIEL 205

best that Kilp not know where she was until she could be disguised and on her way again. Clariel had no idea how long a Charter Magic disguise would take to cast. Hours? She hoped it was quick, or there would be little chance for her to escape.

Three houses up and across the street, she hid by the front door of a darkened house, and watched the gate of the tower. It was only when she tasted salt in her mouth that she realized it wasn't just rain on her face. She was crying, the tears flowing for the father who though he had disappointed her, she had always loved; and for her mother, who she must presume to be dead.

But she could not afford tears, not yet at any rate. Clariel wiped her eyes with her sleeve, and watched again. There was no movement on the street. All was quiet, and most of the nearer houses were dark. She could not wait longer, because any search would undoubtedly come here. Valannie knew everywhere she went, and doubtless she would have already told Kilp's minions where to look.

Clariel crossed the road at a run, went straight to the small portal in the gate, and knocked on it as quietly as she dared. Even so, the knocks sounded very loud in the quiet, dark street. She gripped her dagger harder, ignoring the pain in her hand, tensing for a sudden attack from somewhere. An arrow, or a quarrel from one of the windows opposite, someone leaping out from that doorway—

A head appeared suddenly through the door, thrust *through* the iron-studded timber. Clariel shrieked and jumped back, before she realized it was the Charter sending that had opened the door before. It looked at her, its eyes a bright concentration of Charter marks.

"Kargrin," croaked Clariel. "I need to see Kargrin. Let me in. My name is Clariel. Please let me in!"

The sending's head withdrew. At the same time Clariel heard running footsteps on the street, hobnails sharp on the paving stones. She turned and saw half a dozen guards in goldsmith livery approaching, long wooden staves in their hands rather than more deadly weapons.

"Drop your dagger!" commanded the leader.

The sound of bolts being withdrawn came from within the tower. Clariel backed up against the door and hefted her dagger. The guards approached warily, staves at the ready.

Clariel stamped backward with her foot, hoping the door would budge. But it didn't move.

"Kargrin!" she screamed, as loud as she could. But he didn't answer, and no help came. She couldn't fight six guards, not without help, and the berserk fury that might have made the difference felt far distant, banished by the shock of her parents' death, or suppressed by the aftereffects of Jaciel's spell.

The door groaned open. Clariel turned to duck through it, and in that instant, the guards struck. Several blows rained down on her back and shoulders, sending her sprawling across the threshold of the gate. She tried to crawl through, with the sending just standing there, doing nothing but holding the door open. She felt her legs grabbed as the guards dragged her back out. She twisted around and recognized Linel, who mouthed the word "Sorry" even as she was treading down hard on Clariel's hand to make her drop the dagger, pain stabbing through her half-healed wound.

Too much pain, and too much endured in too short a space of time. Clariel made one last, violent attempt to rise up and spring through the door, but she was held fast. Her arms were brought behind her back and roped together before she was picked up and carried away from her potential refuge, limp and no longer struggling. For a moment she gazed up at the night sky, crowded in by the buildings on the street. The sky seemed darker than it should, till she realized she was swimming in and out of consciousness, and then the darkness was complete.

Magister Kargrin, flying above in the shape of a beggar owl, granted by wearing a Charter skin, saw the commotion on his street from afar, but despite the powerful beating of his grey wings, he could not arrive in time to tip the balance in Clariel's favor. For a moment he did consider a rescue, but there were not only the six guards who had taken Clariel, but another dozen coming up the street. Some were Charter Mages, and there would not be time to argue rights and wrongs, so any aggressive magic he used would be countered or negated by these others, as was the nature of Charter Magic. And he could not physically fight more than four or five guards, on a good day, with luck.

Luck had not been noticeably with him so far that night. He had been spying on the Governor's House, watching the Trained Bands muster, for he knew the soldiers were not being gathered by Kilp to counter a riot in the Flat, since it and all other parts of the city were quiet. He'd seen Clariel come bursting out of the gate, but had lost her in the alleys, and then had lost precious time going to her home, not guessing she would go to his own tower.

He was wondering whether he should follow the guards taking Clariel back to the Governor's House, and attempt a rescue there, or do something else, when he caught the sound of a distant horn blast.

The great baritone boom of the Charter-Magicked horn that hung on chains atop the gatehouse of the Palace.

The Palace was under attack.

Kargrin let out a screech that was the owl equivalent of violent swearing, and swooped up to catch the wind that would speed him to the northwest, to defend the King. He took one last, yellow-eyed look at Clariel down below, a forlorn figure carried on the shoulders of the guards like a casualty of battle.

They would not harm her, he thought. Kilp needed Clariel, or her mother. Surely, they would not harm her . . .

Clariel came back to consciousness in slow starts, like a fish rising to a baited hook with slow circling and tiny nibbles, till at last it struck, and she, just like that hooked fish, was hauled out of comforting dimness and into harsh light.

She was on a low truckle-bed. Her hands were freshly bandaged, as were her feet, and she had on only the innermost of her long silk tunics, four layers of gold and white removed.

The bed was in a small, circular room. Clariel sat up and looked about and corrected that observation. It was not a room, as such. It was either the base of a small round tower, or a circular pit. The walls stretched up thirty feet, and ended in a slanted glass ceiling, which was currently admitting a lot of light, so the sun must be nearly directly overhead. Which meant it was late morning, or early afternoon, presumably the day after—

"The day after my parents were murdered," whispered Clariel. But she could not continue with that thought, or dwell on it, because if she did she thought she might never pull herself together again. Instead, Clariel slid out of the bed and stood up to take stock of her limited surroundings. There was the bed, a simple chest at its foot, and a small table that from the characteristic scorch marks on its top had come from a goldsmith's forge. There was an earthenware pitcher on the table, with a tin goblet next to it, and a lidded chamber pot under the table.

She couldn't see any entrance. There was no door or hatch, in wall or floor.

All in all, it was clear she was in a prison. A moderately comfortable prison, with sunshine above, a bed, and everything to meet modest needs. But nevertheless a prison.

It was even shaped a little like a bottle, Clariel thought, remembering Aziminil and her plea not to be caught. The lower part of a bottle. Narrow and tall, with the walls pressing in and the air still and stagnant . . .

A shadow crossed the floor, and Clariel looked up. Someone was looking down through the glass ceiling high above, but the glass was cloudy and she could not make out who it was, till the central pane was lifted up by unseen hands, and there was Kilp staring down at her with his horrible eyes.

"Lady Clariel."

She didn't answer, just stared back at him. He was leaning over and partially into the window, so there was some sort of walkway up there, suggesting she might be in the base of a tower and not a pit. Though she supposed it still could be a pit, with a raised upper portion. Like a well. It could be a well. A very wide one. Which might mean it extended much deeper below, and that could be useful . . .

"Lady Clariel," Kilp said again. "May I say that I regret the circumstances that have led you here. They were not of my choosing."

Clariel didn't answer. She looked away from him, up and along the brickwork. The bricks were small and very tightly packed, with hard mortar in between. But perhaps if she could pick that mortar out, to make toe- and fingerholds, then she could climb to the skylight window above. If she had something hard she could turn into a mortar-picking tool . . .

"Regrettable things have happened," continued Kilp. "But let me assure that your mother is receiving the best care, a healer—"

"What!" exclaimed Clariel, goaded into talking to him. "Mother's dead."

"No, she is badly wounded, I grant you, but the healer says she will live," said Kilp. "And your father's death *was* an accident. If only we could have all just talked about it!"

"Talked about consorting with Free Magic creatures," snapped Clariel. "Against every law of the Kingdom and all common sense!"

"In many ways I am now the law of the Kingdom," said Kilp. "And this so-called Free Magic, how does it differ from Charter Magic really? I employ Charter Mages. Why should I not employ a Free Magic entity?"

"Because they are inimical to mortal life," said Clariel.

"That is a story we are often told," replied Kilp easily. "But Az, as we called it, never harmed anyone, and it did much useful work."

"And how did you pay her . . . pay it?" asked Clariel. "Blood?"

"No, no. Some gold, some gems, nothing much different than any other in my employ."

"You're lying!" screamed Clariel. "Lying about everything!"

"No," said Kilp. "I speak the truth. I deal with the world as it is, not as some would wish it to be. I would like to make an arrangement with you, Clariel. One of benefit to both of us, as all good trades are. But we cannot talk about it while you are in this aggressive frame of mind. I will come back tomorrow. And to help you concentrate your thoughts, I think we'd best give you more shade down there."

He snapped his fingers. Guards moved up next to him, lifting across large sections of planks. Shutters, Clariel saw with dread, shutters that were quickly fixed across two of the panes so that only the central, open window still admitted any sunlight.

"I understand you are not the mage your mother is," said Kilp. "Even so, you should know that Charter Magic will not help you escape this particular place. It was made so, long ago, and then forgotten. Till Az showed us. You see again how useful the creature could be? Think hard about being more conciliatory, young Clariel. As I said, we can help each other. Deal with what is, not dreams and fancies."

He stepped back, and the last shutter was fixed in place, plunging the deep chamber into total darkness.

Clariel felt her way slowly back to the bed and sat on it.

Could her mother still be alive? Kilp had sounded convincing, but she felt sure he always did. Surely, there was no way Jaciel could have survived, charging toward so many enemies, so many weapons raised and ready. They would have had no choice but to fight against her, for she would have given them no quarter . . . but Clariel had not felt her die, not as she had felt her father's death. Perhaps she had been too far away . . .

But what if Jaciel *was* alive?

Clariel rested her head in her hands, massaging her temples, as if she could somehow force the memories of the night before out of her mind, make it as if it hadn't happened.

But it had happened, and she *was* sure both her parents were dead. Even if Jaciel had miraculously survived, that didn't matter now, Clariel decided. She was never going to enter any arrangement with Kilp, no matter what. The only thing she would do with Kilp was hunt him down and kill him, and Aronzo too, as if they were crazed stoats that had to be got rid of before they killed again.

That meant she had to escape, and soon.

To test Kilp's last comment, Clariel tried to conjure a Charter light. But when she sketched the first mark in the air and tried to draw it out of the Charter, she couldn't make it appear. She could feel the Charter, could sense the flow of it, but she was somehow cut off, as if it could only be observed and not interacted with at all. At the same time, she became aware there were Charter marks deeply woven into the bricks, thousands and thousands of them, all joined together in some great and terrible spell. This place had been made by Charter Mages to contain one of their own . . . a nasty thought. But she supposed Charter Mages must go crazy from time to time, or otherwise need to be confined. Though it was surprising this prison wasn't part of the Palace.

So Charter Magic was out as an escape method, though to be honest with herself Clariel had not really considered that a likely aid in any case. She just didn't have the knowledge or skill to cast anything very powerful.

She would have to escape by more mundane means. Up to the skylight and out through the windows and the shutters. Or down, hoping to find a tunnel, a sewer or something that this well connected up with. If it was a well, and if there was a way to get through the floor.

Clariel stamped her feet, hoping that the groan and creak of timbers would answer. But there was the dull, leaden sound of stone instead, and she hurt her feet testing it. To make sure, she got up and slowly stomped around, feeling her way with her outstretched hands. With every stomp she hoped to hear an echo or some give in the floor, indicating a trapdoor under a thin veneer of stone, or a timbered portion in one corner or something.

There was no such echo. Even checking under the bed confirmed that the floor was stone, and solid stone at that. Her fingers told her there were four great slabs, each covering a quarter of the room, and they were butted up so close together she couldn't even get a fingernail between them. Each one would be far too heavy to lift or move anyway, even if she could find some purchase.

That left climbing. Clariel sat down again and thought about a tool for picking mortar. It would need to be metal, and there was nothing metal in the chamber. She crawled over to the chamber pot to confirm that it was a soft terra-cotta, as was its lid and the water jug. So breaking them wouldn't even provide a useful shard.

The bed turned out to be pegged together. Clariel felt over every part of it, without finding any nails, screws, or bolts.

She went over to the wall and felt the bricks and tested various lines of mortar. None were crumbly enough to pick out with just fingers. A metal tool was absolutely necessary. Even then, the bricks were so close together that if she did somehow manage to pry out the mortar, the toe- and fingerholds would be thin, and extremely precarious. It was thirty feet to the top, and a fall from even halfway might be fatal . . .

Clariel was thinking about that and regretting the absence of anything even vaguely useful when she remembered her silk tunic was fastened at the back of the neck with a metal button. Quickly, she felt for it, fearing it might have been torn off. The buttons looked gold, but they were only gilded, iron coated with a thin layer of gold. Jaciel did not approve of using soft gold for such utilitarian purposes as hidden buttons.

Or rather, she hadn't approved . . . Clariel fought against the hope that her mother was alive. She was certain Kilp had told her this to weaken her, and she would not be drawn into believing it.

Jaciel and Harven *were* dead, and she was alone.

Clariel tore the button from her tunic. She almost started to scratch at the mortar in a brick in front of her, but a moment's thought sent her over to the bed, in her enthusiasm going too quickly and running into it, barking her shins. Hopping and cursing, she levered the bed up on its end and pushed it against the wall. Then after removing the water jug and chamber pot, she slid the table against the vertical bed to hold it in place, and clambered up. It was difficult to judge how precarious it all was without being able to see, but it felt solid enough.

Clariel climbed on the table and then pulled herself up to crouch on the bedhead, now a kind of shelf seven feet up the wall. It shook a little but the table seemed to be holding it firm, so Clariel stood up.

With that head start, she began to scrape away at the mortar around a brick at waist-height. This would be her first toehold, she thought, and she would have to make fingerholds as high as she could reach. It would get much, much more difficult after that, because she would have to hold on and scrape one-handed, making small advances up the wall.

Even if she did get to the top, she might not be able to open the shutters, or the windows for that matter. But that was another problem, to be surmounted when she made the climb.

It was likely she would fall, she knew, but Clariel almost welcomed that. Better to die trying than to just lie in the dark, remembering what had happened, over and over again.

Chapter Nineteen

A MOUTHFUL OF EARTH

C lariel did fall. Twice. Both times she landed on the table, which was a small blessing compared with hitting the floor, though in the second fall she also struck one of the stumpy legs of the bed on the way down.

After the second fall, Clariel didn't have the strength to start climbing again. Nursing her bruises, she dragged the table slowly back into place and tipped the bed back down. Sitting on it, she drank some water and dabbed a little on a strip of cloth torn from a bed sheet to wash her bloodied fingertips and toes. Then she used the chamber pot and laid down, the precious metal button under her pillow.

She didn't mean to go to sleep, and would have thought it impossible, as her mind still grappled with the enormity of what had happened, with her parents' deaths. But sleep did come, almost as soon as her head went on the pillow.

It was a restless sleep. Clariel woke several times, each time in panic, raised from a dream of death, her heart pounding with terror. It was made no better by waking in complete darkness. Each time, she calmed herself, following the breathing and mental exercises outlined in *The Fury Within*.

When she finally awoke properly, there had been no change in the darkness. Clariel had no idea how much time had passed, save that she needed to drink again and use the chamber pot and that she was hungry, though it was the kind of nervous hunger that says your body needs to be fed even though you are too upset to eat.

She washed her fingers and toes once more. They felt sore, but she couldn't really tell how badly bruised or cut they were. There were scabs and extra sore places, but no free-flowing blood. Even so, she didn't think she could try climbing and mortar-scraping for a while.

Clariel was thinking about that when there was a thud on the shutters high above, followed by a sudden, narrow shaft of sunlight. She cried out as much from relief as from the sudden pain in her eyes, but stopped herself from leaping up and showing too much gratitude for the light. Deep inside, she knew that if this continued for too many days, there would come a time when she would beg for any chance of fresh air and sunlight, even whatever little might come down to her prison from above.

"Stay on the bed!" ordered a voice from above. Clariel recognized it, not favorably, as Reyvin. Once her guard. But she obeyed, blinking as the other shutters were raised, the central window was opened, and then a long, thin ladder of what appeared to be lashed-together bamboo was lowered down.

The ladder was held at the top by Reyvin and another guard, but the person who started climbing down with a large basket on her back was too small to be a soldier. Just a young girl, perhaps nine or ten years old, dressed like a kitchen servant in a plain tunic and apron with wooden clogs that were giving her some trouble on the ladder. She stopped halfway down and looked fearfully at Clariel.

"You won't kill me, will you, milady?"

"No!" protested Clariel. "Why would I do that?"

"They said you might," said the girl, gesturing upward with her head. "To try and get up the ladder. But there's lots of them up there, milady, and I'm the only one in the family has a job now—"

"You're perfectly safe from me," said Clariel. "Look, I'll sit cross-legged here on the bed. Are you bringing me food?"

"Yes, milady," answered the girl, continuing her descent. "Simple fare, and new water. I'm to empty your chamber pot too, even though I'm not a night-worker. I'm tenth in the Governor's kitchen."

"What's your name?" asked Clariel. She leaned back as if to yawn, and took a look at the wall to see if her handiwork of the night before was noticeable. It wasn't too visible, not on the wall itself, but she was disturbed to see spots of fallen mortar on her blankets and sheets. In the daylight, the sprinkled mortar was quite a bright yellow, possibly even obvious enough to be seen from above.

"Can't say," said the girl cautiously. She shrugged the basket off her back and set it on the floor.

"Sharrett!" roared Reyvin from above. "Don't talk to the prisoner!"

Sharrett sighed and rolled her eyes. Clariel winked at her, and the girl smiled. She took a small loaf of plain bread and a round of soft cheese out of the basket and put them on the table, filled up the water jug from a bottle, and with her face screwed up and nostrils clamped as best she could, tied a string several times around pot and lid of the chamber pot to make sure it would stay shut in her basket and swapped it for a new one.

"Thank you," said Clariel quietly. She was thinking about when she had been Sharrett's age and much more carefree than this streetwise urchin. She had worshipped her father, and been both afraid and respectful of her mother, and the world had seemed an open, easy place. Even back then she had been drawn to the wild, and had spent many happy hours in Estwael's parklands. In retrospect the age of nine or ten had been among the happiest times of her life.

Sharrett finished sorting out the chamber-pot swap, and crouched down to settle the basket on her back before starting up the ladder. When she got to the top, she was helped up over the edge and then the guards pulled up the ladder. As they began to fix the shutters closed again, Clariel called out.

"Hey! Can I have a candle and some friction lights?"

"No!" shouted Reyvin. "Orders!"

The final shutter came down, and once again the prison was locked in darkness. Clariel shivered. With the dark, she felt the walls come closer, the air grow more still and dead. Worse still, she couldn't imagine a way out. It felt like she had reached an ending in her life, that it had stopped with her parents' death, and this was just a short continuation . . .

"Enough!" Clariel told herself. She got up and stretched, then carefully found her way to the bread and cheese and forced herself to eat and drink some water. Then she took a deep breath, stripped the bed of sheets and blanket—pausing to consider that it was surprisingly warm inside this prison, when it should be dank and cool—put the linen in one corner so it would be away from any falling mortar, moved water and chamber pot, dragged the table over, lifted the bed, took up her button, and once again resumed the making of finger- and toeholds.

Clariel did better this time, and several hours later made it to the top. There were beams there that supported the slanting roof, and she was able to hook a leg up and over one and pull herself up. She lay at a full stretch along the beam for a long time, her fingers completely numb and her muscles aching. Eventually, she forced herself to feel the window above her. Given that no one could expect a prisoner to climb up, she hoped they might not be locked, bolted, or barred on the outside, and that the shutters above might be simply planks laid on top of the glass.

Clariel pushed up. Shutter and window moved together, opening enough to admit a slight breeze, but no immediate light. She was puzzled for a moment, but as she peered through the gap she realized it was a little lighter outside. But it had to be early in the morning, likely just before dawn.

Clariel held window and shutter open for some time, drinking in the breeze that came through. She also heard human noises carried by the wind, a yawn or exhalation of breath, then a muttered comment, answered a moment later by someone else. Guards, she thought. Perhaps a dozen yards away, not right outside the window.

Eventually Clariel slowly closed window and shutter. She lay on the beam and thought about what to do next. There was a good chance she could surprise whoever was directly outside, but she had heard at least two guards. She couldn't fight two armed and armored enemies, no matter how much she surprised them. But there was the faint possibility she might be able to sneak out in the night, if it was dark enough.

Reluctantly, she concluded for the time being that she had to climb back down again to disguise the fact she could reach the top.

If only I'd got here earlier in the night, she thought, feeling frustration and anxiety in equal measure.

Clariel sighed and swung her legs over, feeling the wall with her toes. At least it would be easier to make the ascent the next time, since she'd dug out the finger- and toeholds. She could make them deeper and longer, perhaps even loosen some bricks enough to pull them out entirely, and a loose brick would be a weapon as well.

She was about to start down when she heard an almighty crack below, like the sound of a flawed crucible breaking apart when it was quenched.

"Clariel?"

Clariel didn't answer. The voice was monstrous and rasping, as if shaped in a larger and stranger mouth than any human could possibly have.

"Clariel. Do not be alarmed. It is Kargrin. I am wearing the Charter skin of a giant mole. Where are—ah, I sense you. How did you get up there?"

"Kargrin?" whispered Clariel. It was still pitch black, but she could hear scuffling, and earth falling.

"Yes. Come down! Quickly! We must be away!"

The descent was difficult. Clariel had stiffened up, resting on the beam, and was more tired than she'd thought. She almost fell twice, the jolt of sudden fear providing just enough energy to keep her going. She was shaking by the time she put her feet on the raised bedhead and had only just begun to feel the relief of something solid under her when the bed suddenly moved. Surprised, Clariel lost her fingerholds on the wall. She teetered atop the upended bed for a second, then fell, crashed onto the table, bounced off it, and rolled onto the floor.

Or what used to be the floor. It was no longer level, one of the huge stone slabs had lifted up at one end. Clariel slid down it, scrabbling for a hold, successfully resisting the urge to scream. She ended up against the wall and crouched there, feeling out all around her, her hands sliding up the slab to discover it was on an angle of more than forty degrees from the horizontal.

"Over here! They will have heard the stone crack above, I'm sure. Clamber over to me—I cannot come closer, or my Charter skin will be frayed by the prison's spells."

Clariel heard the sound of the shutters being lifted up above. She hurtled forward on all fours, up and over the tilted slab and down into the muddy, bristly grip of something bestial, which held her tight and pulled her farther down into a hole, and despite being *almost* certain that it was Kargrin in another shape, Clariel couldn't help but struggle and cry out.

"Keep still!" came that strange voice. "Hard enough to carry you as it is. Tunnel. I just dug it."

Clariel forced herself to be still, feeling carefully with her hands, trying to get a tactile picture of whatever was carrying her. She could feel thick hair or fur on an arm that was as broad as her waist, and there was the same hair above her, undulating as muscles worked . . . she grimaced as she caught on that she was clutched to the belly of some giant ratlike creature . . .

But it was taking her out of her prison.

"Nearly there. Collapsing tunnel behind us. Hold your breath, shut eyes!"

Clariel held her breath and shut her eyes. She felt soft, sticky stuff on her back that rose up around her shoulders and ribs and spread over her face, going up her nostrils and between her lips, no matter how tight she tried to keep her mouth shut. She started to panic again, thinking that she was going to be smothered in this dirt, or mud or whatever it was, and then she felt the hairy arm or paw or whatever it was let her go and she dropped a few inches, her eyes and mouth opening with the sudden shock.

There was light, and air. She choked and spat out dirt, and looked up at a red-eyed rodent creature the size of a horse that was looking back at her with a self-satisfied expression.

They were in what appeared to be a cellar, because it was full of barrels. The light was coming from a Charter mark that had recently been cast into the timber frame of the door at the top of the five or six steps that led out. There was a huge mound of fresh earth in one corner, and a hole in the floor that they had just come out of, the exit to the tunnel she had just been dragged along.

"I have *got* to take this off," said the giant mole-rat. "Clothes and such over there."

It gestured with one huge, muddy claw at a pack leaning up against the steps. Clariel limped over, brushed dirt from herself, and opened it up. There was a rough woolen robe and a pair of wooden clogs like Sharrett had been wearing. Clariel hesitated for a moment, then whipped off her dirt-smeared silk tunic and dragged on the robe, the kind of super-fast dressing she did on hunting expeditions, so as not to give the men ideas. But when she turned around, Kargrin was busy with his own undressing, taking off the Charter skin, and very strange it was too. Clariel stared at the weird combination of man and beast. It looked as if Kargrin was either being vomited out of the giant mole or was being eaten by it, since the top half of him was struggling out of . . . the back half of the mole. As he climbed out, he rolled back skin and fur, but as he rolled it tighter the very concrete illusion of that skin and fur instead became tightly interlocked Charter marks, thousands and thousands of marks all woven together.

"Got to fold it up properly," grunted Kargrin. "Might need to use it again. Put on the pack. There's a knife in the side pocket."

Clariel opened the pocket and took out a simple, short knife of the kind anyone might have, in a plain leather scabbard on a cord. She hung the cord around her neck and put on the pack.

"Where are we?" she asked.

"Cellar of an inn near what was once the Winter Palace, when the current Palace was smaller and only used in summer," said Kargrin. He was nearly completely out of the Charter skin now; it looked like he was standing on a pair of giant mole feet that had been cleanly separated from the rest of its body.

"How did you find me?"

"My rats followed Kilp," said Kargrin. "I knew about the prison holes, from when I was Castellan. They were filled with rubble when the Winter Palace was demolished more than a century ago, but yours was dug out by Kilp's people. Fairly recently. I doubt it was planned for you. I suspect he probably had me in mind for it. How are you feeling? Up to running?"

"Yes," said Clariel. "And fighting, too."

"We'd best hope not," said Kargrin. He had folded the Charter skin down smaller and smaller until it was no larger than a pocket handkerchief. He carefully put this in a pouch on his belt—the Charter skin had been worn over his clothes, even including his sword and boots—and wriggled his shoulders and shook his feet. "Always feel grubby after wearing the moleskin. When we get the all clear we can go upstairs. The innkeeper is a former Royal Guard, he's shut up for the day. We can look out on the street from the common room, there shouldn't be too long to wait. I hope."

"To wait for what?" asked Clariel.

"Bel is going to land a paperwing in the street and pick you up," said Kargrin.

"Really?" asked Clariel. She had seen paperwings a few times. They were magical craft made of laminated paper, every inch of their fabric deeply imbued with Charter marks. They flew like birds, and could carry two or even three people, presuming the Charter Mage flying the craft could successfully work the wind. "Is Bel strong enough to be doing that? Where could it land? The one I saw in Estwael came down in the park, it glided along the ground like a . . . a pelican landing on water."

"I *hope* Bel is up to it," said Kargrin. "I would not ask it of him save that there is no one else who can fly the paperwing. As for landing, we're on Old Nevil Street here, it's broad and straight, and there are few people about since Kilp announced a curfew and restricted the day workers to the Flat."

"What is happening?" asked Clariel. "Kilp told me my mother survived, but I'm sure she couldn't have."

Kargrin rubbed his nose and wrinkled it up and down a few times.

"Mole lingering. Hmmm. That is interesting to know. What *did* happen at the Governor's House?"

"Kilp . . . he . . . they killed my parents . . ."

Clariel found it very hard to say those words.

"Go on," said Kargrin gently. "I wouldn't ask if it wasn't necessary. I had a rat there, looking through a crack in the wall, but its view was very limited."

"Mother touched a goblet Aronzo made, or said he made," said Clariel. "Sparks flew, white sparks . . . Mother said it wasn't made by any mortal hand but by Free Magic . . . Kilp tried to talk about it, but Mother . . . she wouldn't talk, she just never *compromised*, it was always *her* way and nothing else mattered—"

Clariel burst into tears, full-blown crying, her breath coming in racking sobs that shook her whole body. But in just a few moments she had it under control again, was forcing her breathing into a regular pattern and wiping her eyes.

"She was an Abhorsen again, in the end," said Kargrin gravely. "I hate to ask you . . . but are you sure both your father and mother were killed?"

Clariel nodded once, then hesitated.

"I . . . ah . . . I saw Father, and I felt him die," she said slowly. "He was hit by a quarrel, in the chest. Mother was charging at least half a dozen guards, flames in her hands, they were hacking at her . . . she made me run, I didn't see . . . but she must have been killed."

"You felt your father die?" asked Kargrin. "You have the Abhorsen's death sense?

"I suppose so . . ." faltered Clariel. "I never realized before that's what it is . . ."

"But you didn't feel your mother die," said Kargrin. His forehead was crinkled with concern, and his voice showed he was trying to be kind, but was desperate to know the answer.

"No," said Clariel. "But I was already on the stair. Her spell forced me to go. Otherwise I would have stayed to fight. I would have!"

"I'm sure you would," said Kargrin. "But better you didn't."

"Is there . . . *could* Mother have survived?"

"I don't think so," said Kargrin heavily. "Kilp was ever a master of misdirection. He's put out a broadsheet claiming the King is dead, killed by insurrectionists, which is false of course. It also says that the King named Jaciel as his heir, with Kilp as 'Lord Protector,' his name for an all-powerful Regent. The coronation of the new Queen will take 'some time' due to the 'rebellion,' which is being suppressed by 'loyal forces' under the Governor's direction."

"So Mother might be alive," said Clariel wonderingly.

Kargrin shook his head. "I very much doubt it. No one has seen her, supposedly because she's grief-stricken over the King's death. I think she *was* killed with your father. I am sorry, Clariel."

"I still can't . . . it doesn't seem real," whispered Clariel. "But how can Kilp say the King is dead?"

"Easily," said Kargrin, with a shrug. "The Governor's story is that rebels have seized the Palace and killed the King. The Trained Bands have surrounded the Palace. It's not quite a siege, not yet, but no one can come out. They're emplacing war engines now on Coiner's Hill, bolt-throwers, to shoot down paperwings, though that will take some hours yet; and several galleys of the Eastern Company are standing off the Palace sea gate. All very well organized, as you would expect from Kilp.

"Of course, none of this would be possible if it weren't for the King's obstinance. If Orrikan would just show himself on the city side of the wall Kilp's nonsense would be obvious to all, and I'm sure there are loyal guildmembers who would turn on Kilp. But the King won't do it. He keeps muttering about letting all the poison out, it will only hasten Tathiel's reappearance."

"But does anyone . . . do the people believe that the King is dead?"

"They don't know he's *not*," said Kargrin. "Which is probably more to the point. He has been so absent these last few years that most of the people accept that Kilp is the power in the land, whether they like it or—"

Three quick knocks sounded on the door at the top of the steps, followed by two more.

"Ah, all clear. Let us go up. Follow me."

Clariel noted that despite the signal knocks, Kargrin went

warily, and she saw the glimmer of Charter marks held in his right hand, some spell that was already partially formed, needing only a master mark to complete it. But the door opened easily, and the innkeeper on the other side led them along a corridor, through a clean and airy kitchen and into a common room that looked snug and prosperous, despite its currently empty benches and tables and dearth of customers.

"Told the regulars my wife's sick and I'm feeling ill myself," said the innkeeper. "She's enjoying playing the part. Gone to bed. I'll join her in a minute."

He indicated the bay window, which had heavy winter drapes of dark, coarse fabric drawn across it.

"Just twitch the curtain aside, you'll get a good view," he said. "And if you don't mind, when you do go, take the side door I showed you, please, Magister."

"We will," said Kargrin. "Thank you, Jezep."

"Honor to serve," said Jezep. "May the Charter be with you."

He bowed, and left. Clariel heard his heavy footsteps going upstairs to join his wife. She hoped that he would be able to claim ignorance and innocence if . . . or when . . . Kilp's people came looking for their escaped prisoner.

Kargrin went to the window, knelt down, and gently lifted a tiny corner of the curtain. Sunlight came through this spy hole, the soft light of early morning.

"Street's empty," reported Kargrin, blinking madly, his eyes tearing up from the sunlight after his sojourn as a giant mole. "Just one pie seller and her cart is set well back off the road. I hope I was right about those bolt-throwers on the hill being slow to set up. And Bel being fit enough . . ."

"Where is Bel going to fly me to? Back to the Palace?" asked Clariel. She thought about where she wanted to go, but there was no obvious answer. She still yearned for the Great Forest, but a part of her now felt that she hadn't . . . earned . . . that. Her parents had been *killed*, and their murderers still lived. That needed to be rectified. The Great Forest would have to wait.

Kargrin shook his massive head.

"No," he said. "We have to get you safe. If your mother really is dead, then Kilp will want to see you set up as Queen, married to Aronzo, and safely under his control. Bel will fly you to the Abhorsens at Hillfair."

He rumbled up and gestured at the spy hole.

"Have a look, get both eyes adjusted to daylight," he said. "If you see the paperwing, tell me immediately. Do you want a glass of wine?"

"No, thank you," said Clariel. She sat down by the window and looked out. Going to the Abhorsens at Hillfair. To her grandfather and aunt, and apparently a multiplicity of cousins. Who all thought her mother was a kinslayer . . . it was not an attractive proposition. Except that the Abhorsens would surely gather a force to combat Kilp, so she could at least join in that . . .

Clariel sighed and blinked. Even though the morning light was diminished by a band of clouds, it was still harsh on her eyes. The street looked much like any other street in Belisaere, paved with grey stone and bordered by the deep but gently curved gutters built to cope with the torrential rain in spring. This road was wider than the streets on Beshill, but the houses opposite, though as always faced with white stone, were only two or three stories high and in general looked less well-kept.

There was no one on the street, which was very unusual in any part of the city. Clariel saw the pie seller diagonally opposite, leaning against her handcart, looking disgruntled. She wasn't even bothering to keep the firebox going so the pies stayed hot, judging by the lack of smoke from the slim bronze chimney at the front of the cart. No point wasting money on fuel as well as a barrow-load of unsold pies that would have to be sold for animal fodder. Unless the citizens of Belisaere were less discerning than those in Estwael, who could detect a day-old pie at first glance, let alone first taste.

Clariel was thinking about the pies in Estwael when a long shadow flitted along the street, raced up the walls of the house near the pie cart, then turned and went back along the street again. The shadow was followed a moment later by the paperwing that had cast it, the aircraft banking and looping around to land into the wind, coming down to swoop along the road a mere fingerbreadth above the stone paving, before sliding to a very neat halt three or four houses to the right of the inn.

"Paperwing's landed!" shouted Clariel, jumping to her feet.

Chapter Twenty

H e has flown swiftly!" said Kargrin. He set his wineglass down on the closest table and took Clariel's hand. "Come on!"

They went out the side door of the inn into a narrow alley crowded with empty barrels stacked high against one wall. Clariel's shoulder bumped against them as Kargrin dragged her along. He increased his pace to a full-out run as they reached the street, running to the paperwing, the pie seller staring with her jaw open, her lack of sales now partially made up for by a story she could tell over many drinks.

The paperwing was smaller than Clariel had expected. She'd seen them flying before but in the far distance, which made it hard to gauge their size and shape. This one had a body rather like a slim boat, tapered at each end, with a hole in the middle where the occupants sat. Its hawklike wings stretched out and back from the middle. They were partially folded for landing, but when fully extended would stretch for forty paces a side, or perhaps even more. The whole craft was made of paper, Clariel knew, layered and bonded together with secret glues and considerable Charter Magic. The outer layers were colored in glorious reds and golds, in swirls, dots, and circles, save for the front where dark, very lifelike eyes looked ahead on either side.

Bel was standing up in the middle of the craft, slightly hunched and favoring his left side. He was wearing his gethre plate armor, one plate holed near the shoulder, over hunting leathers. He had a heavy wool cloak on as well, despite the warm and humid morning.

"Clariel!" he shouted out, combining a wave with sitting down in a clumsy motion that obviously hurt, for he gasped in pain before adding over his shoulder, "Quick!"

Clariel tried to run faster, but she wasn't used to wooden clogs, and almost fell over. Kargrin held her up as she kicked them off and he almost carried her as they ran on. He did pick her up as they reached the paperwing, lifting her high but lowering her very slowly and carefully in behind Belatiel. As soon as he had done so, he turned back and reached up with both hands. Glowing Charter marks fell from his fingers like a sudden, fiery rain. He gripped apparently empty air and hauled on something invisible. A moment later a cool breeze slapped Clariel in the face and sent her hair flying back.

Kargrin was calling up the wind.

"Hang on!" shouted Belatiel. He pursed his lips and whistled, a long, clear note, his exhaled breath full of Charter marks. Kargrin's wind answered to it, swooping down under the paperwing, which shivered as if in anticipation of sudden freedom from the earth.

"Go!" roared Kargrin. He swung both arms down and swept them at the paperwing's tail, a great gale bursting from his hands, picking the aircraft up so violently the craft rolled and pitched as it ascended, only kept true and level by Bel's whistling and the lesser winds that answered him, pushing left and right and up and down as was required.

Clariel was about to ask why there was such a hurry when she saw a crossbow bolt fly past. It was flying back to front, overturned by the wind, but it supplied the reason for Kargrin's haste. Holding on tight to the rim of the central well where she sat, Clariel cautiously looked over the side of the paperwing. They were already several hundred feet up, and for a moment she had the horribly dizzy sensation that she had become unfixed from the world and was falling upward and would so do forever. But it passed as she focused on the world below. There was Kargrin, running up the street, close to the houses, and there were guards in pursuit of him, and others with their crossbows pointing up, but iron springs could not propel the quarrels fast enough to compete with the spelled wind that was rushing the paperwing away.

As Clariel watched, Kargrin turned to face his pursuers. Her heart leaped into her mouth, thinking she would see him killed. But instead there was a bright flash, and a sudden eruption of smoke or dust. A huge cloud filled the street and rose up to the rooftops before it too was caught by the wind. As it cleared, Clariel, now looking back over her shoulder, saw the pursuing guards all knocked down like bowling pins. A broad swathe of the street's paving stones was broken to the bare earth, and there was no sign of Kargrin at all.

Clariel turned back and settled down, noticing for the first time she was sitting in a kind of hammock or netting chair set into the central hole. Bel, still whistling steadily, was sitting in a similar one just ahead of her, and her knees were almost touching his back.

There was a rolled-up cloak and a leather water bottle near Clariel's left foot and what looked to be a loaf of bread or perhaps bread and meat wrapped in a muslin cloth by her right foot.

She looked over the side again and was shocked to see how much higher they had flown in such a short time. She could see all of Belisaere below, the whole city sprawled on the tip of the peninsula, with the Sea of Saere all a-silver around it. They were so high she could only make out the larger buildings, the smaller houses blending into large masses of red-tiled roofs.

Looking down on Belisaere, she felt a slight lift to her heavy heart. It was not the way she wanted it, but she had at last escaped the city. The walls no longer held her in, the masses of people no longer thronged around, the air was sweet, the sun unshadowed.

But she knew she hadn't really escaped. Not completely. There were unseen shackles of grief and duty that still tied her to Belisaere.

The paperwing, which had been sharply angled up toward the sky, started to level out, and a minute or two later Bel stopped whistling and slumped back in his hammock, colliding with Clariel's knees. She drew them back as he lurched forward again and twisted around, gasping in pain and holding his left shoulder.

"Sorry," he said.

"Don't be," said Clariel. "Thank you for flying to my rescue."

"I was . . . happy to be able to do so . . ." said Bel. He twisted back to the front. "Please forgive my rudeness . . . but I can't really turn around at the moment."

"Are you all right?" asked Clariel, struck by the sudden anxiety that he might pass out from the pain of his past wounding, or that it might reopen. Then they would both be in dire peril, so high in the sky with Clariel having no idea how to control the paperwing.

"Yes," grunted Bel. "Stupid wound isn't healed and the windworking takes it out of me even when I'm fit. Not made any easier by that great gust Kargrin called up. Mind you, we wouldn't have got away so quickly without it. Did you see what happened to him? I saw some guards—"

"I think he got away," said Clariel. "He made the street rise up. All the guards chasing him were knocked down, and when the dust cleared I couldn't see him."

"Trust Kargrin," laughed Bel. "I wonder what that spell was? Must ask him next time I see him."

"I hope you do get to see him again," said Clariel, all too conscious of those she would never see again.

"Yes," said Bel, the laughter gone as he caught her mood. "I um . . . Kargrin said he thought your parents . . . that they were . . . were killed . . . I don't know . . ."

"Yes," said Clariel quietly, almost to herself. "They are dead. It was all so very quick. We were at this dreadful dinner, and I was thinking about how soon we could leave, and how soon I could leave . . . I mean leave the dinner and also leave Belisaere altogether. Aronzo was annoying and Kilp scared me, but I never thought . . . I never thought anything could *happen*, not like that . . ."

"Then the world was changed, all in a few moments," said Bel. "I never thought Kilp would try to take the Palace either. If Gullaine wasn't so suspicious, I'd be dead too."

"Why? What happened?"

"The Abhorsen's rooms are in the lower west court," said Bel. "Much easier to attack, but almost completely separate from the rest of the palace. They broke in there and I suppose they thought there'd be an easy way into the palace proper. The first I knew about it was Gullaine shaking me awake just after midnight and rushing me along a maze of secret ways, with guard sendings popping out the walls and floors and growling off behind us, and then there was Anstyr's horn echoing everywhere. There was no chance of them taking the Palace after that, though they did try an escalade on the lower wall by the gatehouse. Not one ladder reached the top. It was horrible, not least because so many of the guild's people were clearly halfhearted, unsure what was really going on . . ."

He fell uncharacteristically silent. Clariel didn't think she'd ever heard Bel stop speaking without someone asking him to, or some other interruption.

With Bel not talking, Clariel noticed it was much quieter than she had expected. They were borne up by the breeze and carried along by it at a pace far swifter than any horse could gallop, but she could only hear a dull humming sound, and that was almost more a vibration felt rather than heard.

"Why is it so quiet?" she asked.

"What? Oh, we are inside the wind, carried with it, rather than having it pass across us," said Bel. "But the paperwing is also imbued with charms to still the air here where we sit, and to make it warmer as well. Though if we go much higher, you'll still need your cloak. It gets very cold, like being up a mountain."

"Kargrin said you are to take me to the Abhorsens," said Clariel.

"He thinks that will be the safest place for you," said Bel. "Gullaine agreed. She let me take this paperwing, it's one of the royal ones, though I guess you knew that from the color."

"What if I asked you to take me to Estwael?" asked Clariel, suddenly struck with a guilty, but almost overwhelming desire to get to the Great Forest, to the only place she truly felt at home. If she could get there, then somehow everything that had happened could be dealt with, or the effects lessened. "We could fly there, couldn't we?"

Bel didn't answer for a moment.

"I suppose we *could* fly there," he said. "Though chances are we'd get lost. As it is, I can only find my way to Hillfair by flying west by the sun till we see the Ratterlin, and then follow that south. The flying part is relatively easy. The navigating is hard."

"We could follow the Yanyl from the Ratterlin," said Clariel. "It rises close to Estwael."

Bel shook his head.

"I'm sorry, but I'm under orders from Kargrin *and* Gullaine. I have to take you to the Abhorsen. Besides, you probably wouldn't be safe in Estwael. Kilp controls all the royal officials in the towns."

"I would be safe in the Great Forest," said Clariel. She hesitated for a moment, before adding, "I really don't want to go to the Abhorsens."

"The Abhorsen is your grandfather," said Bel tentatively. "I guess . . . he would be your closest relative . . . uh . . . now—"

"I have my aunt Lemmin in Estwael," snapped Clariel. "And I'm old enough to live on my own anyway."

"Yes, of course," muttered Bel. "It's just that with your mother being declared Queen by Kilp and everything—"

"My mother is dead," said Clariel bleakly. "But I understand. I am a card to be played, and Gullaine and Kargrin and probably my grandfather too wish to hold me in their hand."

"I would take you to Estwael if I could," protested Bel. He half twisted around to look at her before a sudden sharp pain reminded him why he couldn't. "If the Abhorsen lets me, I'll fly you there. I promise."

"If he lets me," said Clariel. "There is small chance of that."

Bel didn't answer. After a moment, seeing his downcast head and slumped shoulders, Clariel added, "But thank you. If the opportunity arises, I will take you up on your offer, and have you fly me away again. But I fear that it might need to be more of an escape than anything. If you don't think you can fly me there now, I doubt things will be different later."

"You never know," said Bel. "Just like it says in *The Book of the Dead*, 'Does the walker choose the path, or the path the walker?'"

"What does that mean?" asked Clariel. "And what is *The Book of the Dead*? You mentioned it once before."

"It is the book that teaches every Abhorsen the secrets of walking in Death, of the bells we wield, and the mysteries therein," said Bel. "But I have to confess that I've never been exactly sure what the path and the walker thing really means. Only that perhaps it means something in between, that even if there is destiny, you get to choose to take it on or not. The path is your choice, but once you tread there, you have also chosen where you will go. I think."

"Hmmm," said Clariel. "How long will it take to get to Hillfair? We seem to be traveling very fast, faster than a horse can gallop."

"It is faster, but not quite as fast as it looks," said Bel. "We'll have to land at a way station before dark; paperwings won't fly at night unless there's a full moon and a clear sky, and . . . uh . . . I'm getting a bit . . . a bit tired anyway. If we get a good start tomorrow, we should be at Hillfair by early afternoon, I guess."

"A way station?" asked Clariel. "Kilp could have sent a message-hawk to have me arrested. Would a hawk get there before us?"

"Yes," said Bel. "But since the King stopped looking after them a

few years back, the way stations south of Belisaere have been run by
the Abhorsens and those north by the Clayr. The one I'm thinking
of is between Orchyre and Sindle, so even if Kilp sent guards from
either town, they couldn't get to us before morning."

They were flying over farmland now, a patchwork of well-
ordered fields bounded by low stone walls beneath, with occasional
stands of woodland and every now and then a village or a large farm-
stead. A shepherd waved to them from atop a low hill, her flock of
sheep on the slope below being gathered by a dog darting hither and
thither to drive them to some new pasturage.

They flew in silence for some hours after sighting the shepherd,
Clariel lost in her own thoughts and sadness, Bel intent on flying the
paperwing. The sun rose in the sky to its zenith, and then began to
fall again.

Around the middle of the afternoon, the land some way off on
their left-hand side began to change, fields giving way to a long
fringe of trees that soon gathered together to become a forest that
marched for miles to the south, the paperwing taking a path almost
parallel to its northern border, though several leagues distant.

Clariel stared at the green expanse of woods hungrily.

"That must be the Sindlewood!" she exclaimed, sitting up
straighter and leaning out the left-hand side so suddenly that the
paperwing rocked.

"Careful!" exclaimed Bel. "Slow movements, please. You really
don't want to fall out, you know."

"Sorry," mumbled Clariel. She gazed out at the vast green mass
of the forest. The Sindlewood was the closest major forest to Belisaere
and though she had never been there, she had read about it, and heard
about it from the Borderers who had been stationed there before
their time in the Great Forest.

"The way station shouldn't be too far ahead," said Bel about five
minutes later. He sounded slightly anxious, and was moving his head

from side to side, peering at the ground below. "Can you see any-thing?"

"What am I looking for?" asked Clariel.

"A low hill, like where the sheep were, but flatter on top and longer," said Bel. "There's a tower, not very tall, it should have a big flag on top so I can see where the wind's blowing from down there . . . surely I couldn't have missed it . . ."

Clariel looked away from the Sindlewood off in the distance and focused on the ground closer ahead and to the sides. It was still settled farmland beneath them, the patchwork of fields continuing up and down and over the slight rolling hills, dotted occasionally by copse or small wood, house or steading, with bare earth roads between. The only major paved road in the area was farther north, joining Belisaere to Sindle and parts east, the road that ultimately led to Estwael.

"We could follow the road," Clariel said suddenly.

"What?"

"We could fly along the main west road," said Clariel. "To Estwael. You wouldn't get lost, we wouldn't have to follow the Yanyl."

"We're not going to Estwael, and roads are harder to follow than big rivers unless you go low, which is dangerous," said Bel wearily. "We really need to find that way station. I'm getting tired and the paperwing will get very difficult if we're not down before dark."

"Right," said Clariel. "I'm looking."

They flew in silence again, but it was less companionable than before. Clariel's eyes kept following the road that headed to the west, to Estwael and home. Bel looked down, anxiously searching for the way station.

"I'm just going back the way I flew in last year," said Bel a little later. "But everything looks the same, there's no decent landmarks. If we don't find the way station soon we'll just have to set down wherever we can. We do have some food but it's nothing fancy . . ."

"I don't need fancy food," said Clariel. "Could you . . . could you land near one of these small woods? I would like to be among trees again. The night will be warm, we won't need to be under a roof."

"I suppose so," said Bel. "But it's always easier to take off down a hill. And the way station has actual beds."

"A scrape in the ground filled with fern and grass is quite comfortable," said Clariel. "And we have our cloaks."

"We are definitely going to have to land anyway," said Bel, with an anxious glance ahead at the westering sun, which would soon be setting. "How about by that farmhouse over there?"

"Surely it would be better no one knows we have passed by," said Clariel.

Bel nodded reluctantly.

"Look for a large, flat field," he said. "Without big stones. We'll swoop over low to look closer and then turn back and land."

"There," said Clariel, pointing over Bel's shoulder. Up ahead there was a larger field than usual left fallow, so it currently sported short pale green and yellow grasses in tufts between patches of dirt. At its northwestern end, it abutted a low, forested hill of old, lichen-covered oaks, accompanied by chestnuts and birches of lesser ancestry. It was clearly tended by foresters, for it was more open and sparse than any ancient forest, but even so it called to Clariel.

"Looks all right," confirmed Bel. He pursed his lips and blew. At first nothing came out and he looked disturbed, even frightened, then he managed a whistle. It was soft, but true, and infused with Charter marks. The paperwing heard it and angled down, till they were swooping along only twenty or thirty paces above the ground, their speed much more apparent to Clariel now, as were the various stone walls, stumps, trees, and other obstacles they could run into and be smashed to pieces.

But their chosen field looked safe enough, the plow marks still present, indicating it had been turned over in the spring, if not replanted. Bel whistled again, the paperwing rose and veered to the left, away from the forest, rising a little to circle back the way they had come.

"Can you see from the treetops which way the wind is blowing?" asked Bel.

"From the south," said Clariel. "Not very strong."

"Hold on tight for the landing," said Bel as the paperwing completed its turn into the wind and began to descend. "Could be bumpy."

But it wasn't bumpy at all. The paperwing skimmed over the grass, occasionally touching to lose speed, before coming down to skid some twenty paces through loose soil, sending a spray of dirt to either side but barely rocking its two passengers.

Bel's head dropped onto his chest and he let out a long sigh. Clariel waited a moment to make sure the paperwing wasn't going to move again, then climbed out, stretched her arms up, and unkinked her back.

"I am *very* tired," announced Bel. He struggled to stand up and would have fallen over if Clariel hadn't lunged forward to steady his elbow. "I hope your forest beds are as comfortable as you say."

"If you're that tired it won't matter," said Clariel. "How's your shoulder?"

Bel moved his arm slightly and winced.

"It's just stiff," he said. "I was supposed to stay in bed for another week. But I can do that once we get to Hillfair. I'm sure I'll be fine to fly in the morning."

He stepped out of the paperwing and started to turn and bend down to get something from inside the hollow nose, but stopped suddenly, his face showing intense pain.

"Ah, if you wouldn't mind . . . could you fetch my sword? And the food and water by your seat? I'm just going to sit down over against that tree . . ."

He walked very slowly toward one of the lone, outlying trees of the wood, a younger oak, its trunk merely spotted with lichen. Clariel picked up his sword, an ordinary-looking weapon in a plain scabbard on a simple leather belt, albeit with a gold-chased buckle. She strapped it on herself, then bent down again to take the water bottle and the muslin-wrapped bread.

There was something else there too, wedged almost in the nose of the paperwing. A silver bottle wreathed in gold wires. Clariel reached down to pick it up but as her fingers closed there was a flare of Charter Magic. Pain shot through the bones of her hand to her elbow, and she flinched back.

With the pain, she heard a distant, despairing voice.

The voice of the Free Magic creature.

Aziminil.

"Help me! Help me . . ."

Clariel's hand stayed frozen near the bottle. She stayed completely still for a few seconds, the sound of Aziminil's voice receding till she heard it no more. Once again she felt the desire to help the creature, to free it from its prison, a desire made stronger by her own experiences as a prisoner.

But there was a stronger emotion. She remembered the thrill of incipient power, when she had almost dominated Aziminil, when her will had closed like a fist upon the creature's mind and she had been on the brink of seizing it, of using its sorcerous gifts. If she released it from the bottle, Clariel could force it to obey, and then it could help her. Who knew what she might be able to do with the creature's powers at her disposal?

But the thing had tried to kill Bel before. Everyone said Free Magic creatures were evil. Yet against that, Kargrin himself said they were not evil as *such*, and surely that meant it was all about what you did with them—

Clariel withdrew her hand and shook her head violently, as if she could clear it of unsuitable thoughts. Grabbing the water and the bread, she went after the staggering Bel, catching up just in time to help manage his controlled collapse, getting his back against the trunk and slowly bending his knees till he was sitting down.

"I'll be fine after a rest," he whispered. "I did say that wind-working took it out of me, didn't I?"

"You did," replied Clariel. She set the food and water by his side.

"Thanks," asked Bel, his eyes half-shut. "I'm glad you're here with me."

Clariel did not answer. She looked back at the paperwing and then over to the shadowed edge of the wood proper, with the dusky light coming through the trees. She felt the trees beckon to her, inviting her in.

Here she had a real choice, for the first time ever. Her parents were gone, the ties of love, affection, and duty broken by their violent deaths. She had not wanted that, and she felt guilty at the thought that they could no longer hold her back from living the life she wanted to lead.

Against that, even in death they had set a very strong obligation upon her. They had to be revenged, and she was their daughter; surely this was her task.

But even as Clariel thought this, some small part of her was whispering away, suggesting that they would be avenged *anyway*, no matter what she did herself. The Abhorsens and the Clayr and Captain Gullaine and Kargrin would deal with Kilp and Aronzo. Besides, what did the living ever really owe the dead?

That same sly internal voice suggested Clariel could and should simply go into the forest here. This was a small wood, perhaps only a league from side to side, but it would be a stepping stone. She could head west on foot, there would be other small forests to hide within, she would cross the Ratterlin somehow . . .

Clariel paused, forcing herself to make a realistic assessment of her chances. She had neither the gold nor the disguise promised by Kargrin, and without either she would be taken easily at the ferry by the guards there, who would answer to Kilp as Governor or Lord Protector or whatever he called himself now. Besides that, she would have to survive forest and road, weather and ill-chance, barefoot, dressed in just a smock and cloak, with only the small knife around her neck and, if she could sink so low to steal it, Bel's sword.

Furthermore, this little wood was nothing like the Great Forest. It would have few animals to hunt, or woodland foods to gather. She would have to beg or steal from the surrounding farms, and with every contact the chance of running into guards searching for her would increase, or word of her passage would get back to them.

But it was possible . . .

Bel groaned in his sleep, and his mouth twisted as if he were about to whistle, before relaxing again.

Clariel looked down at him. He was unconscious and even paler than usual, so white that if she hadn't met him before she would think him sorely wounded and losing blood.

She frowned and quickly knelt down. Rolling Bel to one side, she unlaced his hauberk enough to get her hand inside the neck, so she could gently probe his wounded shoulder. The bandage there was damp but not wet, and when she withdrew her hand she saw her fingers only tinged with pink, a mixture of sweat and a little blood. His wound had not reopened, as she had feared for a moment. But he was still so pale. She put two fingers on his neck to feel his pulse. It was steady, if not strong. She felt his forehead too, which was cool but not clammy, confirming that he was simply exhausted, and not struck down by fever. He would be better for a sleep, and she felt confident he would be able to continue in the morning.

If she left, he would fly on to Hillfair, thought Clariel. No doubt sadder but none the worse.

Bel would tell the Abhorsen what had happened. He would

avenge her mother and father. Kilp and Aronzo *would* have to pay, and pay with their lives. But as everyone said, revenge was a dish best made with care. Better to go to Estwael and take the time to plan and prepare, rather than rushing back to Belisaere. Besides, Clariel told herself, she didn't care how Kilp and Aronzo died, provided someone killed them.

The forest and freedom was so close, and she could make it to Estwael . . .

"I will go," whispered Clariel, almost as if Bel could hear her and that made it more honest. "I'll have to borrow your sword and your money, if you have any . . ."

Since she was stealing his sword anyway, it made sense to search him for a purse. He didn't have one, but there were three gold bezants and five silver deniers in a pocket at the top of his left boot, and a knife in the top of his right boot. Clariel left him the knife and one of the bezants.

Though the night was warm, she put on the cloak. It was dark, unlike her smock. Pursuit was unlikely, but you never knew what might be lurking in the woods. It would be better to at least try to remain unseen.

She also left the food and the water bottle for Bel. Though it had been a hot summer she had seen many small streams from the paper-wing, so finding water would not be a problem. Food might be more of an issue, given the ordered nature of the woods about, but there were farms. Now she could buy food as well as steal it.

The biggest problem was simply the distance to Estwael. More than two hundred leagues and that barefoot—though she could per-haps buy some shoes, or make rough sandals from bark, or slippers from animal skin. All the while having to avoid contact with other people as much as possible.

It was not going to be easy, but Clariel knew she could do it.

She looked up at the darkening sky. There was no moon yet, but the stars were becoming visible. There, low on the horizon above the wood was the bright red star Uallus, and three fingers left of that was north. From there she looked halfway across the sky to find the six stars that made up the great sickle, the tip of the handle a pointer to due west, or close enough. Halfway between was her best course, she thought. Northwest through the wood. If she reached the edge of the forest, or at midnight in any case, she would stop and sleep, and in the morning progress onward from copse to small forest, though she would also have to cross open fields. Getting over the Ratterlin was going to be difficult. She couldn't take the ferry and would have to steal a boat . . . but this was a problem for another day.

Unless . . . Clariel thought again of Aziminil. She looked back to the paperwing, now just a dim silhouette, barely visible in the fading light. Though the bottle was hidden in the aircraft's nose, she could almost feel the Free Magic creature's presence, almost hear the plaintive cry to be released.

Clariel wondered if Aziminil knew that she was being sent to the Abhorsens. There could be no other reason the bottle was in the paperwing. She wondered what they would do with it. Possibly the Abhorsens could actually kill Free Magic creatures, and Aziminil was being carried by Bel to her execution. Or maybe just to be stored, kept prisoner somewhere safer than Kargin's tower in the city.

Was Kilp right that Free Magic was just another kind of magic that could be used as required? It seemed that Aziminil had worked for the Governor and his son without compulsion, even making Aronzo the golden cup. That didn't sound "inimical to all life" as Free Magic was often described. Aziminil had fought on the Islet, but they had been trying to capture her; surely anyone would fight in such circumstances?

With Aziminil's aid, the journey home would be so much easier . . .

Clariel shook her head, even harder than she had after almost touching the silver bottle in the paperwing. This temptation had to be cast out of her mind.

"No," she whispered. Better to stick to what she knew. She took one last look at Bel, and bit her lip. He looked so weak and defenseless lying there, and she was going to abandon him.

Bel made a whimpering sound in his sleep and his face twitched in pain. Clariel looked away and shut her eyes.

"I have to go," she said. "Forgive me, Bel. This might be my last chance."

She did not look back after that, but struck out for the wood.

It was cool and dark under the trees, but the forest was open enough to admit starlight. Clariel's eyes adapted to the gloom, and there was a path that headed roughly in the right direction. She walked slowly, listening to the small, quiet sounds of tree, bird, and beast, a feeling of peace coming over her as she went deeper into the forest.

But she had only gone a few hundred yards when the quiet sounds suddenly stopped, a sure sign of some incipient trouble. A few moments later she heard different noises, louder sounds. Something was moving through the undergrowth behind her, something large enough to break twigs and crunch leaves underfoot. Clariel stopped, her hand on her sword hilt, and listened. It was large enough to be a boar, or a wolf. She heard more sounds of movement, spread over a larger area. There was more than one of whatever it was.

Clariel drew her sword. There were Charter marks on the blade. Simple marks for sharpness and durability, probably cast on the blade by Bel himself. They glowed softly, shedding a little more light than the stars above.

Wolves, she thought, or perhaps wild dogs. A small pack, only three or four animals. Nothing she need fear, not with the sword. In any case, the sounds were growing fainter. They were moving away from her . . .

Back toward the unconscious Bel.

Clariel wavered for a moment, but only for a moment. It was one thing to leave Bel in safe farmland. It was another to desert him when she knew there was a pack of wolves or wild dogs close by. Even though the animals would be cautious, his lack of movement would eventually lure them close. He was so exhausted, so deeply unconscious, he'd have no chance when they finally decided to attack. They'd rip his throat out before he could even wake.

She turned around and went back along the track. The moon had finally risen, so she could see her way more clearly, the clear silver light casting shadows from the trees, black lines crosshatching the ground.

In the fringe of the forest, she saw what she expected. A group of wild dogs, four of them, not even enough to be called a pack. They were brindled, shaggy, and clearly feral, and they were heading toward the unconscious Bel.

Clariel pushed her cloak back over her shoulders and tapped the flat of her blade hard against the nearest tree trunk, the whap of it loud in the still of the night. The four dogs stopped as one, ears pricked, heads turning in her direction. She stalked toward them, slapping the flat of the sword against every tree as she closed, tilting it so the steel caught the moonlight.

The dogs were wary of an armed human. They waited for a few moments to make sure she really was coming after them, then broke and ran, at first into the field and then back into the woods.

She chased them for a while, making a lot of noise, but there was no chance of catching them on foot. So there was a strong possibility that if she left then they would come back, and Bel would still be vulnerable.

Clariel sighed, the longest sigh of her life. She stared up at the sky for a long, long time before finally starting to gather ferns for bedmaking. Combining the fern fronds with large armfuls of grass, cut ignominiously with Bel's sword, she made two beds next to each other in a slight hollow between some exposed roots of the lone oak, and when they were ready, dragged Bel over and laid him down.

She found herself quite tenderly tucking his cloak over him, and drew her hands back. Was this the beginning of caring for someone? Of falling in love? If she let herself go would she become like the girls in Estwael, fussing over their lovers?

Clariel scowled at the notion and told herself she cared no more for Bel than she would for any wounded animal.

"You could be a fawn and I'd treat you the same," she said to the sleeping Bel, somewhat belying her words by straightening out his legs so he would be more comfortable.

Bel did not answer, only shifting slightly in his sleep. Clariel lay herself down on her own bed, the sword at her side. She watched the stars and moon above, framed by branches, and listened to the small sounds of the forest and meadow return now the dogs were gone. The light breeze ruffling tree branches; a barking owl flapping overhead; a single small animal, probably a fox, coming close but not too close; the yip of that same owl over in the field as it caught a field mouse . . .

Slowly the tension that had been held inside her for all her time in the city drained out into the good soil beneath her bed of fern and grass. As Clariel let it go, sadness welled up, and tears began to slide down her cheeks, tears for her slain parents and tears for herself.

But she cried silently, without moving, and eventually exhaustion overcame emotion, and she went to sleep.

Chapter Twenty-One

HILLFAIR, HORSES, AND DOGS

lariel woke first, just before the dawn, in that cool half-lit world where shapes begin to become clear again. Mist was already rising as the dew felt the warmth of the as-yet unseen sun. The sky was clear, with the promise of blue, and looked to be warm. Clariel got up, strapped Bel's sword back on from where it had lain ready to hand, wrapped her cloak around herself, and went into the trees for her toilet.

When she came back, Bel's eyes were open, but blearily, and he had his cloak pulled up to his nose. He pulled it down just enough to expose his mouth and said, "Good morning. I say that, though I have had better mornings."

"We're alive, and out of Belisaere," said Clariel shortly. She sat down and investigated the muslin bundle, which proved to contain a loaf of bread, gone stale on one side and slightly mushy on the other, and a small wheel of hard cheese, protected in red wax. She broke the bread in half, and took out her knife to slice the cheese open. "Breakfast? I could go and find some berries and such, but it would take some time."

"No, we'd better get aloft as soon as we can," said Bel, taking a proffered piece of bread in his right hand and a triangle of cheese in his left, though he grimaced as the movement made his shoulder twitch. "We can have a proper meal at Hillfair. The Abhorsen doesn't stint anyone at his table."

"What about his prisoners?" asked Clariel. "As I am like to be."

"What!" exclaimed Bel, almost choking on his bread. "You're

the Abhorsen's granddaughter! You won't be a prisoner!"

"I hope not," said Clariel. "But if he thinks Mother is alive, and has agreed to be Queen with Kilp as temporary Regent or whatever . . . it won't look good for me."

"I'm . . . I'm sure he wouldn't be so . . . stupid . . ." said Bel, but his words lacked conviction. Clearly he did think the Abhorsen could be that stupid.

"You know how I said I couldn't tell you about why my mother fell out with Tyriel," said Clariel.

"Yes?"

"He thinks my mother killed her brother."

Bel choked again, this time quite seriously, so Clariel had to clap him on the back, dislodging the bread and jarring his wound.

"Ow! No! What?"

"I wondered if you were just pretending not to know the other day, and whether the . . . um . . . rank and file Abhorsens knew," said Clariel. "I guess not. I only found out myself recently. She told me that he was already dead, inhabited by a Free Magic creature, or something Dead. So Mother only killed the body. But her father . . . my grandfather . . . he didn't believe her, and banished her as a kinslayer."

"I'm sure most of the family have no idea," exclaimed Bel. "I never even heard a whisper of it, and there are always enough rumors and gossip going round about everything else! Whenever Jaciel was mentioned, which wasn't often, people just said she'd had a falling-out with the old bastard . . . I mean the Abhorsen. Which is easy to do. I fell out with him too. But I'm sure you'll be all right . . ."

"Maybe," said Clariel. "Let's get it over with, anyway. You think we can reach Hillfair by early afternoon?"

"If I can put myself together," said Bel, slowly tottering to his feet. He stretched tentatively, favoring his left side. "I've . . . got to find a tree, back in a minute."

In fact it was late afternoon by the time Clariel had her first sight of Hillfair, the sprawling nest of houses and outbuildings that an Abhorsen of three generations gone by had begun by building a summer lodge on the western ridge that ran along and above the river Ratterlin. Hillfair was three leagues north of the much older and enormously more defensible Abhorsen's House, but that was smaller and more inconvenient, occupying an island in the river on the very brink of the great waterfall where the Ratterlin fell twelve hundred feet to the lowlands below.

"There it is," said Bel. "Hillfair."

His voice was weak and strained, his lips dry and mouth parched from too much whistling. Though they had generally followed the Ratterlin south for more than two hundred leagues, requiring little change of direction, the vagaries of the wind meant Bel had needed to change altitude. And they had also flown much higher approaching High Bridge, to give the place a wide berth in case the town authorities reported their passage or had been ordered to shoot them with the large bolt-throwers that adorned the guard castle there, relics of the long-ago days of Kaelin Scaler and her river pirates.

Clariel leaned around Bel and looked ahead. They were still two or three leagues away, and at that distance Hillfair looked like a small town. There were at least twenty buildings, some of stone and some of wood, spread out on the flat top of the ridge and down to the river, the latter on terraces that had been carved out of the rocky hillside.

"How many people live here?" asked Clariel. "And how many belong to the family?"

"Five or six hundred, I guess," replied Bel. His voice was scratchy. "And at least half that number are Abhorsens, one way or another, though most are distant from the main line. Just call everyone cousin and you'll be right enough."

"It's a daunting prospect," said Clariel. "I hope the Abhorsen will let me go soon."

"I will fly you to Estwael, if I'm allowed," promised Bel. He hesitated, then added, "Though I might need a few days' rest first. I haven't been this tired since . . . forever, really."

"Thank you," said Clariel. "I hope I do get to fly with you. You've been a good friend."

Bel mumbled something and the tips of his ears turned red, the blush easy to see on his pale skin. Clariel noticed the blush and perceived she was meant to hear the mutter, no doubt a protestation about "mere friends" or something like that. Bel wanted more, obviously, but she did not. She liked his company, and he was a friend, as she judged things, proven by his actions. But she felt no passionate attraction, no giddy desire. She'd never felt that, though she'd heard enough about it from other young women in Estwael. She had always presumed it just came upon them, but she did wonder now if it might grow from a small spark of friendship. But it didn't matter. Not now.

"A good friend," she repeated.

"I know," sighed Bel. "If I had a denier for every time I've heard 'let's be friends' I'd be richer than Kilp."

"Come on, Bel," said Clariel, suddenly cross with him. "Denima was falling all over you. She's prettier than me, and smarter too, I'd say."

"I wouldn't say so," said Bel stiffly. "Either one."

"I'm just not . . . not interested in men," said Clariel.

"Oohh," said Bel, blushing again.

"Or women either," added Clariel. She felt a strong desire to slap him around the ears a bit and if he hadn't been wounded might have done so. "Think about the situation I'm in, will you! How could I be thinking about . . . about kissing and bed games with everything that's happened . . . that is happening?"

Bel was silent. Evidently he had no trouble thinking about such things at all, at any time.

"You'll be safe here," he said hesitantly. "Maybe after a—"

"Will I?" asked Clariel. "Let's see. But in any case, let me say again to be perfectly clear, I am not interested in jumping into bed with you or anyone, or sighing and cooing and playing at romance, or planning a marriage or any of it. But I do value you as a good friend. All right?"

"Perfectly clear," said Bel. "And understood. Sorry."

"Good," said Clariel. "I need my friends, few as they are."

"I'm glad to be one," said Bel, with forced cheerfulness.

Clariel wondered if she'd really made her point, or if Bel's natural optimism would break out again in a few days. She really didn't want to have to keep rebuffing him, because he was a friend. But she also didn't want any further complications in her already troubled life.

"You didn't tell me we had that Free Magic creature aboard," she said, going for a change of subject. Clariel had tried not to think about Aziminil, trapped in the silver bottle, but she had found it difficult. Even now, she thought she could almost hear a despairing cry for help, on the very edge of audibility.

"Oh," said Bel. "You saw the bottle . . . Kargrin told me not to tell anyone, including you. It's spelled so only an Abhorsen can touch it."

"Hmm," said Clariel noncommitally. She wondered if Kargrin had worked out that she had let the creature escape on the island. But that seemed unlikely. Maybe he was just being secretive in general. "What will happen to her . . . that is . . . it?"

"It'll go down to the Abhorsen's House," said Bel. "The original house, you can't see it yet. It's in the river, as running water defends against the Dead, and you don't get much faster running water than in the middle of the biggest waterfall around. See that huge low cloud up ahead, past Hillfair?"

Clariel did see the cloud. She had wondered why it sat so low and alone, with the rest of the sky so blue.

"That's from the waterfall? And the house is there? It must be damp."

Bel shook his head, a litte too vigorously, and winced at the pain.
"Not at all," he said. "The mist doesn't fall back on the house. A
spell, I suppose. The whole place is wreathed in spells. Even the river
currents are ensorcelled, so you can get there by boat without being
taken by the waterfall. Presuming you've been invited, of course."

"Why doesn't the Abhorsen live there anymore?" asked Clariel.
"I've only ever heard people talk about Hillfair."

"Take a look along the ridge road," said Bel. "You'll see."

Clariel frowned in puzzlement, but looked. There was a long line
of people on horseback moving toward the closer buildings, but they
were still quite distant so she couldn't make out more than that.

"Riders," she said. "Might be a hundred of them, I suppose.
What of that?"

"The Grand Hunt, returning to Hillfair," said Bel. "I hope they
had a good day, it always puts Himself in a better mood."

"I still don't understand," said Clariel. She knew about Grand
Hunts; there was one in Estwael three times a year, she'd even ridden in a few. But it was a ridiculously overdone show, in her opinion,
with massed riders and packs of dogs all getting in one another's way,
and foolish rituals, and it depended on weeks of work beforehand
from foresters and the Borderers, and beaters on the day. "I heard the
Abhorsen likes to hunt . . ."

"*Loves* to hunt," said Bel. "Twice a week, if not more. And
everything is about the hunt. Half the buildings in Hillfair are horse
stables or dog kennels. That's how it got started, in the first place,
with the Abhorsen Kariniel . . . let's see, she was Tyriel's great-aunt,
so your great-great-great-aunt . . . she was hunt mad and you can't
keep horses in the old house, and the island is inconvenient. So she
built a lodge and stable and called it Hillfair."

"But, isn't the Abhorsen meant to travel about the Kingdom
making sure the Dead stay Dead, that Free Magic creatures like the
one we faced don't appear, and so on?" asked Clariel. "I know there

hasn't been trouble, but if he's hunting all the time instead . . ."

"Exactly," said Bel darkly. "That's always been my point, that there might be all kinds of perils slowly brewing. But no one down there wants to know, they simply don't believe that things could turn back to the bad old days. Like I said, I doubt if Yannael has even read *The Book of the Dead*. Maybe even Tyriel hasn't himself. I can't remember ever seeing him wear the bells. That's why I'm getting ready, so at least *someone* is prepared."

"Prepared for what?" asked Clariel. As she spoke, she felt a shiver pass through her, and the paperwing's shadow cut like a knife across the silver waters of the Ratterlin below.

"Whatever happens," said Bel. "Take that Free Magic creature in Belisaere, for example. The Abhorsen should have come to deal with it straight away, not left it to Kargrin and Mistress Ader. And why would something of that power be free now? I bet there's more, or more coming. I wouldn't be surprised if the Clayr have already warned Tyriel and he's just ignored it, like the King ignores everything he doesn't want to know about. Charter save us from old men!"

"I hope you're wrong," said Clariel. "It seems to me there's enough trouble with Kilp, let alone anything worse."

"True," said Bel. "But Kilp at least is a purely ordinary, mortal problem. At least he is now that his allied creature is safely imprisoned. He shouldn't be too difficult to defeat. If the Abhorsen takes even a hundred Charter Mages north, and the Clayr come south in force—there's thousands of Clayr—no ordinary army will be able to stand against them. Kilp doesn't realize what a big group of really powerful mages can do. He should have been shown, then he wouldn't have dared to do anything."

"Maybe," said Clariel. "I doubt it will be that easy."

"It will," said Bel confidently. "Oh, thank the Charter! There's the landing lawn, finally! I could sleep for a week."

The lawn he was referring to was a long swathe of well-cut grass between the river and the road that ran along the ridge and up to Hillfair itself. There was a tall pole at one end, the flag on it spread by the westerly wind to show the silver keys of the Abhorsens on a blue field.

"We're going to land around the same time the Hunt goes by on the road," said Clariel cautiously. "The paperwing won't scare the horses?"

"No . . . I think . . . they should be used to paperwings," said Bel. "Besides, I really have to get us down. I'm feeling very . . . very tired . . ."

His head slipped forward as the words drawled out of his mouth. Clariel felt her heart leap into her throat as she gripped his good shoulder and shook him, only to let go as a dry chuckle emerged and he sat up again.

"Don't worry, only jesting," he said. "I am tired. But I can stay awake long enough to set us down."

He pursed his lips and blew a series of rising and then falling notes, pure and strong. Charter marks flew out with the music, and mingled with marks that shone from the paperwing's nose and wings, wreathing the aircraft in light. It slanted down toward the lawn, sideslipping a little across the wind as it descended.

They landed smoothly enough, but Bel was just plain wrong about the horses and dogs. As the paperwing's shadow passed low over the rear of the line, the dogs that had been loping next to the road in a semi-organized pack all began to bark and jump up, before falling down and over one another, and racing around all over the place, including in front of the horses. Many mounts spooked and shied, with several riders falling off or being suddenly bolted with along the road, causing more problems. The orderly procession of a minute before became a riot of horses, dogs, fallen riders, hunters, and dog handlers, with whistles and shouts and bellowed orders and screams of pain and whinnying horses and barking dogs.

The paperwing came to a stop about a hundred yards ahead of the front of the returning hunt. Clariel looked back at the shambles their arrival had caused, noting that half a dozen riders from the vanguard of the hunt were now galloping down the lawn toward them, and not in a way that suggested a sudden happy desire to welcome the newcomers.

Bel didn't even try to look around. He hunched down in the paperwing and put his head in his hands. Clariel thought she heard him say something that might have been "oops," but she was already climbing out. She presumed from the quality of the horses and richness of their attire that the silver-haired man who was charging down toward her on a surprisingly small chestnut horse was her grandfather, the Abhorsen Tyriel; and the tough-looking woman with the black hair who closely resembled her mother was almost certainly her aunt Yannael.

Clariel didn't want to meet them sitting down. She didn't want to meet them at all, and she wished Bel had not made what was already a difficult situation for her even worse.

For a moment, it looked like it might not be a meeting so much as a trampling, but Clariel was pleasantly relieved to see the riders expertly bring their mounts to a fast, wheeling halt right in front of her, incidentally cutting up the lawn something terrible.

"Bel, you're an idiot!" called out Tyriel, the finely worked collar of silver keys on his chest confirming Clariel's guess. She knew he was a similar age to King Orrikan, but he didn't look it. His hair was silver, but cropped short, and his close-shaven face, though lined and weather-beaten, was not fallen or shiny, as the king's had been. His hands were stained to the wrists with the blood of a stag, and he wore no sword, only a hunting dagger at his waist. "And you, I suppose, are my granddaughter Clariel?"

"Yes, I am Clariel."

"Come here," said Tyriel. He bent down from his horse as Clariel approached and reached out with his hand toward her forehead. She stood still as he gently placed two fingers against the Charter mark on her forehead. He did not lean down so far that Clariel could return the gesture, as was polite. Consequently she felt only a faint, distant connection with the Charter from the brief contact. Evidently whatever Tyriel felt, he was satisfied that she was indeed his granddaughter.

"What's wrong with Bel?"

Bel remained hunched forward, and had not spoken. He had either really fallen unconscious from weariness or was pretending in order to avoid getting into trouble over disrupting the hunting party.

"He was badly wounded a few days ago," said Clariel forcefully. "Fighting a Free Magic creature. He's still recovering and he's worn himself out flying here. He needs help."

"I had a message about his wounding," said Tyriel. He didn't sound like he was particularly concerned. "One of many messages in the last few days. He can't be too sorely hurt if he managed to get here. Siranael, go get some of your people, have them carry Bel up to the infirmary."

One of the riders behind wheeled his horse about and rocketed back toward the main body of the Hunt.

"There is also a silver bottle," said Clariel. "Charter-spelled. It holds a Free Magic creature."

"Oh, yes," said Tyriel. "Cursedly inconvenient. I suppose I'll have to take it. Pass it up."

"I can't touch it," said Clariel. "Magister Kargrin—"

"That's right, I forgot," said Tyriel impatiently. He swung his leg over and slowly lowered himself down from his horse, the smell of stale sweat preceding him. He went to the paperwing, lifted Bel's head, and looked at him with what seemed casual indifference, then bent down and rummaged around. Finding the bottle, he picked it up as if it might be a flagon of ale, tucked it under his arm, and remounted. His movements were quite stiff, but very practiced.

"Yannael," he said, to the hard-faced woman. "Take your niece up behind you, see that she gets properly dressed and so forth. Bring her to me when you're done."

Yannael didn't speak, but merely nodded slowly. In any case, Tyriel hadn't waited for an answer. He chirruped to his horse, gave it a touch of his heels, and was away again.

"Come on, girl," said Yannael. She took her foot out of her stirrup so Clariel could use it as a step. Like her father, she stank of stale sweat, blood, and horse. "Get up."

Clariel reluctantly got up behind her. She did not feel welcome, but it was worse than that. She felt like she was about to enter another prison. There might not be endless walls like Belisaere, but it would be a prison, sure enough.

Chapter Twenty-Two

THE ABHORSEN DECIDES

annael did not speak to Clariel on the short ride up to Hillfair. The place *was* like a small town, except that all the outer buildings appeared to be stables, kennels, and barns. It also didn't have a perimeter wall or even a palisade, which Clariel presumed was because all the other towns she'd seen were much older, and so possessed defenses that had been built long ago in more troubled times.

The road followed the ridge line, with the buildings spread out on either side, most of them on the flat, but some on the terraced hillside above the river. Clariel kept expecting to stop outside one or other of the stables, where grooms aplenty were waiting to take the horses from the returning hunters. But they kept going along the road, till it ended in a grassy courtyard surrounded by buildings. The chief of these was a great hall whose lower two stories were stone, but with four or five levels above that of blue-painted timber. Unusually for Hillfair, at least what she'd seen so far, Clariel couldn't see an obvious stable. But when Yannael pulled the horse up in front of the hall's great arched doors, a groom emerged from somewhere off to the left and took the reins.

"Get down," said Yannael, once again allowing Clariel her left stirrup. When the younger woman had alighted, she jumped down herself. "Follow me."

Clariel opened her mouth to protest her aunt's rudeness, but shut it again. There seemed little point, and there was always the slim possibility that Yannael was always like this, and it was not meant to be insulting.

A porter opened the front door, a tall gate of pale timber, which was adorned with hundreds of small keys of beaten silver or to Clariel's trained eye more likely some cheaper, silverish alloy. It opened directly into a vast open space, a true great hall, though crowded with four lines of long tables already loaded with food, and servers scuttling about with even more, platters of meats and fish and bread, with the meat in preponderance. Though the benches next to the tables were empty for the moment, it looked like several hundred people would be served a meal there soon. There was a dais at the far end, with a high table draped in blue velvet, a thronelike chair of gilded wood in the center and several smaller and somewhat less ornate chairs on either side.

There were tall windows behind the dais, but a great deal more light came from the thousands of Charter marks embedded in the hammerbeam roof high above, something that must have taken hundreds of mages years to place, and would require constant effort to keep the spells at full strength. Just getting up there would be no small feat.

Yannael led Clariel along one side of the hall, the servers ducking out of her way, bobbing their heads as she passed. At the far end, near the dais, the older woman opened a door and they went through into a corridor that ran at right angles to the hall. There were numerous doors leading off the corridor, all painted blue with silver keys.

"Private quarters for the main line of the family," said Yannael. Her face showed no friendliness or indeed, any emotion. She might have been a superior kind of servant giving directions to a not particularly notable guest. "You will have your mother's old room. Third along. Have a bath. I'll send someone with clothes. Get dressed and wait for me."

"My mother's old room," said Clariel. She felt the anger stir within her. "You know she's just been killed, don't you? Your *sister*?"

"She's been dead to us for a long time," said Yannael. Her eyes flickered with brief emotion, quickly quelled. "Just as my brother, Teriel—who she slew—has been dead a long time. Third door along."

She turned on her heel and strode away, the single spur she wore on her right boot-heel clinking. Clariel stared after her, feeling the rage deep inside her kindle and burn higher. She took a deep breath and slowly exhaled, and thought of her calm, willow-bordered refuge in the forest. The fury could not help her now. She had to keep it suppressed. Breathing in, breathing out . . . slowly she felt the anger subside, till it slept again.

But it was not gone. It was always there, no matter how deep she pushed the feeling. Always there, a fiercely hot spark waiting for the slightest fuel.

Clariel took one last very deep breath and breathed it out very slowly while she walked along the corridor to the third door. As she passed the first two, she saw they had small bronze nameplates, clean and bright. She didn't know who "Enriel" or "Harmanael" were, but the third door along . . .

She touched her finger to the small plate that had "Jaciel" engraved upon it. Unlike the previous two doors, the plate was tarnished and dull, but the name was still clear. It was also slightly different in design, the letters were more finely cut. With a slight shock Clariel recognized that this was her mother's own work, probably made when she was just a girl and beginning her training as a metalsmith. Now, it was a slight remnant of a whole former life that Clariel knew nothing about, and would never know, because she could not talk about it with her mother.

"She is dead," whispered Clariel. She closed her eyes and let her forehead rest against the door. "My mother and father are dead."

Saying it aloud didn't make it feel any more real, though she knew it was, that no matter what lies Kilp was spreading, there was no chance of it being otherwise. But some part of her also simply couldn't accept it, that her parents were dead, and she was in Hillfair, and the future looked grim and complicated.

But that future had to be faced, and the first step was to get cleaned up, ready to talk to the Abhorsen. Clariel straightened up, turned the handle, and went into her mother's childhood room.

If the room, in fact a whole suite of rooms, had once held personal things to identify it as Jaciel's there were none there now. The first chamber was completely bare apart from a single chair that didn't look like it belonged there anyway. The inner chamber had a bed with no linen, and a chest with a padded top that was empty. Beyond this room there was a kind of antechamber entered via a doorway with a curtain rod but no curtain, which contained only a bathtub and a chamber pot.

None of the rooms had windows, but they were quite light, again thanks to Charter marks in the plastered ceiling and stone walls.

Clariel had just finished reviewing this unpromising accommodation when there was knock at the door, followed a moment later by a whirlwind of people in blue aprons coming in with loads of sheets, blankets, towels, a more comfortable chair, a writing desk, a velvet lounge, a standing mirror, several baskets of clothes accompanied by a seamstress, and a whole gang of young girls and boys equipped with steaming cans of hot water, which they proceeded to pour into the bath.

All of this happened under the direction of a middle-aged woman with a cheerful face and untidy hair, whose blue apron was trimmed with silver, setting her apart from the others. She nodded to Clariel and said, "I'm your cousin Else . . . Elseniel, that is, but no one calls me that. I'm the keeper of the house, so if you want anything within these walls, come to me. Salleniel here has some clothes that will probably fit with a bit of a tuck or adjustment, so take your pick. Yan said to have you ready within the hour, so pop in the bath right away. The water cools quickly anyhow, so get the best of it. Off you go now!"

"Uh, yes," said Clariel. "Um, thank you, cousins."

They might be cousins, but there were too many of them crowded around, in too small a room. Clariel fled into the antechamber, and drew the newly placed curtain shut. She could hear general milling around and bedmaking noises going on, but mercifully no one followed her in.

The bathwater was still very hot, but it was welcome. Clariel hadn't realized quite how dirty she had become in the prison cell, a state that had not been helped by a night under a tree. There was new soap on the bath rim, good soap scented only slightly with lime. She used a lot of it, and turned the bathwater the color of a mud puddle, before she climbed out feeling much cleaner and considerably more refreshed.

Salleniel the seamstress was the only person still in the other rooms. She hardly spoke, her mouth full of pins already, but she had a very good eye as proved by her choices of linen undergarments and a leather hunting tunic that turned out to be very near a perfect fit. The knee-length leggings of doeskin were slightly long, but still only needing a quick turn and a rapidly stitched hem.

"Are hunting clothes suitable?" asked Clariel. "I mean, I saw there is to be a feast in the hall . . ."

"Hunting clothes are always suitable around here," mumbled Salleniel through her mouthful of pins. "Himself never wears anything else, and what he wears is what we all wear. You'll need some boots made, cousin, but there's soft slippers here, which I can pinch in at the toe if needed, just slip your foot in, there . . . hmmm . . . not so bad. Stay still!"

Salleniel made no comment when Clariel, fully dressed and ready to go, put the short knife Kargrin had given her through her belt. Almost as she did so, there was a perfunctory knock at the door and

Yannael—or Yan, as it seemed most of the Abhorsens called her—came in. She was bathed too, but not so much changed as simply wearing clean versions of her previous hunting leathers.

"He's in the message-hawk mews," said Yan, without preamble. "Come on."

"Thank you, cousin," said Clariel to Salleniel, who smiled and waved.

Clariel followed Yan along the corridor, but instead of turning left to go back into the hall, she stopped at the end and stood in front of a large painting, a hunting scene, that had been done directly on the plastered wall. For a moment Clariel wondered why her aunt was just standing in front of it, before she saw her move a horse's head in the painting, sliding away a cunningly matched lid of paint and plaster to reveal a tiny keyhole. Then she extended an equally tiny key from the ring on her finger and turned the lock. The whole wall, painting and all, pivoted inward as she pushed against it, revealing a narrow stair. Not a dusty, unused stair, Clariel noted as she climbed up. It was lit by Charter marks, and was as clean as the rest of Hillfair, so it was perhaps not meant to be all that secret. At least not to whoever mopped the floors. Yan, as Clariel had come to expect, did not explain why they were taking this stair.

They climbed up past several other doors, two of which looked ordinary enough and one like the painted wall below, though on this side Clariel could see the faint outline in the stone wall and the grooved arc cut in the floor where the wall slid back. Then they went along another enclosed corridor, around a corner and up again, this time a larger, straight staircase of polished wood.

Finally, five or six levels up this stair, Yan opened a door onto a long verandah or wide balcony. Heads turned as they came out, the heads of half a dozen message-hawks, their fierce yellow eyes fixed on the arrivals for a moment before they lost interest and looked away. Message-hawks, bred and trained with the help of Charter

Magic, were never hooded, and they stayed on their perches without
the need to be tethered by jesses. These ones, on their perches out on
the verandah, were ready to go at a moment's notice, as soon as they
had a message imprinted in their minds.

There were a dozen more message-hawks on their perches inside
the mews behind the verandah, a large, fairly dim room that looked
like it had been added on to whatever building they were in—which
wasn't the hall, because she had seen the roof of that from the verandah. Despite that, Clariel wasn't sure which end of the hall she'd
been looking at. Hillfair could prove just as easy to get lost in as the
city, she thought, and she liked it no more than she liked Belisaere.

The Abhorsen Tyriel was sitting at a writing desk in the middle
of the room, reading a transcribed message. A clerk with inky fingers
sat next to him, writing with a quill but not looking at what he was
writing, because his eyes were fixed on the message-hawk that sat
on its perch two inches from his face, something you would never
do with a hunting bird. Hearing a confidential message, Clariel
presumed. She knew the message-hawks could speak if they were
so instructed, but it wasn't unusual for them to carry messages that
could only be "heard" inside the mind, and only then if the correct
marks or passwords were given to the hawk.

"Ah, Clariel," said the Abhorsen. He had changed, but like Yan,
only into a different set of hunting leathers. He still wore the collar
of silver keys. At least he didn't smell of horses and blood anymore,
Clariel was pleased to note as she approached his desk. "We'll talk
outside. You may return to the feast, Yannael, and give the toast. I
may be some time."

"Yes, Father," said Yan. She shot her niece another swift look that
defied interpretation but was probably just pure meanness, Clariel
thought.

"Come," said Tyriel, walking out to the verandah with Clariel
close behind. The hawks once again turned their heads in unison,

one look at the moving humans and then back again, out toward the open sky. Though their behavior was controlled by Charter Magic, Clariel thought they still had the primal urge to fly. Only now all they could do was look, until they were dispatched upon their next mission.

"I have had a lot of messages about you," said Tyriel. "Messages from Kargrin, and Captain Gullaine, and Governor Kilp."

"Kilp!" spat Clariel. "He killed my parents!"

"So Kargrin says," said Tyriel. "But Kilp claims otherwise. Indeed, he sends to ask for my help, or at least to stay my hand—in the name of my daughter, who is now Queen."

"What!" said Clariel. She clenched her fists, blood rising in her face. "She's dead. I was there! I saw my father killed. Mother made me run with a Charter spell, and then . . . then she charged Kilp's guards . . ."

"Go back," said Tyriel. He made no move to comfort Clariel, or wipe her tears, or anything a real grandfather might do. "Tell me everything, as you saw it."

"Why do you care?" asked Clariel bitterly. "You thought Mother was a kinslayer. *Aunt* Yannael said she's been dead to you for years."

"Yannael feels deeply, and holds on to pain," said Tyriel. "I do not, and as the years have gone by, I have wondered . . . even now, I hold a small hope that Jaciel lives, that we might talk again, neither of us in anger."

"I do not think there is any hope," said Clariel. The anger was flowing away, like water from a holed vessel, she had nothing to contain it now.

"Tell me," said Tyriel.

Clariel told him. How they had visited the King, and the kin-gift, and then to the Governor's mansion. Jaciel touching the goblet, the sudden fight, her flight and capture, the prison hole, the paper-wing flight to Hillfair.

"So," said Tyriel heavily, when at last she had finished. "I believe you are right, and now only one of my three children lives."

"Can't you . . . go into Death to see?" asked Clariel. She was remembering what Bel had said about Tyriel never wearing the bells, perhaps not even having read *The Book of the Dead*.

"No," replied Tyriel, very shortly. "Death is not to be entered save when . . . needs must."

"What are you going to do about Kilp then?" asked Clariel. She felt two conflicting urges inside her. One was as it had always been, to get back to the Great Forest. The other was the desire to destroy Kilp and Aronzo, to take revenge for her parents' deaths, to join the force of Abhorsens that was surely going to help the King.

"We must consult with the Clayr, and Gullaine and Kargrin in the palace," said Tyriel. "There is also the matter of the Summer's End Hunt, one of the most important in our year . . ."

Clariel felt some of that anger that had leaked away return. How could the Abhorsen be concerned with a ceremonial hunt, when there was urgent business at hand? The Borderers didn't go hunting stags for pleasure when there was a wolf pack in the Forest.

"There is also the question of what to do with you," continued Tyriel. His voice held no menace, but even so, Clariel found his gaze upon her very disquieting.

"I would like to go to Estwael," she said quickly. "To my aunt Lemmin, my father's sister."

"That, at least, is out of the question," rumbled Tyriel. "You would not be safe. Kargrin says that Kilp needs to establish you as Queen under his control. A puppet, if you will, for he cannot continue to claim Jaciel will take the throne. No one will believe him if he cannot show she lives. Kargrin also told me . . . about your encounter with the Free Magic creature."

"What's that got to do with anything?" asked Clariel. "She . . . it's captured. You've got it stuck in a bottle."

Tyriel didn't answer for a moment, but kept looking at Clariel, his eyes unblinking. She tried to meet his gaze, but eventually found herself casting her eyes down.

"Kilp may have other such allies," Tyriel said finally. "I think we must keep you somewhere safe, in case of abduction. Or if things change and Kilp needs all of the closest royal heirs dead, safe from assassination."

"I'd be safe in the Great Forest," said Clariel desperately, seeing yet another prison looming in her future. The city had been one, albeit a relatively open prison, and then the pit . . . and now . . .

"You most assuredly would not be," said Tyriel. "Have you considered that the Borderers get their orders from the Governor, or as he now styles himself, the Lord Protector?"

"No . . . but I know the Borderers near Estwael," protested Clariel. "They wouldn't . . ."

"There is already a warrant out of the city calling for you to be found and 'helped' to return to Belisaere," said Tyriel. "Apparently you took flight when the King was killed by rebels and did not know your mother has become Queen. Kilp is a glib hand with such stories."

"But if I told Sergeant Penreth the truth, she wouldn't—"

"Would she be able to ignore a properly sealed warrant from Belisaere, backed up by the gold that Kilp has spent widely to buy people in every city watch, among the Borderers, and in the Wall Garrison? No, you must be kept safe until we are ready to move against the traitors. You will go to our old house, and the sooner the better. I will take you there myself."

"But . . . how long will I be there?" asked Clariel.

"As long as is necessary," said Tyriel. "As I said, there are many matters to be considered. The King is secure in the Palace, there is no need for precipitate action. A few months, perhaps more—"

"A few months!" exclaimed Clariel. "No! I can't be shut up again!"

She turned to run and found herself caught by the wrist. It hurt. The pain shot through to her elbow, and then to her chest, and it was as if a friction light had been applied to a line of resin and pitch, flames flaring all along the way, heading for that secret, internal place where her berserk fury was contained, but the bonds were weakening . . .

"No!" said Clariel. "No! Not now!"

She was talking not to Tyriel, but to herself. Frantically she tried to slow her breathing, to keep that breath inside, and not take another one too soon. Where was her calm place, the willow arches, the stream in the forest? She couldn't see it, she could only feel the pain, and the fire inside and then—

The rage came, roaring up unstoppably inside her. It filled every muscle with sudden, furious energy that could not be gainsaid. Clariel jerked her arm and Tyriel's grip came free. She howled and drew her small knife as everything turned red and she saw a shadow ahead of her, knowing it only as an enemy, not as a person.

An enemy who must be killed.

Clariel struck, but somehow her target twisted away, making her angrier still. She charged forward, hitting strange objects whose tops erupted into flurries of movement and piercing cries, confusing her as they flapped about, and behind them her foe kept backing away. There were strange flashes of light, and trails of glowing sparks that lashed her, but still she went forward, her knife slashing. Then the trails of light wrapped around her, trussing her up like a spider securing its prey. She was suddenly down on the floor, shaking and gibbering, her hand jerking as even then she still tried to stab the enemy, the enemy who must be killed . . .

So you do have your mother's fury," said Tyriel.

Clariel opened one eye, and saw the Abhorsen looming above her, a red-streaked sky and a hawk on a perch behind him. She opened the other eye, and saw more perches. She was still on the balcony of the mews, but it was some considerable time after her last conscious memory, for the sun was beginning to set.

There was something soft under her head. She reached back for it and felt a pillow, realizing with the motion she was not bound, as well as she might have been after trying to kill her grandfather. They could bind her easily enough now, thought Clariel, for she felt as if she could hardly move, there was no strength in her at all.

"The rage crops up every now and then among us," said Tyriel. "I have had some practice in dealing with berserks. I saw you try to hold it back. I suppose I should have expected something of the sort, for it often gets out of control after . . . things that stir the emotions . . . deaths and trouble . . . and Kargrin *had* told me you had the rage."

He was sitting on a wooden stool, the kind milkmaids used, Clariel saw. It looked rather incongruous. He saw her staring at the little three-legged affair, and added, "My knees aren't what they were, and I didn't want to leave you. It's best to let a berserk stay where they fall, they come back to their senses faster that way. How do you feel?"

"Weak," whispered Clariel. "And foolish."

"You should not feel foolish," said Tyriel. "The rage is both curse and blessing. Learn to rule it, and it can aid you to incredible feats of strength and daring. Let it rule you . . . I'm sure you can imagine how that would end."

"I can," whispered Clariel. "I won't let it."

"There is an excellent book that has proved to be very helpful for our various berserks," said Tyriel. "I believe there is a copy at the house, I will send word to have the sending librarian find it for you."

"I will not stay there," muttered Clariel.

"You will," said Tyriel. "It won't be as bad as you seem to imagine. The Abhorsen's House is very pleasant, it has gardens, there is fishing, and a multitude of sendings to tend to you. Some of them are even remarkably fine cooks."

"And jailers?" asked Clariel.

"For your own safety, they will make sure you do not leave the House," said Tyriel. There was a tone in his voice that brooked no further questions. Clariel sighed and let her head slump back.

"Can you walk? I expect you would feel more dignified than if you have to be carried to a horse—I presume you can ride, for that matter? Your mother loved to ride."

"Did she?" asked Clariel woozily. She rolled over and managed to push herself up to a sitting position. "She never got on a horse unless we had to travel. But I can ride well enough. And walk . . . just give me a minute or two."

"Take your time," he said. "It's a short ride along the riverbank."

When Clariel was ready to walk, they didn't go back down the secret or semi-secret stair, but instead down a broad and open staircase at the far end of the mews balcony. This went all the way down to ground level, ending in a kind of alley between buildings. There were grooms waiting there holding horses, and a dozen or so people already mounted. Half of them wore gethre plate hauberks, with shields, helmets, spears, and swords; and the other half in lighter mail without shields, but they had short bows in saddle-cases above their left knees and quivers on their right. They were the first inhabitants of Hillfair that Clariel had seen not wearing hunting clothes.

"I doubt that there are any assassins lurking so close," said Tyriel. "But I am a great believer in caution, it cannot be overrated. You are sure you can ride?"

"Yes," said Clariel. She felt less shaky now, and was determined that she would not be treated any more like a prisoner—or a parcel—than was absolutely necessary. And if there was even the slightest chance she could get away . . . she would take it.

"The bay mare there is yours," said Tyriel. "She's called Digger, after an incident long ago, but she has a sweet nature now."

"Sweet nature" meant sluggish and docile, Clariel realized as she mounted. Digger didn't want to do more than a walk, and had to be strongly encouraged when Tyriel and the entourage broke into a trot as they cleared the stables on the northern end of Hillfair. Clariel noted that the heavily armored guards stayed close around her and the Abhorsen. Shielding them from arrow-shot, no doubt, but also making sure Clariel couldn't gallop off. Something Digger couldn't or wouldn't do anyway, the choice of such a mount surely intentional.

The road wasn't much more than a track, but it had been raised and roughly guttered, and was broad enough for six to ride abreast. Past the buildings, the ridge was covered in a low heather, which looked rather too perfect for an assassin to hide in, though only a suicidal one would attempt a shot. They would be ridden down or shot themselves all too soon.

The river below and to their left was running fast, with a great deal of white water. The cloud of mist from the waterfall loomed up ahead, far larger and more imposing than it had seemed from the paperwing, particularly as the western edge of the white expanse was now stained with red from the setting sun.

Set against the middle of this vast white backdrop, cradled between two arms of the river on the very lip of the massive water-fall, Clariel saw the Abhorsen's House.

It was built upon a rocky island, enclosed on all sides by a high white wall. A tower loomed above the red-tiled roof of a large house, the top of a very tall fig tree visible behind it, hinting at the garden Tyriel had mentioned. There was a narrow wooden bridge from the riverbank across the now fast-rushing Ratterlin, a bridge built upon a line of low stones, each about four paces apart, that could only just be seen above the surface of the water.

In other circumstances, she might have been excited and amazed to see and visit such a place. But with the prospect of being trapped there for months, Clariel felt only dread, that she would soon be con-fined behind high walls again.

The road continued along the ridge toward the Long Cliffs, where it turned westward, but there was a narrow bridlepath that diverted down toward the river and the bridge. The company sorted itself out into a single file, with Tyriel and Clariel in the middle, and they slowly descended. With every step, the roar of the waterfall grew louder. It was so loud by the time they reached the riverbank that Tyriel had to shout.

"We leave the horses and everyone else here. Go ahead of me, and hold the handrail on the bridge. If you go in, there'll be no sav-ing you."

Clariel could well believe that. The river was a mass of white here, streaming around the stones under the bridge and splashing the timbers in a great spate of furious energy.

The bridge itself didn't look very secure or easy. It was only three planks wide, not much wider than Clariel's two feet side by side. There was no handrail on one side, and the one on the waterfall side looked like it had been made with broomhandles lashed together. The whole bridge looked very makeshift.

"Are you sure it won't fall apart?" she shouted.

"Yes!" boomed Tyriel. "Count yourself lucky. When I was a boy there was no bridge, just the stepping-stones."

He had dismounted already and handed the reins of his horse to one of his followers. Reaching into one of the saddlebags he took out a familiar silver bottle and tucked it under his arm.

Aziminil's prison drew Clariel's attention like a dog catching sight of a morsel about to fall from the dinner table. She had to force herself to look away.

"Walk the horses," Tyriel shouted to his company. "I won't be long."

Clariel dismounted clumsily, but pushed away the helping hand of one of the guards and Tyriel's too, when he tried to steady her as she staggered over to him. She found it impossible to think of him as her grandfather, or even a relative. He was just another old, powerful man who was determined to control her life.

Just like Kilp.

"Remember to hold on!"

Clariel nodded, and preceded the Abhorsen onto the bridge. She gripped the rail immediately and was relieved to find it felt more secure than she'd expected. Similarly, with the river roaring past underneath and the spray flying up she'd expected the planks to be wet, slippery and slimy. But they were perfectly dry. As she stepped forward, still looking down, Clariel saw small Charter marks glisten in the wood under her shoe, and understood why the bridge was dry and hadn't been carried away. Its strength lay not in carpentry, but Charter Magic.

Halfway across the bridge, a hundred yards from the riverbank, the roar of the waterfall was so loud that even a shout would be lost. The mist hung above them like a great, grasping hand of white, forever reaching in. But it was held back, assuredly by more magic, and there was no spray on Clariel's face or shoulders, not even a single drop.

Though it only took them a few minutes to cross the bridge, it felt longer to Clariel, and she was relieved to step off onto a much more strongly built and permanent-looking landing stage of dressed stone. Curiously, the river here was completely still, though the current raged only a foot away. There was a boat tied up there, a small sailing craft, its mast shipped with no sign of sail bags, oars, or any other equipment.

Clariel looked at it, and then at the narrow channel of slack water that followed the side of the island northward. Again, magic must be employed to allow boats to come and go without being taken by the river and then, very swiftly thereafter, the waterfall. So it was possible to leave the island by boat . . .

Tyriel saw her looking and shook his head. Crooking one finger, he pointed to the gate in the white wall ahead. Clariel shrugged and continued on, the gate opening without visible intervention by anyone as they approached.

As she stepped over the threshold, the roar of the waterfall stopped as abruptly as if it had been simply turned off. Clariel rubbed her ear, thinking she'd gone deaf, till she heard the birds calling in the orchard to her left, and Tyriel clearing his throat. She turned to him, but he was facing the wall, his hand raised, a silver ring on his finger catching an errant ray from the setting sun.

Puzzled, Clariel looked around. The place was more pleasant than she'd feared. There was the orchard to her left, heavy with late summer peaches and apricots. A long lawn was divided by a bricked path, with the great fig tree she had glimpsed in the northern section, and a fountain in the south. Beyond that was a small grove of oaks, with a strangely thin and stunted tower set into the perimeter wall beyond.

"This is my granddaughter Clariel," said Tyriel. "She is to be accorded the respect due one of the family and guarded as such. But she is not to cross the bridge, take a boat or a paperwing without my direct permission, or that of the Abhorsen-in-Waiting. Is that understood?"

Clariel had turned to see who the Abhorsen was talking to, since he was still facing the wall. She stepped back instinctively as she saw a shape in the stone, moving under the whitewash, a long blade in its hand. But the sword moved in salute and she saw that it was a sending coming out of the wall, the thousands of Charter marks that outlined it growing brighter as it emerged. Standing before them, the marks dimmed, and the sending took on a more normal appearance, that of a tall man in helmet and long hauberk, a great two-handed sword now resting on his shoulder. He bowed low to the Abhorsen, turned slightly, and bowed again to Clariel, only not so low.

"You will tell the other sendings?" asked Tyriel. "The House lacks for nothing to provide for her comfort?"

The sending nodded in answer to the first question, and shook its head to the second.

"Right," said Tyriel, turning around to clap his hand on Clariel's shoulder. It had more the feel of a man grabbing a dog he was about to instruct than anything familial. "That's settled. You'll be comfortable here, and more important, completely safe. I will visit you as soon as matters allow."

"You're just leaving me here?" asked Clariel. "Are there . . . does anyone else live here?"

"Only the sendings," said Tyriel. "Kargrin's letter said you found the city too busy, you liked solitude—"

"In the Great Forest," protested Clariel. "Of my own choice!"

"I'll send Bel to visit when he's well," said Tyriel. "I will visit myself when the opportunity presents . . . as I said, it will only be for a few months, three maybe . . ."

"Months with you doing nothing to avenge my parents," said Clariel. She could feel the rage rising in her again. It was unbearable to be treated in such a way, to be put somewhere safe without any thought for her own desires and feelings. She took a deep breath and managed to hold it, Tyriel watching her carefully, his sun-wrinkled eyes narrowed.

"Caution is a virtue," he said, as she finally let the breath out, very slowly. "Kilp will pay for his misdeeds in due course, but you must be patient. Read the book on controlling your rage. Rest. Enjoy the gardens, and the fishing. Grieve for your parents."

"I will," said Clariel. "That I will certainly do. But I will not stay here. No matter what you think."

The Abhorsen sighed.

"You will. You might even thank me in time."

He took a step toward the gate then paused, looked at the silver bottle under his arm, and handed it to the sending.

"Take this to the usual place."

The sending took it, with a curious meshing of the Charter marks that limned and defined its fingers with those wreathing the bottle. Tyriel looked at Clariel again, gave her a glance she couldn't decipher, and went out. The sending closed the gate after Tyriel, before striding off quickly toward the house, carrying the bottle at arm's length.

"Where do I go?" called out Clariel. She tried to lift the bar on the gate, as a test. It was stuck fast, so immobile it might as well all be one piece that never moved, even though Clariel had seen it open easily enough a few moments before.

Another sending appeared at her elbow, coalescing out of the path of rosy, faded bricks. This one had the appearance of a cowled figure, only its hands and a shadowed face visible under a dark robe. It appeared human save to close inspection, when the Charter marks that made up its strange skin and even its clothes could be seen.

The sending beckoned, and started toward the blue-painted door of the main house. Clariel looked at the gate and the sky above, then followed wearily.

The house did look comfortable, Clariel thought as she went in. Charter marks for light sparkled in the ceilings, brightening as the day grew dim outside. The sending took her through a hall and up a central stair, and then to a large bedroom that had windows that looked out over the curtain wall to the river. The walls were of painted plaster, in light blue with silver details. There was a fireplace, with no fire set, but it would not be needed for some weeks yet. The large bed had four posts, each beautifully carved with the key motif of the Abhorsens; with a fat feather mattress, as evidenced by a half-escaped goosefeather at the foot. There was a silver washstand in the corner, with a large porcelain basin under two bronze tubes with screw-wheels, which Clariel recognized as one of the relatively new-fangled arrangements for supplying hot water. She was surprised to see this because the Abhorsen's House was otherwise clearly very old.

The sending indicated the basin. Clariel shook her head. She'd just had a bath and had not gotten very dirty or sweaty on the short ride over. The sending gestured again.

"No, thank you," said Clariel. "I'm going to have a look around."

She turned about and went out the door. The sending scurried after her, carefully shutting the door.

The sending stayed at her heels for the next two hours. Clariel found the main hall first, with its floor-to-ceiling stained-glass windows showing shifting scenes of the Wall being built. She watched this for some time, trying to catch the movement in the scenes, but it never happened in the actual pane she was focused on. Needless to say, on close inspection the windows weren't really glass, stained or otherwise, but very complex Charter Magic spells. It was also hard to remember exactly what she'd seen, save the Wall itself.

The hall had a table almost as long as the room, groaning under the weight of silver and gold salt cellars, dishes, jugs, plates, platters, decanters, and other objects. Some of it looked like Dropstone work as far as Clariel could tell, which reminded her of Jaciel and made tears come to her eyes, as well as wonder why her mother had never spoken of the Abhorsen's House. If she had known this was all here she would have set up a forge out on the lawn and never left. But even growing up at Hillfair, she must not have come to the older house. It was as Bel had said. The Abhorsens had abandoned their responsibilities, and with them, this house.

After the hall, Clariel prowled through the kitchen, where a great many sendings all came to attention, stopping in the middle of cooking a dinner for at least a dozen people, which made Clariel worried there would be company after all. Feeling very much in the way, she quickly glanced in the buttery and larder and hurried out again.

She went to the tower next. The ground floor was a library, with floor-to-ceiling shelves all the way around, a table, and what looked to be a very comfortable padded armchair for settling down to serious reading. A cowled sending came out of one of the bookshelves as Clariel entered, bowed low, and gestured at the books all around.

"Um, do you have a copy of *The Fury Within*?" asked Clariel. She wondered what had happened to the copy Gullaine had given her, left somewhere in the Belisaere house. Doubtless it would have been seized by Kilp's people, with all her other things, her mother's gold and silver works, the strongbox with the family gold, the paper records . . .

All gone now. Gone forever.

"I forget the subtitle . . ."

The librarian sending bowed, whisked across the room, and shinnied up the bookshelves almost to the ceiling, more like an insect than a person. It didn't seem to have any feet under its robe. As with the other sendings only its hands were fully visible, and its shadowed face when seen from directly in front. It took a book from the shelf and came back down again.

It was a slightly different edition of *The Fury Within: A Study of the Berserk Rage and Related Matters*. This book was larger and printed on thicker paper with slightly bigger type. Clariel took the volume and she and the sending bowed to each other as she backed out. As she did so, something made a hissing noise behind and below her, the unexpected sound startling Clariel so much she dropped the book, whirled around, and reached for her knife.

A small white cat was sitting in the doorway, twitching his tail, his bright green eyes fixed on Clariel with an unnerving directness. There was a red collar around his neck that gleamed with Charter marks, and a tiny bell that Clariel knew instinctively she never wanted to hear ring.

"And who might you be?" asked the cat.

I think you should be answering that question," said Clariel, edging back into the library. She glanced at the librarian, but it did not appear perturbed by this cat-thing, which was clearly not a cat at all. It had to be a Free Magic creature, though the Charter Magic collar was curious . . .

"Let's see," said the cat. "You're neither the Abhorsen nor the Abhorsen-in-Waiting, not least because they never set foot inside this house if they can help it, but also because you're too young. You remind me a little of . . . Teriel . . . but you can't be his sister, also because you're too young. Did Teriel have a child before—"

"I meant who are *you!*" interrupted Clariel.

The cat drew himself up and puffed out his chest.

"What do you mean? I am Mogget, of course. The one and only Mogget. Though I have had other names."

"What are you?" asked Clariel. "Why don't the sendings . . . do something about you?"

"Why would they?" asked the cat, with a yawn. "I am as much a slave as they are; we are old companions. Only I wasn't made by an Abhorsen, just forced into slavery by one, with a bit of help. It's an ancient tale and new ones are so much more interesting. Like your story. Tell me who you are."

"I am Clariel. Jaciel's daughter. The Abhorsen's granddaughter."

"A pleasure to meet you," said Mogget. "It is awfully dull here, and my collar itches me so. Perhaps you would be kind enough to take it off for a few minutes?"

"I don't think so," said Clariel slowly. The Charter marks on the collar were fading now, sinking back into the red leather, but she thought she had recognized at least one Master mark of binding. The mere fact she couldn't recognize any of the others indicated their power. What's more, the bell was obviously a small version of one of the Abhorsen's necromantic bells. "Why do you say you are a slave?"

"Bound by magic to serve the Abhorsen till the sun grows cold and dies?" asked Mogget sourly. "What else would you call it? If you won't loosen my collar, can you at least fish?"

"What do you do for the Abhorsen?" asked Clariel.

"I asked you first," said Mogget. "Can you fish?"

"Yes," replied Clariel. "What's that got to do with anything?"

"I like fish, fresh-caught," said Mogget. "The sendings rarely give me any. I thought you might—"

"What do you do for the Abhorsen?" repeated Clariel.

"Nothing for the last sixty years or more," said Mogget. "Tyriel, like his predecessor, hardly ever comes here. Spends all his time riding around that ridiculous Hillfair like an idiot, wreaking havoc on the deer. I haven't even been taken outside since Feriniel was the Abhorsen, and she was . . . let's see . . . Tyriel's great-great-uncle's daughter . . ."

"What *did* you do back then?"

"Oh, the usual," said Mogget slyly, his emerald eyes narrowing. "Sage advice, the wisdom of the ages, that sort of thing. Not that many of them listened. What are you doing here?"

"Being imprisoned," said Clariel shortly. "Temporarily, if I have anything to do with it."

"Tell me more," said Mogget encouragingly. He tilted his head in interest, and Clariel had to stop herself from instinctively reaching down to scratch under his chin. As she half extended and then pulled back her hand, Mogget stood up on his hind paws, pink nose sniffing.

"Interesting . . ." he said.

"What?" asked Clariel.

"Oh, the scent of the outside world," said Mogget. "So you're a prisoner?"

"For my own protection, or so I am told," said Clariel. She bent down to pick up the dropped book, keeping a careful eye on Mogget. She was trying to remember where she'd heard the name before, or some part of it . . . and then it came to her. Bel, talking about books in the Abhorsen's House, and someone called "Mog," his voice trailing off with the name incomplete . . .

"Do you know Belatiel?"

"Ah, the delightfully enthusiastic Bel," said Mogget. He was looking at the book, whiskers twitching. "So keen, so unencumbered by experience. Yes. He is one of the few members of the extended family who come here, and even then I think he has to sneak away to do it. You are . . . familiar with Bel?"

"He's a friend of mine, if that's what you mean," said Clariel. "From Belisaere."

"So Belatiel has been in Belisaere," said the cat. "How appropriate. It has been long since I visited the city. Long indeed. So you come from Belisaere."

"Only most immediately, before that I was . . ." said Clariel. Her voice trailed off and she shook her head. "Why am I telling you anything? I can see you're a Free Magic creature."

"But not the first you've met," said Mogget slyly. "Or held, by the faint trace I discern upon your hands. But have no fear! You've seen my collar, proving my . . . *utter* faithfulness to the Charter that binds me. I am but a slave of the Abhorsen, currently your grandfather, and thus by extension of you. You have but to command me and I will obey."

"You will?"

"Possibly," answered Mogget, yawning to show his very sharp white teeth. "It all depends. I do have to obey the Abhorsen and the Abhorsen-in-Waiting, but as neither has given me any orders for such a long time I fear I am out of practice. You could ask me nicely. Promise me a fish."

"You can show me the rest of the house to begin with," said Clariel. "Please."

"If we converse along the way," said Mogget. "That would be acceptable."

He sidled out of the library, tail high.

"I suppose we could," said Clariel cautiously.

As they wandered upstairs she found herself telling Mogget about her life in Estwael, the move to Belisaere, and the events of the last week. But she gave a highly abridged version of her encounter with Aziminil, very light on details, specifically not mentioning her mental conversation with it or how she had let it go.

"I know of Kargrin," said Mogget, as Clariel looked in the armory on the second floor. It was very well-stocked, and perfectly clean, but it had an air of disuse. Everything was just too perfectly put away. As with elsewhere in the House, a sending appeared as soon as Clariel entered, this one gesturing at the racks of swords and the stands of bows and spears with what might almost be construed as a beseeching gesture. Clariel shook her head, though she took note of several weapons of interest. If there was any chance of getting away, she would need to be better equipped. There were complete arrays of armor there too, on stands, including a short shirt of gethre plates that looked like it would fit her.

"What was that about Kargrin?" she asked Mogget as they left. She hadn't been paying attention and he'd said something else about the magister.

"His teacher's the one to watch for," repeated Mogget. "The old witch."

Clariel stopped. "Who?"

"Ader, she calls herself, or did," said Mogget. "But she was Maderael when she was the Abhorsen."

"What!"

"When she was the Abhorsen," said Mogget innocently.

"But . . . she's still alive," said Clariel. "I thought you only got a new Abhorsen when the old one died . . ."

"Ah, the lack of education among you young ones," sighed Mogget. "Abhorsens can abdicate their authority. The trick is fooling . . . convincing someone else to take over."

"You mean she was the Abhorsen before Tyriel?"

Mogget shook his head and gave out a rather alarming caterwaul-like chuckle.

"Oh, no, she was one back again, the Abhorsen before Kariniel, almost a hundred years ago."

Clariel shook her head. "She can't be that old."

"Can't she?" asked Mogget. "Charter Magic can do many things. She was very young when she took the bells, and very young when she gave them back again."

"Why?"

Mogget looked away from her and batted at the air with his paw, as if an errant fly was passing.

"How would I know? I'm just a slave, remember?"

"Look, I don't even want to know this!" protested Clariel. "I don't care who's the Abhorsen now or then or whenever! I just want to go and live my life in the Great Forest and be left alone!"

"Well why don't you?" asked Mogget reasonably.

"I just told you," said Clariel crossly. "Governor Kilp wants me to be a puppet Queen. Gullaine wants me to be some kind of Regent. The Abhorsen wants to keep me out of the way while he dithers about not actually doing something about anything. And I'm a prisoner here!"

Mogget's ears went up, expressing an opinion Clariel interpreted as mild contempt, and padded out of the room. Clariel followed him, treading heavily, and wondered why she'd bothered to tell the creature anything. But he had made her think.

I won't accept my imprisonment here, Clariel thought. I would have escaped the bottle cell in Belisaere even without Kargrin's help, and that really was a prison. Surely I can get out of here as well. And once out, then I can decide what to do myself. Whatever I want to do. Whatever I think must be done.

From the open doorway of the room opposite, evidently another armory or a store of some kind, Mogget gestured with one paw. Clariel frowned, but bent down on one knee. Mogget gestured again, so she leaned forward, close enough for the cat to butt his head against her chin.

"You're thinking of escaping, aren't you?" whispered Mogget.

"No . . ." said Clariel unconvincingly.

"Yes you are," said Mogget.

"If I was I wouldn't tell you!"

"But you should," purred Mogget. "I'm the only one here who might be able to help you."

"Why would you do that?" Clariel whispered back. "Besides, aren't you a slave who has to do what he's told? The Abhorsen told the sending to tell everyone not to let me out."

"I don't take orders from the sendings, and the Abhorsen said nothing to me," said Mogget, very quietly. "In fact, no Abhorsen has told me to do anything for a long time, the consequence being that I have . . . ahem . . . managed to get out of the habit of obeying some of the more general commands of yesteryear."

"What do you get out of it?" asked Clariel again, who had dealt with many tricky merchants over the years in her father's counting house. She had never known someone to offer something for nothing, even if it was something intangible or some future favor that was being stored up just in case and might never be used.

"Amusement," breathed Mogget, his eyes wicked. "I told you it was dull here. Maybe more than that."

Clariel stood up abruptly. Her heel-following sending had drifted closer, she saw, as if it had wanted to hear what Mogget said, and some others had literally come out of the woodwork. One of them was the guard sending from the gate, she noticed, unless there was another one exactly the same with a two-handed sword.

"I'll think about it," she said to Mogget. "What's upstairs?"

"Music room, practice room, Abhorsen's bedroom, and in the tower the upper reading room, study, and observatory," rattled off Mogget. "Roof gardens on either side of the tower. Downstairs is much more interesting. The lower levels. What?"

The last word was addressed to the guard sending with the two-handed sword, who had silently moved closer to the cat and was looking down at him, his face stern.

"Go on then," said Mogget to the guard sending. "Report me. But who to, that's the question, isn't it?"

"Report what?" asked Clariel suspiciously.

"Nothing," said Mogget. "Like I said. You going up?"

Mogget was silent as they took the stairs to the third floor, the two-handed sword sending now accompanying them along with the cowled attendant. Clariel barely glanced in on the third-floor rooms. The music room had a clavichord, zithern, and other instruments; the Abhorsen's bedroom was much fancier than Clariel's; and the bare chamber for weapons practice was only made distinctive by virtue of its floor being three inches deep in pure white sand that was so clean it squeaked when Clariel stood on it.

The tower room on this level was again completely lined with books, but there was also a narrow stair cutting through the shelves, going up higher. Clariel looked up and was about to ascend when she heard the sharp note of a gong being struck below. Mogget immediately whipped around and lit out for the main stairs, crying out, "Dinner!"

"What's up there?" Clariel asked her attendant sending. It bowed, then bent to imitate sitting down, and made scribbling motions with its hand across an imaginary page.

"An office . . . a study?"

The sending bowed, straightened up, and gestured urgently toward the main stairs as the gong rang again.

"I'm expected for dinner?" asked Clariel. The sending bowed and gestured again. Though there was no indication it would try to force her to go downstairs, Clariel still felt it was like a prison warder laying down the law. It was dinnertime, and she must follow the routine of her prison.

A comfortable, perhaps even fascinating prison, but a prison nonetheless.

For now, thought Clariel, and went down to dinner.

She was rather surprised to see that Mogget was seated with her at the table in the hall, the cat-creature sitting on a stool opposite her own place, a quarter of the way down from the thronelike chair at the head of the table, in what appeared to be a measure of Clariel's standing in the family. Not one of the titled Abhorsens, but a close connection.

There was a great deal of food, all of it very good, but after assuaging her initial hunger, she paid it little attention. Unlike Mogget, who ate as if he really was a starved cat and not something else that probably didn't need to eat at all. He certainly didn't need duck in a wine sauce and poached salmon, the latter dish being greeted with yowls of almost unseemly enthusiasm, though Mogget then went on to eat it daintily. The cat-shape was clearly not just a mere outward shell, but extended to behavior as well.

Clariel pushed her plate away, deep in thought about how she could escape the House. Even if she managed this, she would then need to evade everyone searching for her, which would include not only Kilp's people, which essentially meant all the organized forces of the Kingdom; but also the Abhorsen's. And probably the Clayr as well, she thought, who might simply be able to look into the ice and see where she was *going* to be and tell the Abhorsen where to intercept her.

It seemed impossible, but she knew that part of her generally defeated feeling was simply tiredness and reaction to everything that had happened. Surely there would be ways to escape the House. The Abhorsen might even change his mind, or could be helped to change his mind.

There was also the Free Magic creature in the silver bottle. It was here somewhere, in the House. She had freed Aziminil once. Perhaps the creature could help return the favor . . .

She looked over to ask Mogget about where the bottle had been taken, only to see a completely bare salmon dish. The cat-thing, all the fish being eaten, had departed upon some silent mission of his own.

Clariel waited for him to come back, but eventually gave up and, after refusing more offers of various desserts, including one involving ice and apricots that looked delicious, started back upstairs. Halfway up, after briefly considering going farther to look at the study and the observatory in the tower, she instead decided that she really, really needed to go to bed.

Chapter Twenty-Five

GONE FISHING

Clariel slept for sixteen hours. When she woke up, sunshine was streaming through the windows, and her attendant sending—or at least one that looked exactly the same— was standing at the end of the bed holding a towel. There was an odd smell in the room, almost like rotten eggs, which surprised and alarmed Clariel until she realized it came from the steaming hot water that had just come out of the pipe into the basin. It was the same smell as the hot springs that could be found half a day's ride from Estwael, a favored spot for the townfolk to ease aching limbs. Some Abhorsen had worked out how to pipe hot water from just such a spring below the House.

As soon as Clariel got up the sending with the towel ushered her over to the basin and, acting more like a nursemaid trying to bathe an infant than a lady's maid, helped her wash and dress. New clothes had been laid out, new linen underclothes and a light woolen dress in blue, with the silver key motif very faintly woven into the cuffs. The improvised leather slippers from the day before were still there, but had been cleaned. Clariel's knife was laid on top, with a knotted black cord provided as a belt to hang it from.

It was very peaceful, Clariel thought, as she tied the cord around her slim waist and checked the knife moved freely in its scabbard. The sun was shining, she'd had a rejuvenating sleep, and there were wonderful smells of fresh baked bread and cooking bacon coming up the stairs.

Mogget wasn't at breakfast, but even after only a short acquaintance Clariel presumed he'd simply had his earlier rather than skipping it. After Clariel had eaten she went out into the garden. It was warmer outside in the sun, but there was a cool northerly breeze blowing in off the river. She walked around the rose garden, marveling at all the different varieties, most of them in bloom. There were red, white, and yellow roses, and even one so dark purple it looked black from a distance. A black rose would be a suitable flower for the Abhorsens, she thought, a death-flower. Not for Tyriel and his hunters, who it appeared had mostly given up the old ways. A black rose for the old Abhorsens, the ones who often walked in Death.

Clariel thought about that as she walked across the lawn to the grove of oaks. She never really thought much about the sensation she felt when an animal died, it was something she had got used to in the forest. But in Kilp's dining chamber, the deaths there . . . it was the same feeling, but magnified many times.

So she had the Abhorsen's Death sense, inherited along with the berserk fury from the royal side. But all the Abhorsens and the Royal Family were great Charter Mages, and she wasn't, as Kargrin had discovered. She couldn't even begin to understand why Bel, for instance, was so interested in the Charter and felt so much a part of it. Perhaps it was because she was an outsider, and *wanted* to be an outsider.

Clariel put her hand on one of the oaks, feeling the strength of it under her hand. It was old, all the oaks here were old. Hundreds and hundreds of years, growing tall and strong. But like her, they were contained within the white walls . . .

"Heading for the fishing tower? Excellent idea."

Clariel jumped at the sound of Mogget's voice. The cat emerged from behind one of the other oaks and sat near Clariel's foot as if he had been waiting there all morning.

"I wasn't," said Clariel. "But I could. I want to ask you some questions, away from—"

"Away from the cruel cares of deciding what to have for breakfast," interrupted Mogget.

"No, I meant away from the—"

"Repressive number of plates of dry crusty things those sendings put out," interrupted Mogget again. "I trust they're looking after you? That one there can be a bit pushy."

"What?"

Clariel turned around. Her attendant sending, who had silently followed her from the house, was standing two paces behind her back. It bowed, the strange face inscrutable under the cowl.

"Oh, do go away," said Clariel.

It didn't move.

"It won't," said Mogget. "Ordered to watch you. Guard you too, I suppose."

"Will it report what I say to the Abh . . . to my grandfather?"

"Yes," said Mogget. He bent forward and suddenly scratched at the ground, clearing away some leaves and fallen acorns to the bare earth. Then, extending one claw, he scratched something in the dirt. It took Clariel a moment to understand that he was writing something. She knelt down to see it better, and briefly saw the words *Sme cn't read*.

"Ah," said Clariel. She arched her eyebrows and jerked her head back a couple of times, indicating the sending behind her.

"There's a fungus on bread that will make you do that," said Mogget. "I believe it is curable."

Clariel sighed and, holding her hand close to her stomach, pointed with the tip of her forefinger at the sending.

"Oh, yes, I think that does apply to the one in question," said Mogget, scrabbling for a moment in the earth as if he'd spotted a tasty-looking bug, but in fact writing another message in shorthand:

I can shw yu how to gt rid of them.

"I think I'd like to look at the study in the tower," said Clariel. "I have some letters to write."

"After you catch me a fish, surely," said Mogget. "It's easy enough, because of the spelled currents, the fish get drawn in around the southern end of the island. There's a pole and hooks and such in the tower, and a sending will bring worms from the kitchen garden."

"I see," said Clariel, who saw very well that Mogget would answer no questions unless she did catch him a fish. "I'll catch you a fish."

Two hours and three long but slim silver fish that Mogget called "skinnerjacks" later, they were crossing the southern lawn going back to the house when the cat suddenly stopped, ears flicking.

"Someone's coming," he said.

"The Abhorsen?" asked Clariel.

"No," replied the cat. "There would be more sendings coming out. I suspect it is your lover. Belatiel."

"He's *not* my lover," protested Clariel. As the actual catching of fish had only taken up some fifteen minutes of the two hours spent fishing, she had spent a lot of the time talking. Mogget was interested in everything that had happened, though every time Clariel had tried to move on to questioning him about the House and how to get out of it he'd changed the subject, apparently because the sending was listening. But she hadn't mentioned Bel's romantic intentions, so either the cat had read more into what she'd said, or he was just making fun of her.

"Your friend, then," said Mogget, as they turned left and followed the path toward the western gate. "Particular friend."

"He's not a particular . . . oh, never mind," retorted Clariel. She looked down at the cat. He blinked his eyes at her, pretending total innocence. "You just like to stir up trouble, don't you?"

"Not as much when it is so remarkably easy," said Mogget. "Though you do offer slightly more of a challenge than Belatiel."

Clariel hoped the visitor was Bel, because he would be vastly more preferable than Tyriel, or, Charter forbid, Yannael.

The sending with the two-handed sword opened the gate as they walked up, and it *was* Bel. He looked pale and drawn, but better than he had when they'd landed the day before, not least because he was wearing fine clothes, similar to the outfit Clariel had seen him in when they first met at the Academy. He smiled as he saw Clariel, a full-hearted smile, which retreated somewhat when Mogget slunk out from behind her legs.

"Clariel! And Mogget . . ."

"Hello, Bel," said Clariel. Mogget merely winked and tilted his head to look at the fish Clariel held by a string through their open mouths. His pink tongue protruded just a fraction as if he couldn't quite hold it back.

"I see you have met Mogget," said Bel. "And he's talked you into fishing for him already."

"She volunteered," said Mogget. "You look sick."

"I was wounded," said Bel. "Clariel saved my life."

Mogget looked up at Clariel, emerald eyes inscrutable.

"You didn't tell me that."

"Twice, really," said Bel eagerly. "First from the crossbow bolt, then she stopped a Free Magic creature that was about to kill me."

"Stopped a Free Magic creature?" asked Mogget. His eyes gleamed in sudden interest. "Fascinating. I wondered how you came to be . . . that is, I understood you are not much of a Charter Mage, as such . . ."

"I held its feet," said Clariel, uncomfortably. "They were like blades . . . anyway, what am I supposed to do with this fish? And what are you doing here, Bel?"

She did not notice Mogget's eyes widen as she spoke, or the

calculating glint that came into them.

"I came to see you, of course," said Bel, as if there could be no question that he would do so at the first opportunity. "I would have come earlier this morning, but ah, I didn't think the Abhorsen would . . . um . . . make you stay here and no one would tell me where you were. I had to go and ask Tyriel himself, which, let me tell you, wasn't easy. I had to submit to a lecture about flying low over horses and dogs."

"Well, here I am," said Clariel. "A prisoner again, as I foretold."

"He told me it's for your safety," said Bel awkwardly. "But it shouldn't be for very long, only until Kilp is dealt with—"

"And how soon is that going to be?" asked Clariel bitterly. "Tyriel isn't going to do anything. Not with the Summer's End Hunt to get through first, and who knows what else he thinks is more important."

"He says the King is safe enough in the Palace," said Bel awkwardly. "And he doesn't take Kilp seriously anyway. I'm sorry, all right?"

"Sorry for what?"

"For not flying you to Estwael like you asked," said Bel. "Though I guess with your aunt being arrested there—"

"What!"

"Maybe not arrested exactly—being taken to Belisaere for her own safety," said Bel quickly. "Didn't the Abhorsen tell you?"

"No."

"Maybe he only found out this morning. There have been so many message-hawks flying back and forth all the pigeons have fled Hillfair . . ."

"She was arrested by Kilp?"

"On the orders of the Governor," confirmed Bel. "The story being that her safety was at risk, with the 'rebels' threatening Queen Jaciel . . . there's still no public sighting of her by the way . . ."

"There won't be. She's dead," said Clariel, stony-faced.

"You can't be absolutely sure of that," said Bel awkwardly.

"The Abhorsen could, though. He can go into Death can't he?"

"Yes," admitted Bel. "But it wouldn't be that easy to find out. If she was killed at the dinner then she would have long since passed the Ninth Gate. So it would be a matter of questioning certain . . . things . . . that lurk in the Precincts between, maybe even go as far as the Sixth or Seventh Gate. Tyriel would never do that. Risky even for a practiced Abhorsen."

"You mean he wouldn't get off his horse long enough to do something useful!"

"It isn't just that," said Mogget. He had found a dandelion and was intent on delicately removing each petal with a single outthrust claw. "He's afraid of Death, afraid of being the Abhorsen. That's why he never comes here, because everything reminds him of what he's meant to be. Out hunting, he can forget."

"What?" asked Clariel. "That can't be true . . ."

Her voice faltered, because she could see from Bel's face that he shared Mogget's opinion. The Abhorsen *was* afraid of Death, and was shirking his responsibilities.

"He's a coward?" asked Clariel. That would explain why he was so slow even planning to take action against Kilp . . .

Bel shook his head.

"No . . . he's as brave as anyone in the hunt, braver. He'll ride anything, face down a boar or a bear . . . but he won't do anything the Abhorsen is supposed to do. Nor will Yannael. I guess they've been able to avoid it, because nothing has threatened them or the Kingdom. Tyriel's been the Abhorsen for nearly fifty years and I doubt he's ever been called to deal with anything. So he has been able to forget it all and devote himself to hunting. That's why I've been training myself, so there *is* a proper Abhorsen when one is needed."

"I thought it was just an overly developed case of curiosity," said Mogget. "The kind that kills cats. Myself excepted, of course."

"I wondered why he would just throw me in here and leave," said Clariel. "But do you think this means he *won't* go and help the King at all?"

"I don't know," said Bel. He looked wretched, as if he was personally letting down the King. "I think he will eventually, because it's not really Abhorsen business, I mean not to do with Death, or the Dead, or anything like that. But the hunt takes up all his mind, and until the Summer's End Hunt is done . . . nothing will even be got ready."

"Is the King really safe in the palace?" asked Clariel. "Kilp has a lot more guards. A lot more."

Bel shrugged unhappily. "I don't know."

"What about Princess Tathiel? Any signs of her showing up?"

"Not that I know of," said Bel. "What are you laughing at, Mogget?"

Clariel had never seen a cat laugh before, and wouldn't have known that's what it was if Bel hadn't spoken. She thought Mogget was preparing to throw up a fur ball, since his shoulders were shaking, his eyes were closed, and he was making a kind of rasping noise in his throat. He continued for a few seconds after Bel spoke, then said with dignity, "I find many things amusing. Abhorsens who are afraid of Death, Princesses who shirk their inheritance . . . it's all quite funny."

"I don't think so," said Clariel. She balled her right hand into a fist and slapped it against the open palm of her left, making a very satisfactory thudding noise. "If I was . . . if I was either the Abhorsen or the Princess, I'd just get on with doing my job."

"Would you?" asked Mogget. "What is your 'job' then?"

Clariel didn't know how to answer that, at least not immediately. When her parents had been killed she had lost her clear and obvious place in the world, but it had been a place she had intended to leave behind anyway.

"I am a hunter," she said slowly. "I belong in the Great Forest. It's the only place where things make sense to me . . . where I make sense. But perhaps that's only what I want to be, and I must become something else instead."

"You'll get to the forest," said Bel encouragingly. "I mean, it may be a while, but I'm sure Kilp will be defeated, and then everything will go back to normal. Like I said, I'll fly you to Estwael—"

"How can you be so sure Kilp will be defeated?" demanded Clariel. She stepped close to Bel, her eyes angry. "No one's doing anything! What about Aunt Lemmin? If they . . . she's just an herbalist, she's kind and wise and she always looked out for me . . . they'll put her in a hole like they did to me, or worse! *Someone* has to do something!"

"Don't get angry," pleaded Bel. He took a step backward, making calming gestures with his hands.

"I'm not going berserk," said Clariel, through gritted teeth. "I can control the rage."

"She's got a book about it," said Mogget helpfully. "Mind you, you should have seen the berserk that wrote it. Huge she was, and if the sendings didn't bring her wine fast enough, she'd pick them up and snap them in half and throw the pieces on the floor."

"How do you snap a sending in half?" asked Bel, easily distracted by some knowledge even more arcane than usual.

"When fully manifested, they are solid, as are their accoutrements," said Mogget. "They may be attacked, torn apart, broken up. If properly made they can be put back together, some can even re-form themselves. It's all covered in *Simple Sendings*, I think—"

"How interesting," said Clariel. "I'm going to leave you two to your lesson. Mogget, I want to talk to you later."

"Clariel! No, wait, I came to see you," said Bel hastily. "I can't stay, Tyriel told me I mustn't—"

"Go then," said Clariel. She had spoken truly about not going berserk, but she was angry. Not with Bel, but with her grandfather, and the King, with all the useless people that had let things get so out of control that her parents could be *killed*, and an innocent like her aunt Lemmin could be swept up, taken away from her home . . .

Clariel stopped in mid-stride, so quickly that Bel, starting after her, almost ran into her back.

"Kilp must want Aunt Lemmin as a hostage," she said. "To make me go back to the city."

"Very likely," said Mogget. "I am interested in this Kilp fellow. Few Governors of Belisaere have had much intelligence, by any measure. Um, perhaps if you could just leave me those fish?"

"Do you know when she was arrested?" asked Clariel. She was thinking about where her aunt might be. If Kilp had sent the order for her arrest the night Jaciel and Harven had been killed, then Lemmin might already be in Belisaere, already in a prison hole.

"No. I suppose I could find out," said Bel. "But there's nothing you can do for her anyway, Clariel. I'm sorry you're stuck here, but there are worse places . . ."

His voice trailed off as he saw Clariel give him a look similar to the one the chief cook at Hillfair used when confronted by a joint of meat that had become seriously maggot-struck.

"Please do find out," she said coldly. She looked at Mogget and threw down the fish. "And tell my grandfather that even if he isn't going to do anything, I *am*."

"But you *can't* do anything," called out Bel, to her rapidly retreating back. "Look, I'll ask him, I really will. I'll be back tomorrow, maybe we can work out something . . ."

Clariel did not reply. She stalked into the house, went to her room to get *The Fury Within*, and stomped up the stairs to the west roof garden. Unlike the one in her parents' house in Belisaere, this garden had green plants. Mostly white rowans in large terra-cotta pots but also some smaller shrubs she didn't know, with broad green leaves and tiny yellow flowers.

The garden offered a great vista over the river to the hills beyond, only slightly marred in Clariel's opinion by the roofs and towers of Hillfair when she looked to the north. Ignoring that side, she resolutely dragged the comfortable bench with its blue and silver cushions around to face the south, toward the mist-cloud of the waterfall, opened her book, and began to read.

She paid careful attention to the instructions in the tome. It had already helped her a little, and she was determined to learn more. The rage frightened her, and Clariel knew she must bring it under control. The book said it was possible to raise it when she willed, and dismiss it in such a way that she was not left so exhausted. But it was not as simple as just reading how to do it. The book offered techniques, things to practice, ways of thinking. But it would take time, and work, and strength of will.

The sendings brought lunch to Clariel when she did not answer to the repeated gongs or the increasingly broad gestures of her attendant sending. It was composed of one of the fish she had caught, evidently rescued from Mogget. This had been grilled with ginger, pepper, and some spice she didn't know, set atop a salad of grains and greenleaf, accompanied by a lightly sparkling clear wine she had to admit was delicious and refreshing.

Reading in the roof garden was also relaxing, but she refused to let either lunch or the pleasant surroundings lessen her fixed decision that she had to get out of the Abhorsen's House.

It was clear that no useful help would be forthcoming for the King. No one would be going to rescue Aunt Lemmin. Kilp would just get away with what he was doing.

Someone had to do something.

I have to do something, thought Clariel.

She put the book down and walked over to look down at the river roaring past; and then switched her gaze over to the northwest, in the rough direction of the far-off Estwael. As always, the call to the Great Forest was strong in her heart. She yearned to be there, but it was farther away from her than ever.

The Abhorsen wasn't go to do anything. Aunt Lemmin was in danger. Aronzo would certainly treat her badly and she couldn't bear that thought. Kilp might also be able to capture the palace and the King.

But even presuming Clariel could get out of the Abhorsen's House, what could she do on her own? She wasn't a powerful Charter Mage, not a Charter Mage at all really. The fury, presuming she could govern it better, did offer something if it came to fighting a few foes—but she would not be fighting a few foes.

Bel's words rankled, though she had to acknowledge there was some truth in them.

But there's nothing you can do.

Truth, but not entire.

There *was* a power she could wield. It had been on her mind ever since the Islet, a slight, gnawing thing that wouldn't go away. It had been reinforced by the sight of that silver bottle in the paperwing, the bottle under Tyriel's arm, the bottle that was somewhere in the House even now.

There was power there to rescue Aunt Lemmin; power to wreak her revenge upon Kilp and Aronzo; power to set the Kingdom to rights.

Only then could she go to the Great Forest, free of all cares . . .

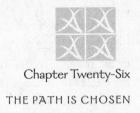

Clariel had almost given up on Mogget by the late after-noon, but he popped up around her feet just as she was closing *The Fury Within*, having read it to the final page. She was thinking deeply about all the things it had told her, of the nature of being a berserk, so she started in surprise when the cat wound himself around her legs.

"You wanted to see me?" he said, with a flick of his ears at the ever-present sending who stood silently behind Clariel's shoulder.

"I did," said Clariel. "You took your time."

"You were so busy reading I didn't want to disturb you. Educational, I trust?"

"I hope so," said Clariel. "But the more I learn the more I find I need to learn."

"Then there is hope for you yet," said the cat. "I believe you wanted to see the Abhorsen's study?"

Clariel saw the glint in Mogget's eye and correctly deduced this was part of his plan to get rid of the eavesdropping sending.

"I would," she said. "If I am allowed."

"I am a great believer that anything not expressly forbidden is explicitly allowed," said Mogget. "What did your grandfather tell the sendings when you first arrived?"

Clariel thought for a moment.

"I think he said I should be treated as his granddaughter and guarded, but not to be allowed to cross the bridge, step into a boat or a paperwing," she said.

"The sendings are very literal," said Mogget. "Hmm . . . 'Not allowed to cross the *bridge*, use a *boat* or *paperwing*.' That was rather lax of Tyriel. I suppose I shouldn't be surprised at his ignorance. Follow me."

Clariel followed the cat into the tower reading room and then up the narrow staircase. The study above was also lined with shelves and many books, but Clariel's attention was immediately drawn to the one glassed-in cabinet set among them, home to a single book bound in pale green leather with silver clasps. It was as if the book were watching her, as much as she was watching it.

Mogget saw her staring.

"*The Book of the Dead*," he said. "Best left alone."

"I am an Abhorsen," said Clariel. She remembered Bel talking about this book, how it contained the knowledge the Abhorsens needed to enter Death and return, how to wield their seven bells to bind and command the Dead. She found the book weirdly fascinating, though she had no particular interest in the Abhorsen's peculiar kind of necromancy.

The book itself was fascinating. She felt like she was watching an animal, waiting to see where it would spring, being on guard in case it attacked but also tensed to pursue if it fled. "Doesn't that give me the right to read it?"

"No," said Mogget. "You're one of the family, sure enough, but only the Abhorsen or the Abhorsen-in-Waiting can read that particular book."

"Bel told me he read it," said Clariel. "And he thought Yannael hadn't, maybe even Tyriel had never read it."

"Like I said," replied Mogget.

"What?" asked Clariel.

"People seem to have got confused about who's who and what's what since I last got let out of this house," said Mogget, which didn't help Clariel at all. "Now, you wanted writing materials, I believe?"

"Um, yes," said Clariel. She was still thinking about what the cat had said. "But everyone calls Yannael the Abhorsen-in-Waiting . . . you mean she isn't?"

"Everything you need is on the desk," said Mogget. "Be *very* careful you don't spill the ink."

Clariel looked at the massive redwood desk. Each corner of the tabletop was adorned with intricately carved dragon heads. The dragons all had individual expressions; she could see the character of each of them: melancholy, angry, happy, and a fourth had its eyes closed, apparently asleep.

For the first time she wondered if dragons had once really existed. These seemed modeled from life. In the middle of the dragon table there was a silver inkwell, very finely made and old, accompanied by several quill pens, a knife to cut them, a sheaf of paper, and a blotter made from the dried sponge she had last seen in quantity, wet, in the fish market of Belisaere.

She pushed one of the high-backed chairs aside and bent down to cut a pen. Inking it, she held it above the paper, while Mogget watched from a safe distance on the other side of the table.

"Oh no, you've got ink on your hand," he said, though she didn't, or at least didn't yet. "Best ask your sending for a wet cloth. Actually a wet cloth and a dry one, and perhaps a small bottle of spirits of hartshorn; that ink is very difficult to shift."

Clariel spilled some ink on her hand, turned to the sending, and repeated Mogget's request. The sending bowed, and drifted out of the room. As soon as it was gone, Mogget leaped over to Clariel and began to whisper, his whiskers quivering because he was talking so fast.

"That'll only get us a few minutes. The ordinary ones aren't very smart, but if it runs into one of the superior sendings it'll be here in an instant. Do you still want to escape from the house?"

"Yes," said Clariel. "But that's not all."

"What else?" asked Mogget.

"I want to know where the silver bottle Tyriel brought has been taken."

"Ah-ha!" cried Mogget. "I knew it. I smelt it on you, the lovely tang of Free Magic, and not just because you're a berserk. Things come together, paths converge—"

"What do you mean?"

"When you held the creature, as Bel says you did, did it tell you its name?" asked Mogget.

"Yes," said Clariel. "Aziminil."

Mogget's eyes widened and his mouth curled up in a smile. He got up and circled around three times, tail almost whisking across Clariel's face.

"Aziminil, Ziminil, Zimminy-Az," he said. "Caught in Belisaere, you say. And now Az is here, and not *completely* put away, and so are you, and you're a berserk and you want to get out when bridge, boat, and paperwing are barred against you."

"What are you talking about?" demanded Clariel. "Quickly!"

Mogget stopped his circling.

"What I mean is that while there are more ways to leave this house than you might think, there is only one way for *you* to leave this house that offers a reasonable chance of success, not to mention survival," he said. "It requires the . . . assistance . . . of a Free Magic creature. But how to do this? Charter Mages can only bind such creatures, they cannot make use of them. But you are a berserk, the Free Magic is strong inside you. Tell me, did Aziminil submit to you when you first met?"

"Something like that," said Clariel. "She—"

"She?" asked Mogget. "Clever Aziminil. Go on."

"She tried to enter my mind . . . to bend me to her will. But I went into *her* mind, and forced her to obey *me*. Then Kargrin speared her and she would have been trapped, so I . . . I let her go."

"You let her go," chuckled Mogget. "Let her go. Ah, there *is* more than mischief to be gained here. Were you in the rage when she surrendered herself to you?"

"Yes," said Clariel. "How can Aziminil help me escape? Where is she?"

"She is down below, where the Abhorsens take their captives and hold them close. She ought to be sunk deeper still, but the sendings only take the prisoners so far. Tyriel should have finished the job, put the bottle out with the rest, but he's shirked it, as so much else."

"How do I use Aziminil to escape?" asked Clariel. "And how can I make sure she doesn't kill me, or . . . do whatever Free Magic creatures do to people?"

"Summon the rage, bend her to your will," said Mogget. "As for your escape, if Aziminil is strong enough she can become a vessel to take you out through the waterfall."

"Out through the *waterfall*?" asked Clariel.

"Yes, indeed," said Mogget. "Az will know how, but it will be a question of strength, for the waterfall is mighty indeed. Aziminil alone may not suffice, you could need more than one of the prisoners to take you through. But one or two or three, *you* can command them. You have the power within you, fueled by your rage."

"Only for a short time," said Clariel. "What happens afterward, when I am weak?"

"Have them swear when you first hold them in your sway," said Mogget, his eyes alight, his claws out. "You can fix them then, make them serve you no matter whether you are weak or not, awake or not, unconscious . . ."

"There is no way they can turn against me?" asked Clariel.

"Any bond will weaken over time," said Mogget. "But it can be made anew."

"I have always heard it said that Free Magic creatures are inimical to life," said Clariel. She was excited by the prospect of freedom, but cautious too. "What exactly does that mean?"

Mogget did not answer immediately, choosing instead to lick one of his paws with intense interest.

"Mogget! What does it mean, that Free Magic creatures are inimical to life?"

"Bah! An exaggeration," said Mogget. He hesitated for a moment, twisting his neck as if his collar had caught on something, before adding more quietly, "I suppose it is true that their substance, the manifestation of their flesh, is corrosive to living things. But it can be contained, avoided, taken care of in numerous ways. Why, the Abhorsens use a kind of Free Magic all the time, in their bells and spells in Death. They used to use it more freely still. You would be no different."

Clariel nodded. She'd been wondering how Kilp and Aronzo had survived if Aziminil really was so dangerous. They hadn't even bound her to their service, she had just agreed to serve them. That didn't sound like a creature "inimical" to all life.

Against that, though, she had to balance the fact that her mother had died fighting against the very idea of working with a Free Magic creature. Jaciel had even slain one before who had assumed the shape of her brother. But then, Clariel thought, Jaciel was not like other people. She never compromised, she would not depart from her chosen path, no matter what. Perhaps if she had talked to Kilp, taken the more sensible approach, then she would still be alive, and Harven too, and Clariel would be on her way to Estwael . . .

Clariel shook her head. There was no point in thinking over might-have-beens. She had to work out what to do now, deal with the situation as it was.

"If a Free Magic creature's touch is corrosive, how can Aziminil take me through the waterfall?"

"The swift water will lessen the effect," said Mogget.

"Lessen?" asked Clariel. "That doesn't sound very good. Is there anything else I can do? I remember Kargrin said something about the

Abhorsens having special robes . . ."

Again, Mogget was slow to answer. It looked to Clariel as if he was struggling with a desire not to answer at all, or perhaps to lie. Even though he was a cat, she'd seen merchants behave similarly, shifting where they looked, hunching their shoulders, even nervously clawing at their collars, as Mogget was doing . . .

"There are garments, robes, masks, and suchlike that provide protection for a time," said Mogget. "For when the Abhorsens used to deal more closely with their prisoners. There should be some such stuff below."

"Should be?" asked Clariel. "I'm not risking a 'should be.' And what does 'for a time' mean?"

"They are there," said Mogget grumpily. "Old, but serviceable. I presume you would not be able to renew the marks within them?"

"No," said Clariel shortly.

"Then once put in use, they will fail at the next full moon."

"Which is in about five days, I think," said Clariel, counting on her fingers. There had been a half moon when she slept in the forest, the night before last. "Not long. If Aziminil can take me through a waterfall, can she also move me swiftly? To fly like a paperwing or become some sort of mount? I need to be in Belisaere as soon as I can. I have to rescue my aunt. And kill Kilp and Aronzo."

"Free Magic can shape itself to almost any need," said Mogget. "Swift travel, unseen passage, impenetrable armor, unbreakable weapons . . . it will all be at your command. You simply will whatever is needful."

Clariel thought of that, for a moment. Sorcery that did not need laboriously memorized Charter marks, learned over years, or the disorienting plunge into the Charter . . . simply to will something, to use raw power. It was a heady temptation. But she must be careful . . .

"What if I need to imprison Aziminil again," said Clariel. "I can't do it with Charter Magic, I do not have the skill or knowledge. Could I force her into a bottle and secure it just by the force of my will?"

"You could," said Mogget. "As I said, I can tell you have the strength. You remind me of some of the earlier Abhorsens, who had much to do with Free Magic entities."

"You remind me of one of mother's apprentices," said Clariel. "All flattery and guile. You said you would help me for love of mischief, and maybe more . . . and I see you think it is more. What do you hope to gain?"

"Freedom," whispered Mogget. "Freedom from my enslavement."

"You mean you want me to take your collar off?"

"Only the Abhorsen can remove my collar," said Mogget. "And the Abhorsen has the means to put it back on again. I need some greater manumission."

"So how will you helping me forward your ambition?"

"A small stone cast from a hilltop may dislodge larger stones," said Mogget with a sly glance. "And the larger stones may move great . . . stones . . . and then the whole hillside might come tumbling down."

"What does that mean?" asked Clariel.

"That things change, and an opportunity might present itself that otherwise would not," said Mogget, his tail twisting around almost as much as his words.

"And what would you do with your freedom?" asked Clariel.

"Who can say?" replied Mogget evasively. "But I would no longer be a prisoner, no longer a slave. I think you understand that, do you not?"

"Perhaps," said Clariel. "But I am not sure I should think of you as I would a person enslaved."

"Why not?" asked the affronted cat. "Am I a piece of furniture? A block of wood?"

"I do need your help," said Clariel. "But I won't do anything actively to release you. There must be a reason you are bound to serve the Abhorsens."

"Reasons can always be found to bind a slave," said Mogget sulkily. He turned away to plonk down in the middle of the table, addressing Clariel over his shoulder. "You have found some for yourself, after all."

"I suppose I have," whispered Clariel. She was thinking about that, and what she might do with Aziminil after she had freed Aunt Lemmin and set matters to rights. The creature had been in Belisaere for months without killing people and causing trouble, surely there would be some way to set her free, somewhere she could exist without being hunted by Charter Mages and at the same time, offer no threat to ordinary people?

"Where is—" Clariel started to ask Mogget, but she stopped as the cowled sending stepped off the top of the stair and slid over to her side, offering several cloths, a dish of water, and a small bottle of hartshorn.

Clariel scrubbed slowly at her hands and wondered how she could distract the sending again. But as she scrubbed, Mogget got up and came over to her, and jumped into her lap. She flinched, but he felt just like any normal cat, even to the extent of him shifting around to get comfortable, not bothering that his claws were doing the precise opposite to Clariel.

When he was settled, Mogget leaned forward and dipped one extended claw in the inkwell. Then he wrote on the paper, in very small, perfectly formed letters.

You must act soon in case Tyriel does recall his duty and put Aziminil under the waterfall. Tonight is best, at midnight. I will distract sendings first and meet you in kitchen store, we go down from there.

Clariel read over his shoulder as the cat wrote. He hesitated at the end, and she felt him wriggle, as if struggling with something. The marks on his collar grew brighter, some spell there coming to the fore. Mogget hissed, and then wrote again, the marks growing brighter still as he did so:

> *Garments not whole protection. You must remember to order*
> *Aziminil not to touch you and—*

With that last word, Mogget yowled and sprang out of Clariel's lap as if he had been singed on the tail. Rampaging across the table, he overset the ink. A great tide of it spread across the paper, blacking out his words. Trailing inky paw-prints, he leaped from the table and shot down the stairs.

Clariel watched the cat go, over the back of the sending who had bent to mop up the spilled ink. She almost got up, but stayed where she was and thought for a moment. It was always advisable when going into the wilds to let someone know your intentions, the path you planned to take . . .

She took up a piece of paper that was only marbled at the edges with ink, cut a new quill, and used the last of the ink in the well to write a short note to Bel. If things went wrong, then he would know what she had done, and why, and perhaps might be able to do something about it.

> *Bel,*
>
> *I am going to release the Free Magic creature we fought on the Islet and with its help escape from here and go to Belisaere. There I hope to rescue my aunt Lemmin. If the creature proves powerful enough, I will use it to slay Kilp and Aronzo and end their rebellion. They are guilty of murder and treason, and deserve no better.*

I almost bound the creature before on the Islet, and I ~~think~~ am
sure I can do so again. Its name is Aziminil. Mogget says there are
special robes I can wear to avoid the corruption of flesh or whatever it
is such creatures do. I don't suppose my actions will spur my grand-
father into doing anything, but if I should fail, I call on you to do
what you can for my aunt Lemmin and also to ensure justice is done.
I am sorry I was cross with you today, you don't deserve it.

    Your friend,

She signed it simply with her name, absently almost added an
"X" for a kiss but didn't, folded it twice, wrote *Bel* on the outside,
and put it in the middle of the desk.

"Leave this here, but tell Belatiel about it tomorrow," she said.
The sending paused in its ink-cleaning duties to bow, indicating it
understood.

"Not when he arrives, when he is about to leave," Clariel added
cautiously. Even a few hours might make a difference, and doubtless
it would be better not to leave a note at all.

But she felt two conflicting emotions battling inside her. One was
all excitement, bursting to get going. To finally do something, to act
of her own volition, rather than being forced into doing what her parents wanted, and then being a prisoner of Kilp, and now effectively a
prisoner of Tyriel. But against that excited, pent-up feeling there was
a much quieter, more sober voice that warned that she might be doing
something stupid. That it was not always better to do something than
nothing. Hunting sometimes required stillness and waiting.

But this small voice was no match for the excitement Clariel felt
rising inside her. She had read *The Fury Within*. She knew how to
raise the berserk anger that would fuel her domination of Aziminil.
She knew where the Free Magic creature was, and that it could not
only help her escape, but speed her to Belisaere.

Finally she would be a hunter again, rather than the hunted.

Chapter Twenty-Seven

INTO THE WATERFALL

After dinner, which she ate in the hall alone, save for numerous sendings, Clariel went to the armory. The sending there once again offered her armor and weapons; this time she accepted them, taking the shirt of gethre plates, which fit quite well over the jerkin she had been given at Hillfair, though it was shorter, hanging only an inch below her hips; and also a short, broad-bladed sword similar to her old falchion.

The sword had Charter marks on the blade, but fewer than some of the other weapons, and she was eventually able to puzzle out that they were relatively straightforward marks for durability and resistance to rust. She did not want a weapon that bore marks she did not understand. For some reason the marks were harder to identify than usual; it seemed to her that they would not stay still. Charter marks always moved and shimmered, but usually they would slow or even freeze for a few seconds when someone was looking at them.

Apart from armor and sword, she discovered a good woolen cloak and a large belt pouch in her room. She filled the pouch with several not-quite-ripe apricots taken from the dinner table, and rolled the cloak up so she could wear it by its cord over her shoulder.

Her attendant sending watched these preparations, but as far as Clariel could tell was not alarmed by them, which was heartening. It seemed likely to Clariel that with an absent Abhorsen all they could really do was watch and report later, though she supposed the superior ones might be able to send messages to Hillfair. But then, if what Mogget and Bel thought about Tyriel was accurate, he would be very slow to do anything that required him to come to the House.

Waiting until midnight was difficult. There was a clock in her room, which had surprised her at first, because she expected one of the Charter Magic time crystals rather than something mechanical like you would find in Belisaere. But on closer inspection she saw that the case contained no clockwork, but instead a kind of Charter Magic imitation of cogs and wheels and chains, driving hands of gold and silver on a face of ivory, the chapters detailed in tiny pieces of jet.

Clariel had been interested in clocks at one time. There were several clockmakers in Estwael and Jaciel had worked with one of them on and off over the years. This timepiece was silent; for all its magical mimicking of clockwork it did not reproduce that comforting, regular sound, so reminiscent of a heartbeat.

Clariel shut the case and went to sit on her bed. She felt nervous and excited, but she forced herself to be calm. Once again she opened *The Fury Within* and read over the chapter on raising the rage, trying not to look at the clock at the end of every page.

The moon climbed higher as she waited, its cool light through her window competing with the warm glow of the Charter mark lanterns. Clariel left her bed to look out, the world outside stark and moon-blue, the river silver. Soon she would be out in that world again, Clariel thought, looking at the clock. She wondered what Mogget would do to divert the sendings, and forced herself to sit back on the bed and read her book.

At five minutes to twelve, she started to suspect Mogget had forgotten, or worse, had betrayed her. At one minute to twelve, she was sure of it, and cursed herself for even thinking for a moment the cat-creature would help her escape.

Then the clock's minute hand moved to the twelve. There was a sudden deep roar outside, akin to the sound of a tea ceremony spirit burner lighting up, but many times louder. The cool moonlight through the window became charged with red, a lurid red that flickered, the light of some sudden, enormous fire.

Clariel ran to the window and looked out. There was a growing cloud of smoke billowing up toward her from the orchard, where three peach trees were alight from root to crown. Sendings were already rushing in, one with an axe chopping at a fiercely burning tree, the others raking back leaves and other litter that might burn.

"Go help them!" ordered Clariel to her sending servant. Without waiting to see what it did, she took up her sword, ran down the main staircase three steps at a time, and dashed to the storeroom next to the kitchen.

Mogget was already there, his white hair slightly blackened and his whiskers perhaps shorter than they used to be. He stood on a trap-door at the rear of the storeroom, between shelves stacked high with hundreds of jars of preserved apricots and peaches.

"Quick, open this!"

The cat leaped aside as Clariel bent down and pulled on the ring. The trapdoor opened easily, revealing stone steps descending into darkness, a darkness only slightly relieved by the Charter marks slowly coming to life on the rough-hewn walls.

"Go!" yowled Mogget, himself streaking down the steps. "Shut the door behind you!"

Clariel obeyed, almost hurling herself into the narrow stairwell. As she turned back to shut the trapdoor, she saw sendings coming out of the shelves, sendings in armor with swords and axes, their faces grim.

"Come on!"

Clariel ran down the steps after the cat. The stair curved around as they descended, not a tight circular stairway but a gentle slice of a circle. Almost before she knew it they passed the first small land-ing and a door reinforced with iron bolts and considerable Charter Magic, marks briefly flaring as they passed.

"How far down?" gasped Clariel. "Will the sendings chase us?"

"Sixth landing," said Mogget. "The ones above won't follow, but there are more sendings below. They should be slow without the Abhorsen to direct them. Sleepy. Speed is of the essence."

Steps and landings flashed by. As they passed the fifth landing, Clariel shivered, for it was frosted with ice and a cold wind blew around it, apparently from nowhere. Then it was behind her, more steps taken at a run. Suddenly Mogget slowed in front of her and stopped before another iron-reinforced door that was also swimming in Charter marks. This one, at least, was not covered in ice.

"Here's the test," he said. "I hope the spell knows you as family, and that is enough. It may need more, but we shall see. Put your hand against it."

Clariel looked at the swirling marks on the door nervously. She didn't know any of them, and all the stories of people burned from the inside out, or turned to sand, or rendered senseless forever from mishandling Charter Magic came back to her.

"Put your hand against it," repeated Mogget. "Quickly! There is little time."

Clariel slowly extended her hand and set her palm against the timber. Sparks flashed as she did so, and Charter marks thronged from the wood and moved up her arm. She gasped, but there was no real pain, just a strange sensation, as if something was moving over her skin.

The door did not move.

"Lean your forehead against it!" urged Mogget, who was now dancing around Clariel's feet. "Tell it open, in your grandfather's name!"

Clariel did so, pressing the Charter mark on her forehead against one of the iron bolts that reinforced the door. Again, she felt the weird, crawly sensation, this time extending all over her face.

"Open in the name of Tyriel, my mother's father! Open!" she said, her voice not as steady as she wished.

There was a resonant click inside the door, and it moved under Clariel's hand and head. She put her other hand against it, and pushed. It moved slowly, like a person who has reluctantly agreed to something but wishes they had done otherwise.

As the door opened, Clariel was assaulted by an incredibly loud noise, so loud it felt almost like a physical blow. The sound of the great waterfall. Kept from the house by magic up above, it was even louder here than it had been going across the bridge in the river. The reason was clear, for a broad cavern in the cliff face lay beyond the door and the far end of it was a gaping hole, with a wall of white water plummeting down outside. Spray was blowing in, making rainbows as it passed across the Charter marks for light that shone in the ceiling and walls of the cavern.

The rough-hewn chamber was empty, save for a massive table in the very center, itself carved out of the rock. One end of this hulking piece of furniture was crowded with several dozen green glass bottles, of differing shapes and sizes, and next to these bottles was a pyramid made of an equivalent number of silver stoppers, a coil of thick gold wire on a decaying wooden drum, a rusted pair of pliers and several other lumps of rust that had once been tools.

At the other end of the table, standing alone, there was the familiar silver bottle wreathed in gold wire that held Aziminil.

Clariel walked toward the table, the door shutting behind her. She reached out for the silver bottle, almost in a trance, but stopped short of it as a cloud of spray hit her in the face. She blinked, and stepped back. Mogget sneezed and stayed behind her heels in an effort to avoid any drop of moisture.

Beyond the table, she saw a jagged, narrow peninsula of stone that thrust out into the waterfall. Barely three paces wide, it was at least twenty paces long, the far end invisible under the onrush of water from above. From a few paces out and then as far as she could see into the waterfall, this strange promontory was wrapped in dozens and dozens of tarnished silver chains, big chains with links the thickness of Clariel's finger, chains that were doubled over this stone outcrop and then stretched down into the maelstrom below.

"What are the chains for?" bellowed Clariel. She had to bend down to hear Mogget's repeated answer, the noise of the waterfall drowning the cat's first reply.

"Prisoners," shouted Mogget. "Free Magic creatures suspended in the waterfall, in bottles of green glass."

"Why green glass?" shouted Clariel.

"Can't question them through silver. They can be heard through glass, silver is only for transport. But there's no time for questions now! Hurry up! There's the bottle! You can do it!"

"Not so fast!" Clariel shouted back. "Where are the garments to protect me from Free Magic?"

"I don't know," spat Mogget. "You don't need them. Hurry!"

Clariel ignored him, and quickly walked around the table, taking stock. The whole cavern had an air of decay and disuse. There was moss growing up almost to the tabletop, and there were more faded or dead Charter marks in the ceiling above than live ones. There was a chest under the table, with a pile of silver chains next to it, and a long stick with a hook on the end, like a fisherman's gaff.

Not without some trepidation, Clariel opened the chest. Judging from the tarnish on the chains, the moss everywhere, and the general feel of the place, she expected whatever had been in the chest was probably a disgusting pile of mold.

But it wasn't. A spell broke as Clariel lifted the lid, Charter marks spilling out everywhere to fade as the complex web of the spell fell apart, leaving the scent of roses. Once again, she didn't recognize any of the individual marks, but it had to be some kind of preservative or protective spell, because the inside of the chest looked fresh, clean, and most important, dry.

There were numerous articles of clothing inside, in different sizes. All were made of some kind of woven stone, or stonelike material, that was light as linen but enormously strong, and there were thousands and thousands of Charter marks swirling within the fabric. Clariel sorted through the clothes quickly, holding them up against her body. She chose a long hooded robe, gauntlets that came almost to her elbows, and curious tall overshoes that puzzled her for a few seconds till she realized they were footwear.

Underneath the clothes, there was a line of bronze masks. Full face masks, which would fit under the chin and extend back to the ears, with narrow slits for the eyes covered in some clear crystal, and a hinged flap over the larger mouth hole. The masks had leather straps with bronze buckles.

"Hurry!" hissed Mogget. "If I thought you'd be this slow I never would have bothered!"

Clariel continued to ignore him. She slipped on the robe, which wrapped around her almost twice and had several ties to make it fast. The overshoes were next, tying off just under her knees, the robe flowing over them down to her ankles. Then the gauntlets, which were also tied to the robe, a difficult operation.

She reached for the mask she thought would fit her best. It was heavier than she had expected, the bronze a finger-width thick. Like the clothes, it too was heavily laden with Charter marks. Clariel slipped it on, grimacing as the cold metal touched her face. She drew the straps tight, then pulled the hood up and fastened it to the sides and throat of the mask using the strings provided for that purpose.

The mask felt even heavier on her face, heavy and repressive. But then Charter Magic tingled, the baptismal mark on her forehead burned for a moment, and for a brief instant Clariel felt herself dip into a great swathe of the Charter, as if a storm composed of millions of marks had swept over her, there and gone in a second. The mask felt lighter and warmer thereafter. She hoped it meant that the protective magic was working, for she knew no way to wake it if it required some spell.

"Hurry!"

Mogget was yowling now, his voice made more distant by hood and mask, even harder to distinguish above the roar of the waterfall.

Clariel bent over the silver bottle and directed her thoughts to the spark that lurked deep inside her, the ember of the rage that she must blow into fire and feed till it became the fury, making her strong enough not only to survive the Charter Magic that kept the bottle sealed, but also to overpower the creature within.

Aziminil.

"Hurry up!"

The words sounded distant, from some other place of no account. Clariel once again ignored Mogget, her mind bent inward. She had found the place where the rage dwelt, and now she fed it, supplying it with memories.

The terrible night when her parents died; the memory of Aronzo smiling his self-satisfied smile; the feel of the knife in her hand when she tried to stab him and Roban had parried it away . . .

Then she bit her lip, right through, the taste of her own blood hot and salty, and she wanted to spill more blood, not her own, the rage rising and rising, spreading through every muscle, every vein . . .

Clariel roared and grabbed the bottle, gauntleted hands gripping the stopper, ripping it off in one swift movement, gold wires and all, Charter Magic spells to chill her bones and stop her heart broken in that instant, marks spinning off uselessly into the air.

With the stopper gone, Aziminil was suddenly there on the table, taloned hands reaching for her rescuer, a spiked foot stabbing out. But Clariel batted the hands away, gripped the spiked foot, lifted the creature above her head, and threw her to the ground, almost to the lip of the waterfall.

Aziminil tried to get up but Clariel was upon her, her gauntlets smashing down upon the creature's bony shoulders, the strength of Clariel's hands and the strength of her mind forcing the thing to kneel. Charter marks blazed bright as stars in her gauntlets and white sparks fountained from the creature, the stench of hot metal a sharp reek that filled the cavern.

Aziminil struggled to rise, but could do nothing against the force of Clariel.

"Obey me!" bellowed the young woman, her voice near as loud as the waterfall itself, infused with all her berserk fury. She felt triumphant, for she could sense Aziminil's mind already bending beneath her will, giving in, surrendering to her as was her right.

"Swear you will serve me! Serve me forever!"

S wear to serve me forever, or be *destroyed*!"

The creature suddenly slumped. Clariel felt something shift inside Aziminil's mind, some last shred of resistance snap.

"I will serve you, Mistress," said Aziminil. She bent forward till her head struck the ground at Clariel's feet.

"Forever, until I release you," boomed Clariel.

"Forever, until you release me," agreed the Free Magic creature.

As Aziminil spoke, Clariel felt a sharp pain in the middle of her forehead, where her baptismal Charter mark was, but the pain was lost as she also felt a sudden surge of power. It was Aziminil's power that she felt, power that she knew she could draw upon, shape and direct as she willed.

Power that would be far greater still if she took off the gauntlets and the robe, the mask and the overshoes, and took Aziminil into her body, there to dwell and be ever ready to serve her mistress.

It was a great temptation, made greater because the *fury* wanted that power, wanted that fuel to become greater still, to become such a warrior that nothing could stand against her and she would wade through her enemies, rending them limb from limb, laughing as they sought to flee . . .

But unlike all previous occasions when she had gone berserk, this time Clariel retained some sense of her own self. She had summoned the fury, but as the book had taught her, had kept back some part of her being. From this redoubt of her true self, she sallied forth, banking down the angry fires that threatened to burn up all the fuel within her, the fires that wanted all Aziminil's power, not just the fraction available to her without being touched, skin to skin.

"No," whispered Clariel. She let go of Aziminil and stepped back. The creature was bound. Nothing more was needed, at least for now. She must resist the temptation for more.

"Clariel! The door!" shrieked Mogget.

Clariel whirled around. The door was slowly creaking open. Beyond it she saw a great crowd of armored warriors, sendings all. Instantly she drew upon Aziminil's power and, gesturing with one hand, directed a great blast of raw sorcery that struck the ceiling above the door and shattered the rock. Huge boulders came tumbling down to block the doorway, a cloud of dust bursting over Clariel and out beyond, only to be washed away by the waterfall.

Clariel smiled and looked at Aziminil, who remained kneeling near her feet.

"It is good," she said. "The power . . . now none shall gainsay me—"

She faltered, words trailing away. The fury was rising again, as was a strange joy in what she had just done, a feeling of near ecstacy. She had merely *willed* something to be so, and it was. The stone destroyed, the way blocked, the enemy foiled . . .

Concentrate, thought Clariel. I must not enjoy this, I must use it only as I need to, I must do only what must be done and no more.

Slowly she forced the fury back, damped down the savage excitement that wanted to unleash more sorcery. She slowed her breathing, and brought up the memory of the quiet calm of the willow-arched glade on the river, and let that gentle flow take the rage away.

She told herself once more: I must use it only as I need to, only to do what must be done. No more.

"Aziminil. I want you to carry me beyond the waterfall, to the eastern bank of the Ratterlin, and then beyond to Belisaere, as safely and swiftly as you may. And should my garments fray, or my skin somehow be shown, you will not touch any part of me. Do you understand and obey?"

"I understand and obey, Mistress," replied Aziminil, lifting her head, the strange void that served as her face directed toward Clariel. A small cloud of mist wafted across her bloodred skin, tiny gouts of steam blowing up as it touched. "But I do not have the strength to carry you through the waterfall alone. It is too great a cascade, the water too swift."

"You must release and bind another creature," said Mogget from near Clariel's feet, his emerald eyes intent on Aziminil. "Draw up one of the chains, open a bottle."

"But which one?" asked Clariel. "There could be anything out there. Is there some record, some register?"

"Once there was," said Mogget. "Long neglected, lost these many years. But you are strong, Clariel. Take any bottle, none within the waterfalls can stand against your will."

"The Mogget's advice is sound, Mistress," said Aziminil.

"I just draw up a chain?" asked Clariel. She looked back at the table, and the hooked stick. "With that gaff thing?"

"Yes," said Mogget. "Best be quick. Rock alone will not stay the sendings long, and a message must already have gone to the Abhorsen."

"Again, the Mogget offers good counsel," said Aziminil.

Clariel looked at the gaff, then back at the waterfall and the narrow chain-wrapped outcrop. Even lying down, it would be very slippery, and she would have to edge some way into the waterfall itself, go into that massive downrush of water. It would be so easy to get washed away. But if Aziminil spoke the truth, then she had to bring up another bottle to make her escape . . .

She could still feel the rage, close at hand. It would not need any great effort to bring it back. She could bind another Free Magic creature, she knew. More than one, if it proved necessary. She could gather all the bottles, bind a score, no, a hundred creatures to serve her, and then none could stand . . .

Clariel lifted her hand to slap herself in the face, but the movement alone was enough to break these runaway thoughts. Which was just as well given she wore a bronze mask. She would have bruised her hand. This made her laugh, and that helped too. She felt more secure, more normal.

But there was still only one way out and that meant getting another bottle, binding another servant . . .

"Aziminil. Go to the rocks by the door and do what you can to slow the sendings coming through. Mogget, you go with her."

"I can help you with the bottles," said Mogget. "Tell you who's inside perhaps."

Clariel shook her head.

"You should stay away from the water," she said, though they both knew this was not the reason. She did not trust the cat-thing, despite his Charter mark collar or perhaps even because of it, for she did not understand where his loyalties truly lay, or what he was. It would be too easy even for a small cat to help her fall from that slippery tongue of stone.

"As you wish," said Mogget haughtily, and stalked away. Aziminil bowed, and followed him, spiked feet striking sparks that leaped and spat and made sharp cracking noises as they fell into the puddled water on the floor.

Clariel picked up the gaff and felt along its length. The wooden shaft had moss growing on it, and a few soft patches, but it felt solid enough. The hook was rusted, but she banged it on the stone table and it rang true.

She took off her sword and laid it on the table. After a moment's hesitation, she also took off the robe, gauntlets, and overshoes and then even her simple leather slippers. The stone was very cold under her feet, but she knew that bare soles would serve her better. She left the bronze mask on, thinking it would offer some protection for her eyes from the force of the falling water.

Taking up the gaff in both hands, Clariel walked to the spit of stone and knelt down. Dragging the gaff, she crawled out of the shelter of the cavern and into the waterfall. It hit her like a bruising blow, all along her back, water gushing around her head so forcefully that it threatened to drown her even as she hunched over, trying to maintain some small pocket of air. It was like being in the heaviest rainstorm ever, one so dense there were no individual drops, just a constant wave of water.

If she had entered it standing up, she would have been knocked over in an instant. Even crawling it was very difficult to keep steady, at least till she reached the first of the chains, which at least offered something to hold on to. For a moment, Clariel thought she would hook that one up, but then she reconsidered. Closer to the edge probably meant more newly placed, she reasoned. It might be a weak thing, insufficiently strong to help Aziminil take Clariel out through the falls. Then she would have to come out this way again to find a third.

No, better to go out farther now. Find something older and more powerful, something that would serve her better.

Clariel crawled over the first chain, holding on to others ahead, and continued on, going farther out and deeper into the waterfall. The crashing waters were really hurting her now, as savage as any blow she'd ever felt, as hard-hitting as the training weapons she'd used long ago with her schoolfellows in the practice yard of the Estwael Trained Band. Still she kept on, till reaching ahead her fingers encountered no more chains, but a jagged edge of rock, so unlike the smoothly worked edges to either side that she thought it must once have extended farther, but had been broken off by the tireless assault of falling water.

The third-last chain would do, Clariel thought, some vestige of caution exerting itself at last. Whatever dangled from the furthermost chain might offer a challenge too great even for her new and much puffed-up confidence. Holding tight, she reached out and down with the gaff, and, after a few attempts, got the hook securely through a link. Then she cautiously drew up a green glass bottle from below, the Charter marks on it glowing so brightly they cut through even the dense wall of water.

She hesitated to touch the bottle. The marks shone so brightly, for the first time ever she felt some fear of the Charter. She had never understood Charter Magic, never wanted to understand it, it was just something that was there in her life. But here, even half-drowned, pummeled by the waterfall, and in a precarious position on a narrow tongue of stone, she felt the awful majesty of the Charter.

I need this bottle, I need the creature within, Clariel thought. I cannot save Aunt Lemmin with Charter Magic. I cannot save myself . . .

There was a pain in her forehead, as if the mask was pressing there too tightly. Clariel really did not want to touch those Charter marks. To delay doing so, she started to shuffle backward, now holding the chain up above her head, so the bottle dangled safely a yard or so above the stone. She did not think it could be easily broken, but she didn't want to put it to the test. If the creature within broke free before she was ready . . .

Halfway back to the cavern floor, Clariel realized the chain was long enough that she could bring the bottle all the way back, rest it near the lip, and then open it. Whatever challenge the spells on the bottle offered, she would not have to confront them out here, under the waterfall. She could do as she did before. Raise the fury and open the bottle as a berserk, protected by her rage.

If she *could* raise the fury.

Clariel felt tired already, not to mention bruised and battered by the waterfall. But she knew there was no choice. As with a wounded deer, even at the end of the day, if it was not finished then you had to go on.

She took a few minutes to rest once she got back to the cavern, just sitting cross-legged on the edge of the cliff. The spray still buffeted her, but it was not too strong. Mogget sat on the table, watching Aziminil, who was watching the falling stones. But the cat did not say anything as Clariel got up and came over to the table. His eyes narrowed, and his tail twitched, but he said no word.

"I forgot to ask," said Clariel, as she wearily put her protective garments back on, fastening hood, gauntlets, and overboots. "Are you coming with me?"

"I cannot leave the House without the permission of the Abhorsen or the Abhorsen-in-Waiting . . ." said Mogget thoughtfully. "But then, no Abhorsen has forbidden me to leave for a very long time . . . I wonder if I can . . . do you want me to come?"

"I don't know," said Clariel. "Maybe. Yes. I just don't know if I can trust you."

"Our interests are aligned," said Mogget very carefully.

"I wish I could ask Bel," said Clariel. "But I know he'd try to stop me."

"There you are then," said Mogget. "The point, in any case, is moot. Neither of us may be leaving, unless you get on with it."

"I suppose so," said Clariel. She looked down at the green glass bottle with its tarnished silver stopper wound with gold wire. "Do you know what . . . who is in this one?"

"There are spells of enquiry," said Mogget. "But I fear you do not know them. It doesn't matter. I am sure . . . I am confident . . . you will prove stronger than the entity within."

Clariel looked over at Aziminil, who was watching the fallen stones around the former door like a cat before a mousehole. Then she looked back at the bottle. Such a small thing to contain a creature of elemental power . . .

"Hesitation oft incurs a price," said Mogget. "One you might not be willing to pay."

"I make my own decisions," said Clariel, and called up the fury.

Mogget backed away as she stood rigid above the bottle, her fists clenched within the gauntlets. Once again she relived the night of her parents' deaths, the smirk of Aronzo, the crushing boot of the guard outside Kargrin's door, the darkness of the prison hole . . .

But the fury would not rise. Clariel bit her lip again, but even the blood in her mouth would not kindle the fire within. She had damped it down too far, and the spark was cold.

Across the cavern, stones rumbled. The helmeted head and sword-wielding arm of a sending thrust out through a hole, to be met by a savage, leaping kick from Aziminil that sent her spiked foot right through the neck of the magical being. Sparks and Charter marks exploded in all directions, the sending crumbling into its component parts. But there were many more behind it, pulling at the edges of the hole, dragging rocks aside, making the way broader, no matter how many times Aziminil hopped and jumped and struck with her savage, sharp feet. There were too many sendings, scores and scores of sendings, more than Clariel had ever imagined could be within the House.

She took off her left gauntlet, fumbling with the knots that tied it to her robe, too conscious of how swiftly the sendings were breaking through. Her hand free, she took up her knife and sliced it across her palm, along the line of the barely healed wound from the Islet.

Pain blossomed, terrible pain that ran from her hand to her arm to the center of her head. Clariel embraced it, drank it in, fed it to the rage.

But still it was not enough, not until she lifted her hand to her bronze-masked face, opened the lid over the mouth-hole and pressed her palm there, blood spilling through upon her tongue.

Then the rage came, so swiftly that Clariel barely managed to do as the book told her, to retreat her conscious mind to an island within. There she used the last of her calm self to slip the gauntlet back on and to force her attention not at the sendings who she ached to fight, but at the bottle in front of her.

Once again, stopper, gold wire, and the sealing spells were no match for a berserk. Clariel felt the bone-snapping and the heart-stopping spells as a mere itch and a pang no worse than indigestion. Flinging the stopper to the ground, she held the bottle upside down and roared, "Come out! Come out, whatever you are!"

But the creature inside was already out, out in the instant Clariel broke the seal. It did not come out fighting, like Aziminil. It just stood there, a few paces from the shouting berserk, as still as if it had been carved from the rock of the cavern.

It was tall, nine feet or more. Its body was manlike, but thin as a spindle, with arms and legs jointed too many times, white bone protruding in lumps through flesh as blue as best azure ink. Its neck was no wider than Clariel's wrist, its head more akin to a wolf than anything else. A wolf's head stretched long and the mouth cut at the corners to fit in more teeth. Its eyes were like Aziminil's face, dark voids of nothing, empty and drear.

Clariel lunged forward and gripped it by those impossibly thin wrists, to twist and bend it to the floor. Sparks and Charter marks flew in profusion, but the creature did not give way. It held fast as Clariel tried to twist its wrists, and she felt its cold thoughts invade her mind, exerting a terrible pressure that seemed to enter through the holes in her mask, as if unseen thumbs were pressing upon her eyes, rough fingers attacking her mouth.

"I am Baazalanan," said a voice that filled the cavern and echoed deep inside Clariel's head, making her cheekbones ache to the very marrow. "Bow down before your master!"

Clariel felt her knees begin to bend, her fingers begin to uncurl where they gripped those impossibly thin, impossibly strong wrists. Her hands were hot, almost burning, and there were fewer Charter marks falling from the gauntlets, the sparks subsiding, as if the protective cloth was already wearing thin.

"Bow down," said Baazalanan. Its voice was soft and slippery, but strong, like a crawling snake that was winding through Clariel's head, flexing and looping, readying itself to crush her and strangle her will. There was nothing she could do, even with the fury stretching every muscle and sinew, concentrating every thought. She could not move the creature, could not free its grip on her mind.

In her berserk state she could not believe this was happening. It was not possible for an enemy to resist her power. But in the small part of her mind that remained separate, she knew it was so, that she had gambled and lost. Mogget and Aziminil had led her on, and her own foolishness had put her feet willingly upon this path.

"I will not give up," she whispered. Letting go of the creature, she stepped back and shouted, "Aziminil! To me!"

As she shouted, she surrendered the small conscious part of her mind to the fury, to become truly berserk. Frothing at the mouth, she smashed her bronze-armored forehead into Baazalanan's middle, and once again grabbed and twisted its wrists. She felt Aziminil close behind her, and drew upon her power, as much as she could through the barrier of her protective garments.

"Bow down," said Baazalanan, but both its audible voice and the mental one in Clariel's head quavered, and there was finally a tremor in its wrists. Clariel laughed, a laugh that was twin to her mother's in Kilp's house, the laugh of someone who has totally surrendered to their rage.

The pressure in Clariel's head began to ebb away, the sinuous grip of the Free Magic creature began to loosen. The narrow wrists were no longer as hard to move as stone, but shifted under her grasp. Clariel twisted harder and Baazalanan screamed, the scream further strengthening Clariel's rage. She dragged the wrists down and the tall stick of a creature followed, its legs bending thrice, each joint making a noise like a snapped green branch as it folded.

"I submit," squealed Baazalanan as it fell down, but Clariel did not answer. Instead she shifted her hands to grip one arm alone, and tried to tear it from its socket. She was lost now, lost in fury, and all talk of submission, of her plan to escape, all of it was gone. She would rend the creature limb from limb, and throw its torn carcass into the waterfall to be destroyed forever.

"Clariel! Stop!"

Something was calling her name, something annoying. Clariel dropped Baazalanan's arm and whirled around. A white shape rose up on its rear legs ahead of her. She roared and charged at it, hands grasping, but it jumped aside and shot under the table. Clariel sprang after it, and almost grabbed a tail, but it was too quick. It ran to its left, and Clariel sped around the table to her right, but when she got to the other side there was no sign of the impudent creature.

Then it called again.

"Clariel, Clariel! Stop! Think!"

She whirled around. Where was it? She couldn't see the pesky thing, and her original enemy was getting up. The tall creature. How dare it get up! She stalked back toward it, on tiptoe, body arched to spring, hands shaking, the froth dribbling down the chin of her bronze mask.

Baazalanan sank back down and bowed its wolf-head, mouth shut to hide its teeth. It laid its long arms out in front, taloned fingers flat on the stone.

"Clariel! Take its submission! That's what you want!" called Mogget.

Clariel stood over the kneeling creature and raised her fist, ready to bring it down on the back of the creature's head, just where it met that spindle of a neck. But as she did so, she felt some of her power ebb. Turning, she saw Aziminil back away, bowing as she did so.

"Mistress, you wished to bind this one, not kill. Make it serve you and we shall all turn against your *true* enemies."

True enemies. Bind to serve . . .

The thoughts penetrated Clariel's enraged mind. The lessening of power from Aziminil took the edge off her rage. She faltered, suddenly unsure of what she was doing. The rage faded a little further, and some rationality returned.

Clariel turned back to the kneeling Baazalanan and laid just one finger on its head. This time, it was her turn to find a way into its strange, cool mind, to extend a mental grip upon its thoughts.

"Swear to serve me forever, or be destroyed."

"I will serve, Mistress," said the creature.

Clariel lifted her finger, and stepped back, her mind withdrawing from the creature as she took the step. She took another, and swayed, and then fell to her knees. Aziminil and Baazalanan did not move, and she still could not see Mogget.

But she could hear the tumble of stones being pushed aside, and looking across, she saw a multitude of sendings gathered beyond the destroyed doorway, the half dozen at the front straining against one enormous boulder that still blocked their way.

"Take me gently through the waterfall and safely to the western shore of the Ratterlin," she ordered. "Do not touch my skin. Be quick!"

The two Free Magic creatures bowed. Sparks of white light began to form upon their strange bodies, small flames flickered from bloodred and inky-blue flesh and then larger flames till with a whoosh both entities were columns of white fire, bright as the sun but completely without heat. The columns moved toward Clariel and began to change again, shaping themselves into two halves of a globe. Clariel staggered to her feet as they began to close around her and looked across to where she had left her sword on the floor. It was too late to fetch it now.

Too late to change her mind.

A white cat erupted out of the open chest that had held the robes and zoomed toward her, jumping at the last second through the gap between the closing hemispheres and into her arms. Clariel caught him by reflex, too weary even to be very much surprised.

"You're coming then?"

"I believe I am," said Mogget. He sounded surprised himself. "Don't touch my collar!"

"Why not?"

"It will break the globe, we will be left here."

Clariel nodded. She barely had the strength to do that, and certainly couldn't keep talking. There was no fury left in her, and her legs felt like they might buckle at any moment. She shut her eyes as the white globe closed around her, and held Mogget close. He surprised her again by beginning to purr, though he stopped almost immediately, perhaps because he'd noticed he was purring.

She could sense the surface thoughts at least of Aziminil and Baazalanan. They were servile, wanting to obey her every command, intent on carrying her safely through the waterfall.

Her servants had done as she bid, and would continue to do so.

The globe rolled to the edge of the cavern, though inside Clariel felt no motion. On the edge it stopped for a second, then rolled again, entering the cascade with a great boom and an explosion of sparks that lit up the whole waterfall and the lowlands beneath for several leagues, as if a small sun had fallen with the river.

Chapter Twenty-Nine

ONCE WERE DRAGONS

A league downstream from the waterfall the globe of white fire rolled ashore and split in half. Clariel staggered shakily out onto a beach of many tiny pebbles that offered uncertain footing, so she had to stoop and put one hand down to regain her balance. Mogget jumped out of her arms and sniffed the air. Whatever he smelled seemed to satisfy him, for he wandered over to the shallows and stared into the water, one paw raised.

Nearby, the fiery hemispheres dulled and shifted, Aziminil and Baazalanan resuming their more familiar shapes. As Clariel stood up, they bowed their heads, the picture of model servants.

Clariel looked at them, up at the moon high above, then back toward the waterfall, a streak of white against the darkness of the Long Cliffs. It was hard to believe she had escaped, that she had two Free Magic servants, not to mention the dubious assistance of Mogget. The way was now clear to go back to Belisaere and do what must be done, and then finally be released to start her proper life in the Forest.

Insects buzzed around her head, midges of some kind, reminding Clariel that her face was bloodied, and her hand. She walked back down to the water's edge, knelt there, took off her gauntlets, and undid the hood of her robe and the straps of her mask. But when she tried to take the mask off, it was stuck fast and wouldn't move. Clariel shrugged and splashed water over it and through the mouth hole, thinking it must be dried blood that held it to her skin. But even then it still wouldn't move, and she began to grow afraid. She plunged her head into the river, into the fast-running water. Holding her breath she worked at the mask, till at last it came free with a sickening pang in her forehead.

Trembling, Clariel touched her fingers to her baptismal Charter mark. It glowed softly as she touched it, but the light that reflected on the river was wrong, not the warm golden glow she was used to. This was whiter, brighter, though still tinged with gold.

Clariel hesitated, then tried to reach for the Charter, to conjure a simple light. It was the first spell she'd learned, something she knew well, and she could nearly always make it work. But the Charter wasn't there, or she could no longer feel its presence. Yet she knew it was everywhere, the Charter made up all things, it described the world and everything in it . . .

Except Free Magic. That was outside the Charter.

"But I wore the robe, the mask . . ." whispered Clariel. She touched her forehead Charter mark again, and once more reached for the Charter. This time, she felt it, but far away. No great drift of marks fell upon her; they stayed as distant as the stars above, and just as out of reach. But even that far-off, momentary glimpse relieved Clariel. She had never really valued the Charter, neither understood it nor wanted to know more, but she felt its absence keenly.

It felt wrong, unnatural.

"Mogget!" she called.

The cat came back from the edge of the river, his paws and face wet and a look of satisfaction on his face.

"Mogget," said Clariel. "My Charter mark . . . something's happened to it, and I can't . . . I can't reach the Charter. You told me the robes would protect me from the Free Magic."

"The Charter and Free Magic are antithetical," said Mogget. "When you use one, you cannot use the other. Binding Free Magic creatures, drawing on their power . . . it weakens the Charter within you."

"You didn't tell me that," said Clariel.

"I thought you knew," said Mogget. He examined his left paw, and licked off a tiny shred of fish. "Common knowledge among real Abhorsens."

"What will happen to me?" asked Clariel, touching her forehead again.

"The Clayr may see your future. I cannot make predictions."

"Mogget! Answer me properly, or I'll . . . leave you behind."

"I really don't know," yawned Mogget.

"I can still feel the Charter, though it is distant," said Clariel. "Does that mean I might be able to . . . to find it again?"

Mogget didn't answer, but continued to lick his paws.

"Mogget! Please! I am an Abhorsen, even if I'm not *the* Abhorsen. Surely that counts for something."

Mogget stopped licking his paws. The Charter marks on his collar grew brighter, and there was the faintest sound of some distant, disturbing bell. The cat squirmed and blinked his green eyes twice.

"Free Magic and the Charter will struggle inside your body," he said slowly and reluctantly. "One or the other will win out. The more you draw the creatures' power within you, the stronger the Free Magic will be. There are healing spells, marks to cleanse the flesh of the Free Magic taint. Touching a Charter Stone would help, one of the Great Charter Stones most of all, of course."

"The Great Charter Stones?" asked Clariel. "Kargrin spoke of them, beneath the Palace. So if I went there, I would be cleansed of this . . . this taint?"

Mogget looked away, his head lunging up as if he was snapping at a tasty moth. He spoke urgently, clearly compelled to speak. The marks on his collar shone brighter still, and once again the faint echo of a bell came to Clariel's ears, making her shiver, and not with cold.

"It is . . . would be . . . very dangerous. You must . . . you must seek the help of a Charter Mage, a magister of the first rank."

Clariel felt a wave of relief pass through her. If there was a means to regain her connection to the Charter then using Free Magic was an acceptable risk. Kargrin—or the surprising Mistress Ader, who had been an Abhorsen—they would know what to do, they would help her.

It would all be worth it, when Kilp and Aronzo were dead, and Aunt Lemmin free, and the path to the Great Forest made clear at last.

"How may we serve you, Mistress?" whispered Baazalanan. It had crept closer to her, Aziminil at its heels. They must have heard everything. "Shall we carry you to Belisaere?"

Clariel let her hand fall from her forehead. She hesitated for a moment, then put the bronze mask back on and buckled the strap, before lifting the hood and making it fast. Her gauntlets went on next. She noted that the Charter marks in the strange, stony fabric were neither as bright nor as numerous as before. Touching the creatures had taken its toll. But she needed whatever remaining protection the garments offered.

"How will you carry me?" she asked. Thinking quickly, she added, "In a globe of white fire again? Remember that you must not touch my skin, nor convey me in such a way that I might accidentally touch you."

"We shall make a chair for you, Mistress," said Baazalanan in its soft but penetrating voice, which sounded neither male nor female. It was simply otherworldly and strange. Clariel knew from her mental contact that Baazalanan was the more powerful of the two, something she saw confirmed when Aziminil took up a subservient position a step behind the taller Free Magic creature. "We will summon metal from the ground. Then we shall join to make a flying mount and set the chair upon it."

"A flying mount?" asked Clariel.

"I think they intend something you might call a dragon," said Mogget thoughtfully. "At least a creature that inspired some of the tales of dragons."

He was lying on his stomach in the grass, watching the two Free Magic creatures. They turned their heads toward the cat and though they did not speak, Clariel sensed some silent communication before they turned back together to look at Clariel. If "look" is what Aziminil did, with her strange oval void in place of a face.

"I do not know what name you would use," whispered Baazalanan. "It is the shape favored by some of our kindred, long ago. Winged Perazinik, Jagdezkal, Tazkehanar . . ."

"Lost long ago, when the Seven made the Charter," added Aziminil. "But we remember."

"As do I," said Mogget. He grimaced and turned his head, licking at his collar.

"A dragon," said Clariel. She smiled under her mask. When she had been six years old her mother had made her a little golden dragon with ruby chips for eyes. Jaciel had taken it back a year later, and melted it down as a punishment for some infringement Clariel could no longer remember. "Can it be a golden dragon?"

"Whatever you wish, Mistress," said Baazalanan in its strange, soft voice.

But Mogget said, "It would be better grey, unless you wish for everyone to know we're coming, Clariel. Grey hides well against any sky."

"Grey, then. Also I will need a sword," said Clariel, suddenly remembering the one she had left behind. The Free Magic creatures had spoken of drawing metal from the ground and Aziminil had made a fine goblet for Aronzo. "Can you make me a sword?"

"Yes, Mistress," said Aziminil. "But not quickly. It will take some little time."

"Better yet, I know of a sword that would serve you well," whispered Baazalanan. "And other weapons. A cache from long ago . . . it lies toward Belisaere, and we could break our journey there. Even for such as we, it is not possible to retain the dragon-shape without rest."

"A hidden sword and a dragon?" asked Clariel. She smiled again, thinking of her eight-year-old self and the stories she used to love, told by her aunt Lemmin, for her mother had told no stories. But the smile faded, for that younger Clariel would not have been able to imagine her present companions, nor would she like them. The eight-year-old would not understand the necessity of using such creatures. "Let us find it then. Make me a chair, and become your dragon. I will rest upon the bank. Keep watch while you work. Wake me as soon as you are ready, but remember you must not touch me."

The two creatures nodded and bent down, their hands plunging deep through the pebbly beach into the earth, already summoning metal from the depths below. Clariel walked up the grassy bank beyond the beach of stones, and laid herself down. Mogget watched her for a moment, then padded back to the creatures. Both stopped their digging and bent their heads down toward the little cat.

If Clariel had been watching she might have wondered whether they were bowing down to offer homage, or simply to hear him better. He whispered something to them, unheard by Clariel, and they answered as quietly. Then Mogget went back to his fishing in the shallows and the creatures began to summon iron from far beneath their unnatural feet.

Clariel lay on her back on the grass and looked up. Her last conscious thought before sleep fell on her like a starving bear was that the moon looked bigger than she thought it should, and that this was important for a reason she couldn't quite recall . . .

The moon was beginning to descend when Clariel awoke, but its light was still clear and bright. It was roughly the third hour of the morning, she thought, still well before the dawn. She lay there, not moving, just staring at the moon for a while, before she remembered the importance of the current phase of the moon. It *would* be full tonight, and if Mogget had told her the truth, her protective garments would completely fail. She had to get to Belisaere and do what was needed before the next moonrise, which would be shortly before midnight.

Groaning a little, she levered herself up on one elbow and saw the dragon. Its head did look like the corners of the Abhorsen's table, but its body didn't resemble any picture Clariel had ever seen in a book of children's tales. It was not sinuous and reptilian, but more like an enormous bat. It was covered in light grey bristly hair rather than scales; its taloned forelimbs were part of its membranous wings, its hindquarters were muscular and rather feline. It didn't have a tail as such, but a stumpy stern like the docked tails of the Olmond hunting dogs. Its head was hairless, more skull than flesh, a thing of bony ridges and deep-set eyes. Eyes that were larger versions of Baazalanan's. Pools of utter darkness, reflecting no moonlight.

It was also smaller than Clariel had expected, only some twenty paces from head to its stunted rear, and its outstretched, leathery wings were only half as long again. The chair the creatures had made was already set on its back, directly behind its head, the legs seemingly fused into the bone beneath. Though they'd called it a chair, it looked more like a throne to Clariel. Made of raw, black iron, its back was high and adorned at the top with flanges and spikes, the armrests were flat plates of the metal, and there was a curving footrest that extended out over the dragon's head like a half helmet. It did not look comfortable at all, but it was imposing.

"We are ready," rasped the dragon, its breath carrying the hot metallic reek of Free Magic, white sparks falling from its long and dextrous tongue. It extended its neck and laid its head on the ground, so Clariel could step over onto the curving footrest without touching its body.

The chair was cold and uncomfortable, and did not feel anywhere near as secure as being in a paperwing. Clariel gripped the arms and wedged herself into the seat as best as she could. A moment later, Mogget landed in her lap and began to tread around in a circle, claws extended.

"Don't tear my robe!" said Clariel sharply. She put her hands around Mogget's middle to put him at her feet, but he immediately retracted his claws and sat down, looking up at her with an innocent expression.

"I still don't know why you're really coming with me," she said. "What happens if the Abhorsen finds you gone?"

"Tyriel?" snorted Mogget. "He could summon me back, and I would go. I cannot disobey his direct commands. But I doubt he will think of me. He never has before."

"He might now," said Clariel. "I left a note for Bel, just in case."

Mogget stood up suddenly, his head butting Clariel under her chin.

"You did what!"

"He won't see it till late today, if he visits like he said he would," said Clariel. "Even in a paperwing he couldn't catch up with us. Besides, Bel would want to help me anyway."

"Would he?" asked Mogget darkly. "Perhaps he might see things differently now. But done is done. We had best make speed. Order your minions to carry us aloft."

Clariel nodded. Whatever Mogget said, she was sure Bel would not try to stop her, particularly not when she was going against Kilp and Aronzo, to save the King.

"Fly carefully," she instructed the composite beast. "Do not allow me to fall, but go swiftly."

"First to find the sword?" asked the dragon. Interestingly, its voice now was not a combination of the two Free Magic creatures, but Baazalanan's alone.

"Where is it?" asked Clariel. "And how fast can you fly? It is near two hundred leagues to Belisaere."

"The sword lies on the foothills of Mount Aunden; we can be

there soon after the dawn. We must rest then, under the height of the sun, but can then reach Belisaere by an hour after dusk."

"But what is your intention, Mistress?"

The voice now changed to Aziminil's.

"We are strong and may pass the water channels, but there are many Charter Stones and many Charter Mages in the city . . . we cannot travel as we are, and should we be seen, they could imprison us once again."

"I am not sure," said Clariel slowly. She frowned, the movement making her mask move as well; it was sticking to her forehead again. "I need to see what is happening. Perhaps we will drop down outside Belisaere, find travelers or farmers, ask what is going on . . . I will decide later. Fly now!"

"Yes, Mistress," caroled the dragon, in its composite voice. It extended its wings, the tips unfolding to a far greater length than Clariel had suspected, beat down with them, and began a lurching run along the pebbled beach, the powerful hindquarters driving it forward at considerable speed. Just before the beach ended in a tall, overgrown bank, the dragon pumped its wings again and lurched into the sky, with Clariel and Mogget holding on for dear life in the iron chair.

Back in the Abhorsen's House, there came a great pounding on the gate. The guard sending hastened to open it, to admit Bel, fully armed and armored in helmet and gethre-plate hauberk. He was even paler than ever and clutched his left shoulder. A message-hawk was asleep on his right shoulder, its head tucked under a wing.

"What in the Charter's name is going on?" asked Bel. There was still smoke billowing up from the now-extinguished fruit trees in the orchard, a drift of it gathered about the House, pale under the moonlight. A line of sendings holding buckets, bowls, and even a firkin stretched from the orchard to the pump in the rose garden. "What's this about Clariel and Mogget? Where are they?"

The guard sending gestured downward, and made several quick signs, Bel watching his flashing fingers.

"They went down and out through the *waterfall*?" asked Bel sharply. There was none of his amiable chatter now, no hint of any smile in his mouth or eyes. "Both of them?"

The sending held up four fingers, then slowly made four signs, one of them a claw.

"Two Free Magic creatures!" exclaimed Bel. He bit his lip and groaned. He guessed at once that one must be the creature in the bottle he had brought from Belisaere. Kargrin had warned him not to let Clariel touch the bottle, that her previous contact with the creature could have made her crave more. But another one as well? It had to be one of the chained, and that was beyond bad news.

"Clariel, what have you done?" he said, tears starting in his eyes. But he wiped them away immediately, for there was no time for tears. He had to do something. But what was there he could do?

A sending tugged at his elbow. Charter marks from its fingers flowed through those in his armored coat, warming the skin beneath. Bel looked at the cowled figure, who inclined its head and offered him an ink-stained piece of paper. He took it, held it up to the moonlight, and read it. For a moment he felt relieved that at least Clariel had written a note.

But something had happened below, for the sending reported *two* Free Magic creatures gone . . . and there was Mogget. Out of the House without permission, and unrestrained . . .

Bel took a deep breath, and stood as tall as he could.

"Ready a paperwing to launch as soon as possible from the platform," he said, desperately hoping the sendings would obey. He was not the Abhorsen, nor the Abhorsen's heir, but surely they would recognize that he was the only one who had the spirit of an Abhorsen?

"Bring me the sword Cleave and . . . and a set of bells."

The guard sending knelt and bent its head, and the cowled one followed, and then the whole bucket line of sendings knelt as well. Belatiel felt the hair stand up on the back of his neck, and from somewhere deep beneath his feet he thought he heard the distant echo of a sorrowful bell.

Already some half-dozen leagues away on dragon-back, Mogget sat up in Clariel's lap and turned his head to the south, ears pricking up.

"What is it?" asked Clariel. She could not sleep, for the wind sped past too briskly, it was cold, and the dragon did not fly as smoothly as a paperwing and she was afraid of falling out.

"A change," said Mogget thoughtfully. "Not unexpected, but sooner than I thought. It is as well we left when we did."

"What do you mean?" asked Clariel.

But Mogget was silent, and did not answer.

Chapter Thirty

AN ANCIENT TREASURE

Clariel came to the foothills of Mount Aunden in the early
morning, well before noon. The mountain itself loomed
up to their right, a great hulking mass of granite, its snow-
capped peak gleaming in the sun. In winter, its upper slopes would
all be under snow, but now bare rock shone there, above the conifer
forests that thronged below the winter snowline.

The dragon tilted its wings and began a long glide down, aiming
for a long flat shelf of grey-green rock, a little way above the treeline.
Just before it seemed to Clariel that they would simply fly straight
into it and all be killed, it beat its wings furiously, so that they almost
stopped in midair. Then, with its rear legs running fast before they
even made contact with the ground, the dragon landed in a lurching gallop that ended not, as Clariel feared, over the edge of the
rocky ledge, but some twenty or thirty paces short. Whichever Free
Magic creature was the guiding force behind the shape the two had
assumed, it knew how to use it.

Clariel climbed stiffly off the chair, stood on the footrest, and
leaped clear of the dragon, Mogget at her heels. Clapping her hands
together, she jumped on the spot, for despite the hooded robe and
mask over her hunting leathers, she was cold. They had flown high
and fast and the chair definitely did not have the warming spells of
a paperwing.

"We will divide," said the dragon. "If you permit, Mistress."

"Do so," said Clariel. She pushed her hood back and continued to stomp and clap her hands as she walked around the ledge. She could smell the pine sap of the trees below, a clean, welcome scent that she drew into her lungs. Once she'd got warm in the sun Clariel thought she might walk down under those trees, since they were going to stay for some hours anyway to allow the Free Magic creatures to rest.

She looked up at the rocks above, more ledges interspersed between high crags, and wondered where the ancient cache of weapons Baazalanan had mentioned might be. There were no obvious caves, nor was this the kind of rock that lent itself to the formation of such things.

"I should have stayed in the House," said Mogget sourly from behind her. "Not even a field mouse to eat up here."

"It's wonderful," said Clariel, stretching out her arms. "No people, the forest just below, the sun on my face . . ."

She faltered and stopped, and lifted her hand to touch the mask. She'd forgotten she was wearing it, and for a moment could have sworn she *had* felt the sun on her face, without the barrier of the mask at all.

"Mistress, the cache *is* still here."

Baazalanan's whisper, close behind her, made Clariel turn swiftly on the spot. The creature was back in its regular form, looming above her, its blue skin bright in the sunlight, though its eyes remained pools of darkness. Aziminil squatted nearby, legs folded twice.

"Where?" asked Clariel.

Baazalanan stamped the ground with one of his clublike feet. An echo came back, indicating a hollow space beneath the apparently solid slab of stone.

"Under this ledge. There is a tunnel below."

It walked along the ledge toward a large outcrop of granite and down a narrow gully between the two. Clariel followed, with Aziminil behind and Mogget bringing up the rear with an air of someone who wishes they had something better to do.

The gully led down to another ledge of folded stone below the one they'd landed on. Baazalanan walked to the interior edge of it, where it ran into the hillside. It looked no different than the stone anywhere else, but the creature reached out with one of its stick-thin fingers and traced a doorway in the stone, sharp nail screeching on the rock.

"You must make the door," said Baazalanan. It gestured at the outline it had made. "Here."

"How?" asked Clariel, even though she already knew. She touched the mask on her face as she spoke.

"Free Magic," said Mogget. "Draw on your minion's powers, cut through the stone. It will only take a moment and use only a fraction of the power you now have."

"But I . . . I don't want to use any more . . . I don't want to make it more difficult to regain the Charter," said Clariel.

Baazalanan and Aziminil squirmed as she mentioned the Charter, and she felt their unease, their mental shying away from the very notion.

"It won't make it—" Mogget started to say, before the marks on his collar started to glow. "That is, it will make it only slightly worse, I'm sure. You will need all the help you can get if you still plan to go to Belisaere. It won't be easy."

"I suppose so," said Clariel slowly. "I guess I've chosen my path, haven't I? Now I need to speed along it."

She looked at her two Free Magic creatures, and then at Mogget and his collar. The marks were fading again, but she felt a longing to touch them, to regain some connection to the Charter.

"What if I touch your collar, Mogget?" asked Clariel. She took off her right gauntlet and bent down toward the cat, slim fingers reaching for the cat's collar. "Will that help me?"

As she spoke, Baazalanan hissed and stood up to its full height as if ready to attack or run, and Aziminil skittered backward on her bladed feet. Mogget didn't move, but Clariel stopped just short of touching his collar, her hand frozen in the air.

"It would help you regain something of your connection to the Charter," said Mogget. "But it would . . . damage your servants, perhaps severely."

"And you?"

"No," said Mogget. "I have worn this collar a very long time. But its purpose is to restrain a Free Magic creature much greater than the two specimens you have bound, and you are connected to them."

Clariel withdrew her hand, replaced her gauntlet, and looked at the cat with new respect and caution.

"And you desire me to help free you?"

"When I am able to think for myself I do," said Mogget. "Anyone would. But as you know, that does not always apply."

"I won't, you know," said Clariel. "You're wasting your time. I'm going to use Baazalanan and Aziminil to help me rescue my aunt and kill Kilp and Aronzo, but that's it. Tools for one particular job, that's all."

"I believe you," said Mogget, with a yawn. "In any case, I find your company more interesting than the sendings back at the house, whatever may happen. Now, are you going to open a way through this rock?"

"I just want you to be clear on what I will or won't do. I'm not releasing you and neither is anyone else," said Clariel. She stood up straight and looked firmly at the two Free Magic creatures. "You have sworn to serve me, and so you will. Acknowledge that."

"Yes, Mistress," chorused the pair. She felt their acquiescence, but kept looking at them, willing them to show further obeisance, until they bowed low. Even then, she kept the mental pressure there until she was satisfied they were totally compliant.

"You may rise," she said. "Aziminil, I will take some of your power, but again, do not touch me."

Clariel stood before the outlined door in the rock face and stretched out one hand toward the stone and the other toward Aziminil. The Free Magic creature crept closer, her head still bowed. Clariel could feel the power within her servant, raw sorcery just waiting to be tapped, wanting to be used. She summoned it into herself, trying to hold back, to draw only just enough, but the thrill of it was so intense she found it hard to resist. With this power she could do anything, anything she could think of, and it was enormously difficult to bring her focus back, to refuse more power and direct what she had against the stone.

Intense white light burst from her outstretched hand, a spear of superheated air that she used to follow Baazalanan's tracery, cutting through stone as easily as a hot wire through gold. Molten stone ran across the floor toward her, but Clariel made a brushing motion with her hand and the spear of white became a broom that swept the creeping lava aside. White smoke billowed out across the ledge, enough to choke any mortal, but again Clariel used the raw sorcery she held to wrap herself in a breeze that took the smoke away.

The stone door fell in with a crash, revealing a tunnel beyond. Clariel reluctantly lowered her hand, and let the power flow back into Aziminil. It ebbed slowly, not least because she had to make a determined effort to let it go. So much of her was screaming to take it all in, to make Aziminil a true servant, to subsume her into Clariel's flesh.

The tunnel did not go far into the hillside. Clariel had to wait until the stone around the melted doorway cooled, but that did not take long. As she went into the darkness, Aziminil followed, her bloodred skin beginning to shine, till it grew bright and lit their way with a red light akin to a storm lantern or a pitch-soaked torch, shadows flickering across the wall.

There was a chamber at the end of the tunnel, a circular cave cut in the granite by sorcery. In the middle of this chamber there was a sarcophagus of bronze carved with symbols that twisted and squirmed, Free Magic parodies of Charter marks. Clariel stopped with a start as she felt the nature of these symbols, for they were the visible remnants of a Free Magic entity that had been stripped and broken apart, its power taken and infused into the metal. Yet something of its identity still lingered, a faint sense of something shadowed and brooding that liked the dark places of the earth, an ambusher and lurker. Even its name felt close, as if it were whispered in the bronze and could be heard if she pressed her ear up close.

But it was what lay on top of the sarcophagus that most attracted Clariel's attention. There was a sword, ostensibly a plain weapon with a blackened steel hilt, the grip wrapped in wire, and an ugly roundel of bronze for a pommel. But it too had the shifting, ugly symbols in its metal, again the legacy of some entity that had been deconstructed and forced into the blade.

Next to the sword there was a bandolier, a broad strap of leather to wear across the chest, with seven leather pouches holding seven bells, their ebony handles projecting out.

Seven bells of increasing size, the smallest able to be cupped in Clariel's hand, the largest bigger than two hands clasped.

"A necromancer's bells," said Mogget.

"Like the Abhorsens use?" asked Clariel. As with *The Book of the Dead*, she felt attracted to the bells, felt her fingers yearn to touch the ebony handles, unclasp their cases, hear their voices . . .

"Like and unlike," said Mogget.

"You may need more servants, Mistress," said Baazalanan. "And the Dead are many."

"I don't know how to use the bells," said Clariel. She kept staring at them. Was it her imagination, or could she hear the instruments faintly humming in their leather shrouds? Calling to her? "I know no necromancy. I haven't read *The Book of the Dead*."

"*You* need nothing but your will and the instinct in your blood," said Mogget. "These bells are Free Magic things, not wound about with Charter Magic. Take them up, speak to them. They will answer to you, teach you their use, their strengths and foibles."

"I could go into Death?" asked Clariel.

"Anyone can go into Death," said Mogget, with a smirk. "Coming back again is the difficult part."

"There are always many Dead who wish to return to Life," whispered Baazalanan. "An army of the Dead awaits you, Mistress. Take up the bells."

"Take up the sword," echoed Aziminil, her voice sweet and cajoling. "Take up the bells."

Clariel took a step forward, and then another. She almost felt like she was out of her body, watching herself walk forward. The sword and the bells called out to her. It was inevitable that she should pick them up, and wield them. She should raise an army of the Dead and lead it against Kilp and Aronzo. She would take Belisaere by storm and put everyone there to the sword, to make more deaths, to raise more Dead, to build an army such as the world had never seen, an army to go forth and conquer till there were none who could gainsay her.

Clariel the Great, deathless and all-powerful, free to *make* her own path—

"No!" screamed Clariel. She snatched her hand away, inches from the bells, shocked to find that she had already taken the gauntlet off, that she would have touched these Free Magic things with her bare fingers. "No!"

Turning, she ran from the room, out through the tunnel, out into the sunshine. But it was stark and hot and hurt her eyes. Stumbling, she went to the gully and found a path down, down into the pine forest, down into the calm, cool world she loved.

Mogget found her there a few minutes later. Clariel was collapsed against the trunk of a great pine, one with a prickly skin. But she had her arms around it, nevertheless, and her head against it, and her legs were buried in the fallen needles as if they could provide a blanket to comfort her.

"If you show weakness, Aziminil and Baazalanan will turn against you," said Mogget conversationally.

Clariel let go of the tree and lifted her head with a jerk.

"What! You told me if I bound them they would serve forever! They promised!"

"They are things of elemental power," said Mogget. "No promise means anything to them, save it be backed by force. They will serve only as long as you are stronger than them."

"You lied to me," whispered Clariel. She felt the rage rising inside her, the sudden fury of the betrayed.

"I am not *your* servant," spat Mogget. "We are, if anything, companions in adversity. You wish your freedom, I wish mine. Running away and hugging trees will not help either of us!"

Clariel snarled and lunged at him, but Mogget danced away.

"That's better!" he cried. "Let the fury come! Take the sword, take the—"

The cat's words ended in a choking cry as his collar suddenly flared brighter than the sun, Charter marks in violent motion, circling his neck. The cat twisted in agony and flopped to the ground, while Clariel held her gauntleted hands to her face and recoiled back behind the tree.

The fury was gone, replaced by a cold determination.

"I'm not taking those bells!" called out Clariel. "But I will use Aziminil and Baazalanan as I see fit, and when I am done you will go back to the Abhorsen's House!"

Mogget gave a pathetic, mewing cry, but it was not in answer to Clariel's words. The blinding light of the Charter marks dimmed, and a woebegone cat crawled around the tree and looked up at Clariel.

"I may be gone sooner than you think," he rasped. His head was bowed, and to Clariel he seemed totally abject, for she could not see the cunning glint in his green eyes, nor the curl in the corner of his mouth. "The Abhorsen has put on the ring, and soon will set out to pursue us. He will return me to the House, no doubt, but what of you? I do not think you will see your Great Forest ever again."

"I will," said Clariel firmly. "Nothing will stop me, not now. I've let too many things get in my way. We will go to Belisaere, and kill the King's enemies, and he will let me go, no matter what Tyriel might say or do."

"As you say," said Mogget.

"I will take the sword," said Clariel suddenly. She got up and began to stalk back up the gully. "But not the bells."

"Not yet," whispered Mogget, so soft that it was barely more than a thought. "But I know a necromancer when I see one."

He padded after her, his pink tongue out a fraction, listening in satisfaction as she called out forcefully to her servants.

"Aziminil! Baazalanan! Make the dragon again, at once!"

Clariel saw the Sea of Saere first, darker and more lustrous than the sky, an expanse of different blue. Then the peninsula, with the great city at its end. From this distance and height it was merely a blob of off-white against the blue of the sea and the patchworked green of the farmlands beyond the walls. There was the Narrow Way stretching rule-straight toward the city . . . and there was something on it halfway to Belisaere, three or four leagues ahead, something that obscured the clean line of the road. Clariel couldn't make it out, it was too far ahead and her eyes were slitted against the wind even with her mask.

"Mogget, what is that on the road? Can you see?"

"I see," said Mogget. "An army on the march. A small army, perhaps five or six hundred all told. There are banners in the van . . . ah . . . there may still yet be time . . ."

"What? Whose banners?"

"Many, some unclear. But I can see the silver star of the Clayr, and the blazons of Navis and the Bridge Company," said Mogget. "Many Charter Mages, some of the greatest power; I can feel the Captain of the Rangers, the Chief Librarian, three of the four Bridgemasters . . . another who I do not know, most powerful of all . . . they are marching fast, as if any delay could brook disaster . . ."

"The Clayr?" asked Clariel. She felt curiously relieved and deflated at the same time, and suddenly uncertain in her purpose. "They *have* come . . . so they will take care of Kilp, rescue Aunt

Lemmin. I don't need to do anything, we could turn away now, fly to Estwael . . ."

The cat stood up on his hind legs, one well-clawed paw hooking into Clariel's leg. He had been sitting at her feet, because the sword with the Free Magic symbols lay across Clariel's knees, the blade naked to the wind.

"I suppose they are hurrying because the Palace is on fire," he said. "That is smoke, not cloud."

"On fire!" exclaimed Clariel. "How . . . how much on fire?"

Mogget shrugged and sat back down.

"There is a lot of smoke. I would guess that Kilp, seeing the relieving army approach, has tried to take it by assault. Perhaps he hopes to face the Clayr with the King already dead, and the evidence of his own crimes wiped clear. Probably including your aunt Lemmin."

"But the Clayr wouldn't treat with him," protested Clariel. "Would they?"

"More to the point, they won't reach the city before nightfall," said Mogget judiciously. He looked up at Clariel, his eyes slitted against the wind, giving no sign of the thoughts that lay behind them. "Even if the city walls aren't held against them, they cannot come to the palace in time. The King's guards may still be fighting, a last, desperate struggle, hoping for reinforcements . . . but who can help them?"

"We can," said Clariel. "Why don't they fly in? The Clayr have paperwings, but I can't see any . . ."

"You told me yourself of bolt-throwers on Coiner's Hill," said Mogget.

"I wonder . . . if we should drop down and speak to the Clayr," said Clariel. She was finding it difficult to think clearly. It was so cold, and her forehead hurt. She could sense an eagerness from the dragon beneath her: Aziminil and Baazalanan wanted to fly faster, to come to grips with the enemy. It was like the fury, but different. And it wasn't just about fighting, they wanted something else, she could feel it . . .

"They will attack you on sight," warned Mogget. "We ride a Free Magic creature, remember! If we do go to the Palace the same applies, we will need to be wary of both sides."

"My robes have Charter marks," said Clariel. She lifted her left sleeve to look at it, and was surprised to see so few marks there, and even these were fading, coming adrift from the cloth. "Well . . . once on the walls, the dragon can come apart, Az and Baaz can stay . . . stay behind me. I will speak to Gullaine, she will know me . . ."

Her voice trailed off. It was so difficult to think! But her path was still clear in her mind. Go to the Palace. Save the King. Kill Kilp and Aronzo, who were bound to be there. Aunt Lemmin . . . she might be anywhere, a prisoner in the same hole where Clariel had been herself, but she didn't really know where that was . . . or in the Governor's House.

No matter, Clariel thought. Kilp will tell me before he dies.

"Fly faster!" she instructed. The dragon answered, its leathery wings moving to a more rapid beat.

"You could call a wind," suggested Mogget. "Take just a smidgeon of power from Aziminil, she has plenty to spare. This shape is easy for the two of them."

Mogget did not tell her that he had an uneasy feeling all along his backbone and up his tail, a feeling compounded by a look around the back of the chair. There was a small speck high on the horizon behind them. It was a long way away, but it was a paperwing, flying as fast or faster than the dragon.

"No," said Clariel. She touched the mask again with her left hand, sliding her gauntleted fingers up the cold metal to her forehead. She could feel nothing behind it, not the faintest glimmer of the Charter. But the baptismal mark must still be there, she told herself. It was just too difficult to feel through the woven stone of the gauntlets and the thick bronze of the mask. Kargrin, or Ader, they could help her, once her task was done. But she must not make it worse.

She had already forgotten the sword she held across her lap, her hand tight around its hilt. There were no Charter marks on that gauntlet now, and the material was becoming thin, her skin almost visible beneath.

"Fly to the west of the city, and approach the Palace from that direction. We must avoid Coiner's Hill and there are . . . there were ships to the north of the Palace, they may also have bolt-throwers."

"We shall go high, with your permission, Mistress," whispered the dragon. It was Baazalanan speaking. "Then drop fast, too fast for bolt or spell to strike us."

"Like a kite upon a vole," said Mogget, licking his lips. "The osprey upon an unsuspecting fish."

"Yes, let us do that," said Clariel. "Look ahead, Mogget. What can you see of the Palace? Does the royal banner fly above the gatehouse?"

"The smoke is too thick," said Mogget. "I cannot see."

"Faster," mumbled Clariel. She said it again, and wondered why her mouth was dry. Then she remembered that she had neither drunk nor eaten since dinner the night before, and now it was the fourth or fifth hour of the afternoon. But she was not hungry, or thirsty, and in a moment she forgot the dryness of her mouth and throat.

She also wasn't tired despite her very short sleep of the night before. But as they flew faster and higher, and the cold gripped her more tightly, Clariel found herself drifting into a kind of fugue, where she was neither asleep nor awake. She knew where she was, in the iron chair on the back of a dragon. But at the same time she imagined herself to be in the Great Forest. In the wintertime, when the forest canopy above was sparse, snow covered the greensward, and ice glazed the edges of the stream where she liked to fish. It was too cold to tickle trout in winter, but there were rabbits to snare, and wild honey to be gathered from sleepy bees without competition from even sleepier bears. She would have a snug forester's hut, with a stove bought from the town red-hot upon its rough-fired clay plinth; a stack of wood as high as the turf-covered roof outside, a larder full of autumn's harvest; winter in the forest could be comfortable indeed . . .

"We are ready to descend, Mistress," whispered the dragon. "On your command . . ."

Clariel awoke fully, the wintry forest landscape banished in an instant. They were in the high waft of the smoke, not so thick that it choked, but enough to cause half-waking dreams of comfortable stoves. As the smoke swirled beneath them, Clariel caught glimpses of the Palace far below, and the sea next to it. There were some people on the walls, but she could not make out whether they were fighting, or who they were.

"Brace yourself, Mogget," she said. Crouching down herself, she set her shoulders against the back of the chair, and her feet hard on the footrest. She placed the sword between her knees and gripped it there, her hands tight on the metal arms of the chair, which for the first time she noticed were lightly rimed with ice.

"Take care not to harm me or throw me out," she said sternly to the dragon. "But descend as fast as you can!"

The dragon pushed its head down, its body following, and folded its wings. Clariel slid down the chair a fraction and her stomach flipped up toward her throat in a moment of fear. She pressed herself even flatter into the iron seat and gripped harder. Mogget was somewhere under her legs. She felt his claws cutting through the overshoes around her ankles, but she couldn't look. The dragon was nearly vertical now, and they were plummeting to the earth, the wind howling past so that their previous speed paled in comparison, as if they had been sauntering across the sky and now were sprinting.

A hundred paces above a broad stretch of the Palace wall they came suddenly out of the thickest smoke into afternoon sunshine. The dragon flung out its wings; there was an almighty crack like thunder, and had they been of normal flesh the wings would have been stripped from the dragon's body by the sudden shock. But they were not normal flesh. The dragon slowed. It reared backward, wings beating, Clariel sliding up the chair back, so she had to arch and twist her legs to keep the sword safe between her knees. Then they were down, the dragon rampaging along the wall till it came crashing to a complete stop by colliding with the door of one of the seaward-looking towers.

Clariel took up the sword and jumped down, Mogget close behind her. With a flash of white light, a wave of heat, and the stench of burning metal, the dragon divided into its two components. The iron chair fell from the back of Baazalanan, hit a merlon with a resounding clang, and fell into the sea.

The door opened, and a frightened man in the livery of the Cobblers Guild looked out, a spear held unsteadily in his hand, unready for any foe. Clariel opened her mouth to speak, but before she could say anything Aziminil lunged past her, her taloned, three-fingered hand piercing almost all the way through the guard's neck. Blood sprayed, Aziminil withdrew her hand. The guard fell choking to the ground, and died a few seconds later.

Clariel felt him die, felt his spirit enter Death. She knew she could catch that spirit, and her hand went to her chest as if to draw a bell. Then she remembered she had left the bells behind, that she was not a necromancer, and didn't want to be one. Neither did she want to kill Guild guards who undoubtedly had no idea that Kilp was really a traitor to the King.

"Do not kill," she croaked. She had to look away from Aziminil, who was licking her fingers clean, a tongue of red fire coming out of the featureless void that was her face. Clariel wished she hadn't seen that.

"No killing, save on my order."

Neither creature replied.

"It is their nature," said Mogget. He jumped up on the battlements and looked back toward the south. The paperwing was close, perhaps minutes away, coming down in a long, fast glide. It couldn't land on the wall like they had, but there was a terrace not far below, out of sight.

"I know," said Clariel. She shut her eyes for a second, then hefted her sword and entered the tower. "But I want the next one alive. I need to ask questions."

The "next one" was a woman as young or younger than Clariel, wearing the badge of the Fishmongers. She came up the stairs calling out to someone, her sword still sheathed. She saw Clariel first and stared, agape, before fumbling at the weapon on her side. When the two Free Magic creatures loomed up as well, she stopped and raised her shaking hands.

Clariel lowered her own sword. It was shifting in her hand, trying to move of its own accord, wanting to taste blood.

"What is happening?" she rasped. "Does Kilp control the Palace?"

"Almost, yes, I think so," blurted out the young woman. "There is still fighting in the Great Hall, and the . . . the leopard-creatures . . . but this side is taken—"

"Does the King live?"

The woman looked confused.

"The King was killed by the rebels, a week since or more," she said. "Least, that's what we were told . . ."

"Where is Kilp? And his son Aronzo?"

"I don't know," sniffled the woman.

"Where!" snapped Clariel. She unconsciously drew on Aziminil's power, her voice compelling an answer. White smoke billowed out of the mouth-hole of her mask as she spoke, though she did not notice it.

"Probably the Great Hall," sobbed the woman. She sank to her knees on the steps, tears gushing down her stricken face. "The Goldsmiths Company, they were the only ones allowed to go there. The Great Hall!"

"Where is that?" asked Clariel, but the woman could only sob and shudder, her voice taken away by terror.

"I know," said Mogget, causing another shriek. He jumped past the woman. After a moment, Clariel followed. She didn't look back, and so did not see Baazalanan effortlessly twist the guard's head off her shoulders as the creature passed by.

"Through here," said Mogget, indicating a door on the next landing down. "Along the corridor beyond, that will come out in the musician's gallery of the Great Hall."

Clariel almost opened the door herself, then thought again, and gestured to Aziminil.

"Open it," she said.

Aziminil didn't bother to turn the ring. She raised one spiked foot, leaned back, and smashed it through the center of the iron-studded, Charter-Magic reinforced door. Oak, iron, and magic shattered under the blow. The creature laughed, an eerie, high-pitched chuckle, then reached in to pull entire planks out, the wood screeching as it bent. Clariel caught a glimpse of several Guild guards hastily retreating down the corridor beyond, and heard their shouts of alarm.

"Go ahead," she instructed Aziminil. "Do not kill them."

Aziminil bent down and rushed through the broken door, spiked feet clattering on the floor, a terrifying sound as she charged after the fleeing guards. Baazalanan followed swiftly on her heels, bent almost double, using its hands like forefeet as it ran. Clariel and Mogget came more slowly behind, Mogget pausing often to look over his shoulder.

"What . . . what can the creatures be confined in?" asked Clariel.

Aziminil and Baazalanan were smashing down another door ahead. Aziminil was laughing again, the sound making the bones in Clariel's face ache under the mask. "Without Charter Magic. Or did you lie about that as well?"

"If you could compel them into a dry well that would hold for a time," said Mogget. "Capped with a heavy stone. A silver bottle, stoppered with melted silver, might last a day or two. Or they could be chained under a river, or a tidal flow, though again that would not last long without Charter Magic."

"We had best hope Kargrin lives," said Clariel. "Or Mistress Ader."

If Mogget answered, it was lost in Baazalanan's howl, a terrible sound of glee and bloodlust. As it howled, the door broke and the creature grabbed a stunned guard on the other side and pulled him through the splintered hole. Still howling, it obeyed Clariel's instruction not to kill, instead breaking both the man's arms and legs as if they were kindling for a fire. Tossing him aside, it tore at the timber to make the hole wider still.

"No!" shouted Clariel. She ran to the door, stepping over the guard who had fallen unconscious to the floor. "No unnecessary harm! Hurt no one unless I tell you!"

Baazalanan and Aziminil turned back toward her. Everything became very still. Clariel could feel her heart pounding, feel the beat of it echoing inside her head, as if it were amplified and reflected by the mask.

"Harm no one without my permission," repeated Clariel.

"No," whispered Baazalanan. Aziminil laughed her horrid laugh. They turned away and went through the door.

"Obey me!" rasped Clariel, holding out her hand as if she might physically claw them back. But she could feel them breaking free of her, could feel their minds turning to some other purpose. They had wanted to come here for their own reasons, some great ambition that excited them. They had always intended to rebel.

Clariel turned to Mogget, to ask him a question, to ask what she might do, but he ran past her and through the door. With his departure a sickening feeling came to Clariel, the dreadful realization that she had brought these terrible creatures to the Palace without knowing what they truly wanted. All along Aziminil had helped Kilp for a reason. Even now she might join forces with the Governor again . . .

"No," growled Clariel. Holding her sword high she ducked through the smashed-open door, out onto the musician's gallery, a long balcony that occupied one end of the Great Hall. Aziminil and Baazalanan were already at the top of a staircase leading down into the hall, but here they had stopped.

One of the guard sendings, the leopardlike creatures, had surprised them. It had its jaws locked around Baazalanan's neck and had borne him to the floor of the gallery, white sparks blazing as Charter Magic fangs rended Free Magic flesh. But Baazalanan had its thin fingers about the leopard's throat, and Aziminil was hacking at the great cat with her bladed feet, white sparks geysering up with every blow.

Mogget was perched on the railing of the gallery, looking down into the hall. Clariel looked too, trying to take in everything she saw. A dizzying sensation of recent death rolled across her, the result of many violent deaths in so short a time. There were dead guards everywhere, guild and Royal. The Royal Guards were fewer by far, but they had killed many more of their foes. Only strength of numbers had overborne them in the end. Most of their dead lay around the dais on the far end of the hall, where they had formed a shield ring around the throne.

But that ring was broken, and the King they had sought to protect was slumped on his throne, with Kilp and Aronzo and a half dozen of their Goldsmith guards around him. A moment before they had been laughing, relieved to have survived a hard-won victory.

Now they were all staring back toward the gallery, at the creatures battling there and the strange bronze-masked apparition that returned their stare.

The rage came unasked as Clariel saw Kilp and Aronzo for the first time since they had killed her parents. It rose in her like a vast wave capsizing a ship, complete in an instant, with no possibility of turning it back. She howled, white smoke issuing from her mask like steam from a kettle. Her sword burst into hot, red flames that sent a sickening metallic stench across the hall.

Ignoring the battle on the stair, Clariel jumped over the railing, down the fifteen paces to the hall below. Her ankles turned as she landed, but the pain was simply taken up by the fury as additional fuel, adding to the rage and hatred that already stoked it high. Striding forward, Clariel called out in a voice that could never be recognized as her own.

"Stand away from the King or die!"

Three of the guards stood away from the King and fled. Of the remaining three, one began to slot a bolt in his crossbow, his fingers trembling. When it fell on the floor, he also ran. But the other two were made of sterner stuff. They edged forward with Aronzo, very slowly, their swords held high.

Kilp drew his dagger and stayed by the King. Orrikan swayed back on his throne and lifted his head, his old nose sniffing the stench of Free Magic in the air, his eyes wide.

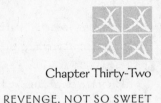

Clariel stormed toward the closer trio, a hooded figure of flame and smoke, her bronze mask gleaming. The first guard tried to parry her sweeping cut but his sword broke and Clariel's weapon cut him in two. Even as he fell she withdrew the blade and engaged the second guard, who stumbled back and turned to flee. Clariel sprang forward farther than anyone could possibly jump and took his head from his shoulders. That left her open to Aronzo, who cut at her shoulder, but through fear or weariness the stroke was short. Clariel whirled and the very point of her sword nicked him on the neck, just above his mail hauberk.

"Father!" screamed Aronzo, retreating fast. He fell over a corpse and landed heavily. "Help!"

Kilp threw his dagger. It struck Clariel in the side, easily parting the protective robes, long since threadbare and bereft of Charter marks. The hunting leathers beneath slowed the dagger a little, but not enough, the blade sinking deep. To Clariel, deep in the rage, it was no more than a pinprick. Ignoring it, she stood over Aronzo. He wasn't smiling now, and she was pleased to see his cheeks were badly sliced, the wounds not healed.

"For my mother," she said, striking down. Her sword pierced Aronzo's mail with a thunderclap, flames licking across the metal. Aronzo screamed again, a bubbling scream that became the choking, rattling cough of death.

"For my father," said Clariel, and she struck down again for the heart, killing him instantly. Clariel felt Aronzo die, felt his spirit cross all uncomprehending to the cold river that would bear him away beyond the Ninth Gate. For a moment she even had a vision of those implacable, rushing waters and once again her hand twitched as if it should be holding a bell.

Withdrawing her sword from Aronzo's chest, she turned toward Kilp. He stared down from the dais. His mouth worked and his eyes bulged, as if he could not comprehend the ruin of his grand plans and the death of his son.

"Who are you?" he shouted, his voice high. He looked over Clariel's head, toward the minstrel's gallery. "Aziminil! We agreed, I said you could have the King! There is no need for this!"

"Have you killed so many parents that you cannot remember their children?" asked Clariel. She wished she could take the mask off, so Kilp could see her face before she killed him. But that was not possible.

Kilp turned to run, but he did not go far. Clariel cut him down at the King's feet, stabbing him through the body. White surcoat and gilded mail offered no protection against her ensorcelled sword.

Kilp died, the look of disbelief set permanently on his once-handsome face. Clariel looked at the blood spreading across the pure white cloth, at the tumbled bodies of a father and son. What had killing them achieved after all? It had not mended the pain in her heart. She knew it had been foolish to think it would.

She felt the rage beginning to ebb away from her, like the wash of a wave retreating from the sand. But she knew she must not let the fury go. Kilp and Aronzo were dead, but this had brought no ending. She could feel the fierce, strident thoughts of the two Free Magic creatures. They had dealt with the leopard sending and were once more intent on their greater purpose, whatever it was.

Clariel had to regain control over them, and quickly.

"Who are you?" asked Orrikan, his voice shaky. "Do you serve

Tathiel? Where is my granddaughter?"

Clariel ignored the King and looked toward the gallery.

Baazalanan and Aziminil were stalking toward her, with Mogget a few paces behind. All that was left of the leopard sending was a smattering of fading Charter marks upon the gallery stair.

"Stop!" ordered Clariel. She had hoped the fury would give her the power to reassert her domination, but she was already out of the full berserk rage. It had begun to fade the moment Kilp hit the floor.

The creatures did not stop. They continued to advance, Baazalanan going to one side and Aziminil the other, as if they hoped to avoid Clariel entirely. Both were circling around to get to the King, Clariel realized. She raised her sword and backed toward the throne, darting glances toward Orrikan. He did not look dangerous, and he had not defended himself against Kilp. But he was a powerful Charter Mage, or he had been once.

"Who are you!" repeated the King.

"I am Clar—" Clariel began to say her name, then stopped. What use was that name now? She felt like her old self was gone, destroyed by her own hand, by her own mistakes. "I am no one. Run, Highness. I will try to stop them here."

"What do these creatures want of me, *Claw*?" asked the King, mishearing what she had said. He sounded as if he might be asking for his tea. There was some remnant of what he had once been, some vestige of power in his voice. It was enough to make Mogget answer, however reluctant he might be.

"We . . . want . . . your . . . blood," said Mogget, each word dragged unwillingly from his mouth. He clawed at his collar, tearing hair and skin. A multitude of marks shone and roiled there now, evidence of some great spell in action. "We want your blood upon the Great Charter Stones in the reservoir below, to break the Charter. To free all of us so enslaved!"

A sharp stab of pain hit Clariel in the forehead as Mogget spoke, blinding her for a moment. Her sword felt slippery and uncertain in her hand, as if it might fly out of her grasp. She gripped it tighter, her fingers breaking through gauntlets that were now like ancient lace, the very threads disintegrating. Stepping up on the dais, she drew even closer to the King. Aziminil and Baazalanan stalked nearer too, watchful and silent.

Clariel could still feel their thoughts, their intent, even if they would not obey her. The connection between them remained. They would not kill the King here. They had to take him somewhere below, for his blood needed to be spilt fresh upon the Great Charter Stones.

"Where is my granddaughter?" asked the King again, as if he had not heard Mogget. The old man looked at the creatures, then at Clariel, his old rheumy eyes weeping, his mouth hanging open. "Tathiel was to come. The Clayr Saw her. Why is she not here, Claw?"

"She sent me," said Clariel. "She awaits you. But you must run now. The Clayr are coming, you will be safe."

"I can't run," protested the King. "I haven't run for years."

"Get behind the throne!" ordered Clariel urgently. She could sense the Free Magic creatures were about to spring. "Crawl if you must."

"I do not crawl!" said Orrikan indignantly.

Baazalanan sprang at the king as he spoke and Aziminil jumped high at Clariel. She tried a stop-thrust but the sword betrayed her, turning in her hand, so she threw herself into a dodge, ducking and rolling away as Aziminil came screaming down, her spiked feet smashing into the wooden dais.

Before Aziminil could strike again, Clariel dove forward, scrabbling across the floor on all fours, the gauntlets falling off her fingers like shredded skin. Mogget was right in front of her, twisting and yowling, and his collar shone brighter than the sun with Charter marks. The spells within it held him fast, held him for Clariel.

She grabbed the cat's collar with both hands.

The Charter exploded into her body, rocketing through muscle, skin, and bone. Thousands, hundreds of thousands, millions of marks burned their way through every part of her body, and into her mind. There the marks found the bridge from her to the creatures, and exploded across to Baazalanan, who held the King; and to Aziminil, just as she was about to stomp down on Clariel once again.

The creatures froze like statues. Twin waterfalls of golden sparks exploded from Baazalanan's eyes. The void that was Aziminil's face suddenly lit with a glow brighter than one of Jaciel's crucibles. Charter marks danced amid the sparks, weaving a river of light between collar, woman, and creatures.

But it was not enough.

All three creatures fought the Charter, and Clariel could not keep her grip. Mogget edged slowly backward, snarling as he exerted his will against the compulsion of his collar.

Clariel could not hold on. As her fingers weakened, so did the stream of marks.

The sparks streaming from Baazalanan's eyes faltered. The creature started to move again, taking a step, the King dead or unconscious in his arms. Aziminil's face returned to darkness, and she jerkily lifted her foot above Clariel's back, a fraction at a time, slow steps toward a killing blow.

Clariel only gripped the collar with two fingers now. All strength had fled from her body. She felt used up, the fury gone, all her hopes and dreams fled. Aronzo and Kilp were dead, but now the King was to be killed, and the Charter broken. Creatures like Aziminil and Baazalanan would roam freely, slaying and wreaking havoc . . .

It was all her fault.

"Stop," she croaked at Mogget, who was ever so slowly continuing to edge away from her, ever so slowly breaking her grip. "Stop,

Mogget. In the name of the Abhorsen whom you serve."

Mogget did not answer. Clariel's fingers slipped again. She held the collar by only one finger now and it was giving way. She could feel the spike of Aziminil's foot against her back, just touching below her shoulder blade. But the pain from that was nothing compared to the other pain in her side, and even that was less than the pain in her forehead. This pain came from the contact with the Charter. It would go if she released her grip, she knew. But still she tried to slide forward, to keep her hold, to keep the marks flowing through her into the Free Magic creatures . . .

This was how Bel saw her, when he came running into the Great Hall, with the sword Cleave in his right hand, the bell Saraneth in his left.

He saw a tumbled, masked figure on the ground, desperately trying to struggle forward as Mogget retreated back, her one finger hooked around his collar. Bel saw the marks flowing from collar to Clariel to the creatures: the dagger-footed one from the Islet, her spiked foot about to deliver a terrible blow; and another, tall and impossibly thin, who cradled the King in its arms, sidling toward the door that led to the reservoir below.

Bel saw it all, and in that instant knew what was happening, saw that Clariel was the dupe of Aziminil and Mogget, and not the deceiver he had feared.

Bel rang Saraneth even as Clariel's finger slipped.

In the moment of its sounding, all became still. Saraneth's deep voice commanded all who heard it to obey. In the echo of the bell's call, Belatiel spoke, the voice of an Abhorsen come fully to his power.

"Stop!"

Aziminil's spiked foot stopped, just piercing the skin of Clariel's back. Baazalanan froze in place. Mogget gave a disgruntled yowl, but he too became still.

Yet even Saraneth could not command a wound to stop bleeding, and the blood flowed without stint from the dagger wound in
Clariel's side.

Bel held up his sword hand. The silver ring that Tyriel had worn
was on his index finger. The ring that sealed Mogget's allegiance.

"Mogget, I am the Abhorsen, and I renew all instructions, orders,
and commands that have been given to thee these many years, and
reiterate them anew."

Mogget rolled his eyes and muttered something that Clariel
couldn't catch. She couldn't hear properly. It was the hood, she
thought, though in fact the hood was in tatters around her head.
Like the rest of her robe, all its virtue lost, all Charter Magic long
since fled.

Only the bronze mask remained, though she no longer felt the
metal on her face.

"Mistress Ader, if you could help me with the creatures?"

Clariel heard that. So Mistress Ader had survived. That was
good, she thought dimly. She knew Gullaine had not lived, for the
Captain of the Guard was lying only a few paces away in front of the
throne, her sightless eyes turned toward the ceiling, eyes that had
once been so alive.

Gullaine had a dozen wounds or more upon her front. They
would all be at the front, Clariel thought.

Charter marks suddenly flew above her, like a flock of bright
starlings come home to roost. She screamed as they struck Aziminil,
as she shared the pain of the creature's binding. Then there was a sudden vacancy in her mind and Aziminil was gone, gone as if she had
never been. Another agonizing stab of pain followed and Baazalanan
too disappeared.

Clariel sobbed from the pain of their absence, and for the loss of
the great power she had never dared fully use. And perhaps most of
all for the power she had used so unwisely.

Finally, Bel knelt by her side. Clariel tried to sit up, or even roll upon her back, but she couldn't move. She craned her neck and tried to speak, the words slow, her mouth strangely dry and twisted.

"Sorry," she croaked. "Thought no one was doing anything. Didn't understand. Free Magic."

"I know," said Bel. He saw the blood pooling under her, suppressed a gasp, and reached for the Charter to choose the marks of a healing spell.

"My aunt Lemmin," whispered Clariel. "Rescue her?"

"We will," said Bel. "There will be no more fighting. Not with Kilp dead, and the Clayr and the others coming through the Erchan Gate."

"The King?" whispered Clariel.

"He's dying," said Bel. He had the marks, the spell was all ready, but it would not leave his hand. The marks refused to enter Clariel's flesh. He looked quickly at the King. "It has all been too much. He's smiling, though. Ader is telling him the news."

"Telling him . . ."

"Princess Tathiel came with the Clayr," said Bel. He grimaced as the spell rebounded again and he lost the marks. "She has been with them all this time. She will be Queen. Much against her wishes."

"We can't all get what we want," whispered Clariel. "I thought it was so simple . . . the Great Forest . . . not so much to ask . . ."

"No, not so much," said Bel.

Clariel didn't answer.

Bel wiped his eyes and reached for the Charter again. Mistress Ader came to his side, and he felt her hand upon his shoulder, lending him strength. But again the marks were repelled and Bel, already weary from his frantic flight in pursuit of Clariel, almost fainted from the effort himself.

"There is too much Free Magic in her," said Ader, her voice kind but sure. "The wound is too deep. You have to let her go, Bel—and we must make sure she cannot come back."

Bel nodded slowly and stood up as if carrying a great weight upon his back. As he did so, Mogget curled around his legs.

"There is a way to save her, you know," said the cat. "Or you should know, if either of you had been properly educated. I suppose I could tell you, now you have recalled me to myself and to make some . . . ahem . . . amends."

"What?" asked Bel urgently.

"The Great Charter Stones," said Mogget. "Your healing spells will work if you draw upon them. Take her down to the reservoir.

"Though it might be too late," he added, pulling one paw back daintily from the spreading pool of blood.

C lariel came to consciousness slowly. For a moment she was disoriented, feeling the crisp linen under her, the sheet and fine wool blanket across her body. Was she home in Estwael, or was she still trapped in the new house in Belisaere?

Her eyes opened to see a circular room she'd never been in before. She was somewhere high up, the narrow window opposite showing only a night sky with a scattering of stars, dim in the light of the Charter marks that glowed softly above her bedhead.

Her side ached, and her face . . .

Clariel remembered. Her hands flew up, to touch nose and mouth, fearing to find bronze but instead feeling familiar skin. She let out a long, shuddering sigh of relief. Slowly she traced her cheek-bones, and then, more hesitantly than ever, touched the middle of her forehead.

This didn't feel the same. She felt no Charter mark, no connection with the Charter. Instead there were two painful welts of new scar tissue, crossing each other to make something like a misshapen, twisted X.

Clariel let her hands fall. She lay there, staring out at the sky for a long time. She had tried to do what was right, but in retrospect so much of it had been wrong. The Clayr would have defeated Kilp without her. All she'd done was help Aziminil get close to carrying out some long-laid plan to destroy the Great Charter Stones.

Even worse than that, she had to admit to herself, was the fact that Free Magic was wonderful. If she had let herself not worry about anyone else, then she could have just used the power of Aziminil and Baazalanan. They would never have dared turn against her without Mogget's help, and her own weakness. She could have flown to Estwael, gone to live in the Great Forest, *ruled* the Forest . . .

"No . . ." whispered Clariel. She sat up in the bed and slapped herself in the head. What was she thinking? She'd been stupid, and would no doubt pay the price. But it was better this way, far better than if she had become a fully fledged Free Magic sorcerer.

Or a necromancer, whispered a voice in the back of her mind, remembering the bells in the cavern on the slopes of Mount Aunden. The bells were still there, even if the sword was gone. It was probably destroyed already, melted down by the Abhorsen and his lackeys. But if she could get to the mountain, or find bells elsewhere . . .

"No," groaned Clariel. She put her face in her hands and tried to think of her place of willow arches by the two streams, her calm and pleasant refuge. But though she could picture it, she could no longer imagine herself there. She was a traitor, even if she hadn't meant to be, and there was only one punishment for that.

A soft knock on the door interrupted her thoughts. It opened, and through the gap she saw a winding stair beyond. She was in a tower room, Clariel realized, probably in the Palace. She had no real memory beyond fading out in the Great Hall, though she had some faint recollection of a place of rippling water, and great stones that thronged with Charter marks . . .

Bel came through the door, his finger to his lips. He was wearing a simple blue tunic dusted with silver keys, hunting breeches, and soft slippers, and he looked much better than he had when last she'd seen him. He moved well, as if his shoulder no longer troubled him. That made her wonder how long she had been unconscious. Such healing as she must have needed did not take place in a few days, no matter how much magic was involved.

"We must be quiet," whispered Bel.

"Why?" asked Clariel. Her voice still sounded raspy, strange to her ears.

"Because I'm helping you escape," said Bel. "I've bespelled the guards below with a misdirection, like the one Kargrin used on us when we went to the Islet."

"Why?" asked Clariel again. She let herself fall back on her pillow. "I know what I've done. I should pay the price."

"I owe you my life," said Bel simply. "Twice. Perhaps I've repaid part of that, and now I would repay all. Also . . . I feel responsible. I should have realized Mogget was wriggling free of his bonds, that three generations of Abhorsens had ignored him to everyone's cost. I should have warned you that he was not to be trusted. And I should have made sure the lower depths of the House were forbidden to you."

"You weren't to know," said Clariel wearily. "Not your responsibility."

"But it was," said Bel anxiously. "I've been the Abhorsen-in-Waiting for years, only I didn't know it. I had only to claim my bells . . . and . . ."

He hesitated, then pressed on. "Tyriel was thrown from his horse the evening you escaped. He was very badly injured—he died later that night—and everyone was milling around in a great panic, with Yannael not doing anything useful. In the midst of it, a message-hawk came to me, to me personally. The most curious message-hawk ever because it didn't say anything, it just drew a picture of the Abhorsen's House in the dirt and a bell with legs on a horse riding to the house. So I went, and . . . it turned out I was the new Abhorsen."

"As you always wanted," said Clariel. She tried to smile, but there seemed to be a problem with the corner of her mouth. "Speaking of aunts, is my aunt Lemmin . . . is she still . . . did they—"

"She's fine, she was treated well," said Bel. He frowned and

hesitated again. "They told her you were dead. They've told everyone. Killed with the King, trying to save him."

"I did try to save the King," said Clariel. "I suppose the rest will
soon be true."

"No," said Bel, shaking his head. He went to the chest at the
foot of the bed and took out a plain woolen cloak. "It is true Queen
Tathiel thinks you should be executed, but that's not going to happen. I told you I'd help you escape. Get up and get this cloak over
your nightgown. Not the best for traveling, but I couldn't risk bringing anything up. There's some other clothing, and money and food
and suchlike in the boat—"

"Bel . . . I thank you for what you're trying to do," said Clariel.
"But I . . . I was a Free Magic sorcerer, and I will be again. If I find
another creature, I am sure I will try to bind it. I want that power
again. Charter help me, I even want to walk in Death! I don't think
I can stop it, not by myself. Best to end it here. I always said Belisaere
would kill me, one way or another."

"You won't become a Free Magic sorcerer again," argued Bel.
"When Mistress Ader and I healed you, we bound that part of you,
wrapped it in Charter spells drawing on the Great Charter itself. You
would not be able to bind a creature, even if you found one. It would
simply kill you, like any other ordinary mortal."

"Spells fade," said Clariel. "Bindings fail."

Bel smiled, a melancholy smile.

"Not in your lifetime," he said. "Nor in mine. Come, the guards
will be out of the spell soon."

"Where can I go?" asked Clariel softly. She could feel tears forming in her eyes, tears for the life offered her, tears for the life she could
never have, her life in the Forest. "A boat, you said. But where can
I go?"

"I've spelled it to take you north," said Bel. "Far to the north.
It will follow the coast, then go up the river Greenwash to where

they're building the bridge. There is a pass allowing you to cross the bridge, plenty of money to buy a horse or mule, anything you need. The steppe lies beyond, but farther still, across the Great Rift there are stories of a forest . . . wilder and more immense than anything in the Kingdom . . . it will be risky, of course, but . . ."

"Thank you," said Clariel.

Not her Forest, but a forest somewhere. That was something to live for. She sat up and swung her legs over the bed. There was something under her feet, something cold and metallic. She picked it up and stared down at the bronze mask. The straps were blackened as if they'd been burned, and the bronze was pitted and scarred.

"I thought . . . perhaps you might want to keep it," said Bel very awkwardly.

Clariel touched her face again, feeling the scars on her forehead and the corner of her mouth that wouldn't move, the many small ridges of scar tissue on her cheeks. She nodded, and lifted the mask to her face, slipping the straps over her hair, noticing for the first time it had been clipped almost to her scalp.

"It doesn't matter to me," said Bel. "Your face, I mean. If you could stay . . . I would still want to . . . well, you know how I feel."

"I know," said Clariel. She stood up and went over to him, lightly touching his own cheek, smooth under her hand. "Marry Denima, Bel. You'd be good for each other."

Crimson dots burned bright on Bel's pallid cheeks.

"I don't think the Abhorsen himself should blush," said Clariel. She took the cloak and swung it over her shoulders.

"This one will," muttered Bel.

Clariel opened the door, went down the first flight of steps, and stopped. There on the landing was Mogget, licking his paws. He looked up at her and shrugged.

"You shouldn't have listened to me," he chided. "I wasn't myself."

"I think you were more yourself than you are now," said Clariel softly. She hesitated, then added, "I don't blame you, Mogget. We all want to be free, but that can't work. I had a puzzle once, when I was a girl, a badly made puzzle. One of the pieces would never fit. I loved it, even though the pieces could never come together as a whole."

"True," said Mogget. "May I say that I approve of a piece that tries to remake the entire puzzle?"

"Good-bye, Mogget," said Clariel. She bent down and scratched his head, the little cat purring. He seemed more cat now, and less something else.

"Charter Magic fades beyond the Rift," whispered Mogget, so softly that only Clariel could hear him. "But there is Free Magic there."

Clariel smiled behind her mask, and scratched him again, taking care not to touch his collar. Mogget purred and pressed his head against her fingers.

"This way," said Bel, opening the door that led out to one of the seaward walls. Halfway to the next tower, some hundred paces away, two figures stood upon the walkway. The moon was above them, and in its light Clariel could see the white hair of Mistress Ader and the tall figure of Magister Kargrin.

"Kargrin!" said Clariel in surprise. She half raised her hand, but then let it fall. She was pleased he was still alive, but doubted he would reciprocate. However, as they drew closer, he also smiled and raised his hand in greeting.

"Clariel," he said softly, giving her a full bow. "I am glad to see you well, and sorry at our parting. Sorrier still that I failed to teach you anything useful, and did not appreciate the danger you were in. If I had not used you to lure the creature—"

"Hush," said Clariel. "I would have come to it anyway, I think. But now I am bound about with spells to keep me from my worse nature and . . . and I am glad of it."

"No, you're not," said Mistress Ader. "You may be, in time. I must also take my part in Kargrin's apology. I should have spoken to your parents, and had you sent to the Borderers. A passion thwarted will oft go astray."

"Does the walker choose the path, or the path the walker?" asked Clariel.

"Where did you read that?" asked Mistress Ader, surprise and suspicion in equal parts in her voice.

"I told her," said Bel quickly. He indicated a rope ladder hanging down the wall, out of the closest embrasure. "We'd best hurry. The Queen's guards will be coming round in a minute, and I'd rather explain this after you're gone, Clariel."

"Good-bye then," said Clariel, her voice breaking. There was a still moment where she almost reached out to Bel, to hug him, to let out some feeling that she had long suppressed. But the moment passed. She ducked her head and lowered herself backward through the embrasure, feeling for the rungs of the ladder. When she had a good footing, she transferred her hands to the ropes and began to climb down.

"The boat is spelled, but I've got someone to help you," said Bel. He was leaning down, his hand outstretched, ready to catch Clariel if she missed her grip. "He'll be a faithful servant, he's magicked to serve you, we didn't know what else to do with him. It wasn't his fault—"

Bel's words were lost in the thud of a long, slow wave hitting the wall below. Clariel looked down. There in the moonlight was a small fishing boat, its sails furled, up against a rectangular rock that formed a makeshift quay. A white-bearded old fisherman was holding the boat there, one foot aboard and one on shore.

He held out a hand to help Clariel as she reached the bottom of the ladder and stepped into the boat. He either didn't notice the mask or paid it no heed.

"Take a thwart, there, milady," he said easily, unshipping an oar and using it to push off from the rock. "Name's Marral. Folk call me Old Marral. We'll row out a bit and get the sail up. Wind's fair for the north, and that young chap said he'd spelled her for a fast voyage. Bit of luck me getting this job, if you don't mind me saying so. I've been sick, you know. But I'm all better now. Don't you worry. I'm all better now."

Clariel nodded and drew her cloak around her. As Marral rowed she watched the dark bulk of the wall grow smaller, and then they were out of its shadow, and she saw the lights of the city beyond. So many lights, brighter and more numerous even than the stars above them.

She watched the lights for a long time, long after Marral had stowed the oars and raised both sails, watched them till the city was just a sparkling jewel on the far horizon.

"Begging your pardon, milady," said Old Marral. "But they didn't tell me your name."

"I'm not sure myself," said Clariel slowly. "I will think of it, in time."

Author's Note

Clariel is of course Chlorr of the Mask, who appears at the beginning of *Lirael*, having been drawn south by the reawakened powers of Orannis. As to what she did in the intervening years between the events of this book and those in *Lirael*, who can say?

The next Old Kingdom novel, which I am currently working on, jumps forward again and continues the story of Nicholas Sayre (and Lirael), picking up their story after the novella *The Creature in the Case*.

I would like to thank the many patient readers who have waited a long time for this book. I am also very grateful for the expertise, advice, and hard work of my publishing partners around the world: my literary agents Jill Grinberg, Fiona Inglis, and Antony Harwood; my editors Katherine Tegen, Eva Mills, and Emma Matthewson; and everyone at HarperCollins USA, Allen & Unwin, Hot Key Books, and my various publishers in translation.

Finally I would like to thank my wife, Anna, and my two sons, who have had to be the most patient of all: not waiting for this book, but for me to stop writing it.

Garth Nix
Sydney, November 22, 2013

Turn the page for a sneak peek
at *Goldenhand*

In the Sixth Precinct, the inexorable current of the river that flowed through Death slowed almost to a stop. It was a natural gathering place for the Dead who hoped to go no farther, and for those who strived to claw their way back through five gates and precincts and out into the living world again.

Amid the myriad Dead who waited, and hungered, and fought against the compulsion to go deeper into Death, there were two *living* people. Necromancers, of course, for no others could be here while still alive. At least alive for the moment, for unwary necromancers going deeper into Death than their knowledge and their strength allowed were the particular prey of the Greater Dead who prowled the precinct, ever eager to consume any scrap of Life that would aid them in their desperate desire to live again.

But in this case the Greater Dead stayed well away, knowing the two women were most uncommon necromancers. Both wore bandoliers containing the seven bells, necromantic tools of power infused with Free Magic, but their bells had mahogany handles rather than ebony, and the silver bell-metal crawled with bright Charter marks.

That alone declared their identity, but it was confirmed by their apparel: armored coats made from many overlapping plates of a material called gethre, with surcoats over the armor. One wore deep blue, sprinkled with many silver keys, the other a coat also with silver keys upon the blue, but quartered with golden stars on a field of green.

The silver keys were the blazon of the Abhorsen, foe and nemesis of all things Dead, and this was the Abhorsen Sabriel, one hundred and eighteenth of the line. With her was her apprentice Lirael, the

Abhorsen-in-Waiting, who also bore the stars of the Clayr to show her own unique heritage: she was not only an Abhorsen, but also a Remembrancer, who could See deep into the past, just as the Clayr could See the future.

"She has evaded us," said Sabriel, looking out over the grey and dismal river. She could feel the presence of the Dead, many of whom were lurking under the water, hoping to avoid her attention. But they were all lesser things than the one she and Lirael had hunted, a long and weary way. The desperately scrabbling small things about would weaken in time, and go on, without the need for interference.

"You're sure it was Chlorr of the Mask?" asked Lirael. She looked around more warily than Sabriel. This was only the eleventh time she had come into Death, and only the second time she had come so far, though once she had been very far indeed, to the border of the Ninth Gate. She was very grateful that Sabriel was by her side, while still not being quite able to quell a feeling of great loss. The last time Lirael had passed through the Sixth Precinct, her great friend the Disreputable Dog had accompanied her, lending the young woman great comfort and strength.

But the Dog was gone forever.

Lirael still felt the pain of that loss, and the dread, grey days that had followed the binding of Orannis were never far from her thoughts. The only slight note of cheer from that time had come from Nicholas Sayre, who had told her how the Dog had sent him back from this same cold river, albeit on the very fringe of Life. Lirael would have liked to talk to Nicholas more about this, particularly if he had seen which way the Dog went, grasping at the hope the wily hound had not gone toward the final gate.

In fact Lirael would have liked to see more of Nick in general, for he was one of the very few people she had ever met who she had immediately liked and had felt some unspoken connection to, or at least the potential for something of the sort.

But Nick was gone too. Not dead, thank the Charter. But returned to Ancelstierran regions far south of the Wall, to get him away from the pernicious magics of the Old Kingdom. He needed to escape the legacy of both Free Magic and the Charter and live a normal life, Lirael told herself.

She must forget him.

"It was definitely Chlorr," said Sabriel, recapturing Lirael's momentarily wandering attention. The older woman wrinkled her nose. "Over time, you'll learn to differentiate the various types of the Dead, and individuals strong enough to earn the description of Greater Dead. You sense it now, I suspect."

"Yes . . ." said Lirael.

It was true she could feel the Dead all around, with that strange sense she had not known she possessed for much of her life. She narrowed her eyes and tried to sort through the different sensations, for that sense was something beyond sight and hearing, touch and smell, but it drew upon them all. There was the hint of something more powerful amid all the Dead about them, but it was the fading trace of something that had been and gone, like the scent of smoke from a fire extinguished some time before.

"Has Chlorr gone deeper into Death?" asked Lirael. She hoped the slight quaver in her voice was not apparent. She was quite prepared to go on if it was necessary. She only hoped it wasn't.

"No," said Sabriel. "I think she was too fast for us, and went sideways and then *back* toward Life. But to do that . . ."

She stopped talking and looked around again, intent upon the placid though still treacherous river. Lirael watched her, once again marveling that the famous Abhorsen, Queen of the Old Kingdom and the subject of so many stories that were already becoming legends, was also her relatively newly discovered half-sister. A twenty-years-older half-sister, though Lirael felt that after the events of the summer past, she was no longer so young herself.

"To do that," repeated Sabriel, "Chlorr must be anchored in Life."

"Anchored in Life?" asked Lirael, startled. Chlorr of the Mask had been an ancient necromancer until she was physically slain by Sabriel. But she had not gone beyond the Ninth Gate, instead becoming a very powerful Greater Dead creature, a thing of fire and shadow that needed no flesh to inhabit out in the living world.

"I destroyed the shape she wore," said Sabriel. "But even at that time I wondered. She was very old, hundreds of years old. I could feel that age, a leaden weight within the far younger skin . . ."

She stopped talking and turned about in a circle, sniffing, her eyes narrowed. Lirael looked around too, listening to the faint sounds of movement in the river, sounds that would normally be obscured by the rush of the current.

"There are various ways to extend a life," continued Sabriel, after a moment. "I was too busy to consider which she had used, and became busier still, as you know. But now I think she must be connected to some anchor in Life. That is why she did not fully obey my bells, and did not die the final death."

"But how . . ." stammered Lirael. "How could she do that?"

"There are a number of methods, all of them foul," mused Sabriel. "Perhaps . . . I must tell you how Kerrigor did so, and there are passages from the *Book of the Dead* which speak to the point, though it may not show those pages to you. As always, it has its own ideas of when the reader is ready . . ."

"It certainly does," said Lirael, who, despite considerable familiarity with sorcerous texts from her time as a librarian, was still unsettled by the way the contents of that strange tome were never quite the same and how, reading it, she often felt the same bone-deep chill she felt in the river now.

Lirael spoke slowly, half her mind still focused on her sense of Death, and the Dead. There were things going on, small movements, like flotsam on the tide . . . it took her a few seconds to work out that the dozens and dozens of lesser Dead were gathering together, massing to form a host.

"We shall have to find out, in due course, but Chlorr by herself is not of primary importance," said Sabriel. "Not now that Orannis is bound again, and provided she stays in the North. There are other, more immediate problems. Some at hand, I would say."

Sabriel unfastened the strap that held her favorite bell quiet on her bandolier, her fingers closing on the clapper, bright Charter marks swarming from the silver bell to her hand. She smiled a slight, quirking smile. "I think Chlorr has left us something of a surprise, even an ambush. It is interesting that these lesser things are more afraid of her than they are of us. We must correct that view."

Lirael barely had time to draw her sword and a bell of her own before the Dead attacked, particularly as her right hand moved slowly. It was still being perfected, the new hand that had been made for her by Sameth of clever metalwork and considerable Charter Magic.

There were more than seventy Dead creatures reluctantly moving to attack. Most were warped and misshapen from too long in Death, their original shapes long lost, spirit flesh unable to maintain even a vaguely human shape. Some were squat, as if compressed to fit some awful container; some were stretched long. They had too many teeth, and shifted jaws, and talons or teeth in place of fingernails. Red fire burned in sockets where their eyes once were, and came dripping from their gaping, overstretched mouths.

Lurching and hopping, darting and zigzagging, they came, building courage as they approached, taking hope from the sheer numbers of their companions. They began to growl and slobber and shriek, thinking perhaps this time, they would feast on Life!

But as the throng of Dead finally charged, Sabriel rang Saraneth in a continuous figure-eight motion above her head. The pure, commanding tone of the bell cut through all the foul noises of the Dead, and at the same time the Abhorsen spoke. Not shouting, just speaking firmly, perhaps as she might to a child, or to a horse. Her words were backed by an implacable will, and the strength of the bell.

"Be still."

The charge faltered and came to a stop, Dead creatures stumbling over one another as those closer came first under the compulsion of the bell. Their cries faded, voices quailed. Even their fiery eyes grew dimmer, quenched by the power of Saraneth in the hand of the Abhorsen.

Sabriel flipped Saraneth and caught it by its clapper, silencing the bell. But its voice remained, a long-sustained echo, and the Dead did not move.

"Good," said Sabriel, noting the bell the younger woman held. "Kibeth. The right bell will often come to your hand, unsought. Send them on, on to the final death."

Lirael nodded, and rang Kibeth the Walker, a lively, leaping bell, so eager to sound that she had to exert herself to ring it true and not be carried away herself. And as always now, she had to steel herself against the sound, for in every peal she also heard the memory of a joyful dog's bark, pleased at the prospect of going for a walk.

The Dead began to sob and groan under Kibeth's spell, and then as one they turned and began to shuffle. Lirael kept the bell ringing, and the Dead started to run and hop and skip, slowly moving into a great circle, a horrible parody of some village dance as performed by monsters.

Twice this long parade of Dead trod around in an ever-closing circle, compelled by Kibeth; the third time the Sixth Gate opened under them with a great roar, drawing them down and onward, never to return.

Chapter One

AN UNLIKELY MESSENGER AT THE GATE
Greenwash River Bridge, North Castle

Winter was hard in the North, beyond the borders of the Old Kingdom. The nomadic clans who lived on the steppe would seek the lower reaches before the snow began to fall, leaving the high plateau. But there was one tribe that did not roam, whatever the season. They lived in the mountains in the northwest, beyond the steppe, and did not ride or revere horses, though they would eat them if the opportunity presented itself.

These mountain-folk were easily distinguished from the other clans because they did not wear the long slit tunics and silk sashes of their nomadic cousins. Instead they favored jerkins and breeches made of patchwork goatskin stitched with thick red thread, and rich cloaks from the fur of the *athask*, the huge cats that roamed their peaks and gave the clan its name. For weddings, feasts, and their own funerary pyres, they donned heavy bracelets and earrings made of alluvial gold from their mountain rivers.

It was unusual to see any of these folk outside their mountains at all, let alone hundreds of leagues to the south and east, so the guards on the gate tower of the Greenwash Bridge Company's north bank castle were understandably both curious and cautious when one such fur-wrapped, red-thread goatskin-patched nomad appeared as if from nowhere out of a swirling wet snowfall on a spring afternoon and shouted up at them, asking permission to cross the bridge into the Old Kingdom.

"You're no merchant," called down the younger guard, who'd

set his crossbow on the merlon, ready to snatch up and fire. "So you have no business to cross the bridge."

"I'm a messenger!" bawled the nomad. She was even younger than the young guard, perhaps having seen only sixteen or seventeen of the harsh winters of her homeland. Her lustrous skin was acorn brown, her hair black, worn in a plaited queue that was then wound several times around her head like a crown, and her dark eyes appealing. "I claim the message right!"

"What's that, Haral?" the younger guard asked his elder quietly. He'd only been with the Bridge Company eleven months, but Haral was an old-timer. She'd served twenty-six years, back into the bad old times before King Touchstone and the Abhorsen Sabriel restored order to the Old Kingdom. Before that restoration, the bridge and its castles on the northern and southern banks and the fort in the middle of the river had essentially been a fortress constantly under siege. It had been much more peaceful since, though there had been great trouble in the south in the last summer.

"The tribes give messengers immunity from challenges and feuds and the like," said Haral. She looked down at this unusual—and unusually attractive—messenger, and thought it was just as well the younger guard wasn't here by himself. People who wanted to cross the bridge were not always what they seemed. Or were not actually people at all, apart from their outward form. "But I didn't know the mountain-folk followed that custom. I've only ever seen them a couple of times before, and they were traders, going northward to home."

"Who's the message for?" called out the young guard. His name was Aronsin, but everyone just called him Aron.

"Must I tell you?" asked the young nomad. It was an odd question, said as if she was uncertain of the etiquette involved, or unfamiliar with dealing with other people in general.

"It would be a start," said Aron. He glanced at Haral, sensing her suddenly straighten up. She was peering out into the falling snow, looking into the distance, not at the nomad below.

"Thought I saw movement," said Haral. She took a perspective glass from her belt, extended it, and held it to her eye. Having one nomad pop up almost at the gate could be blamed on the snow and the fading light, but to have any more get so close would be a dereliction of duty.

"So who's the message for?" asked Aron. He smiled down at the mountain girl, because he liked the look of her and he couldn't help himself. "And what's your name?"

"The message is for the witches who live in the ice and See what is to be," replied the mountain nomad reluctantly. "My name . . . I don't really have a name."

"People must call you something," said Aron. He glanced over at Haral again, who had lowered the perspective glass but was still looking out, her eyes narrowed. With the snow beginning to fall more heavily, and the light fading with it, visibility was ebbing.

"Some call me Ferin," said the nomad, the faintest hint of a smile quirking in the corner of her mouth, sign of a fond memory. "Now, can you let me in?"

"I guess—" Aron started to say, but he stopped as Haral laid a hand on his shoulder, and pointed with the perspective glass.

Three figures were coming into sight out of the swirling snow and the lowering darkness. Two of them were on horseback, nomads clad in the typical long woolen tunics of black and grey, slit at the sides for riding, and wound about the waist with multicolored silk sashes. Those who knew could tell the tribe from the pattern of colors in a sash.

But they were not common nomads. One was a shaman, with a silver ring around his neck, and from that ring a chain of silvered iron ran to the hand of the second nomad, the shaman's keeper.

Even without seeing the neck-ring and silver chain, Haral and

Aron knew immediately who . . . or what . . . the nomads must be, because the third of their number was neither on horseback, nor was it human.

It was a wood-weird, a creature of roughly carved and articulated ironwood, twice as tall as the horses, its big misshapen eyes beginning to glow with a hot red fire, evidence that the shaman was goading the Free Magic creature he'd imprisoned inside the loosely joined pieces of timber fully into motion. Wood-weirds were not so terrible a foe as some other Free Magic constructs, such as Spirit-Walkers, whose bodies were crafted from stone, for wood-weirds were not so entirely impervious to normal weapons. Nevertheless, they were greatly feared. And who knew what other servants or powers the shaman might have?

"The Guard! Alarm! Alarm!" roared Haral, cupping her hands around her mouth and looking up to the central tower. She was answered only a few seconds later by the blast of a horn from high above, echoed four or five seconds later from the mid-river fort, out of sight in the snow, and then again more distantly from the castle on the southern bank.

"Let me in!" shouted the mountain nomad urgently, even as she looked back over her shoulder. The wood-weird was striding ahead of the two nomads now, its long, rootlike legs stretching out, grasping limbs reaching forward for balance, strange fire streaming from its eyes and mouth like burning tears and spit.

The shaman sat absolutely still on his horse, deep in concentration. It took great effort of will to keep a Free Magic spirit of any kind from turning on its master—a master who was himself kept in check by the cunningly hinged asphyxiating ring of bright silver, which his keeper could pull tight should he try to turn his creatures upon his own people, or seek to carry out his own plans.

Though this particular keeper seemed to have little fear her sorcerer would turn, for she fixed the chain to the horn of her saddle and readied her bow, even though she was still well out of bow-shot, particularly with the snow falling wet and steady. Once she got within range, she would get only two or three good shots before her string grew sodden. Perhaps only a single shot at that.

"We can't let you in now!" called down Aron. He had picked up his crossbow. "Enemies in sight!"

"But they're after *me*!"

"We don't know that," shouted Haral. "This could be a trick to get us to open the gate. You said you were a messenger; they'll leave you alone."

"No, they won't!" cried Ferin. She took her own bow from the case on her back, and drew a strange arrow from the quiver at her waist. Its point was hooded with leather, tied fast. Holding bow and arrow with her left hand, she undid the cords of the hood and pulled it free, revealing an arrowhead of dark glass that sparkled with hidden fire, a faint tendril of white smoke rising from the point.

With it came an unpleasant, acrid taint, so strong it came almost instantly to the noses of the guards atop the wall.

"Free Magic!" shouted Aron. Raising his crossbow in one swift motion, he fired it straight down. Only Haral's sudden downward slap on the crossbow made the quarrel miss the nomad woman's gut, but even so it went clear through her leg just above the ankle, and there was suddenly blood spattered on the snow.

Ferin looked over her shoulder quickly, saw Haral restraining Aron so he couldn't ready another quarrel. Setting her teeth hard together against the pain in her leg, she turned back to face the wood-weird. It had risen up on its rough-hewn legs and was bounding forward, a good hundred paces ahead of the shaman, and it was still accelerating. Its eyes were bright as pitch-soaked torches newly lit, and great long flames roared from the widening gash in its head that served as a mouth.

Ferin drew her bow and released in one fluid motion. The

shining glass arrow flew like a spark from a summer bonfire, striking the wood-weird square in the trunk. At first it seemed it had done no scathe, but then the creature faltered, took three staggering steps, and froze in place, suddenly more a strangely carved tree and less a terrifying creature. The flames in its eyes ebbed back, there was a flash of white inside the red, then its entire body burst into flame. A vast roil of dark smoke rose from the fire, gobbling up the falling snow.

In the distance the shaman screamed, a scream filled with equal parts anger and fear.

"Free Magic!" gasped Aron. He struggled with Haral. She had difficulty in restraining him, before she got him in an armlock and wrestled him down behind the battlements. "She's a sorcerer!"

"No, no, lad," said Haral easily. "That was a spirit-glass arrow. It's Free Magic, sure enough, but contained, and can be used only once. They're very rare, and the nomads treasure them, because they are the only weapons they have which can kill a shaman or one of their creatures."

"But she could still be—"

"I don't think so," said Haral. The full watch was pounding up the stairs now; in a minute there would be two dozen guards spread out on the wall. "But one of the Bridgemaster's Seconds can test her with Charter Magic. If she really is from the mountains, and has a message for the Clayr, we need to know."

"The Clayr?" asked Aron. "Oh, the witches in the ice, who See—"

"More than you do," interrupted Haral. "Can I let you go?"

Aron nodded and relaxed. Haral released her hold and quickly stood up, looking out over the wall.

Ferin was not in sight. The wood-weird was burning fiercely, sending up a great billowing column of choking black smoke. The shaman and his keeper lay sprawled on the snowy ground, both dead with quite ordinary arrows in their eyes, evidence of peerless shooting at that range in the dying light. Their horses were running free, spooked by blood and sudden death.

"Where did she go?" asked Aron.

"Probably not very far," said Haral grimly, gazing intently at the ground. There was a patch of blood on the snow there as big as the guard's hand, and blotches like dropped coins of bright scarlet continued for some distance, in the direction of the river shore.

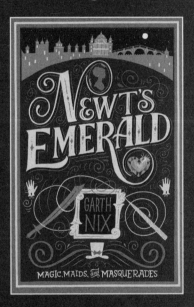

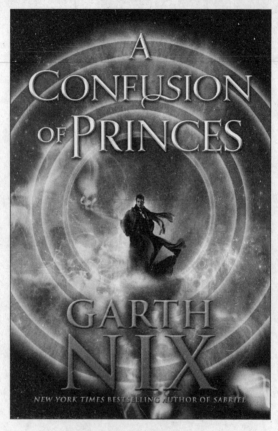